PRAISE FOR *THE WOMAN WHO*
BREATHED TWO WORLDS

"In this vividly drawn, deeply affecting first novel, a spirited girl who is forbidden to attend school as a child is inspired by the warrior myths of her ancestral past told to her by her mother. Though uneducated, Chye Hoon goes on to forge her own destiny as a cook, famed for her savory *kueh* cakes. Author Selina Siak Chin Yoke's special magic draws us instantly and poignantly into Chye Hoon's epic struggle to preserve her family as well as her vanishing culture."

—Laura Esquivel, author of *New York Times* bestseller
Like Water for Chocolate and *Pierced by the Sun*

PRAISE FOR *WHEN THE FUTURE*
COMES TOO SOON

"As Malayan society grapples with the changes brought on by war and occupation, Mei Foong barters away pieces of her existence in order to survive, and rebuild and reclaim her life. She must finally contend with the realization that one could only wholly reclaim oneself by acts of self-assertion requiring greater courage than needed merely to survive. *When the Future Comes Too Soon* by Selina Siak Chin Yoke is an intricately drawn network of human relationships."

—Musharraf Ali Farooqi, author of Man Asian Literary Prize
shortlisted *Between Clay and Dust*

When the
FUTURE COMES
Too SOON

When the
FUTURE COMES
Too SOON

SELINA SIAK CHIN YOKE

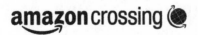

Published by AmazonCrossing, Seattle

www.apub.com

Amazon, the Amazon logo, and AmazonCrossing are trademarks of Amazon.com, Inc., or its affiliates.

ISBN-13: 9781542045759
ISBN-10: 1542045754

Cover design by David Drummond

Printed in the United States of America

Abraham Lincoln once said, 'Fellow-citizens, we cannot escape history.' It was only in writing this novel that I realised how the wounds inflicted on Malaya over seventy years ago have not truly healed. I dedicate this book to my maternal grandmother, Chang Kim Eng, whose experiences served as the inspiration for this story. May her soul rest in peace.

AUTHOR'S NOTE

Some of the conventions adopted in *The Woman Who Breathed Two Worlds* (The Malayan Series, Book 1) are also followed in this sequel.

Dialogue

Most of the characters in this novel are educated and therefore speak in standard English. Where characters have not gone to school, the words in their dialogue are reordered to give a flavour of the local dialects. A sentence such as 'I'll give it to you if you find me something I want' becomes 'You find something I want, I give you'. This convention was used in Book 1 to heighten the sense of place.

Traditional Forms of Address and Family Relationships

Younger characters continue to address older characters in traditional fashion, using titles that indicate the older person's rank and familial relationship: Second Paternal Uncle (father's second brother), Smallest Maternal Aunt (mother's youngest sister) and so on. Older characters, however, address younger characters by name.

Aunt and Uncle

The titles 'Aunt' and 'Aunty' and 'Uncle' are used to politely address people who are not blood aunts or uncles.

Chinese Names

In Chinese names, the family names or surnames come before the name. The protagonist's name is Wong Mei Foong, where Wong is her married surname and Mei Foong her given name.

Malay Names

Malay names take the form of a given name followed by the father's given name. The second name in a Malay name is thus a patronymic. An example is the protagonist's neighbour, Ja'afar bin Abu, meaning Ja'afar son of Abu and typically shortened to Ja'afar Abu. He is therefore called Enche Ja'afar, or Mr Ja'afar.

Old Malay Spelling

Colonial Malay terms and spelling are used in this book.

Malaysian Exclamations

In addition to the ubiquitous suffix 'lah' which Malaysians sprinkle liberally in conversation, characters in this novel use the exclamation 'ai-yahh' denote relief or surprise, as well as exclamations of Chinese origin when asking questions (ah, moh).

Miscellaneous

The characters occasionally use words that would today be deemed politically incorrect.

Chronology

While all of the historical events mentioned in this novel did in fact take place, for literary purposes I have occasionally altered the order in which some of these occurred.

PART I

1

THEY HAVE COME

The thought hit me as my daughter's voice pierced the quiet of that beautiful morning of 15 December 1941. I heard her scream 'Eggs falling on the ground!' and sensed that our lives were about to change irrevocably.

From the bedroom I half-walked, half-ran into the outer hall. It must have taken no more than a minute, though I'd had a bout of morning sickness and my movements could have been ungainly. I was only six weeks pregnant, but being slim and of small build, my baby was already starting to show, a solid presence whose agitation I was convinced I felt from time to time. I had reached the *barlay* – a raised platform made of parquet for sitting or sleeping on – when the first blast came. There was a violent quake. The very walls of our house shook. In front of me, panes of glass on the louvre windows rattled so loudly that I thought they would shatter. Even the trunk of the flame-of-the-forest tree in our garden swayed from side to side, its vermillion leaves rustling shrilly and then dropping as if blown by a strong wind. The hefty front door of our house stood wide open.

As I hurried outside and around the corner, I saw the planes in the distance. But perhaps I did not see them – perhaps I only heard them. I imagined a whole formation, unfurling like a flag in the opal sky. For months, the talk had been of nothing but war and now they were here, the Japanese forces who only the week before, on the night my mother-in-law, Chye Hoon, passed away, had made an incursion into northern Malaya. It had not taken them long to reach our mining town. With conflict on our doorstep, we stood on the precipice of a new age.

In the far corner of our garden, our two eldest children stood beside the gardeners, Samad and Kamil, whose hands were raised to their foreheads as they peered at the sky. I had not taken another step before the second blast reverberated. The ground shuddered and my gut sank, the way it sometimes did during menstruation, as if my innards were being sucked into the earth. I saw the black dashes then, gliding across a liquid sky.

Planes rarely flew over our house; when they did, there was likely to be only one, not an entire squadron. The aircraft could have belonged to our British rulers, but for some reason I did not think so.

It took me a few minutes to understand. We had only vaguely heard about bombs then; we did not really know what they were. The planes made a loud buzzing as they began to swoop. I was frightened and at the same time mesmerised by the sight of the dashes falling, one by one, dropping strange oval balls in sleek lines. Some sank straight to the ground; others moved in curved trajectories, zigzagging, buffeted by invisible gusts. It was only when the balls landed that their terrifying power became clear, and my brain made the connection between the earth convulsing and this strange rain.

At that moment I let out a cry. Although the bombs had dropped some distance away, I could feel grit churning under my feet. I thought the land was going to open up and swallow us all. I imagined the limestone hills surrounding Ipoh being blown apart. My stomach lurched and I felt sick.

From the direction of the town, a column of smoke was rising. My only thought was of getting everyone into the house.

'Go inside! Inside now!' I screamed.

For once, my son and daughter seemed to move too slowly. I remember pulling them by their hands and Samad lifting my eldest son, Wai Sung, while Kamil grabbed hold of my daughter's hand as we scrambled inside through the kitchen door. As soon as we had slammed it, I scanned the room and saw that my second son, Wai Kit, was being cradled by one of the servants. Baby Robert was inside too, in the arms of another servant. But there was still my husband, Weng Yu, who had left earlier for his office in the heart of Ipoh town.

The smoke . . . I need a phone.

I remembered that my brother-in-law Weng Yoon, my husband's fourth brother, who lived next door with his family, owned this modern apparatus.

'Lock all the doors,' I commanded Chang Ying, the tiny girl who had once been my personal maid and now served as cook and amah. Only then did I notice how the blood had drained from her face and how she stood shivering with eyes agog. The other servants were equally stricken, like cats in the midst of being run over. Ah Hong, who had worked in the Wong household for thirty-seven years, began to weep. Irritation surged through me, though I kept my temper. In our inner hall the grandfather clock struck eleven times. I knew I would have to move before it was too late.

'Stay inside,' I said, looking hard at Ah Hong, who had wrapped her arms around my two eldest. I scrutinised each of the servants and they in turn looked at me meekly. Later, they would say that they had never seen me so stern. When I knew that they understood, I ran out of the kitchen door and headed towards the hedge fence that separated our house from my brother-in-law's.

The hedge contained a concealed opening, the 'secret gate' as it was known, which had been conceived by Weng Yoon's wife, Dora, in her enthusiasm for our children to become playmates. Where was the damned latch? I cursed, even though I rarely curse. A secret gate was all very well, I thought, except when one was in a hurry. My hands, I found, were shaking and I could barely prise the latch open. I succeeded only after several tries. Ducking beneath the top of the hedge I found myself in the grounds of Dorcourt, the mansion my brother-in-law had built for his wife.

I had a sudden urge to set eyes on a familiar face, to talk to someone I knew. I was disappointed not to spot Weng Yoon's car. He drove an enormous Humber, which was the envy around town, but it was not in its usual place on the driveway. I hoped Dora was at home. She and I had our differences, but at that moment I needed her company.

'Oh, it's you, Makche, thank goodness, we all so scared, so *takut-lah!*' said the Malay woman who opened the main door. Though clearly agitated, Rokiah managed to give a graceful wave of her hand, indicating the downstairs library. 'Puan is in there.'

I rapped twice on the reddish teak door and turned the knob without waiting for an answer. Dora was sitting behind her husband's mahogany desk, listening to a wireless set. On catching sight of me she rose; then, rushing forward, she grasped my hands in hers and almost knocked me down. She had never been so warm. Later, when I thought back to those moments in Dorcourt's library, I realised how I must have looked standing next to Dora. The oversized dress I was wearing covered my rounded belly, but in my hurry to get into our house when we first heard the planes, I had ripped it on one side under the armpit, all the way down the torso. The hairpins I normally used had somehow become dislodged, so that strands of hair were falling in front of my eyes and I had to keep sweeping them up over my forehead. I did this without thinking, as if I had a nervous tic. In contrast, my sister-in-law stood with her usual poise: elegant bun resting neatly on top of her head, chiffon tunic and sarong unruffled. It was only her ashen face which betrayed signs of turmoil.

'Oh, Big Sister Mei Foong, this is terrible,' she said in English, her voice thinner than I had ever heard it. 'What do we do now?'

'Any news on the radio?' I replied, also in English.

'No, no, not yet. I don't think London knows that Ipoh has been bombed. They may not know for a while. Isn't that awful? The Japs have hit Old Town.'

This was exactly what I feared. Old Town was where my husband's office was situated. For a minute I could not breathe; I wanted to cry, but the sound stuck in my throat. I held so tightly on to Dora's arm that when I released my fingers, a purplish bruise revealed itself.

'Do you want to call Big Brother?' she asked softly. 'Go on,' she said, virtually pushing me out of the library and into the living room where their solitary telephone was located. Only later did I learn that my brother-in-law Weng Yoon had already tried reaching his brother, to no avail. Had I known this then, I would have lost my mind.

Weng Yoon and Dora owned an old-style Bakelite telephone, the circular dial of which I turned tentatively. My head for numbers has never failed me; instantly recalling Weng Yu's office number, I dialled first a 4, then another 4, then 1, and finally 2.

He was not there. Where, I wondered, was that useless assistant of his? No one picked up the receiver. 'If a telephone line has been cut off, does it continue to ring?' I asked Dora, as if she would know. She gave me a blank look.

There was only one way to find out.

Through the windows of Dorcourt, gunfire and the howling of dogs could be heard. 'You can't go out!' Dora said in a horrified whisper, her face whiter than before. 'Not in your condition.'

'But I must, Dora. I have to find him.'

I hurried away before she could reply – and before I lost my nerve. I had to force myself down the street, aware of my fitful breathing and the violent thumping of my heart. We lived in a new suburb called Green Town, whose pockmarked roads were deserted that day, save for packs of stray dogs. But even the dogs were scared: they ran away when they saw me, instead of barking and snarling as they often did.

In the distance I heard the pounding of a thousand feet. The main thoroughfare into town was clogged by smoke, and I did not notice the limbs scattered about. Only in the days afterwards, when others described what they had seen, did I realise what I'd missed. There were people running hither and thither, but in eerily quiet fashion, as if under the command of an invisible hand and as if they knew where they were going. In truth, most were like me, with a vague destination in mind, but with our spirits so fraught that simply walking and running consumed all of our energy. We did not know anything: what we were doing, where we were really going, and if we would ever reach our destinations.

Alongside pedestrians were the rickshaw pullers, none of whom would take me.

'Lady, cannot go into town-lah! The Japanese in Ipoh already! They bomb, now machine-gunning the streets!'

The puller whom I had hailed, a toothless Chinese man with skin the texture of leather, was shouting at me. He did not stop shouting even when his face was just inches away, his grimace full of disdain. It did not occur to me then that I must have looked a little mad – a pregnant woman all on her own, face blackened by grime. With my light-blue dress so badly torn, the puller probably mistook me for one of the deranged tramps who wandered around town.

'I must find my husband!' I said. 'Please, take me! He is in town, on Hale Street!'

'What? You think I crazy-ah? You no can go!'

The man ran away. The other pullers did not even respond to my frantic waving.

For the next half hour, I walked. Ambulances ferrying people to the District Hospital near our home blared their sirens, but no one paid them any attention. The vehicles ended up crawling with the rest of us, along streets so jammed that no one could get anywhere fast, not even if they made as much noise as the fire engines, which were equally stuck. Every few hundred yards, one of the red trucks would grind to a halt and the firemen would jump out to point their feeble hoses at the hundreds of small fires flaring up. The men left behind plumes of white smoke, which stung our eyes and choked us as we fought our way through. At the main intersections, there stood the usual policemen, Malay and Indian, who moved gloved hands mechanically and blew whistles in futile attempts at directing traffic.

The further I walked, the more resolute I became. By the time I reached the Kinta River, the border between New and Old Town, I was already thinking clearly when I heard a familiar voice.

'Puan Wong!'

It was Ja'afar Abu, a policeman who lived in an adjacent house in Green Town. He had set up a checkpoint just yards before the Birch Bridge and was busy cautioning anyone attempting to cross.

'Enche Ja'afar!' I shouted, relieved to spot a face I knew. 'So glad to see you!'

'Oh, Puan Wong, things very bad-lah!'

I did not know Ja'afar and his family well; it was my late mother-in-law, Chye Hoon, who had been their friend. However, they lived only next door and I said hello to Enche Ja'afar, his wife, and their four children every day. I had always found him to be a reticent man, but on that morning he could not stop blabbering.

'The Japanese planes flew very low. I even saw one of their logos – the red sun – on the side of a plane. Hugh Low Bridge has been bombed. Many shops also bombed. At first we didn't know they were Japanese planes, we thought they were British. Many people went out to look and were killed. Then they started firing machine guns. So many wounded. *Habis*. We are finished.

'Puan Wong,' the policeman said, suddenly recovering himself. 'Where are you going?'

'To Hale Street, to find my husband.'

'But you cannot, Puan Wong! It is dangerous there. Someone was shot on that street . . . err . . . ah . . . ah . . .'

When he realised what he had blurted out, the policeman's bloodshot eyes became more prominent. He searched for words and then mumbled, 'Look, Puan Wong, it isn't safe for you to go there. I'm sure Enche Wong will make contact soon. He is probably just . . . just . . . *takut*, scared, like us all.'

Ahead, I saw a stream of pedestrians and cyclists crossing the Birch Bridge. With cast-iron lamps dotting both its sides, the structure must have been visible from the air. I was amazed that the bridge, unlike the British Resident after whom it had been named, was still standing. It was one of the main links into Old Town. On the other side of the bridge, cyclists were dismounting and doing a little dance near one of the balustrades, to avoid what looked like a missing section of the bridge.

I turned back to our neighbour. 'Enche Ja'afar, I have to find Enche Wong. I'd better go,' I said with a quick nod, 'since the planes are no longer here.'

Even as the words tumbled out of my mouth, my heart raced. I departed, walking as fast as I could across the Birch Bridge. Visions of the planes with red suns kept going around in my head; if they returned I had no idea what I would do. I swallowed the lump in my throat. Near the spot around which pedestrians were moving with circumspection, I saw a semicircular crater. I stopped in spite of myself, to join the throng gasping in awe at the steep drop next to the riverbank. One small step was all it would take, and any one of us could have ended up in the silt-filled Kinta River below.

Further along, I passed a cavernous hole in the middle of the road. Opposite, a row of Chinese shop-houses lay in ruins. I could see only foundation bricks; the facades had crumbled into greyish-white powder. I was acutely conscious that Weng Yu's office lay inside just such a shop-house and that he had not phoned. My left hand covered my mouth as I imagined my husband's blackened face underneath rubble. I stifled a sob, my eyes filling with tears. Clouds of dust and acrid smoke were still rising from the cinders. As if to confirm my fears, two pairs of orderlies appeared just then carrying bloodied stretchers. A lone man followed with a child in his arms. The stranger's head and face were covered in dust and soot, and the front of his shirt was soaked through by a spreading circle of pinkish red. It was evident that he was Chinese; he had Chinese eyes, narrow and slanted and burning with urgency. He seemed unafraid.

'Where are you going, madam?' he asked breathlessly in Cantonese, flicking those eyes over my belly.

'Hale Street, to find my husband.'

I averted my head to avoid looking at the mutilated bodies being placed inside the ambulance. When I turned back, the stranger had handed the child in his arms over to one of the orderlies and stood staring helplessly at me. His muscular arms now dangled by his sides, ending in a pair of enormous hands.

'You should not go on your own, madam. Find someone . . .' When he swung around he became quiet. Besides the ambulance men, not a soul could be seen. 'I – I cannot come with you. I'm sorry. I . . . ,'

The orderlies were already heading back into the crumbled ruins. One of them threw the man with the piercing eyes a glance as he shouted, 'Hey, mister! Quick please, we need you!'

The stranger spun around and was gone, as suddenly as he had appeared.

I stumbled on, half-blinded by anxiety, towards the corner of Hale Street, where the family shop-house stood. As I approached my husband's office I felt a surge of relief – the buildings were intact. Then I saw another ambulance with its swivelling light, the driver's path blocked by the hordes running in all directions. I searched for a familiar face in the crowd, but could not find even one. The people seemed to be passers-by, not Hale Street residents.

The ambulance finally moved, leaving detritus in its wake. A mist of fine dust hung in the air. On the ground were metal fragments stuck within viscous pools of red. I remembered what my policeman neighbour had said, that someone had been killed on this very street. There was blood congealing not only along the tarmacked road, but also on the five-foot ways – the verandahs running in front of the shop-houses. I thought I would faint; I was only able to take quick, shallow breaths. Before me was my husband's office. Somehow I managed to climb the few steps up to the blue front door. Without bothering to knock, I lowered the handle and pushed.

It was dark inside. The electric lights were off, the window blinds drawn. I smelled the alcohol at once. Behind the desk which I knew stood in a corner, I sensed a familiar presence and, in the stillness, could hear his breathing – a rhythmic sharp intake followed by a long release. My husband's cowering silhouette gradually emerged before my eyes. After I flicked on the electric switch, I saw that his forehead, which was beaded with sweat, had a greyish pallor, but his cheeks were flushed. In one hand he held a tumbler of whisky.

We stared at one another for a good minute, each as shocked as the other, neither of us able to speak. I was the first to find my voice, which emerged as a strident hiss ricocheting around the walls. My words seemed to come from someone else.

'Have you gone completely mad? Why didn't you come home? Or call your brother? Didn't you think we would worry about you?'

Without looking at me, Weng Yu lifted his tumbler and poured the contents into his throat in one gulp. When he rose from his chair, a small black-and-white photograph fell on to the floor. My husband picked it up swiftly and held its yellowed back to me so that I would not see the image on the other side. He shoved the photo into one of the pockets of his khaki trousers.

'It was horrible, Wife.' His voice was a shocking croak, not the fluid baritone popular with Ipoh's ladies. The deep-set eyes looked right through me towards a distant point, as if I were not there.

Was this the same man who had once turned my head? I could scarcely believe it. Yet there had been signs, even on our wedding night, that Weng Yu loved himself above all others. But I was only eighteen when we married and in love, or at least convinced that I was.

At twenty-six, the mother of our four children and carrying a fifth while bombs were falling around us, I could no longer ignore the reality before my eyes. I wanted to grab hold of my husband by his broad shoulders, to shatter the tumbler in his hand into a thousand splintering pieces. I longed to see that horrible pungent liquid spill from its bottle all over the grey concrete floor. *What about us?* I yelled, but only into the spaces inside my own head.

As our eyes met across the desk, I knew that nothing could ever be the same again. I wished later that I had seized the moment rather than letting it pass. But when it came, I could not find the courage to ask whether he loved me. I did not realise how seminal that moment was, that I would never have another opportunity. Events became my master, not the other way around. Once again in my life, the future arrived before I was prepared.

'Husband, we have to go home,' I said lamely. 'To the children. We must decide what to do. You said this would not happen, but it has. The war has come.'

2

That night the skies opened to a veritable Malayan downpour. The dark canvas hanging over the Kinta Valley was lit up by a ferocious web of hairline cracks that flashed and crackled intermittently with terrifying energy. Thunder rolled and rain came, not in individual drops but as torrential sheets obscuring all before it. In such inclement weather, we were surprised to hear a car pulling up outside. The gentle knocking that followed – rap, rap, rap – confirmed the presence of a visitor. But who would be out in such a thunderstorm? Could it already be . . . ?

I inched open a set of the louvre windows in our outer hall and peeked out. In the darkness and blinding rain I could see little. Visibility had been reduced to mere yards. Certainly, there was another car on the driveway behind Weng Yu's Austin, and people – more than one individual – hovering about, clambering for shelter under the porch. Who they were, I could not say. The knocking became louder, more insistent.

My husband, when he appeared at the doorway of the inner hall, had that serene look which came over him whenever he indulged in the artistic pursuits he loved, be it singing or watching a movie or a play. The record which he had been listening to on the gramophone could still be heard. I recognised the voice as that of an English soprano whom Weng Yu had discovered during his student years in London, where he had gained his civil engineering diploma. Violet Essex was singing an aria from Puccini's opera *La Bohème*. In our inner hall the grandfather clock ticked; outside rain beat down. Meanwhile someone was pounding on the front door.

When Weng Yu realised that it would fall on him to open up, the sensitivity that had won me over disappeared from his face. He turned pale. He had already endured the most trying of days, and the tension was evident in his angular jaw. Despite his masculine physique, my husband would gladly have let me open our front door, had his ego permitted. I had been aware that Weng Yu stood apart from other men, but until the planes came I had not understood what this meant. His difference had remained an abstract fact in my arsenal, one which I barely acknowledged, and if I did, it was to celebrate the fact, alongside his smooth looks, broad shoulders, and lean body, and yes, that he possessed British qualifications, at a time when such a thing was still a rarity. But when I saw the reluctance with which Weng Yu dragged his five-foot-ten-inch frame towards the front door, I felt shame and something close to revulsion. As my husband's eyes darted aimlessly about, I instructed our Malay gardeners, Samad and Kamil, to stand by with wooden bats.

Our heavy front door, made of *chengai* wood and carved with a pair of ornate dragons, was opened using an old-fashioned iron key. In the pelting rain, the ceremonious groaning of the door's hinges was barely audible. Weng Yu slid the door open with caution, prising it ajar just enough to let the arc of electric light from our vestibule penetrate the shadows outside.

We stared in disbelief at the diminutive gentleman before us – my father, so drenched that the colours of his Chinese tunic and trousers could not be distinguished. Though he was standing beneath a paper umbrella, Father's gold-rimmed glasses were spattered by rivulets that slanted transversely across the lenses. He hurried inside with a defeated look. As soon as he had removed his glasses, I saw the weariness in his narrow eyes. His shoulders sagged, and he seemed somehow diminished, a fraction of the man who had been to see us only days before with my uncle from Belfield Street and the troop of cousins visiting from outstation.

Three other figures scuttled in. Like Father, they stood in the hallway with drenched garments. First came Muthusamy, or Mutu, the Indian man who doubled as Father's gardener and driver. In one hand Mutu held a paper umbrella and in the other an unwieldy suitcase. Both were dripping. Mutu gave my husband a questioning look, as if unsure what to do. The two women who followed, one behind the other – Father's faithful servants – were each dragging two large suitcases. The load was clearly beyond either woman's capacity, and a veritable waterfall trailed behind them.

'They're leaving, Mei Foong,' Father said in a voice full of sorrow and accusation. 'We've been betrayed.'

I thought Father was going to cry. When I caught hold of his left arm, the sleeve was soggy, soaked through and sticking to his skin. He was shivering. I led him quickly down the long central vestibule towards the bathroom.

'Come with me!' I shouted to the others. 'Li-Fei, we need towels!'

My husband hurried into our bedroom. When I heard the scraping of hangers and drawers being opened, I knew that he was rummaging through the Italian almerah in which he hung his shirts and trousers. Minutes later, Weng Yu appeared at the bathroom entrance. He thrust into Father's hands a dry white shirt and a homely green-and-white-checked sarong.

'Father, please, take this,' Weng Yu said, his voice a little tremulous. 'I'll find some other clothes for Mutu.'

While our guests dried themselves and changed into whatever fresh clothing we could muster up, old Ah Hong boiled water for tea. The maid was accustomed to dealing with emergencies, having served the Wong family since 1902. Already in her mid-fifties, a lifetime of toil was reflected on Ah Hong's face. A web of cracks broke out at the corners of her eyes whenever she smiled, which was often, and though not quite toothless, Ah Hong had lost enough teeth, including many at the front, to warrant dentures. This was a notion she rejected out of hand. 'I eat with my own teeth or I no eat,' she declared stubbornly, as if eating with one's own teeth was a badge of honour.

Twenty minutes later, our guests were settled and warming themselves. The servants sat in the kitchen while my husband and I were with Father at our long dining table. Despite the violence of the night – with a thunderstorm in full swing – following on from a brutal day my abiding recollection is of Father lifting a teacup to his lips. I have to marvel at the tricks our memories play. The teacup had belonged to my mother-in-law; it was one of her most treasured, and its green dragons and pink borders had faded from wear. In my image Father is handling the vessel cautiously, as if elevating droplets of gold to his mouth. He then began to draw in the brown Pu-erh tea in loud slurps. My husband sat grimacing while Father was lost in another world.

'What are you thinking, Father?' I finally asked. Father's well-coifed moustache twitched. For a good while he said nothing.

'I . . . look I know you have a full house here, Mei Foong . . .'

I said quickly: 'You know you're always welcome in our house, Father. Isn't that right, Husband?'

The shadow of a smile formed on my husband's thick lips. 'Of course, Father, this is your home too.'

I was thankful that Weng Yu had spoken. Our offer was more than simple filial duty: we owed it to Father. Had he not been one of Weng Yu's clients, we might never have met.

The first time Weng Yu arrived at our house for dinner, I was overwhelmed by nerves. Father had tried to make the evening seem like a casual matter, but it was obvious why the young man had been invited. Father took great pains to point out not only how well-qualified Mr Wong was, having been trained in London as a civil engineer, but also that he was enterprising. When the colonials refused to employ him, he had applied for an architect's licence and commenced his own business.

Weng Yu made an impression as soon as he strolled in, with his freshly laundered shirt and khaki trousers, mauve silk tie and imported leather shoes. I had never seen such finely chiselled cheekbones on a man. I wanted him to admire me and worried that he would not. I feared he might consider me too thin, with my somewhat elongated face and slender neck. Though I'd been told often enough that I was pretty, I was conscious of my impediments. I felt vulnerable as soon as I was shorn of the foreign make-up and perfumes which Father's wealth allowed me to purchase. I thought my complexion fair, but not porcelain enough, even if others praised it. My eyebrows, distinctively dark and thick, seemed a much better proposition except that they remained unruly no matter how carefully I plucked them. My best asset was my hair: healthy, silky, and black as the night sky. My hair was still long when I met Weng Yu – falling past my shoulders – and tied into two plaits each morning with Chang Ying's help. It was hard to know what Weng Yu thought. Unlike the other young men who called at our house, he hardly spoke. At some point in the evening he looked across the table and threw me a dimpled smile, and I saw from the glint in his eyes that he was pleased. I knew then that I would see him again.

Father himself was well satisfied with his matchmaking efforts. 'This boy has prospects,' he confided. He was no doubt impressed by Weng Yu's British diploma, as I was. It helped that Weng Yu turned heads, with his beautiful manners and honeyed voice. When I was with him I forgot any ambition I had of becoming a mathematics teacher and dreamt instead of a life together. The prospect of having a marital home much smaller than the mansion in which I had grown up did not deter me. Weng Yu was starting his career; he would move up in the world. Nine years later we were living in the house his mother had built, with lime-green walls, lovely in its own way, but far from what I had imagined for a British graduate in 1940s Malaya.

'Father, you know you can't all have your own rooms. Is that okay?'

My father's narrow eyes rested on me. The heat rose in my cheeks and I looked away, through the open dining-room door towards the kitchen. 'You can take Mother-in-Law's bedroom, and the servants can sleep on the *barlay* in the outer hall.'

A silence ensued. We must have resumed conversation at some point, but I have no idea what we talked about. I remember only a heady, expectant air, the febrile atmosphere and the feeling of crushing impotence inside me. Things were happening over which we had no control. We did not know what would come next. We whispered to one another though no one had told us to. It simply felt safer to speak in a low voice, despite the rain beating down outside.

There came a murmur from the kitchen. The servants' voices were drowned out by the deafening noise of rain crashing against the corrugated zinc roof which someone, probably Li-Fei, had pulled over the air well in the middle of the kitchen. The open air well was an outlet for the dense smoke that our servants produced in copious quantities whenever they cooked. Wood-fired stoves were commonplace then, and mealtimes always saw one or the other of the servants fanning leather bellows while another manoeuvred a metal spatula around the enormous black wok.

Every now and again Li-Fei's voice rose above the murmur. She was the strongest among the servants, and also the loudest. She had worked in the Wong household for almost as long as Ah Hong and thought that she knew best how to run the place. Through the years, we had arrived at an uneasy accommodation. I had no intention of sacking her, not least because my husband would have objected. Besides, Li-Fei was a good Hakka worker, endowed with the dark skin and large feet characteristic of her ancestry, and the only woman in our house capable of pulling the air well cover unaided. Also, the children liked her; she was the boisterous one who yelped and made them giggle.

Amidst the low voices and the pelting rain, I thought back to Father's words as he was entering our house. When I asked what he had meant, he cleared his throat twice, in rapid succession. Father had been making the same deep throttling sound for as long as I could remember. It made me think of male aftershave and Pears soap, and my skin tingled. Once again I was an eight-year-old on his lap, engulfed in a haze of mathematical facts and fantastical stories and the cloying smoke of his opium pipe.

But Father did not smile. He leaned forward to whisper, 'You know, I never thought I would say this. I think the Japanese are going to win this war—'

'We mustn't jump to conclusions so quickly, Father,' Weng Yu interrupted. My husband bolted out of his chair and paced the dining room, his voice loud and unnaturally harsh. 'The British will regroup, you'll see. London will send help. Don't forget, America is now in this war. There is no way the Allies can lose. Japan will be defeated.'

I looked up, wondering whether Weng Yu had forgotten the morning's events. Though an intelligent man, he was clearly swayed by the British propaganda he read in the *Times of Malaya*. For weeks, he and his brother next door had assured us that the Japanese would be no match for the British. Yet the Japanese had landed on Malayan soil and taken less than a week to attack Ipoh. Days earlier, while we were still in the midst of welcoming mourners to the three nights of wake we had held for my late mother-in-law, two British battleships – HMS *Prince of Wales* and HMS *Repulse* – were sunk off Malaya's eastern coast. No one until then could have imagined Japanese fighter planes destroying a single British battleship, let alone two on the same day. The Japanese were said to possess machines of subpar quality, unlike the white man's armaments. But after what I had seen, I was not sure that Japanese weaponry was so inferior.

Father gazed calmly into Weng Yu's wild eyes. His voice was impassive when he said, 'I hope you're right, my son, but I cannot share your optimism. I have seen them leave.'

'Who, Father? What are you talking about?' I asked.

'Our European neighbours. Many are packing up, not openly, of course – in secret – but since it is the maids who have to do the packing, word has spread along the houses on our part of the Gopeng Road. It wouldn't surprise me if by morning there are no Europeans left in Ipoh. They will go tonight, under cover of darkness and this storm.'

'But, Father, surely not all will leave?'

Father looked me squarely in the eye and said, 'I believe all will go, Daughter.'

'But . . . What about people like the Stanleys? Mr Stanley has been here forever. I mean, this is his home, his children were born here! They can't pack up just like that.'

The Stanley family lived two doors from Father, next to the Lees. Mr and Mrs Stanley had met in Malaya. I had known all three of their boys and also the girl, Elizabeth, who was two years my junior. We weren't playmates – the whites kept mostly to themselves – but we knew each other by sight and always greeted one another. Unlike me, Elizabeth enjoyed sport, in particular the climbing of trees. There came a day when she fell and broke her arm. Neither Mr nor Mrs Stanley was at home, and a servant ran to us in panic. Mr Stanley was so grateful to Father for taking Elizabeth to the hospital that he came the next day with a bottle of brandy under his arm. Elizabeth and I became friends of sorts, never close, but my sister and I were invited to the tea party they hosted every May before leaving on their English holiday. Elizabeth had always lived in Malaya; was she leaving too?

'The Stanleys and the others on Gopeng Road are not the only ones packing up,' Father said. 'The folks behind us along Tambun Road are doing the same. Remember old Mr Leong? He telephoned this afternoon to tell me that his planter neighbour, Mr Maxwell, who has been here twenty-five years, was filling up whole trunks. His wife and daughters are going, of course, and so is that, er, pretty maid of his, who we all know is more than his maid. She is very excited, as you can imagine. Although, I somehow doubt she will be allowed on to the boat.'

'Boat? What boat?' my husband and I exclaimed at the same time.

'My children, the whites are setting off from Penang, but there won't be enough space for everyone. Those who don't get on to boats there will go to Singapore, where they hope to gain safe passage to Australia.'

'So they're leaving, just like that,' I said aloud, to no one in particular.

I rose from my chair. My husband seemed deflated; he sat down and did not move. I threw him a contemptuous glance. At that moment I blamed him too: by supporting our British rulers so unreservedly, it seemed only right that he share the responsibility for this imminent desertion.

Stroking the curved ends of his moustache, Father said, 'I've been thinking, Mei Foong . . . You know, Ipoh may not be the safest place now. Especially here in Green Town, with the army barracks so close by.'

A stubborn light shone in my father's eyes. I had seen that determination many times; I knew what it meant. Without warning, Father turned to Weng Yu and asked, 'What do you think, Son?'

My husband's cheeks reddened. 'I – er, I . . . well . . .'

As the seconds passed, Weng Yu became increasingly agitated. When Father did not drop his gaze, my husband knew he would have to reply. He waved his hands nervously.

'Well, it's certainly true that the barracks aren't far, Father, but I can't think where else would be safer. Really, I'm less pessimistic than you. I mean, civilians may be fleeing, but the British army is still here, there are convoys moving up and down the country. Why, we tuned in to the MBC broadcast earlier. Our troops are fighting tenaciously in Penang!'

Father did not reply. He seemed to be listening to the rain outside, which no longer fell in sheets. Large droplets were trickling down; in between loud plops on the metal roof over the air well, Father expelled a sigh.

'You may be right, Weng Yu, you may be right . . . ,' he began slowly. From the timbre of his voice I could tell how disappointed he was; once again I thought he was going to cry, but his eyes remained dark and empty. When he next spoke his tone had hardened.

'My son, even if you are right, we know that the Japanese will come first to Malaya's towns, not to the countryside. And that means that the towns will be the most dangerous places. We should get away from here. You must think of the children.'

Father trained his eyes on me. 'Mei Foong, your uncle on Belfield Street left for Pusing this afternoon. He called me as soon as he could, to ask after everyone. He probably would not have gone if he didn't have to take the visiting cousins home. But then, when we started talking, we both agreed that we should all leave town. We tried to think where you and the children could go.

'You may not remember this, Daughter, but I took you to visit a tin mine once, a long time ago – near Lahat. You were small then, no more than five. The mine belongs to my uncle, your second grand-uncle. He still lives there with your grand-aunt. It's in the middle of nowhere: no army would be interested in going there. And it hasn't changed. He has kongsi longhouses, and there are farms nearby. Weng Yu, you can park your car in the jungle. Uncle will put us up, I'm sure.'

I thought back to that visit twenty-one years ago. I had not seen Second Paternal Grand-Uncle and Grand-Aunt since. The memories which my mind conjured up were hazy but happy. My younger sister and I had sat in the rear of Father's Ford with one of the maids while Mother was in the front beside Father, beautiful and distant, her delicious perfume wafting into my nostrils. The journey seemed to take forever, an adventure along dusty roads. It was the first time I had left

23

Ipoh town. Once we were in the countryside, I was surprised by how the bullock carts and their drivers – men in turbans – and the hordes of cyclists, all disappeared, and there was nothing for miles around save the Malayan jungle, thick with its trees and noises. There was so little traffic in those days that we barely met a bus or another car. When we arrived at a fork in the road, Father turned right. We went down a laterite track, bypassing cultivated land and dwellings that were no more than wooden sheds. We saw two enormous ponds, and in the distance, on top of a hill, Second Paternal Grand-Uncle's house beckoned.

But I was a child then, only five years old, a time when the whole world had seemed magical. Now I was an adult with a growing family to care for. With Father's arrival, our household had exploded from eleven to fifteen people. How would we all transport ourselves to such a remote corner in just two cars? The mere thought gave me a headache.

'I need time to think, Father,' I said, rising from my chair. Feeling a migraine coming on, I went to the window and held the louvres ajar. A wind was blowing in from Ipoh's limestone hills. I took a deep breath, to let the chill air wash over me. Goose pimples rose on my flesh and I shivered, but it felt good to smell the earth and the fresh wetness of rain.

'We can't go yet, Father,' I whispered, formulating my thoughts as I spoke, 'not with the young ones unprepared. It's too late in the night. Also, I haven't finished sorting through Mother-in-Law's things – you'll see when you get to your room. It needs a proper clearing out. No hurry, is there? We don't need to decide right now, do we?'

Father peered at me above the rim of his cup. His eyes narrowed into a sharp warning. 'Don't leave things for too long, Mei Foong. The Japs will be back, if not tomorrow then certainly the day after. And they'll keep coming back. They'll flatten the town if they have to. We must take the children away – to safety.'

That night I could not sleep. The horrors of the day kept flitting through my mind, and there was nothing I was able to compare them to, no barometer I could have used. For a while my husband also stayed awake, though he was far from me in the inner hall to which he had returned, where he sat listening to music and sipping whisky. By the time Weng Yu stumbled into our bedroom, his breath stank. He fell asleep at once, rigid on his back. There were moments when I longed to hold him. I nearly took hold of his hand at one point, but at the last second turned away. On the wall above, a house gecko darted and clacked before scuttling off. I thought of our British rulers; I was furious with them, angry at my husband too. When Weng Yu began to snore, I almost hit him. How dare he fall sleep, abandoning me on such a tumultuous night.

I turned my back on my husband and faced the door. From the way Father had looked at me, I knew that he was willing me into a decision. Yet, whenever I thought about fleeing, an ache came into my head. I twisted from side to side, trying to imagine what the future would bring. I stayed on my side of the bed, far from Weng Yu, until the mosquito coil had burnt itself down and the dawn light crept in.

3

Next door at Dorcourt, my brother-in-law Weng Yoon had begun preparing for the long haul. On entering the garden through the secret gate, Weng Yu and I found him and his driver, Ali, digging a trench. It was 16 December 1941, the day after the Japanese dropped their first bombs on Ipoh. By the time we appeared, Weng Yoon and Ali had created a tomb-like crater in a corner of their grassy lawn and were standing inside the hole with their heads down and *changkols* – large Malayan hoes – in hand, shuffling soil.

It was nearing eleven o'clock. The coolness of the Malayan morning had subsided, and the air was beginning to steam. Ali was shirtless, his legs wide apart. He seemed in his element as he lifted the head of the *changkol* high into the air and then lowered it in a smooth arc. Ali tended Dorcourt's large garden when he wasn't waiting for his boss in muggy heat. His physique was rugged from the work and his naturally bronzed skin glistened under beads of sweat as we approached. On the grass beside him sat the heap of black soil he had dug up.

Next to him, Weng Yoon looked out of place, like an actor who had forgotten his lines. He lifted a scarlet face to us. Weng Yoon was a man of naturally generous girth who had put on even more weight in recent years. By then he was one of Ipoh's preeminent lawyers, and clearly more accustomed to the ventilated cool of the High Court than to toiling over trenches. He did not have time for his garden, other than to stroll occasionally among the flowerbeds.

When my brother-in-law saw us, he stopped digging and muttered a gruff hello. Perspiration oozed out of his pores. I watched the coalescing pools on his temples as they expanded, threatening to engulf both cheeks.

'What's all this for?' my husband asked.

Weng Yoon raised a bushy eyebrow. 'What does it look like, Big Brother? We're digging a bomb shelter, of course.'

'Ha!'

Nothing further was said for a good minute. As if to urge himself on, my brother-in-law emitted a groan, planted his *changkol* deep into the bottom of the trench, and proceeded to fling an enormous spadeful of damp earth on to the grassy verge. He hurled the hoe with such force that the pinkish-red soil on it scattered into clumps and fell near my husband's feet. Weng Yu jumped backwards, only just avoiding a couple of fat black worms as they slithered away in terror.

'Watch it, Weng Yoon!' my husband screamed. 'I didn't come here to be covered in dirt!'

'Sorry, Big Brother.'

The mumbled apology sounded forced and half-hearted. Weng Yoon planted the head of his *changkol* aggressively into the earth before dropping his hands to his sides. The puddles on his temples had broken loose and were streaming down his cheeks. He took out a green handkerchief from the pocket of his shorts and started wiping his face.

'Look, stop a minute, will you?' my husband said irritably. 'We came to talk about something.'

I glanced to and fro between the brothers' stony faces. Weng Yu had raised his voice; from the tightening of his jaw, I could see that he was displeased. He would certainly have taken his younger brother's barbed replies as an affront. The tension between the two had been simmering for months, and now it seemed on the verge of erupting.

My husband glared. Weng Yoon, for his part, glared even harder. The lawyer was a tiger, having inherited from his mother a withering look that bored through your skin. I often thought how frightening it would be to encounter him in a court of law. There were traces of Weng Yu in his face – in the way his eyes were planted deep in his skull, in the angular set of his jaw, also in the long and unusually high nose, though the fourth brother was shorter, heavier in build, and ferocious, like his mother.

From within the trench, Weng Yoon looked at my husband as if he were an annoying ant. The lawyer sighed, consulted the gold watch on his left wrist, and then asked, 'Will it take long? We still have a long way to go on this trench and—'

We heard the buzzing before he could complete his sentence. We did not see the planes – the sun was too bright by then – but we could tell that they were coming closer. When the air-raid siren from the army barracks on Ashby Road began to sound, we knew that the enemy had returned. The thought crossed my mind that I should go home to the children, but I turned instinctively towards Dorcourt's open front door, knowing that I would never reach our own house in time. Ali jumped out of the trench and supported me on one arm while my husband took my other arm.

We struggled into the interior of Dorcourt, where my sister-in-law Dora and their servant Rokiah were flying between windows, shutting them as fast as they could. The women looked up in shock. 'When did you arrive?' Dora asked when she found her voice.

'A few minutes ago,' I said, feeling somewhat faint.

'Big Sister, you can't sit here, we have to go into the secret room.'

'The secret room?' I repeated, breathless. The aeroplanes were already above us.

'Yes, yes,' Dora replied, glancing at the ceiling. 'Quick, Ali and Rokiah, help Kakak. Weng Yoon, come, we'll close the other windows. The children are already in the chamber.'

With Ali supporting my left arm and Rokiah leading me by my right hand, I walked from Dorcourt's main hall and dining room into a long, narrow corridor. My husband followed. Our nephews' bedrooms were located off this corridor. Each bedroom door was open, exposing wooden beds already made up and the blue walls they favoured. Beyond this corridor was an annexe that housed a large garage, its sides lined with storage shelves made of coarse wood. The garage had been conceived primarily for Weng Yoon's lumbering black Humber – one of the few in town then – which stood proudly in the middle.

In the far corner was a narrow door leading into Ali's bedroom. I had never had reason to enter his room and now saw that it contained not only a single canvas bed, but also, rather curiously, a *barlay* – the wooden platform once ubiquitous in Chinese households in Malaya. Ali's *barlay* was similar to the parquet platform my mother-in-law had installed in the outer hall of our house, except that his had wooden shelves above it. The shelves, in turn, were stacked with old books, magazines, comic books, and even ancient copies of the *Law Society Gazette*, all arranged haphazardly as if they had been dumped. The location of the shelves was odd because their presence made a good portion of the *barlay* unavailable, which seemed to defeat its purpose as a communal sleeping space.

Ali smiled at my puzzlement. 'You will see, Aunty,' he said in Cantonese. Ali, although of Malay ethnicity, had taken it upon himself to learn the Chinese dialects spoken in the Wong household. After five years of service, he spoke passable Hakka and excellent Cantonese and Hokkien, with hardly a trace of accent.

He sprang into action, striding towards the shelf which held the thickest books. As I approached, I saw that the hardbacked tomes were legal reports dating back to 1900. With Rokiah's help, Ali began removing some of the copies. They took the books off the shelves, one by one, until bare patches of cream wall could be seen behind. The servants then stood with their legs slightly akimbo and leaned the weight of their bodies – from the soles of their bare feet to the tips of their long brown fingers – against the wall. The shelves began to revolve. I watched with mouth agape as the entire shelf unit rotated on an axis, exposing a small room in the rear from which three cheeky young faces peeked out.

'Big Uncle! Big Aunt!' shouted the twins, Frankie and Freddie, jumping out of their chairs.

'Shush! Quiet!' Rokiah said, hissing like a Siamese cat. 'Frankie, give your chair to Big Aunt.'

Rokiah had also spoken in Cantonese, and she pointed an index finger towards the chair which the elder of the twins – by ten whole minutes – had vacated. Frankie stole a glance at the servant. Observing that her lips were sealed shut, he placed himself meekly on the floor. Rokiah in a determined mood was a force to be reckoned with.

The room we had reached – Dorcourt's secret chamber – was literally tacked on to the *barlay*. The *barlay*'s parquet wood formed its floor while the rotating wall of shelves provided a cleverly concealed entrance. Being raised and hidden, the secret space was small, its ceiling low. I, who stand only five feet and three inches tall, was able to hold my head upright, but my poor husband had to stoop. When he crouched to help me in, his face had turned so white that I thought he was going to collapse. Crawling slowly, he managed to inch his way into a space not far from the swivelling door.

Outside, the air-raid siren continued sounding. The circling planes had loud engines and seemed to be hovering, searching carefully for targets, biding their time. I could not recall how long they had remained the previous day, but it had felt like eternity. I was thankful for Frankie's canvas chair.

The boys' younger sister, Mary, sat nearby on the floor, perched on top of a brown cushion, with a frozen grin on her face. The thought of our own children next door whimpering and hiding under tables made me sick.

'I don't know, these three, they do what . . . ,' Rokiah muttered under her breath. 'One minute also, we cannot leave them alone!'

'Me do nothing, Rokiah,' Mary declared in her tiny voice. 'Me good!'

'Shush, quiet,' said their father, who had by then entered the secret chamber. He and Ali returned the entrance door to its original position, shutting us in brutal darkness. Not even a blade of light protruded. It was, I imagined, like being inside Ipoh's limestone caves at night; I could almost smell the bats and the swifts. Within this tiny rectangular space, larger only than a shed, Weng Yoon's voice reverberated eerily. We were cowed into silence.

From somewhere in the distance came a thundering boom. The bare walls enclosing us shuddered. There followed a vicious stuttering, which was to become familiar – the chilling noise of machine guns spewing their diarrhoea of bullets. In between the pounding of my heart, I could hear my husband's heavy breathing, in out, in and out, like a panting dog.

When eventually the machine-gun fire ceased, Weng Yoon whispered, 'What was it you wanted to discuss, Big Brother?'

For many minutes my husband was unable to find his voice. When he did, it was thin and crackly, a far cry from the rich, mellow tones we were used to. 'Look, we're thinking . . . uh, uh, we want . . . We want to leave, for the countryside.'

'Big Brother, are you mad?' Weng Yoon shouted.

I was taken aback by my brother-in-law's agitation, which struck me as odd, even if I could not put my finger on why. Weng Yoon's voice continued to get louder. By the time he asked, 'And why on earth do that?' his decibel level had risen by several notches.

'Keep your voice down,' Dora said drily. 'This is a small space, there's no need to shout.'

To my great surprise, the lawyer heeded his wife. 'You'll be safer here, Big Brother,' he said, much more gently and with feeling. I had only been able to influence my husband early on in our marriage, and marvelled at the power Dora continued to wield inside her house. I wished I had the same.

A rumble sounded in the distance, like remnant thunder, but it soon died away. The seconds passed, and still my husband did not speak. Eventually, he said, rather defensively, 'Actually, leaving town was my father-in-law's idea.'

I waited for Weng Yu to explain, to persuade. After further time elapsed, I looked to my right, where I discerned his outline in the gloom and could hear him swallowing. I imagined the throbbing flesh at the front of Weng Yu's neck and the exquisite lines of his mouth.

I was surprised that he said nothing more, and yet also not. It suddenly occurred to me that my husband was intimidated. I recalled an incident earlier in the year, at the grand feast which Weng Yoon had thrown to celebrate his mother's sixty-third birthday. The talk had been mainly of war, but the event was a happy one. There had been an ample table, countless children, and even a Japanese photographer, who had taken the only printed image in existence of my late mother-in-law. In between conversations about Churchill and the siege in North Africa, Weng Yoon calmly announced his appointment to the state legislature.

The congratulations had been effusive. Everyone clapped and shook my brother-in-law's hand. On turning to my husband, I noticed how grudging his smile was; he hardly moved his lips. When he spoke, his voice seemed to be trapped within his throat.

Weng Yu's reticence would not have been obvious to anyone else. It was generally assumed that the two brothers were close, having been the only family members to have studied in Britain. But my husband treated Weng Yoon the way he treated all his siblings: in an offhand, slightly disdainful fashion, which he regarded as his right, being the eldest son and his mother's favourite. With their mother's passing away, it should have occurred to Weng Yu, as I was by then sure it had to

Weng Yoon, that the time for change had come. After all, the latter was the more successful of the two, a man not to be talked down to.

There was scraping on the chamber floor. I heard my brother-in-law ask, 'Big Sister, what do you think?'

'Well, Father was quite forceful in his arguments,' I replied, remembering the regard Weng Yoon had for Father. 'You know, we're not far from the army barracks here. The Japanese will know where the barracks are, but there's nothing to bomb in the countryside.'

'But Big Sister, now is not the time to leave,' Weng Yoon said, his voice pained, as if our leaving constituted a form of treachery. 'There will be troop reinforcements, you'll see.'

'From where, Weng Yoon? They've been talking for months about troop reinforcements. They haven't come though, have they?'

'There were fresh troops yesterday travelling north on the trunk road from Kuala Lumpur.'

'Fresh troops? Yes, they were fresh all right – fresh out of school. They were just boys! Weng Yoon, I tell you, Britain is fighting in too many places. They have kept their strongest and best for Europe. Home is more important; don't you see? Father thinks it's all over, that Japan will win this war.'

At that moment a detonation shook Dorcourt's walls. On the other side of the entrance door, we heard the crash of books against the *barlay* floor. I could feel Weng Yoon recoiling. When his daughter started to cry, there was a flurry of movement.

At length, Weng Yoon asked in a quiet voice: 'Your father doesn't really believe that the Japs will win, does he?'

'I think he does.' I sighed. 'But you know what? You should ask him yourself. The question is: where would be safer? Here in town, or somewhere in the countryside?'

From a far corner we heard Dora's quivering voice, 'Oh Lord, ah – I hope your father is wrong, Big Sister, I really hope so . . .'

I turned in her direction. My sister-in-law appeared to have planted herself diagonally across the room. This was perhaps no more than an unfortunate choice, but it illustrated the parlous state of our relationship. Though she had been warm the previous day, Dora had never liked me, and I had given up trying to fathom why. We should have been the best of friends, being of similar age and background. In the early years I kept asking myself whether it was something I had done or perhaps said. We did speak often, living just next door. Having both been educated in missionary schools, we were able to converse in English as well as in the Chinese dialects and spent hours talking about family. She would tell me about her relatives in Penang while I shared stories about mine in Ipoh. I learnt that both her parents had been taught in English and that her entire family had become converts to Christianity. The pride with which she said this left me with a sense that my own Chinese gods were inferior, my Chinese-educated parents even more so.

Yet it was Dora who was prickly. Her animosity could not have been due to envy, because Dora, with her lusciously creased eyes and smooth cheeks, was considered a great beauty. Perhaps it was my status she resented, for I was already well-established in the Wong family by the time she arrived in 1938. Having married Weng Yu, the favourite Wong son, in 1933, I had secured my place as the eldest daughter-in-law and enjoyed a certain respect.

Rank, however, did not prevent Mother-in-Law's preference for Dora from being evident. The old lady's fondness for the new family member was hardly surprising: Dora, like Mother-in-Law, was a Nyonya, a female descendant of Chinese traders who had arrived long ago and who, in marrying local Malay women, had spawned a culture that seamlessly mixed both sets of ancestral traditions. Mother-in-Law and Dora wore the same Malay bajus and sarongs and lifted their hair in chignons, which they pinned on top of their heads. Coming from Penang, they even spoke the same brand of Hokkien. It was inevitable that they would share an affinity from which I was excluded.

Mother-in-Law's obvious approbation failed to improve relations between Dora and me. Even when we were inside our cimmerian cave, I could feel a current of antagonism.

'What do you think, Dora?' I asked.

There was a long, ponderous pause.

'I – I think you have a point, Big Sister,' she finally said. 'About the whites.' I had never heard Dora refer to our colonial rulers as 'the whites'; she had always called them 'the British'.

Her husband waded in. 'And what point is that? As an ARP warden who patrols our streets at night, I have more information than most. I know what Britain is doing, and I tell you, they're doing their best, fighting tooth and nail for this country.'

'Fighting tooth and nail? Fighting tooth and nail?' My voice pulsated. In the quiet it sounded tinny, as if I were shouting into a hollow jar. 'Every day comes news of yet another retreat, and you call that fighting tooth and nail? Just wait, Weng Yoon, they'll keep retreating, retreating, retreating – all the way down to Singapore! That's all they care about, Singapore! Fighting tooth and nail, my foot!'

There was a stunned silence. No one had ever heard me shout. They did not know what to say.

When the words tumbled out of my mouth, I had not given the matter much thought. I certainly had no feelings of prescience. How could I, an ordinary housewife in Malaya, have known that our colonial rulers would do exactly that – withdraw further and further, running south with their tails between their legs?

When he next spoke, Weng Yoon was conciliatory, and seemed almost sorry for his earlier brusqueness. 'Big Sister, Pearl Harbour was bombed. America has joined this war. It is impossible for the Japs to win.'

'Remember what you've been telling us, Weng Yoon. You said they would not dream of invading Malaya. Well, that has now happened.

Who knows what else they may be capable of? Anyway, I was asking Dora what she thought.'

I turned once again in my sister-in-law's direction. 'Dora, you don't think they'll defend us, do you? Are you still planning to stay here?'

In a strained voice, Dora replied: 'Big Sister, we can't leave this large house empty. Besides, with three children, where can we go?'

4

The air raid lasted an hour. When we emerged from Dorcourt's secret chamber, it was early afternoon. Our eyes were dazzled by the bright light, our buttocks sore from sitting. My husband's face had taken on its calcified appearance of the day before. His complexion was as pale as a cadaver's and, despite the heat, his teeth were chattering. When he began moaning, I held his arm, but he was unable to speak. As soon as we were in the safety of our garden, Weng Yu rushed to one of the rose bushes Kamil had planted for his deceased mother and bent his head low. Out of his mouth came a necklace of saliva dotted with yellowish-grey lumps.

When my husband had finished, I led him to the front of our house. The street had the hushed stillness of a graveyard: beneath our flame-of-the-forest, not a sound could be heard. I walked Weng Yu to the front door. He was so pale that I shouted for help. Li-Fei had only just come forward when a shriek reached my ears.

I turned to see one of our neighbours, Mrs Lim, a lady of perenni-ally cheerful disposition, struggling down our street. This hefty woman was impossible to miss: her shoulders were fortresses, her cheeks rosy moon-cakes. She dragged her feet in a curious manner, as if she had been running for her life and would expire any minute. It was then that I glimpsed the spatters of blood on her abdomen. The red circle in the middle of her oversized tunic, which was soaked through, grew larger as she approached. Thinking she had been shot, I half-ran to meet her on the street.

'Mrs Lim, are you all right? What happened?'

'My husband, my husband,' she moaned. As soon as she stopped, her bulwark shoulders heaved; she stood panting, unable to say a word. Our servants had come out by then. Everyone surrounded her. Samad and Kamil were there too, all of us trying to ascertain what had happened. But Mrs Lim, who was known in Green Town for her volubility, was so flustered that she could give only monosyllabic replies. It took many minutes before we realised that it was not she who was in danger but her husband: he had been shot by a bullet.

'Where, Mrs Lim?' I asked for the umpteenth time. 'Where is Mr Lim?'

'There!' the woman replied, pointing a finger bedecked with rings upwards at the sky.

'Which road, Aunty?' Samad asked.

Mrs Lim convulsed into sobs.

'Mrs Lim, you must tell us the name of the road,' I said with urgency.

'Ashby.'

'Ashby Road? Near the army barracks? Is that where he is?'

Mrs Lim nodded weakly, using her finger again to point towards a road some ten minutes' walk away. If Mr Lim was injured, it would be best if we went in a car, but my husband was in no state to go anywhere. For the first time, I wished I had learnt to drive.

'I can drive, Aunty,' Samad said. Samad had indeed used the car once or twice, illegally of course, since he had no licence. But with bombs falling, who was going to care about a short journey to Ashby Road and thence to the District Hospital?

I climbed into the Austin with Mrs Lim and Kamil. Samad took the helm. We spotted Mr Lim on a grassy kerb by the main road near the army barracks. He could not open his eyes; when he did, only for a few seconds, his eyeballs rolled about. Blood was pouring out of a gash in his abdomen. Through the exposed skin, a pale red organ throbbed. I had never seen a human organ in its place inside the body – alive. My head spun and I could not breathe, I had to look away. It was fortunate that my husband was not with us, for he fainted at the sight of blood. Our gardeners were thankfully unfazed. They injured themselves often enough, and Kamil was used to treating his and Samad's cuts and grazes. Kamil now tore off his shirt to use as a tourniquet.

'*Mesti chepat*,' he told Samad with a plea in his eyes. Mr Lim groaned as he was lifted into the rear of the Austin. He remained conscious, but only barely; he was losing a lot of blood.

With Mr Lim sprawled out at the back, there was no space for us all in the car. In any case I had plenty of work to get on with at home, and so I went back on foot.

A flustered Samad returned to the house after just twenty minutes. 'Aunty, you must come,' he said, dragging me by the arm. Samad's face was full of fear, but also of excitement, in equal measure. I could not imagine what else would have happened.

'Don't tell me, Samad,' I said.

'No doctor at the hospital, Aunty.'

'No doctor? What do you mean?'

'European doctors. They all gone!'

I stared at him, my mind suddenly blank.

'You're joking,' I said, in a peculiar voice.

Samad and I arrived at the District Hospital minutes later to an unnerving scene. Everything looked familiar, yet nothing was quite the same. On the grassy lawn in front – usually kept empty – cars were parked, more cars than I had ever seen at the hospital, but they were arranged in haphazard fashion. Inside the hospital itself – comprising a series of low brick buildings with tiled roofs and slatted folding doors that doubled as windows – there was movement and noise instead of the quiet order which usually prevailed. My back stiffened when a fearsome howling pierced the atmosphere. I put my hands to my ears. Whoever was screaming was fighting for life; there was urgency in the very air we breathed, a potent anguish which made the hairs on my arms stand on end. Large numbers of people in ordinary clothes were milling around helping patients, but no one paid any attention to the shrieking. Some of the patients, still in their bandages, were being led out of beds and through the open concertina doors. There were patients crying and screaming, and women in white uniforms doing what they could to help, though they seemed as shaken as their patients.

We entered the main reception area, hoping to gain information at the front desk. There was no one there. Along the corridor on the right, which led to the second-class ward where Samad had left the Lims, we bumped into their daughter, Choy Yoke, who was then training to be a nurse at the hospital. She looked out of breath and harassed.

'Choy Yoke,' I said, gripping the girl by the arm, 'how is your father?'

'Ah, Mrs Wong, you will not believe it! Father is all right, Dr Pillay just told me.'

'Where is he?'

'Just out of the operating theatre. He will be sent home soon.'

'But he can't go home yet!'

'Mrs Wong, you don't know the half of it! The Europeans have gone. They took the machines and a lot of medicine with them. The X-ray machine is gone. We don't even have enough needles. How Dr Pillay is operating, I don't know. Everyone is screaming. Father was screaming too . . .' Choy Yoke shivered, her fulsome body seeming somehow constricted in the white nurse's uniform with its blue belt.

'But Choy Yoke, have all the Europeans really left? What about the patients in the European ward?'

A strange light flitted through Choy Yoke's eyes. She had unusually large eyes for a Chinese girl: they were staring earnestly into mine, glassy and innocent.

'Well, there are only two beds in the European section. There were two men there yesterday evening when I left, but when I arrived this morning, both had disappeared! There was some sort of evacuation last night.'

'Evacuation?'

It was the first time I had heard the word used to describe Britain's abandonment of Malaya. I knew what 'evacuation' meant: to remove to a safer place. But such safety was to apply only to a chosen few.

As I took in what was happening, I tried to recreate images of the white doctors and nurses I had known. There was the matron, Mrs McDonald, who had delivered our four children, and the Chief Medical Officer, Dr Osborne, a friend of Father's. I tried to imagine Dr Osborne fleeing with Mrs McDonald, their equipment in tow, but the pictures would not come; my mind could not conjure them up.

I continued staring into Choy Yoke's face. For a fleeting moment I was transported to another world – a time when I was as youthful as Choy Yoke and my whole life lay ahead. I marvelled, though only for a split second, at the beauty of soft, unblemished skin. I forgot where we were. In the months to come I would try to relive that moment, to remember a past when life was not about war. Time, I discovered, could not be bottled. Every moment slips inexorably away. That moment, like all the other moments in my life, passed and was gone, leaving only an imprint of its memory, and a feeling of searing desperation.

◆ ◆ ◆

Samad and I helped Mrs Lim to get her husband into the back of our car. Asking Samad to take them home, I walked. As I approached our house I spotted, on the neighbouring driveway, a figure with a black songkok on his head, the tall hat favoured by Malay men. Ja'afar Abu, our policeman neighbour, was in the midst of strapping two heaving suitcases on to the roof of a decrepit Morris Minor. The vehicle wasn't his – Ja'afar did not own a car. He must have paid handsomely to borrow it.

'Enche Ja'afar!' I called out. '*Apa khabar?* Are you going somewhere?'

The animated conversation I'd had with Ja'afar – when had that been? Only the previous day, I now recalled, the words we'd exchanged being still fresh in my mind. It was unnerving to see him with suitcases. I felt like one half of a pair of conjoined twins being pulled in two different directions, each path as dangerous as the other. I had entered Dorcourt in the morning confident that we should abandon our house in Green Town temporarily. Yet by the early afternoon, when Weng Yu and I exited the secret room, this certainty had evaporated. What if my brother-in-law was right and well-trained reinforcements were indeed sent? It was difficult to imagine where they would come from, but you just never knew. And now this: a policeman packing up. The sight of it added to my mounting sense of calamity.

On seeing me approach, a frown of displeasure crossed Ja'afar's face. His complexion was deep brown, a colour he shared with many of his Malay compatriots, and after years under the country's sun, it had taken on a mottled appearance. It was hard to read his sentiments, and I could have been mistaken about what I thought I saw. His inscrutability was reinforced by the way he directed his eyes obliquely past me.

This brusqueness was new and rather astonishing. Ja'afar Abu had always been friendly. He had been his usual self only the day before, when he had warned me against going into Old Town. But now, beside a car which was not his, the man did not even stop what he was doing. He ignored me and continued wrestling with the bulging suitcase on the roof.

'Do you need more rope, Enche Ja'afar?' I asked. 'We have some in the house. Let me ask Samad to bring it.'

'No, no thank you, Puan Wong,' the policeman grunted, breathing out while pulling his load tight with heroic effort. 'I think I can do it. There, *habis*!'

His shout of triumph brought a woman to their front door – his wife, Husna, whose head of tiny black curls suddenly appeared. On catching sight of me, Husna ran on to the driveway in her bare feet and wrapped my hands in hers. 'Oh, Mei Foong, *apa khabar*? Are you all okay? Isn't it terrible? We are so *takut*!'

Husna's smile stretched her mouth fully, exposing lovely white teeth, which fitted together perfectly from end to end. I smiled in response, suddenly conscious of my own, rather smaller mouth – shaped like a rosebud and petite, like the rest of me. Husna held me captive with her enchanting smile and her eyes, beautiful brown eyes, which told me how glad she was to see me. A wave of feminine empathy passed between us.

'Are you leaving, Husna?'

'Yes, Mei Foong, we are going to my uncle's house near Kampong Kepayang. We can stay for a few days. There we will always have food. You know, many people already leaving town.'

I could feel something sharp – her husband's eyes – stabbing me from behind.

Husna gave him a momentary glance but did not stop speaking. 'Husband says there are troops on the Gopeng Road, many of them. But you know, in the convoy also many civilian cars, with Penang number plates.'

'Penang number plates?'

'Didn't you know, Mei Foong? Penang has been badly bombed.'

'No! Really-ah?'

'Yes, I tell you, things there are bad. My brother-in-law Hamid passed by this morning and gave us the news. The *orang puteh*, the white people, they are evacuating.'

There was that word again: evacuation; it made me feel ill. Everything Father had predicted seemed to be coming true. For the first time, I had a heavy sense that all was lost. A sharp pain rose up from my gut; I wanted to lie down.

Husna placed her hand on my arm. 'Are you all right, Mei Foong?'

I gave her a feeble smile. Penang, an island off Malaya's western coast, was one of Britain's crown jewels – the Pearl of the Orient. It had things of value to our white rulers: a telecommunications station, a port, wharves, and the godowns which stored the commodities they ferreted away. We had relatives there: Mother-in-Law's younger sister and Dora's family. I would have to tell Dora.

I began to wonder if what Husna was saying could really be true. I focused on its source: her brother-in-law Hamid, whom I had met only once. I remembered him as a lean and clean-shaven boy, young but trustworthy. He was a member of the Royal Malay Regiment, which had been fighting battles with the Japanese. If anyone would know what was happening in the rest of Malaya, it would be Hamid.

'Husna, where is your brother-in-law going?'

'Somewhere south, he doesn't know where.'

'South?'

'Yes, Mei Foong.' Beckoning me closer, Husna added in a low whisper, 'Mei Foong, if I were you, I would leave Ipoh. Isn't that right, Husband?'

I turned to Ja'afar Abu, who had remained upright beside the Morris. His posture was rigid. Eventually he sighed as if overcoming an internal struggle. Thereafter, Ja'afar hunched his shoulders. When he finally looked at me, his eyes had a coldness I had not noticed before.

'Puan Wong, the world has changed. Malaya has changed. I have seen things these past two days I never thought I would see. This country will not be the same. Your mother-in-law, may she rest in peace, was always kind to us. In her memory, I tell you this: you have children, take them and leave. It will be safer for you out of town.'

I looked directly into Ja'afar's eyes. 'Enche Ja'afar, if you leave, and other policemen leave, then who will take care of law and order?'

Our neighbour did not flinch. 'Puan Wong, there are reasons why I'm telling you and Enche Wong to go. Do it now, before it's too late.'

Thanking him, I cupped Husna's hands in farewell. 'Good luck, Mei Foong!' she said as she waved me away.

I headed to Dorcourt, which I accessed via the secret gate. I hoped I was not too late. Weng Yoon and Ali were still in the garden, sweating over their trench in the afternoon heat. Through the open front door, I entered the cool of the main living room, where I bumped into a surprised Rokiah.

'I need to use the telephone, Rokiah. Enche Ja'afar says the *orang puteh* have left Penang. I must call Third Maternal Aunt. Dora should call her parents.'

'Penang? Our beautiful Penang given up, you say? No!'

Rokiah batted back tears with her long eyelashes. I nodded, touching her arm. The maid stood with hands clasped helplessly while I picked up the heavy Bakelite receiver and spoke into its mouthpiece, asking the operator to patch me through to number 3325 in Penang.

'I will try, madam,' replied a woman who spoke English with an Indian accent, 'but Penang has been under heavy shelling. I may not get through.'

'Do you know how bad things are?'

From the silence on the other end, I drew my own conclusions. The operator finally said, 'I've heard there are many wounded. But I will do my best, madam. Now put your phone down. I'll call you back when I get through.' With that she hung up, and I was left with an interminable wait.

Rokiah promptly disappeared, I assumed to pass the news to Dora. I found myself alone in Dorcourt's vast living room, a grand space with double-height ceilings reaching the roof. On the first floor above, a mezzanine balcony around three sides gave a commanding view of the

45

entire living area. I remembered standing on that balcony on my first visit to the house, soon after Weng Yoon had brought his bride home, and being entranced by the shafts of light coming in from Dorcourt's tall windows. The windows were high and, though somewhat narrow, let in more light than our own windows next door. They reminded me of windows in a church, which had perhaps been my brother-in-law's intention. Weng Yoon had become a Christian without his mother's knowledge. For many months he had not dared tell her, fearing one of her famous eruptions. Two months before his marriage he finally revealed his secret, only to be surprised by his mother's muted reaction. The old lady, being no fool, must already have guessed. If a man vanishes each Sunday morning at regular hours, where could he be going?

Rokiah returned to the living room with a tray in her hands. My sister-in-law followed closely behind, her crescent-shaped eyes wide with anxiety. She gave me a wan smile. 'Have they called back yet?' I shook my head.

Rokiah set her tray down on the rectangular coffee table. Puffs of steam rose out of the spout of a metallic blue pot, filling the air with the smell of freshly brewed Malayan coffee. Thanking Rokiah, I grabbed a coffee cup off its saucer and helped myself to three heaped teaspoons of sugar. 'Dora, won't you join me?'

My sister-in-law had moved towards one of Dorcourt's large windows and was muttering to herself. From the divan I caught only snippets: '. . . the hospital store-room . . . can't go now . . . my parents . . .' But her final expostulation, in an anguished voice – 'Oh Lord, why are you letting this happen?' – was quite audible.

I rose from my seat and handed Dora the coffee I had just poured. 'Here, Dora, have this, you'll feel much better.'

Without a word she took the proffered cup and seated herself in an armchair opposite. I poured another cup and then played with my wedding ring, stroking the sparkling gem at its core for no reason other than to give my itchy fingers something to do. I was glad when the phone rang.

'Madam, I've managed to get through. Penang, are you there?'

I heard a cough on the other end and a muffled yes. The voice belonged to Mother-in-Law's younger sister, my husband's third maternal aunt, but she sounded faint and far away.

When she spoke her voice was barely a murmur. 'We do what, Mei Foong? We do what, I ask you?' The old lady began moaning.

'Third Maternal Aunt, please tell me what happened.'

'They bomb, they bomb, Mei Foong, every day. Until now I not even know what bomb is! How they can do this to us, I ask you, how? We also Asian, just like them.'

'When did they come?'

'Today, yesterday, few days already very bad. Every day they come, many dead.' The old lady began sobbing. 'Our neighbour next door, Mr Ang, he died. Opposite, Mrs Phua, she – she . . .'

Third Maternal Aunt's plaintive cry was so loud that Dora heard it through the telephone earpiece. She reached instinctively for my arm with tears in her eyes. When the pain became too much, Dora put a hand over her mouth and fled. Third Maternal Aunt resumed her story: 'First day, we all go to look. Servant Mui Fah also go look. Inside I hear loud boom. Everyone scream. On the roads, they bomb, got fire, very noisy, fire everywhere. They kill Mr Ang next door. They kill him, Mei Foong!'

The memory of Mr Ang's demise brought a torrent of bawling. The old lady began to hiccup.

'Third Maternal Aunt, you need water. Maybe we should stop talking.'

'No, Mei Foong, must tell you!' Panicked by the idea of not finishing her tale, she made a concerted effort to steady her voice. 'Mr Ang die that time still got doctor. Next day many planes come. You remember my friend Mrs Phua? Her house fall down. She not inside, her daughter inside, no one come to house, still got fire now, cannot see road. Mrs Phua, she die outside. She now dead, Mei Foong, she dead . . .'

Third Maternal Aunt began wailing again. In between she managed to say, 'No one pick her body, Mei Foong. Mui Fah say still on road. Penang, how can be like this?'

As the old lady wept, I pictured her surrounded by crumbling houses, with just an aged servant for company. My eyes misted up and feelings of impotence overcame me. There were no comforting words, or if there were, I could not find them. Everything that came to mind sounded immeasurably hollow. In later years we were to learn that Penang's Chinatown had been mercilessly bombed; it was a miracle the family shop-house on Ah Kwee Street survived. I did not have the heart to tell Third Maternal Aunt that similar things had happened in Ipoh. I wondered how many unsuspecting people all over Malaya had had their lives curtailed in this way, gathering to look up at the sky and then being killed when the Japanese planes had dived, dropping bombs and spraying their machine guns.

'I'm sorry to interrupt,' the operator's voice interjected in English. 'I will have to cut short this call.'

'Excuse me, but why?'

'We have orders to evacuate our posts.'

'To evacuate? But, where are you?'

'In Penang, madam. It's no longer safe for us to be here. After today no one will be able to call Penang.'

I translated this for the benefit of Third Maternal Aunt, who was now whimpering. I knew that our goodbye would have to be quick. I told Third Maternal Aunt to take care of herself, that we would surely see each other again. Promptly switching into English, I asked the operator whether she could patch one final call through.

'We need to go, madam—'

'I understand, but my sister-in-law's family lives in Penang, and I know that if you were in my shoes, you would want to know that they were safe. She'll be quick, I promise.'

In the ensuing silence, I sensed the operator struggling with her conscience. After a minute, she relented. 'All right, but be very quick.'

I yelled out for Dora. When she came, I thrust her the telephone mouthpiece. Rokiah stood behind her mistress, her face stony but resolute, defiant almost. We held each other's hands, neither of us saying a word, and then I walked back to our house.

5

For three days, the Japanese bombed Ipoh; for three nights, I did not sleep.

I would leave my husband in bed, slide open our bedroom door, and seek solace in front of the prayer altar in the inner hall. The altar was a dark lacquered table of elm, on top of which sat a porcelain image of Kuan Yin, the Goddess of Mercy. It was my own mother who had taught me to pray. When the bombs started falling, I did not know where else to turn. I stood meekly in front of the Goddess, surveying her enduring posture of repose: left leg bent at the knee, tucked beneath her right leg. The years of smoke curling up in ringlets from Mother-in-Law's joss-sticks had stained the Goddess a yellowish brown. Below the altar table were the plate of oranges and teapot that my maid, Chang Ying, had not forgotten to lay out.

When I thought of dear Chang Ying, I realised that the decision I had to make was as much for her and the other servants as it was for me and my children. Chang Ying had arrived in our household when I was seven. Until then, other amahs had come and gone, women for whom I had not felt the same affection as I did for Chang Ying. She was the first person who truly looked after me. As a result, she filled the childhood memories in which Mother merely drifted in and out. It wasn't that Mother did not love me; rather, that she preferred adult company and spent her time visiting friends or entertaining them in our grand living room. Chang Ying, in contrast, was absolutely dedicated to me. She belonged to the sorority known as the 'black-and-white amahs', women who had taken vows of celibacy and who wore spotless white tunics with tiny Mandarin collars that matched their loose black trousers. Whatever I now chose, I knew I could count on her support.

Chang Ying had been born in Kwangtong, to a family working in the paddy fields. When she arrived at my parental home on the Gopeng Road, she bore only the name Ah Ying, or 'flourishing'. Precocious child that I was, I took to calling her Chang Ying, for in my mind the maid, with her long hair tied into a single plait, was lustrous. Ah Ying, who at four feet nine inches was short even by the standards of the day, did not seem to mind. She served as my personal amah, her only tasks being to see to my every need. Each morning she would brush my hair from its roots down to its very tips. At the time my hair fell below my shoulders, and Chang Ying spent time pulling the strands into two ponytails which never looked right, no matter what she did. As I grew in height, combing my hair became more arduous, though Chang Ying never complained: grumbling was not something servants of that era indulged in. Whenever we went out, she would hold a paper umbrella over my head so that my skin – especially the precious unmarred skin on my face – was shielded from the Malayan sun. To cool my beads of perspiration, Chang Ying kept a Mandarin fan tucked inside the shopping bag she always carried. The fan, which had been given by Mother on the occasion of my thirteenth birthday, was made of sandalwood. Its slats were painted in a polychrome of vivid blues and reds, and it was emblazoned with a turquoise image of Au Chin, the Dragon King of the South Sea, in between white cranes and nine-tailed foxes. To this day I still carry Mother's fan. It has been with me at every significant moment in my life. I carried it the first time I ever entered my husband's house, when my tongue was set on fire by Mother-in-Law's dishes and Chang Ying had to fan my brows.

As I stood before Kuan Yin's enduring image, I thought about how Mother herself had trembled in front of a similar statuette and how, after praying, she would retreat into a state of Zen. Mother-in-Law's zeal had been just as great. Most likely it was this unshakeable belief in omnipresent gods and goddesses which sustained her through a host of ordeals, or so it seemed to those of us observing. Mother-in-Law would clasp three lit joss-sticks in her hands and shake them for hours while reciting soothing sutras. The ritual gave her strength and a tranquillity that had not been there before. I marvelled at such faith; I could not feel a similar confidence. My spirit, clouded by the certainties of pure numbers and algebra, had more in common with the spirits of my husband and my father, to whom religion mattered only half-heartedly, if at all. Like most Chinese men, Weng Yu and Father never bothered with prayer. They were happy to leave this unedifying occupation to the women in the family.

Which of course meant me, and with Mother-in-Law's passing away into the next world, the Wong family women were looking to me to set an example.

For three nights, while our world turned upside down, I attempted sutras before Kuan Yin. Alas, as I watched the red embers flickering on my joss-sticks, my mind refused to remain on the task. I pictured our children instead. I would see our quiet eldest son, Wai Sung, the hair on his seven-year-old head still shining as brilliantly black as it had on the day he was born. When I cast him out of my mind, it was not the Goddess who drew my attention but our other children: Lai Hin, then only five, as boisterous as her elder brother was quiet, and also our second son, Wai Kit, three years old, who was my favourite among the children. Though I had told no one this, the servants must have observed how I encouraged his easy smile and his good nature.

Then there was Robert, a baby barely a year old, who was still feeding from a bottle. Could we really flee with such young ones in tow? But if we did not, how would we keep them safe from the bullets and the bombs? This and a thousand other questions bounced around inside my brain, arriving in chaotic, disjointed snippets. Every time I tried to regain the thread of my prayers, I failed. With nirvana out of reach, I grew vexed, the more so as the Goddess remained stubbornly silent through my hours of struggle.

Afterwards, with the rest of the house still deep in slumber, I would step on to the *barlay* and surreptitiously open the window overlooking our front garden. There was only one way to calm my heart: by gazing at the night sky, dense with stars. A curfew was in force, and the whole of Ipoh lay in darkness. Not a single electric light could be seen anywhere. In the firmament beyond, the stars looked like pinpricks, but there were so many of them, uncountable millions, that they had the appearance of jewels cascading across a velvet curtain or of a sparkling river in heaven.

The first time I had beheld this wondrous sight I was a child of five. Father had taken my sister and me for a walk and had pointed out the constellations. We lived, he said, in a galaxy called the River of Heaven. Father then pointed to the stars. Their exotic names – the Small Bear, the Black Tortoise of the North, the Tiger of the West – made my spirit soar. Later, at my missionary school, I was taught that these same constellations were actually called Ursa Minor, Pegasus, and Andromeda, names which had no meaning for me. Worse, we did not live in the River of Heaven, but in something called the Milky Way. Though I continued to regard the skies with fascination, my enthusiasm for astronomy was never the same.

An almost perfect ball of silver hung in the sky on those three nights, like a globe suspended in air. From where I stood, I perceived watery patches, which were perhaps oceans on the moon. On its bottom half, a vast tract radiated light, which illuminated the clouds. Every now and then, white clumps drifted by, casting bluish-white tentacles across the sky.

◆ ◆ ◆

On the fourth night, after another day's bombing, we fled. We were guided by the glow of a full moon. Samad drove the Austin 8. My husband had chafed at not being the one to drive his family, but when I pointed out that one of us, either he or Father or I, should stay with the children at every moment, Weng Yu seemed almost relieved.

It was pitch-black when we left. The car's lights, sitting atop its bonnet like the eyes of a frog, had to be kept extinguished throughout the journey – we could not afford to alert the enemy. The night outside had the sticky blackness of tar. Fragments of moonlight peeked through only when the clouds parted.

As we trundled along on the narrow road, I glanced often to my right, watching our gardener's long, burnished fingers as they gripped the steering wheel. Samad's hands, creased from age and toil, seemed remarkably steady for a man who had never driven more than a mile or two, and only during daylight hours. To keep awake, he had consumed several cups of coffee. And unlike our other gardener, Samad had chosen to stay.

'Are you sure, Samad?' I had asked him earlier in the day, just after Kamil announced that he would be returning to his kampong. Kamil's Malay village was not far from Slim River, about sixty-five miles south of Ipoh. With the buses and gharries no longer operating, he would have to hitch a ride or walk.

Samad, who was in the midst of lifting a box of provisions from the kitchen floor, drew himself up to his full height – barely two inches taller than me. His curly hair was tousled. 'Makche, Sumatra very far. There also I have no family. Here I have family, family you.' He heaped a big smile on me, showing off teeth that were a walking advertisement for the makeshift sticks and powdered charcoal he used to clean them.

Inside our car, Samad's face was full of the same loyalty and kindness I had seen that morning, but it now bore the determination of a man locked in concentration. He drove the Austin at a steadier pace than my jittery husband would have done, without jerking the vehicle forwards or grinding it to a sudden halt or swerving it from side to side on winding roads.

The car was endowed with old-fashioned windows, and though they could be wound down we kept them firmly up, in a feeble attempt to shut out the night. There were so many passengers and appurtenances crammed into the interior that it smelled clammy and dank, and saturated with the sweat that oozes out when fear creeps through your pores. Our terror spilled out uncontrollably, mingling with the rank odour of the dried salted fish which Li-Fei had stuffed into every bit of spare space.

We made our way in a convoy of two. Each of our vehicles carried in its rear seat a child sandwiched between protective adults. In Father's car, our second son, Wai Kit, had been thrust into the back with Father's old but trustworthy servants. The old man himself was in the front beside his driver, Mutu. In my own car, my daughter, Lai Hin, was watched over by Ah Hong on one side and Chang Ying on the other, while baby Robert nuzzled close against my chest in the front passenger seat.

Both vehicles were bursting at their seams, with every cubic foot of space inside crammed full. Only Robert – because he was a babe in my arms – and Samad, who had his hands on the wheel, did not hold bags. Everyone else, including five-year-old Lai Hin, carried an item on their lap.

The other three members of our household – my husband, the servant Li-Fei, and our eldest son Wai Sung – had had to remain behind. Samad was to make a second nerve-racking journey. Father's driver, Mutu, gallantly agreed to accompany our gardener, and Mutu's empty car proved a blessing. Into the boot Mutu was able to stuff sacks of rice, bags of salt and sugar, yet even more bundles of dried salted fish, as well as a myriad condiments and canned goods – all hauled from our pantry. On to the seats he laid the bags of clothes our servants had already pre-packed, but for which we had found no room in our already heaving cars. Mutu took extra mattresses too, stringing them over the top on the outside, secured by coir rope.

We drove through a ghost town, dingy and deserted, our only company the desecrated bodies in the ditches and by the roadsides, which no one had had time to clear away. The uncovered mounds were not obvious from inside the Austin, but I nonetheless hung garments up at the rear windows to shield my daughter from the sight of corpses. I hoped that Father and his entourage would have the common sense to do the same.

On the Menglembu Road, half an arm – perfectly cleaved at its base – lay beside the road. Gnarled fingers winked at me under a shaft of moonlight. I could swear, as we passed, that the index and second fingers curled and uncurled of their own accord. I gasped without meaning to, my whole heart thumping so loudly and so fast that I was sure I would awaken Robert. I blinked once, closing my eyes. I could feel my eyelashes scrape against the lower lid. Taking a deep breath, I forced my eyes open again. The fingers were still there, in the rigid attitude of the dead. I looked down at Robert, whose head was resting against my breasts. He remained fast asleep, thankfully oblivious to the horrors we faced. But there was my daughter in the rear. I jerked around.

Lai Hin was the child I worried most about, the only one of my children who had fought her way into this world a whole month early. The girl had announced her arrival by shrieking at the top of her voice even before her bottom had been slapped. She emerged with a ready-made mop of hair, straight and hard like the bristles on a broom. Her mouth, rosebud-shaped like mine, belied its projective power. In the Green Town neighbourhood, Lai Hin was already known for her heart-stopping screams. As I expected, the girl's eyes were wide open. In the rear of the Austin, she began to sob.

'Shh!' I said quickly, concerned about the commotion which could follow. 'Don't make a noise, otherwise the Japs will hear you.'

Our old servant Ah Hong, who was sitting beside Lai Hin, put her free arm around the girl's shoulders and pulled the whimpering child towards her. The servant seemed to have taken the place of the grandmother Lai Hin had lost; for this, I was secretly glad. It wasn't that I did not love the girl; of course I did, but when a child is prickly, it's difficult not to favour the easier children.

My daughter calmed down and buried her face in Ah Hong's shoulder. Only the back of Lai Hin's head was visible, and I was once again surprised by my daughter's hair, lustrous even in the dim light of the night, a shine she had inherited from me. The texture, however, was strictly her grandmother's: stubborn strands which refused to lie flat, insisting instead on sticking upwards and sideways.

I turned back towards the road, which was uncannily peaceful in the tenuous moonlight. It had been different during the day, when Ipoh had seen a battalion of cars moving south. There had also been men in distinctive black caps, shaped like the Malay songkok, but with three rows of alternate black-and-white-chequered squares on the fronts. On their epaulettes, boars' heads and wildcats in wreaths stared at us. The men, I was told, belonged to the Argyll and Highland regiment, and they were heading in the opposite direction to the cars – northwards.

'See, fresh troops!' my brother-in-law Weng Yoon had gloated when we went to Dorcourt to say our farewell. 'Britain is defending us!'

I cast a dry look in his direction. Penang had already been evacuated of all its European residents. Newspapers were no longer being printed; our sole source of news was the MBC's five o'clock service. The broadcasts spoke daily of 'strategic retreats', yet the MBC announcers continued to discuss the war as if British troops were winning. My feelings sank like stones to the pit of my stomach when I realised the extent of the lies we were being fed.

Even Weng Yu's protests became muted and half-hearted after Penang.

'I can't believe it! I can't believe it!' he had muttered repeatedly in a fit of coughing. 'How could the Japs have taken over the island so soon?'

Afterwards, when I spoke of what we would need to do for our own escape, he no longer argued. My husband, it seemed, was even more afraid of dying beneath a pile of rubble than of being bombed in the open countryside.

His brother, on the other hand, remained convinced that we were making a mistake. 'It's cowardly to run away,' Weng Yoon declared.

'Ha, you can say that again!' I retorted, unable to contain the bitterness I felt.

'The British haven't run away; they will come back!'

Of course they will, to reclaim the tin and rubber which has made them rich.

When I observed Weng Yoon, contempt and pity surged in me. He was a smart lawyer, yet he could not see the wood from the trees.

His wife, I could tell, was embarrassed; Dora's cheeks were red and she could not stop asking about our imminent departure. Finally I said, 'Dora, we need to leave.' Bidding them and Rokiah the usual 'See you again', we walked out of Dorcourt's front door.

Meanwhile, Ipoh town continued to empty. Most inhabitants left on foot or on their bikes, lugging cloth sacks for the short time that they imagined they would be away. Despite the absence of newspapers, there was no shortage of news. What people could not confirm, they made up. From passers-by on the roads, I heard all manner of stories. The Japanese had already taken over Penang and were just fifty miles north of Ipoh; this was why the Europeans were all running away. As if to confirm the rumour, we spotted the last Europeans leaving town: stragglers from the hospital, lugging even more equipment; the last two engineers from the Public Works Department; a handful of school-teachers, dentists, architects. In short, anyone of European or mixed descent who, with their families, would be the only passengers allowed on to the boats departing for the safety of Australia, were heading out.

Overnight, Malaya was full of refugees. Everyone went somewhere they thought would be safer, without any idea whether they would reach their destination or how long they would be away. Some never made it; they were killed in their cars by stray machine-gun fire, which the Japanese, paying no heed to civilian life, unleashed.

A Malay man was the hero in our own exodus. If Samad had not run out of petrol, he would have made a third trip to transport more of our family's belongings. But there was no petrol to be found. Slowly but surely, like a sieve through which traffic temporarily flowed, Ipoh emptied.

PART II

6

We met again in the middle of the night. When I saw his eyes, narrow and slanted, I recognised the stranger whom I had encountered near Hale Street, the man who had been carrying a child. The expression of urgency had disappeared from his eyes, which were now mischievous and slightly mocking. They rested on me for just a few seconds longer than etiquette permitted. My husband, who stood beside me at the time, did not notice. Weng Yu was in a sour mood, exhausted by the journey. I was equally tired, though not in ill humour. I was thinking about our wireless set.

We could not unpack then. It was too dark and somehow also too frightening. The jungle seemed alive, every thicket ringing with a cacophony we never heard in town. There was a perpetual whistling from creatures we could not see, a rhythmic croaking and hooting which never stopped. Worst of all was the high-pitched hissing, as if the foliage around us seethed with slimy, red-eyed amphibians. The noise drove me crazy after just a few minutes. I did not know how I would survive it.

I thought that if I did something, I would feel better; at the very least it would take my mind off the unearthly noise. I remembered that our wireless set lay inside the Austin 8, which Samad had left parked on the dirt track above. It seemed a good idea to fetch it.

I glanced at the side of the hillock up which I would have to climb to reach the car. 'Come with me, Husband,' I said, giving Weng Yu a light nudge on the elbow.

He looked at me as if I were mad. 'This time, you really must be joking! You're the one who wanted to bring it along. You get it from the car.'

In the still of the night, Weng Yu's vowels exploded in the air and slapped me in the face. The man from Hale Street took in the scene; I could feel his narrow, slanted eyes boring through me. For a moment I thought he would offer to help. A broad smile formed on his small mouth, but then he saw Samad walking up. Still smiling, the man turned away. There was a spark on his face, just before he turned, a strange mixture of sympathy and tenderness and also understanding, as if he had known me all my life. No man had ever looked at me like that, not even my husband. I shivered from the chill of the Malayan night and the vicarious thrill running through my bones.

It took a while before Samad and I were free to climb the gravelly slope leading to the track where he had left our car. First had come the myriad introductions, for we were far from the only ones who had sought refuge at Grand-Uncle's tin mine. In fact the place was buzzing. At that hour, greetings and hellos were the last thing I wanted or needed, but it would have been rude to claim our sleeping places without finding out who our neighbours would be. The words we exchanged were cursory. I was too exhausted to care about names or faces, until I glimpsed relations of ours: Liew Chin Tong, who had been married to my husband's second sister before her untimely death, and his sister Liew Yuk Moi, a spinster who had once been my teacher.

Weng Yu and I almost stumbled as we approached them. I sometimes saw Second Brother-in-Law and Miss Liew as I went about my business in Ipoh. We always exchanged greetings and news, but I never imagined that I would bump into them at the tin mine, of all places. Chin Tong, who worked as an interpreter in Ipoh's Magistrates' Court, told us that he had met Grand-Uncle in the courthouse, where he had helped him get off a parking fine. My grand-uncle, being a generous man, never forgot a favour. He had invited Liew Chin Tong and his sister for a meal as a way of thanking him, after which the families had become friends.

In addition to the Liews, there were the Teohs, the Chuas, and the Chews, families which, like ours, were stretched to a size unimaginable today by the inclusion of elderly parents, aunts, uncles, cousins, and gaggles of servants. When we were finally introduced, just before I went off with Samad to fetch our Philco set, I learnt that the stranger's name was Chew Hock San and that he was there with his wife and three children. As we said hello, his fiercely pomaded hair gleamed in the torchlight. He was squat, much shorter than my husband and rather heavyset, with robust biceps flaring out from beneath his short-sleeved shirt. His wife Kit Mei, who spoke only Chinese, looked a few years younger than me. She regarded me with curiosity. I smiled and saw that on her otherwise beautiful face she sported a black mole on the cleft of her right cheek, towards the edge of her lips. As Samad and I headed to the car, I could feel Chew Hock San observing us. Samad paid no attention, but I had to shrug off the man with the disconcerting stare.

◆ ◆ ◆

When we fled Ipoh, I had been adamant about taking our Philco 444 wireless, a mournful-looking set encased in black Bakelite. My husband was less than happy with the idea: not only were we fleeing to the jungle, a decision he did not wholeheartedly support, but I was asking to take an absurdly bulky item.

'We barely have space in the Austin,' he said through gritted teeth.

Father agreed with Weng Yu. 'Mei Foong, we'll be away only a few days at the most.'

For some reason I refused to relent. It was the first time I had ever pressed an argument with both my husband and my father at the same time and won.

In the end, Weng Yu wedged the contraption under my knees, locked into position against my calves. There was no wiggle room in the car for my legs, nothing I could do to battle the pins and needles which settled an hour into our journey. I could not even stretch my limbs.

But the next day, when the male voice with its British accent came on air and I saw my husband among the audience gathered in the large dining room, I felt vindicated.

'. . . reorganised and refreshed after their bitter battles in the jungles of north-eastern Malaya, the British forces are awaiting the expected Japanese advance southwards towards Ipoh and Singapore . . .'

This pronouncement elicited a storm of groans. Teoh Wai Fong, a garrulous mother of four, flicked her head backwards. The large cowlick of her permanent wave was quivering as she demanded, 'Why are they saying that? Don't they know that everyone has already left Ipoh?'

I pressed an index finger to my lips. When I caught Wai Fong's eyes, her response was a sardonic smile. There was something coarse in the unabashed redness of her lips and the powdery white of her face, though the men seemed to find her alluring. Instead of being annoyed, my own husband's eyes flitted casually over the woman each time she threw her head back and interrupted the broadcast.

Around the enormous dining table there was sudden shuffling. The legs of benches scraped against the planks as an expectant hush descended. Everyone leaned forward when we heard the name of Singapore's Governor.

'Sir Shenton Thomas has declared Penang's evacuation to be absolutely necessary from a military perspective. The Governor has said that he was given no prior knowledge of the evacuation, nor was the Colonial Secretary.'

A volley of cries filled the room.

'No prior knowledge?' shouted a male voice.

'What is this, man? How can they say things like that?' yelled another.

'Ai-yahh, what kind of governor is that?'

This last rebuke, said very softly, had come from a woman who hardly ever spoke. Chua Yik Wei and I had attended the same missionary school, though we had not been close. Until we met again in that unlikely spot in Lahat, I had not seen Yik Wei since we graduated with our leaving certificates. Nonetheless I remembered her well: it was hard to forget a Chinese girl who possessed a European's translucent skin.

'Sickening!' a voice thundered down the room. The ramshackle table shook. All heads turned towards the man who had pounded its surface with his balled-up fist. With his crooked smile and mocking eyes, the impression Chew Hock San gave was of easy joviality, and my heart pounded when he bellowed, 'It's enough to make me want to fight the Japs!'

When Hock San thumped the table a second time, we shrank back as if we had been hit. The mockery in his slanted eyes had dissolved into an intense and rather terrifying passion.

At the time, none of us thought it possible to fight the invaders. Cocking her head to one side, Teoh Wai Fong said, 'Really? And how are you going to fight them? We have no guns, no training, nothing.'

After a minute, she added, 'Besides, the British are finished. What's the point of fighting? If we have new rulers, we have new rulers. Better to get used to them.'

An inchoate murmur permeated the dining hall. There were nine of us huddled down at one end: four women and five men – the sum total of English speakers out of the sixty or so who had descended on Grand-Uncle's tin mine. Among the women, the raspy voice of Miss Liew, Chin Tong's sister, could easily be made out in the low burbling. Because she had once taught me English, she remained Miss Liew in my mind, and for as long as I had known Miss Liew, she had sounded as if she had a sore throat. Her timbre became increasingly crackly as her sentence progressed; with every word she uttered, I feared her voice would break.

Further along the table where the men were sitting, Teoh Wai Fong's husband whispered into my own husband's ears. A look of scorn appeared on Weng Yu's face, but on glancing at Chew Hock San, the triangulated snarl on his lips transformed into a smile of effortless charm. Mr Teoh's remark, whatever it was, had been caught by the man sitting on Weng Yu's other side. This happened to be our brother-in-law, Liew Chin Tong, who, on straightening his back, turned sharply towards his right and retorted, quite loudly, 'I think Mr Chew is right. If the British won't fight the Japs, we must. We need to defend ourselves!'

Once again all heads turned, this time towards the older Liew sibling. The court interpreter, a soft-spoken man who wore gold-rimmed glasses, was better known for his storytelling and his jokes. His skinny frame lent him an air of vulnerability; I could not see him holding a rifle.

By the time the MBC broadcast ended, we had been given no further details of what help would come from Singapore. A glum silence overwhelmed the table, fanned by the breeze seeping in through the flimsy planks of our kongsi house. When I took in a deep breath, my lungs filled with pristine jungle air that smelled of earth, unspoiled leaves and wet rain. A robin's shrill trilling penetrated the hush. Outside I could hear dinner being prepared by the servants and whoops from the group of men playing cards under the trees.

Conversation eventually resumed around the long dining table, as it had to, and we split naturally into two groups. The men remained where they were while we women moved to the other end, away from their abstract talk of war. In the early days the men were not able to let the idea of battle go and insisted on useless speculation over what would happen next. We women had more immediate concerns, such as the next meal, how to manage the supplies we had brought, and, of course, our children and our worries for their safety. We had already noticed the fast-flowing stream behind the two kongsi houses, where the hills began to climb and the jungle thickened. A makeshift bridge had been placed across the body of water, and we feared that the rotting planks would prove too tempting, especially to our boys.

'Mrs Chua, now is a good time to teach your children to swim!' Wai Fong chided my school friend Yik Wei, whom I remembered as a shy and timid girl. She appeared to have changed little; though she had married in the intervening years, she remained just as bashful, and coloured furiously at Wai Fong's remark.

'It's not so easy-lah, Mrs Teoh,' I said, coming to my schoolmate's rescue. 'I myself cannot swim. How am I to teach my children?'

'We have to place a guard near the bridge, maybe one of your servants?' Miss Liew interjected, looking directly at me.

'Good idea, Miss Liew. I will ask Samad and also Mutu, my father's driver. Between them, they should be able to keep an eye on the young ones.'

The conversation turned to more mundane matters. Even Yik Wei joined in, mentioning in that timid voice of hers that a new coffee shop had recently opened on Leech Street which served delicious chicken rice. With no warning, Yik Wei asked, 'Do you think we'll be here long?' She did not look anyone in the eye but made a strange clacking noise, a sound I associated with the wetting of a very dry mouth. None of us knew what to say; we glanced nervously at the cracks in between the wooden planks or up at the thatched ceiling and at the bumps which had been hewn into the table through the years.

In the ensuing silence I felt a pair of eyes on me. Glancing down towards the other end of the table, I found Chew Hock San surveying my figure. What surprised me was that he did not stop, even after he realised that I had seen him. Such brazenness was new, at least to me; the men I came across averted their eyes when caught. I was at first embarrassed by the man's breathtaking calmness and then angry. Our eyes locked, until the full weight of his frank assessment penetrated me. At that point I looked away, annoyed but also confused by how thrilled I was.

Teoh Wai Fong's small, alert eyes darted back and forth. She had caught my interaction with Hock San and took in my fluster. The European-style curls on her head bounced up and down as if they were taunting me. I felt compelled to say something, so I asked where she had her hair done. I mused about getting a perm when we returned to Ipoh.

◆ ◆ ◆

By the second day, my ears had become accustomed to the noises of the jungle. We were in a tranquil and starkly beautiful spot – one which encouraged dark dreams. My mind ranged repeatedly over the bloody scenes that had led to our flight from Ipoh.

The moments the first bombs fell. Bomb: until then an alien word, one which I had only read in the newspapers, without any idea what it really meant and what being under one would feel like. The walk from Green Town to Old Town, through the running hordes and the plumes of smoke, the anguish and naked fear and the protractedness of it all, also the helplessness, not knowing whether my husband was dead or alive or when the Japanese planes would come back.

And then, finally finding him holed up in his office drinking whisky. I had refused to see that the man I married was a coward, but there was no longer any avoiding this unwelcome fact. My mind, filled with stories of heroes and princes, did not have a picture of what a coward looked like, but now I knew that he was no shrivelling devil, rather a handsome man who dressed well and loved culture and kept a black-and-white photograph in his wallet. This photograph, I was quite sure, was the same photograph his mother had told me about. It would surely be of Helen, the English woman whom he had fallen in love with while a student in London, and who was, by all accounts, a pretty woman. Mother-in-Law had even said that she bore a resemblance to me, though her shoulder-length dark hair was wavy.

'Same perfume even!' Mother-in-Law had laughed when she said this, as if it was funny. 'That rose-scented water you use before, she also like.'

I recalled the sound of Mother-in-Law's guffaw, a deep-throated laugh ringing with sincerity which was at once kind and formidable, in the same way that her speaking voice had been. Next to her I felt small, and the more I recalled of what had taken place in Weng Yu's office, the more ashamed I became. I berated myself for being such a mouse, unable to express what I really felt in our marriage. I could not understand where the confidence I'd had as a girl had gone. I did not even have the courage to tell Weng Yu that I knew about Helen. How difficult was that? It had not been so during our courtship or the early years of marriage, but being with Weng Yu had ground me down. I now clammed up whenever a sensitive subject came up between us. Something stopped me from speaking, some fear of exposure, or perhaps of rejection, as if rejection were a foregone conclusion. My silent acquiescence had never mattered before, but with Malaya's streets soaked in blood, it suddenly seemed important that I find my voice.

Within days I had my first victory. The result sat in one corner of our wooden kongsi house – the Philco wireless set I had insisted on bringing, which provided daily accounts of how the war was progressing. My confidence surged further in the jungle, where, in addition to taking charge of our provisions, it fell on me to manage my husband's moods.

Weng Yu was a creature of habit and a lover of luxury; he simply could not get used to the wildness of the jungle. Bereft of his beloved routine – his music and his breakfast of eggs and bacon – he became morose. Granted, none of us liked jungle life, but physical discomfort did not affect me in the same way. He grumbled about his shirts, which he disliked wearing because they could not be crisply ironed.

He complained about the plank bunks we used as beds, which had of course been made with coolies in mind. Though Weng Yu put a mattress on top of his bunk, the bed was still too narrow, too hard, and not sufficiently long; it gave him a backache and horrible dreams, and his feet stuck out. He hated the makeshift bathroom and decided to grow a beard. For his daily shower, he insisted that Li-Fei boil hot water to be mixed into the tub of cold which he then splashed over himself with a pail, as was done at home. It was not just talk: I could see my husband suffering. Bags grew under his deep-set eyes and he began to lose weight.

The lack of privacy inside our kongsi house did not help. There were two such houses at Grand-Uncle's tin mine, each long and narrow and made entirely of rough wood with a thatched roof. Inside our kongsi house were crammed not only the townsfolk who had descended on the tin mine, but also my Grand-Uncle and Grand-Aunt and their own entourage. The family had abandoned its property, a lovely colonial house at the top of the hill, when Grand-Uncle realised what a sitting target it made.

To steal a few minutes together, Weng Yu and I had to wander out along a dirt track, past the second kongsi house, into which a hundred coolies were packed like fish in a tin. We would meander in the hope of spying a clearing. There, in a dank, dark place, we would light a mosquito coil while keeping an eye out for the leeches, which threatened us in mid-embrace. We were not always so punctilious; sometimes, when we were awakened by the groans of our fellow refugees in the middle of the night, Weng Yu would reach out to me, and I would pretend that we were already back at our house in Green Town. Father, who slept inches away, never said anything, nor did anyone else, though they must have heard our soft moaning and the rustling of sheets.

Once, when we were on our way back from a clearing, we bumped into Chew Hock San. Even on the days when I did not talk to him, I was aware of his presence, looming behind me like the jungle, and like it, full of mystery. I remember having trouble breathing, though that may simply have been because the pure jungle air hurt my lungs. As my husband and I continued walking, I absorbed the beauty around me for the first time, noticing how the leaves of trees clambered over one another, in places falling like malachite waterfalls, in others standing stiff, reflecting dapples of yellow as they had done for millions of years. How indifferent the jungle was to all that was happening. I took in small breaths of air, as if sipping tea. I did this often, conscious of my nose and mouth and every orifice in my body, training myself to take the air in slowly until it no longer hurt.

7

'Planes coming! Everyone quick, into the shelters!'

I heard his rousing cry before anything else, even before the buzzing in the sky. The next minute came panicked shouts and screams. Somewhere a man waved his arms about. With the enemy raids getting longer and more vicious, everyone ran towards the large hole in the ground which Samad and Mutu had dug on the day the planes first appeared over our jungle canopy.

'Faster!' Hock San yelled in Cantonese to our servants. Holding on to the hands of our eldest three children, they seemed to be making their way towards the makeshift trench at a worryingly slow pace. 'Hurry, hurry, many planes coming!' Hock San screamed. Then he added in broken Malay, 'Samad, Mutu, come help me!'

Everything must have happened very quickly, yet my memories have a watery quality to them. The noise was loud as I peered upwards to scan the skies. I recall a huge formation flying past, with individual planes breaking off on strafing runs. It was a clear, sunny morning. I had an unimpeded view of the strafing planes, huge metallic pterodactyls with red circles painted on their sides, and presumably they had the same view of us, despite the curtain of leaves beneath which we were hidden. On the ground we, the main actors, seemed to wind our way like snails. I was standing near the edge of the trench, holding baby

Robert in my arms, watching our servants hand the children down to Samad and Mutu, one by one, when a blast appeared to shatter my limbs.

In the aftermath, time slowed. I gave an involuntary cry, though I did not hear it. My ears had been deafened by the roar. I could not feel my limbs, yet I was aware of every bone in my body, of how they were clacking, gyrating like wound springs just uncoiled. I thought we had been hit by a bomb. When I checked, my eyes were open; my limbs and arms still there. I was standing on both feet, definitely alive. There was no smoke, just a melancholic cry from somewhere in the distance, from either an animal or a person, I could not tell which. I heard soft moaning beside me; on looking up I realised it was our servants Ah Hong and Li-Fei, who looked overcome and were wobbling like jellyfish.

'Ohhh . . . , ah-h . . . we are all going to die,' Ah Hong sobbed.

'Get into the trench now!' Hock San commanded. There was a sharp edge in his voice.

He stood over the gaping trench with his legs apart. Placing both hands on Ah Hong's waist, he was ready to lift her down. Before they had time to even move, a second explosion reverberated. This time, I thought my eardrums had been torn apart. Smoke rose above the trees. The smell of burning filled the air and I longed to cover my nose, my ears, even my eyes with both hands, but I could not, as I was still cradling Robert. The silence dragged, as if the jungle itself needed time to take in what had happened. Baby Robert was the first to react: he began to bawl in my arms. His cry released us, gave us permission to howl. The world seemed to mourn with us; everything trembled: the ground on which we were standing, the trees with their leaves, even the hill beside which the kongsi houses had been built. When I heard the sound of falling rocks, I thought that the hill itself had collapsed and that a yawning gap would open up below, sucking us into the very core of the Earth. I cried as clods of soil fell along the sides of our trench. The children wailed louder too, Lai Hin most of all.

Hock San moved swiftly. Within seconds he had forcibly lowered Ah Hong into the shelter, grabbed Li-Fei's shoulders and also my maid Chang Ying's. The latter did not even wait – she threw herself into the crevasse and had to be caught by Chin Tong and Samad.

Next it was my turn. I felt his hands on my waist and when I turned found myself nose to nose with him. We had no choice but to look into one another's eyes; I saw that his were filled with scalding urgency, as they had been when we met near Hale Street. At that moment, he and I were the only people on this Earth, and he had to get me down. Baby Robert began to scream, to kick and flail in my arms. One of the servants took him from me, though I don't remember handing him over. I did not know what was happening. I was afraid of being killed and of dying, but mixed in with the terror was something I could not name. It passed quickly. The next minute, I was swung precariously into the pit.

Much later, I marvelled that all of us, even Father, managed to clamber into the trench without breaking any bones. After we had descended, I realised that Weng Yu was already in the shelter. The trench was still bathed in light at the time, its roof not having yet been made. In the sunlight my husband's prominent cheekbones showed in uncompromising clarity, also his figure, cowering on the folding canvas chair that he kept stored permanently in the shelter. He must have slipped in while Hock San and the others were still assisting us and the children, at a moment when no one else was watching.

Rage surged inside me, compounded almost at once by frustration and shame. Then, like a large wave, it came crashing down, at which point all I could do was cry. The tears drained out of my soul. I was gripped by the same hopelessness I had felt when I had found him in his office with his glass of whisky. Except that now, he had shamed me in front of everyone else, and my despair was worse. I no longer knew what to do, or what was happening to me, or what would become of us. I cursed my husband; I could have pummelled him with my fists.

Everyone was wailing then, or at least, we women were, and I moaned with them.

We heard a sharp crackle above – the breaking of a twig. Hock San had entered the shelter, followed closely by Samad, who had jumped out to gather foliage and was draping a nest of leaves and branches across the mouth of the trench. The smell of damp engulfed us. With a single swoop, the gardener dragged palm fronds over the top of our heads to complete a natural curtain, shutting out almost all light.

In the darkness I rocked baby Robert, whom I found nestled miraculously near my chest. I have no idea how he got there. Overhead, planes continued to circle; we could hear their engines. We never did become accustomed to the sounds of war, no matter how many times we heard them, even if they came at moments that were not unexpected. When the shelter rumbled, my poor baby gave a piercing yell. My own teeth clattered. After the shuddering, staccato bursts came. Nothing could have prepared us for their inhuman echoes zipping from one wall of the trench to the next in haphazard fashion, as if a line of firecrackers had been strung across. We crouched lower, hugging our bodies so that we were curled up like foetuses, as if this would save us from imminent death. At any moment we imagined that soldiers would be heard trampling above. In later years I was to have recurring nightmares in which our camouflage of foliage and twigs was torn asunder, and the soldiers would look down on our bodies, coiled pathetically inside our hole like Malaya's giant squirrels.

As suddenly as the planes had appeared, they left. When the machine-gun fire ceased that morning, we were still sobbing. After ten minutes, nothing stirred overhead. With great caution, Samad shifted a single palm leaf. No footsteps sounded; all we could hear was the rustle of Samad's leaf. A thin blade of light peeked in. Shielding his eyes with one hand, Samad squinted up into the canopy of trees. There were no longer any aircraft, only a thick, acrid odour seeping relentlessly into our chamber.

'*Alamak!* I hope they haven't bombed the kongsi houses!' Hock San said, trying to maintain an aura of calmness. He pulled on Samad's elbow. 'Samad come, we better go out, just you and me. I'll help you.'

Samad nodded. While Hock San held the gardener's waist, Samad grabbed the top of the trench with both his hands. Hock San pushed him out before rising himself, aided from below by Mutu. Through the small exposed corner of the trench we watched the two men, who soon disappeared from view. They were gone for what felt like a long time.

Our shelter remained tomb-like in its silence, no one daring to move or speak until a thin voice asked, 'Ma, when can we go out?'

It was our daughter, Lai Hin, surveying me with what in the gloomy light looked like barely veiled impatience. She was still at that age when she thought her parents would have the answers to all questions, when time meant little and five minutes felt like eternity. Lai Hin, wrapped within old Ah Hong's arms, began to stretch her limbs. The stretching would soon turn into squirming, and if we did not move, trouble would brew. In the dim light I thought I saw Ah Hong glancing in my direction, but I could not be sure. The next minute I heard her voice.

'One day, long time ago, got one poor farmer in China. He in his field dig up a barrel made of clay . . .'

The servant's low voice was oddly melodic and spellbinding in the dusky light. Her story – *The Magic Barrel* – an old Chinese fable, captured our attention, especially the children's, and for that, I was grateful.

'The farmer wife, she use brush to clean the barrel that time, her brush fall inside . . .'

As Ah Hong continued with her tale, she stroked Lai Hin's head. Her musical voice was like a balm, though what it raised within me was a tempest. I could not help thinking back to the days when we did not have to hide from bombs, when our lives were normal and temptation involved simple delicacies, like chocolate.

'One day a coin fall inside the barrel. Then the barrel always got many coins inside, because is magic barrel. The farmer now take out many coins, so he get rich . . .'

Robert began nibbling against the folds of my tunic. I looked down at the one-year-old, at his perfect baby skin and his tuft of soft black hair. He had stopped crying by then; his eyes, I knew, were open, and because he could smell me, did not mind the gloom. I imagined his look of adoration as he waved both arms in the air. This, I thought, was my life: that of a mother, a woman married to a British-trained civil engineer in Malaya in early 1942. I cradled Robert even more tightly.

Just then we heard the crunching of leaves. The figures of Hock San and Samad lurked overhead. Kneeling, they pulled aside the palm leaves and assorted greenery, which Samad had previously taken such pains to stack.

As Hock San removed a large branch from the mouth of the trench, he announced that the kongsi houses were intact. 'We still have rooms for the night.' Then, in a gentle voice to his five-year-old son, he said, 'Don't be afraid, they've gone, it's safe to come out.'

The trench gradually brightened as its roof was removed. The Malayan sun, filtering in through apertures in the jungle canopy, cut a path straight to our heads. It must have been noon by then, and hot. After Grand-Uncle had been lifted out, panting, Hock San said in a gloomy voice, 'Uncle Kwok, you'd better come with me.'

Grand-Uncle nodded. Silently taking Mutu's proffered hands, he followed Chew Hock San. My brother-in-law, Liew Chin Tong, remained inside the pit to help the rest of us out while Samad stood in readiness above, by the side of the trench. When it was my husband's turn to climb out, he shook his head resolutely. 'Look, Husband!' I said, pointing towards our sons, Wai Sung and Wai Kit, who were already sauntering towards the kongsi houses. 'It's safe, really.'

But Weng Yu's handsome cheekbones remained tense. He was in the state that had occasionally caught hold of him since the start of the war, when he could not move or speak. I tried cajoling him one final time. 'They've gone, Husband!' I yelled.

Our brother-in-law, Liew Chin Tong, gave me a hard look before touching my husband's arm gently. 'Yes, the coast is now clear, Weng Yu, it really is safe.'

The lean man on the cream canvas folding chair blinked, but did not move his head. He was clearly not going anywhere.

My brother-in-law hauled himself out of the trench. Looking down into the hole, he circled it once, and then, apparently having made up his mind, pulled a canvas chair out of the trench on to the grass beside him and sat on it. I exchanged a mildly embarrassed glance with Liew Chin Tong before shrugging. What else could I have done? I headed for the hill, to Grand-Uncle's property, from where much shouting could be heard. The smell of smoke still pervaded the air. My heart beat in its cage.

A laterite path had been forged from the tin mine to the top of the hill where Grand-Uncle and his family normally lived. With no one tending it, the ferns, lichens, and liverworts growing wildly on either side had invaded the path. There was also *belukar*, of course, that ubiquitous weedy grass with blade-like leaves which thrives on this land. On the sides of the rising hill were the jungle trees, the oaks and chestnuts and massive *tualang*, clinging on to the soil and towering over us.

After a gradual incline, the path ran steeply up over the last half mile. Struggling under the extra weight of our fifth child, I was near collapse when I spied, in the distance, the haunting grandeur of what had once been Grand-Uncle's house. The intensity of the fire had died down, but charred planks of wood continued to smoulder. The house had been blasted clean away on one side – there was no longer a roof or walls to be seen, and it was difficult to tell that it had once been a colonial-style mansion. Beneath it, the bombs had carved out a circular crater with uneven edges that spread all the way out to the very edge of the hill, where loose rocks remained.

Grand-Aunt and her daughter, who were standing in front of the remains of their porch, dabbed at their eyes with handkerchiefs. Grand-Uncle stood slightly apart, contemplating their loss with a stony face. He had arrived in Malaya with nothing other than a small cloth sack of belongings and a few dollars in his pocket. The house had been his dream, his whole life's work, for which he had sweated years, toiling as a coolie before rising to the position of foreman. When the opportunity of a mining concession had come up, Grand-Uncle had taken the plunge, borrowing from my grandfather to purchase the machinery he needed. The gamble paid off. His mine in Lahat became a steady producer, not the largest, certainly, but profitable enough to allow Grand-Uncle to realise his dream of living in a splendid mansion with a car and servants. Now all that was left were the burnt-out cinders before us. I dared not touch Grand-Uncle's arm, for fear that he would burst into tears.

At that moment, life seemed as cruel as Malaya's midday sun. For a man of Grand-Uncle's age, already past his seventy-second birthday, there was little question of starting again, and for what: what good did it do the Japs to destroy his home, when the British had already gone? My chest burned with anger at this new invader, even though I had yet to set eyes on one.

As we trooped back down the hill to the kongsi houses, I was aware again of Chew Hock San's presence behind me, the stocky body and muscular arms taking up more space than my own willowy husband's. When we reached the mine, we found Weng Yu where I had left him, enthroned on his chair inside the dug-out shelter. Liew Chin Tong was no longer sitting above the shelter, but was pacing the earth nearby. He surveyed the jungle, contemplating the hills behind as if they were guiding stars.

8

The air raid was a chilling reminder that the Malayan jungle was not altogether the haven we had assumed. Thereafter, our children took to waking in the middle of the night. Once, when they began screaming as if surrounded by a ghostly miasma, I went to the bunk bed in which our eldest son, Wai Sung, slept and found him sobbing into his pillow. He pressed both hands against his ears to shield them from the noises in his dreams. As I wiped away the tears on his face, he kept mumbling, 'Machine-guns, Mama, machine-guns, they were coming for us.' I had never mentioned the word in his presence; he must have heard it from one of the other children. Wai Sung's crying had set his siblings off; in the neighbouring bunks I could hear Ah Hong and Li-Fei comforting our daughter and second son and Chang Ying's whispers as she rocked the baby.

When I went back to the sleeping partition I shared with my husband, he found my hand in the dark. Weng Yu never talked about the air raid, but I knew that he felt ashamed. As if to make up for his behaviour inside the trench, he began to take an interest in our eldest son. They went on walks together, and some mornings would find my husband at the edge of a clearing watching the boy play football. My husband would no doubt have preferred an artistic performance, but that was not the sort of boy Wai Sung was. I suspect that Weng Yu, who knew little about football, quite enjoyed the games, or at least was proud of the athletic dives his son made. Wai Sung was supposedly a good goalkeeper, a position which gave him ample opportunity to hurl himself at the flying projectile. Whenever his attempts proved successful, he earned manic cheers from the rest of the field, especially from Chew Hock San who, together with his own boys aged five and seven years old, never missed a football game. The activity gave me plenty of opportunity to observe him, for he was one of these men who forgot everything else as soon as football came along. Hock San's performance on the pitch was clumsy at best, but this did not stop him. He laughed when his foot swiped air instead of the ball and clapped madly for those whose play was superior. The ad-hoc games brought life to our jungle refuge. Even Hock San's four-year-old daughter caught football fever and, to my surprise, was allowed to chase after a ball and kick it with her brothers – an activity which I forbade our own daughter, Lai Hin. I wanted Lai Hin to grow up like a proper girl, as Mother had wanted for me.

After the air raid, Hock San began engaging in furtive discussions with my brother-in-law Liew Chin Tong. Their furious whispers would cease as soon as someone else approached. All of us, by which I suppose I mean all of us women, burned with curiosity as to what the two could possibly be discussing.

'What are you talking about?' I asked one morning when I caught them beside the stream. Chin Tong, as usual, had his sight trained on the hills to the rear of the tin mine. Hock San, on the other hand, allowed himself a moment of distraction. He cast me a sideways look, which I thought about for days afterwards. I feigned indifference at the time, but this only amused him. He curved his lips, which were beefier than my husband's, into a playful smile as he said, 'We are discussing men's business, Mrs Wong.'

Liew Chin Tong eventually turned around. The half-smile he threw me was an uneasy one, mixing confusion with wariness. He looked exhausted. It was a sweltering day, and both men had been keeping watch for many hours. Chin Tong's face was wet and steamy from the heat; his round-rimmed glasses, which were the worse for wear, kept slipping down the bridge of his nose. There was something in his countenance which suggested that he would have been happy to reveal their secret, if it were only up to him. I left soon afterwards, determined to catch my brother-in-law when he was on his own.

I could have asked his sister, Miss Liew, what she knew, except that she was my former teacher and I retained a certain reserve with her. When Liew Chin Tong rose from the dining table after lunch one day and went outside, I followed, hoping that the other kongsi inhabitants would succumb to post-prandial drowsiness.

My brother-in-law headed towards a clump of trees at the edge of the clearing and sat down. I strolled casually after him; without a word, I took the chair beside his. Liew Chin Tong acknowledged my presence with a smile. Then, giving a shrug of both shoulders, he expelled a long, sonorous sigh that sounded almost like a kettle boiling.

'This war is dragging on, isn't it?' he said.

I nodded and then, looking directly at him, replied with a question, 'Second Brother-in-Law, what do you think will happen?'

He kept his eyes straight ahead, away from the kongsi houses. 'I think the Japs will conquer Malaya.'

He said this quietly, in a voice tinged with disappointment. By the time he added, 'I think our lives will never be the same,' it was clear that he had hardened, for there was a steely bitterness in the way he enunciated his words.

I should have asked there and then what he meant, but I never got the chance because the very next moment Chin Tong said, 'Who would have thought it would come to this? I never would have imagined it. Mind you, when we were growing up, there were many things we couldn't have imagined.'

Without any prompting, he launched into a story I had not heard, one which I was sure my husband did not know. Liew Chin Tong recounted the twists and turns of his life in a flurry of words that did not cease until he paused for breath. Something drove him to speak that afternoon, a compulsion with the force of a runaway train travelling through every hill and valley because it must. He seemed to have a destination in mind and was determined to reach it quickly. Since I knew nothing about his life, he had to start at the beginning – a wooden shack outside a one-street town I had only passed through, a place called Gopeng, twelve miles south of Ipoh, where he grew up with his sister. Their mother had been a washerwoman who woke before dawn to trudge the streets; their father, equally unskilled, had served in a coffee shop.

I lost count of time as I sat listening to Liew Chin Tong. He was a natural storyteller, speaking in the manner of a man who expected to be listened to. He attenuated his voice to hold my attention, threw out his right hand every now and again with palm upwards to emphasise a point, before snapping me back to attention with his bone-cracking third finger. His face was sombre when recalling their poverty. He told me how both he and his sister had learnt to hold a *changkol* when they were still children, so that they could till the land in their parents' absence.

I looked at the man before me in a new light, as if I had never taken in his hardy chocolate complexion or his air of perpetual humility. His sister, my former English teacher, Miss Liew, had also inherited the farmer's tanned, blotchy skin and the subservience of one who felt unequal everywhere except inside her own classroom.

My husband did not know the Liews well. Chin Tong had become first a friend and then a member of the Wong family during the years when Weng Yu was away in London. The young interpreter had gained favour quickly with my husband's second and favourite sister, Hui Ying. The two, who were married before Weng Yu's return, had chosen to follow the Nyonya custom of a *chin-chuoh* marriage whereby he had moved into my mother-in-law's house immediately after the wedding. The arrangement, though already highly unusual in those days, pleased the old lady. It meant that she kept her daughter by her side and was able to influence every decision the newlyweds made.

One minute merged into the next, as Liew Chin Tong recounted his happiness. 'It's a shame you never met my wife. She was . . . a lot like her mother, maybe less bad-tempered.'

At that, Chin Tong threw his head back and laughed. The round-rimmed glasses oscillated on his nose, slipping slightly. Almost at once, his voice became taut and he paused, staring into the empty air as if visions haunted him.

'I should never have agreed to the home birth.'

When my brother-in-law resumed speaking, it was to tell me about his wife's pregnancy.

'Things were fine at first,' he said, looking into the distance again. 'We were so pleased. But in her fifth month, something changed. She was just . . . not comfortable. She couldn't sleep at night, nothing helped. I had a hunch that things were not right. My feelings became stronger as time went on. I sensed something terrible was going to happen. I wanted my wife to go to the hospital, but she wouldn't hear of it. "Mother won't like it," she told me.

'I respected her decision, but I now regret that. I wish I had argued more forcefully. I could have done something . . . even at the very end, on that last night . . .'

Chin Tong's eyes were hazy as he relived the screams emanating from their bedroom and the blood-sodden rags he saw being brought out.

'The Malay midwife did the best she could. Later I found out that she was not the same midwife who had delivered the Wong children. If only I had known before. The midwife kept whispering to Mother-in-Law in one corner. They wouldn't tell me what they were discussing.

But I saw it in her face, the midwife's face. She had known that it would be a difficult birth. Mother-in-Law chose not to tell me. And I didn't pry. For that, I blame myself. I was her husband, for goodness' sake, I could have insisted on bringing a doctor! I was partly responsible for what happened. I suspect your husband thinks so too.'

'Second Brother-in-Law,' I said quickly, 'you mustn't blame yourself. I don't think my husband does.'

I was not at all sure what Weng Yu thought, but saw no harm in reassuring Liew Chin Tong. My husband rarely mentioned his sister's demise; whenever he did, it was to rage at his mother. 'He blamed Mother-in-Law, not you.'

Liew Chin Tong sat quietly for a while, staring listlessly into the distance. We were all pensive in those days, given to aimless moping. The shock of war had made us morose, and the air raids themselves were constant, blunt reminders of how fragile life was. We were terrified, though we never used the word; we had run to the jungle where we thought we would be safe, only to learn that in war, there was no such thing as safety. Liew Chin Tong's voice was just a whisper when he said, 'Yes, the old lady made a few mistakes.'

He emitted a snort before turning to me. 'You remember Weng Koon, the second brother? He came to his mother's sixty-third birthday party.'

I cast my mind back to the old lady's final celebration. The event had taken place only months before, but it felt as if decades had passed. Greeting Weng Yu's second brother had been a welcome diversion after the hours in Dorcourt's kitchen where I'd had to put up with Dora's fastidiousness. Weng Koon surprised me with the charm he deployed on every woman present. Even my maid, Chang Ying, giggled in his presence.

'I remember him well, yes,' I said mildly. 'He always brought his three children with him.'

'Well, you know that the old lady didn't speak to him for years? That birthday of hers two years ago at the Kum Loong Restaurant was the first time she'd ever set eyes on those grandchildren.'

'Really? No, I never heard the whole story. Mother-in-Law didn't talk much about Weng Koon.'

'Of course not. I think she regretted what she did. The thing is, she was too old-fashioned for her own good.'

Liew Chin Tong stopped abruptly, suddenly remembering himself. 'Look, I don't mean to speak ill of the dead. Mother-in-Law was one of the shrewdest people in town, everyone says so, and courageous too – few would have dared start a business when she did. And raising ten children so successfully, what can I say? She was definitely some woman!'

'Yes she was, Second Brother-in-Law,' I said. 'I know you mean no disrespect. She talked about you.'

'Did she?' Liew Chin Tong laughed nervously. 'I won't ask what she said. I was fond of her, you know. We used to take tea every night when I lived in their old house. But in the end, some of her ideas were too fixed. Like where babies should be born. She hated hospitals. She didn't want my wife to go to a hospital.

'And it was the same with Weng Koon. He became a teacher in Seremban and then went and got married behind the old lady's back. She could not stomach this. When Weng Koon and his wife asked to come to pay their respects, Mother-in-Law refused outright.'

'Really?' I asked, unable to imagine the scene. I had never detected vindictiveness in the matriarch.

'Mother-in-Law would not hear of accepting his wife. And then the news came that the girl had passed away from cancer of the womb. By then she and Weng Koon already had their three children. Mother-in-Law was truly sorry. If she had still been able to walk, she would have gone to Seremban for the funeral. But it was too late, she was already frail.'

I felt a sudden sadness for Weng Koon and his children, and the years they had lost. Weng Koon's eyes, which were as deep-set as his brothers', had glinted as he touched my arm lightly and laughed. With his easy manner and the trademark Wong looks, he should have no trouble finding another wife.

'Second Brother-in-Law, have you heard from Weng Koon?'

'No, I was going to ask you the same.'

'My husband isn't that close to Weng Koon.'

Chin Tong turned his swarthy face to me and smiled. 'No,' he said with a thoughtful look. 'Funny man, Weng Yu,' adding quickly, 'I like him, don't get me wrong, just that he talks so little.'

I smiled back. There was much else I wanted to ask my brother-in-law. But it would have to wait.

◆ ◆ ◆

One morning, Liew Chin Tong and Chew Hock San wandered into the hills and did not return for the start of the MBC broadcast. The audience had dwindled by then to only six regulars; without Chin Tong and Hock San, we – the quartet of English-speaking women – found ourselves alone at the long communal dining table.

'Eh, where have they gone?' Wai Fong asked, addressing me directly in her high-pitched voice.

'My brother-in-law doesn't tell me everything, you know,' I said, annoyed by her presumption.

'Oh not him, I meant the other guy-lah!'

'The other guy? Who, Mr Chew? What makes you think he would tell me anything?'

Narrowing her small eyes, Wai Fong gave me a sly smile. 'No reason. I just thought he might have.'

'Well, he hasn't.' Turning my back, I lifted the Philco set on to the table, inadvertently chipping off part of the underside of its Bakelite casing. I could feel Wai Fong's eyes on me.

'Ai-yahh, no need to pretend-lah, we're all friends here, and all ladies! You think we don't have eyes-ah? Can you blame him, with that wife of his and you, so beautiful? Yik Wei, don't you think that Mei Foong is the prettiest lady here?'

'That is a cruel thing to say, Wai Fong,' I retorted, watching my poor school friend's alabaster cheeks turn crimson. 'Kit Mei is beautiful and very sweet, too.'

'Sweet, my foot! Just because she never says a word, you think she's sweet! Ha, she—'

The MBC signal tune sounded just in time. We hunched closer to the table, every one of us on tenterhooks. We knew that the British had retreated all the way to Johore, Malaya's southernmost state. Any further withdrawal would force them across to the island of Singapore, at the tip of the Malay peninsula.

'The public has been warned that congested areas in Singapore may be bombed at any time. Fighting is taking place on a line from Nee Soon Village through Peirce Reservoir and . . .'

Bewilderment stretched across Wai Fong's and Yik Wei's faces. Their mouths hung wide open. I must have looked equally stunned.

'But that means – that means,' I cried out, not quite believing my own words, 'they're already in the town! The Japs are on the island!'

'Oh my God,' Yik Wei said in her low whisper. 'It's all happening so fast.'

There was a distracted absorption on her face as she repeated the phrase mindlessly. Sitting up, she suddenly fixed her large brown eyes on me. 'What do you think will happen in Singapore?' she asked as if I were a fortune-teller.

'I think the British will make a stand. It's their last chance – they have to.'

At the time I really believed what I said. I did not expect Singapore to fall; none of us did. We continued to retain a child-like naivety in what the colonial government told us. It had generously described Singapore as an impregnable fortress, and we took this as a given, in the same way we accepted that the Earth rotated around the Sun. Even though I had seen the Europeans leave with my own eyes, and despite our colonial rulers allowing the Japanese Imperial Army to march down almost five hundred miles of our land within days, I continued to assume that the British would, at some point, take a valiant stand.

There were beliefs we did not question.

When Hock San and Chin Tong finally appeared, neither would say where they had gone. They were cradling bunches of wild tubers – fat yams dripping with earth and clumps of tapioca hanging like phalluses protected by star-shaped leaves.

'Ai-yahh, you expect us to believe that you've been picking yams and tapioca for six hours-ah?' Wai Fong exclaimed.

Hock San grinned while Chin Tong grunted, both of them bowing their heads in front of the yams as if they were gods.

'What, you won't tell us where you went?' Wai Fong asked a second time.

'There's not much to tell, Mrs Teoh. We found a jungle path, the Orang Asli must have used it, and we just followed. Whenever we saw yam and tapioca, we collected them.'

'You walked so much and you didn't get lost?' I mused aloud. 'Don't the trees all seem the same?'

Liew Chin Tong gave me a strange look. 'Remember, my sister and I grew up in a jungle area,' he said quietly. 'We used to play among trees like these every day.'

The colour on the men's faces changed when we told them that the Japanese had infiltrated Singapore. Hock San's became a pugnacious red, but Chin Tong's turned grey and he withdrew into himself.

Conversation around the table was desultory. There did not seem much to say.

As I combed my hair that night, my mind kept hovering over the day's events. I held in my hands a small round mirror, one of the few luxuries, together with my comb and Mother's fan, which I had taken into the jungle. I examined the mirror, wondering whether it could be true.

'You are a very pretty woman,' Yik Wei had said that morning, on a rare occasion when we found ourselves alone inside the kongsi house. Though I had been given the same compliment often enough, it was reassuring being told it again, as I did not feel pretty, or clever, or classy – the words people used to describe me. 'You have good features,' Yik Wei continued in her low, whispery voice. 'Nice thick eyebrows, not like some women who could pass as ghosts. They're well-shaped too. You don't even need to pluck them. And a thin nose, which is rather high, like a white devil's. And you're so petite and slim, even after four children! How do you do it? That's what I want to know!' she'd said, pointing towards her own rounded paunch.

I looked again, but failed to discern the beauty which others saw. Perhaps I would never see it. That night I let the matter rest. I thought of the British stragglers who remained in Malaya and wished they would hurry up and head into Singapore. I wondered where Matron McDonald had fled to. I had dreamt about her after the air raid, my bad conscience haunting me in the shadowy black of the jungle night. I would see, sprawled before me, the tins of luncheon meat and soup, the sardines and pilchards, coffee and sugar, and the gunny sacks of rice we had taken from the hospital's store-rooms.

My husband had initially demurred from such an enterprise. 'That would be looting,' he'd announced, rather smugly.

But I had pursed my lips. 'How can you say that? Have we run away? No. Who asked Matron to give Lim Choy Yoke the store-room keys? Did we ask for them? No.'

Weng Yu had agreed to accompany us only after my father had chided him about our food supplies. The shops were already empty by then, and we would need food. Thus we had exploited the unasked-for opportunity, making several trips in the Austin 8, filling the whole car and its boot up with provisions for ourselves and the Lims.

But even while we stood on the premises gathering the Fray Bentos corned beef, which my husband adored, and KLIM powdered milk for the children, I was convinced that I had seen Matron's stout figure outside. When we walked through the door with our booty, there was no one there, but every afternoon in the jungle, as the ocean of emerald around me turned cerulean, I wondered what Matron McDonald would have said if she had seen us at the store-room. Her store-room.

Eventually, I had to admit that my husband had been right. I confessed this one day while we were walking back from a clearing, when he was in an unusually good mood and I felt close to him. 'You know, Husband, I have a bad conscience about taking those goods from the hospital store-room. It was looting.'

I thought Weng Yu would be pleased; instead he stopped walking and his jaw tightened. Looking ahead into the distance he said, with a loud sigh, 'Who is to say, Wife, what is right any more? They left . . .'

As we walked I could feel him slipping away, and the moments of intimacy we had just shared dissolved into nothingness. I wondered whether he was thinking about her, the woman whose photograph he continued to keep in his wallet. I imagined someone with striking beauty and a slim figure, a woman of typical European boldness who spoke her mind, as they all did in our country. If Weng Yu had married her, he too might have been evacuated and allowed on to the boats. Was that what he regretted?

The question burned on my tongue, but once again my courage failed me. I could not bear to know the truth. Fighting to have a radio was one thing; fighting this woman was harder. I never asked the question because I had no wish to hear the answer. Helen joined the set of words I should have spoken, but did not. I stored her name away, alongside a jumble in an empty corner of my brain, where it built up over time and leached out to corrode my heart.

In that foreign space where cicadas screamed, rest did not come to us. If it came at all, it came only to the very young and the very old. Sometimes there were planes in the distance. Their low droning hurried past. The MBC stopped making reference to help arriving in Singapore.

And thus we waited.

◆ ◆ ◆

One afternoon in the middle of February 1942, twenty pairs of eyes were on me as I tuned in to our Philco wireless set. With the heightening tension, many more of our fellow kongsi inhabitants came to hear the news, including a few who spoke no English and relied on translation. Singapore had already been under curfew during the previous fortnight. The MBC broadcasts, read by a newsman known for his equanimity in the direst of circumstances, were sounding increasingly pessimistic.

In the near silence of the Malayan jungle, we heard that British forces had surrendered unconditionally. Lieutenant-General Arthur Percival, the dour voice told us, had met with Lieutenant-General Yamashita Tomoyuki on the previous day at the Ford motor plant at the foot of Bukit Timah, to sign the document of surrender. As a result, fighting had stopped along the entire Malayan front at 10 p.m. local time.

We looked at each other with glazed eyes. No one said anything; even Wai Fong was wrung dry of words. My friend Yik Wei disappeared into her family's curtained off section. We could hear the workings of her hands from behind the partition, quietly sweeping up her family's belongings. I could not move from my chair. I had thought I would be happy, but instead I felt strangely miserable. Now that the Japanese had finally taken over, I had a yearning to have the British back. My eyes misted like the morning dew.

It was the sixteenth day in February 1942, and we had been in Lahat for two months. It was time to go home.

PART III

PART II

9

The pounding was followed by a squeak. From the outer hall there came an excruciating cry and the patter of footsteps. Within minutes my maid Chang Ying stood at the threshold of the kitchen courtyard, staring at us with the gaping mouth and frozen eyes of a netted fish.

'They come! They come!' she said breathlessly.

It emerged later that she had leapt from the *barlay* and run along the vestibule. In the kitchen, Ah Hong, Li-Fei, and I were having a discussion about our food stocks, and my head was swimming with hard thoughts about where we would find the money for provisions. The servants, meanwhile, were fretting about how to stretch what we had left. We were in a sombre mood and quite unwelcoming.

'Outside!' Chang Ying shouted once more as she waved an index finger towards the front door. 'They come already!'

When the rapping began, there was no mistaking its menace. Tap-tap, tap-tap: hard rapid knocks, executed to a sinister beat.

I followed Chang Ying into the vestibule, not tarrying, yet at the same time trying to contain the anxious beating of my heart. My husband appeared at our bedroom door with a sheepish glance. He was too proud to apologise, but I could tell from his greenish pallor and his stooped shoulders that he was feeling a little foolish.

The house we lived in was known as the Green House for good reason. It had lime-green walls, which my mother-in-law, a flamboyant Nyonya of the old school, had insisted on. Being the only house in town with green walls, it had always stood out. In days of peace this conspicuousness had pleased me, but with the town under a swirl of Japanese troops, the attention our green walls attracted was disconcerting.

We had not been at home when the enemy marched – or, more precisely, cycled – in, towards the end of December 1941. In Ipoh, as everywhere else in Malaya, the Japanese had succeeded in confounding our colonial rulers with their widespread use of the humble bicycle. People throughout the land recounted the surreal sight of soldiers trooping in on their two-wheeled vehicles, like herds of well-trained cows, with sweat-stained cloths tied around their heads. The Japs displayed iron discipline. Their bicycles were perfectly arrayed alongside one another, in columns stretching for miles. It was the bicycle which allowed the Japanese Imperial Army to do what everyone else had said was impossible: traverse virgin jungle. This they had accomplished quickly, collapsing time like a concertina.

When we finally returned to Ipoh, the Japanese soldiers were already everywhere. Not only had they taken over the barracks on Ashby Road as Father had anticipated, but they also occupied every building of repute. Groups of soldiers even patrolled Green Town, and whenever they did, they would point to the walls of our house.

'Husband, you should have those outside walls repainted,' I said to Weng Yu more than once. A fortnight passed, and my husband made no effort to see whether Samad could procure a can of paint.

Now it was too late. They were already here, ready to bludgeon their way in. 'Coming!' I shouted in Cantonese, as the rapping turned into thumping.

My husband dragged his lean body towards the heavy front door. His whole posture was one of reluctance, his angular jaw rigid with fear. Weng Yu lifted the door's wooden bolt and then pulled the door ajar. Its hinges creaked as always, and as soon as the door was fully open, he and I bowed our heads low. We had already heard rumours that others were being beaten for lesser offences. For an instant I was blinded by a glint of silver. I blinked, resting my eyes on the coir mat just outside our front door. Inches from its coarse fibres stood the blunt butt of a rifle. Upon then raising my head, I came, for the first time in my life, face to face with the sharp end of a bayonet. A chill ran through me. The sight of the blade, shiny in the Malayan sunlight, was at once malevolent and beautiful.

Outside stood three men: stiff, upright and short, all much shorter than my husband, one barely reaching my height. They looked a sorry sight. Their uniforms, unlike their rifles, were stained and crumpled; instead of boots, they wore coir shoes on their feet, with separate bindings for their big toes and the rest of their toes. Had the men cycled the length and breadth of our country in such makeshift apparel? Clumps of dried mud lined the sides of their shoes. It was hard to believe that these were our conquerors.

The soldier standing in front uttered a hoarse shout. 'Chinese man! All Chinese man come!'

The command was at once guttural – emanating from somewhere at the back of his throat – and cruel. The pronouncement, though made in broken English, could have been spoken in any language at all and there would still have been no doubt about its intent. The cloth cap the soldier wore cast a shadow, and it was a while before I could make out his face. When my eyes adjusted to the sunlight, I saw that he was merely a boy, with the tanned, unblemished skin of a teenager. I judged him to be all of eighteen. Already, his eyes were dark; I searched their depths for an ounce of empathy and found none. Pushing past me, he barged into our house in his shoes, leaving a trail of brown flakes on our polished wooden floor.

'Chinese man come!' he repeated, pointing to my husband.

'My husband, yes.'

'He come!'

Weng Yu and I understood that he was to follow the soldiers, though we had no idea where to or what for.

'Other Chinese man?' the boy asked, surveying the interior of our house.

I bowed low a second time. 'Sir, only my father, but he is sick. And old.'

'Father, where?'

I hesitated for a second, long enough to infuriate the soldier, who spewed forth a stream of abuse mixed with spittle. I sensed that deceit would be unwise. I led the soldier into the rear bedroom that had once belonged to Mother-in-Law. Father seemed to be asleep, or was perhaps pretending to be asleep; in any case he had the sheets pulled over his head and was taking long, deep breaths.

The young soldier, with a single sweep of his left arm, dragged the blanket off the bed, at the same time shouting, 'Up! Come now!'

Father turned his body slowly, with no haste whatsoever, as if being shouted at in the morning was the most natural thing in the world. The old man appeared to have been expecting this visit. He lay supine on the bed, a smile on his wrinkled face.

'Good morning,' he said to the soldier.

In reply, the boy removed the wooden baton that was hanging from a belt around his waist. 'Get up!' he screamed, using his baton to butt Father in the side of his abdomen. 'Up now! No got all day!'

An involuntary gasp escaped my lips, and I covered my mouth with both my hands. *He is sixty years old.* I kept repeating this to myself, as if the more I said it, the more likely I was to transfer the mantra telepathically.

Father hobbled out of bed in his silk pyjamas, which were of a very dark blue. 'Sir, please, can he change first?'

'No got all day!' This too came out as a screech.

'Then sir, can I give him a stick? He is old, he cannot walk without a stick!'

The boy grabbed Father's walking cane – the *chengai* stick with a dragon carved at the head of its rounded end – and tucked it under his own arm. Before Father had even reached the front door of our house, the boy had used the cane to prod the old man in the back. 'Faster!' he cried. 'No got all day!'

Father stumbled but continued walking. My husband held on to the old man's arm. Beyond the driveway, my brother-in-law Weng Yoon and the other Chinese males of the neighbourhood had also been gathered and were traipsing silently towards their unknown destination.

Shortly after the men disappeared from view, the cuckoo bird on our grandfather clock stuck its head out ten times. I remember it being a still morning, with not even the hint of a breeze. I know this because the wind chimes above the threshold of our house, which we hung to guard against evil spirits, remained steadfastly silent. On mornings when the wind chimes were mute, we knew that once the cloud cover in the sky had dissipated, we would have weather in which even strong, healthy men would be tested.

I paced the house, clenching and unclenching my hands. I could not put the images of Father and Weng Yu out of my mind. Each was feeble in his own way: one already advanced in years and barely able to walk, the other quite unathletic and terrified of the midday heat. What could the Japs possibly want with them?

A knock on the kitchen door made us jump. Li-Fei opened it to find Weng Yoon's driver Ali outside, his normally bronzed face a touch pale.

'Aunty Mei Foong,' Ali whispered in Cantonese, looking straight at me, 'I go with Samad to see where they take the men. Aunty Dora worried.'

Our gardener, Samad, who happened at that moment to be standing in the air well which ventilated the kitchen, nodded repeatedly.

'Good, good,' he mumbled in Malay while watching to see if I would give my consent.

'Thank you, Samad, thank you, Ali,' I said, almost crying with relief. Why hadn't I thought of it? Neither Samad nor Ali next door had been rounded up with the other men; at the time I thought this was because the Japs were interested in property owners, not their servants. Being still free men, Samad and Ali would be able to wander through town – not with impunity exactly, but hopefully with sufficient ease as to be able to find out what was going on. Not wanting to be left out, Mutu, Father's Indian driver, who had also been spared, jumped up to volunteer himself.

'No, Mutu,' I said firmly, 'we are now a house of women and children. We need a man here too!'

Li-Fei chose that moment to announce that lunch would soon be served. She pointed to the rice she had prepared and the piles of diced chicken and finely chopped vegetables she was about to stir-fry. In those first few weeks after our return from the jungle, there was no shortage of anything; indeed, Ipoh was awash with produce. 'Eat first, then go!' she said, looking at the would-be spies. But no one was hungry, least of all the two reconnaissance men. Instead of lunching, Samad and Ali rushed out of the house.

I could not eat either, despite not having had breakfast. Strolling up and down the inner hall, I returned always to the altar table, where I lit one joss-stick after another with shaking hands. I did not expect answers from the Goddess, but I could not think what else to do. Whenever I pictured my husband and father in the hands of Japanese soldiers, I had to sniff back tears, which threatened to spill out.

Ali and Samad were gone for longer than I had expected they would be. Finally, at around three o'clock, squeaks were heard on our driveway. From the *barlay* window we saw Samad, sweaty and flustered, dismounting from his bicycle. He seemed shrunken; his posture sagged. Without bothering to look around, he began to push his vehicle towards the back of the house. A noise next door told us that his compatriot had also returned to Dorcourt.

Samad took his time taking off the wooden clogs he was wearing and arranging them on the step outside the kitchen door. The clogs were of the type that slipped off easily enough, but Samad seemed intent on bending down to remove them with his hands. His cheeks had the texture of a film over water – tight, yet vulnerable if pricked. I thought it best to give him time.

When I could wait no longer, I rushed outside. 'Samad? Please, tell me everything.'

The gardener raised his head to meet my eyes, though it was clear he would have preferred not to.

'They are at the Padang, Aunty,' he said very slowly. This was the large field in the part of Old Town which had been the heart of the English quarter, where the previously whites-only club and administrative offices were located.

'What are they doing there?'

'Standing, Aunty, many men, like big sea in the Padang.'

'Like a big sea? How many men are there?'

'Many many, cannot count. And at this time, very hot-lah!'

I tried to picture the scene: the Padang, previously the official cricket pitch and therefore devoid of shade-giving trees, awash with men who had not had food or water for many hours. The Japs had chosen the hottest part of the day for this inexplicable exercise, a touch of brutality that I found incomprehensible.

'Aunty,' Samad said, 'men all Chinese. No Malays or Indians in the Padang.'

'All the men were Chinese? Are you sure, Samad?'

'Yes, Aunty, very sure. I also surprised.'

I made a mental note of Samad's observation without knowing what to think. At the time, China had been at war with Japan for several years, and young Chinese men from Malaya had been known to head to

China to fight the Japanese enemy. But these young men were a minority. Was the Japanese Army going to punish us all? Until the arrival of the Japanese occupiers in Malaya, I had not thought much about the fact that we were Chinese. My family had already been in Malaya for four generations, Father's grandfather being the first to arrive in 1853. I was sure that my husband, with his love of things British, felt even less affinity for China.

'Did you see Father at the Padang? Or Uncle?'

Samad threw his arms up. 'No Aunty, sorry, cannot see-lah! So many men! Really many – hundreds!'

'Hundreds of men, and they are all just standing there?'

'Yes, but must stand straight, you know. If not, guards hit you.'

'Are there many guards?'

'Many guards, Aunty, one row of men, two or three guards. Guards walk up and down the rows. Very many rows, men close together.'

I tried to imagine my husband in the midday heat without the beige-coloured *topee* he always wore and the canteen of water he liked to carry. I feared the worst; Weng Yu would surely have fainted by now. As for Father, he was still in his silk pyjamas. I began to wonder what they did to men who were too weak to survive the heat.

'Did the guards take anyone away, Samad?'

The gardener hesitated.

'Samad, you must say!'

'I not there long, Aunty, but no, when I was there, I not see them take anyone away.'

'Are you sure?'

'Yes, Aunty.'

'But you say some men were hit?'

Samad swallowed before replying, his voice much thinner. 'Yes. Sorry, Aunty. *Terok!* It was not nice. If a man falls, guard hits him. Also . . .'

At that point Samad's voice trailed off. His eyes grew red, and then dewy. Finally, unable to control himself, the gardener sat down at the round table in the kitchen. With shoulders hunched, he buried his head in his hands.

I blinked. Was Father still alive? Placing myself on a chair opposite, I said, as gently as I could, 'Samad, if you saw something, you must tell me, no matter how horrible it is.'

With both palms covering his face, Samad shook his head from left to right and then, with a sign of his outstretched palm, let me understand that he would speak. He lifted his face slowly, focusing his eyes directly ahead, refusing still to look at me.

'When we were cycling, Aunty, we met a friend, Yusof. He said, "*Alamak*, you been to the Central Market-ah?" We said no, and he said, "Must go-lah."

'We told him Uncle Weng Yu and Uncle Weng Yoon taken away, and Yusof said, "Oh, they will be at the Padang." So we went to the Padang and the men all there-lah, the Chinese men, standing under the sun.'

'And then what happened, Samad?'

Continuing to avoid my eyes, Samad said, 'We stay at the Padang, but no can see any person. So we go to the Central Market. There, at the front gate of the Market, Aunty . . . two heads . . .' His voice broke.

'Two heads?' I repeated, as if they were alien words. 'Real heads? People's heads? Just their heads?'

'Two men,' Samad replied in a shaky voice. 'Chinese men. *Terok*.'

'Where were the heads, Samad?'

'On spikes, one head, one spike.'

There was a strange noise behind me, as if someone had choked. I had to stroke my own forehead with a hand, I felt so faint. In a voice I could barely recognise, I heard myself ask, 'Were they . . . people we knew, Samad?'

'Not the name, Aunty, but one I seen before in town . . .'

Samad buried his head once more, and this time, his shoulders began to convulse. 'Japanese say they traitors, Aunty. And they will kill traitors!'

A hush fell. Our mournful, terrified silence lasted hours, until a low muttering was heard from the street. I have no idea where those hours went or how we spent them. The air was already cool when the bedraggled lot of men appeared on our road, their shirts spattered with dirt and looking so drenched that the singlets they wore underneath had become fully transparent.

I rushed to the front door. On opening it I saw Father struggling up our driveway, devoid of his glasses. His eyesight being so poor, he would have been almost blind without them. He was held on one arm by Weng Yoon and on the other by my husband. Despite their support, Father's knees seemed to buckle. Weng Yu himself looked as if he could have fainted at any minute.

But it was the state of the old man which shocked us all. He had a bluish bruise across his left cheek; when we looked closer, we saw that his silk pyjamas were ripped across the torso. When he swayed momentarily, I glimpsed a slice of raw skin on his back.

'Oh my God . . .' I stood immobile, unable to think or act.

'Water, please,' Father managed to mumble before collapsing on to the floor.

'Maternal Grandfather, Maternal Grandfather!' Lai Hin yelled in her booming voice. Before I knew what was happening, my daughter had crawled out of Ah Hong's clutches and was running towards her grandfather.

The child's reaction broke our collective stupor; we adults followed, a touch shamefaced, until we had encircled the three returnees. Father's own servants began making him comfortable, to the extent that this was possible. I handed them my fan while Ah Hong brought a pillow and Chang Ying appeared miraculously with a pitcher of water.

Little Lai Hin continued to cry over her grandfather's wounds in the hours which followed. The day after the Padang incident, she knocked on Father's bedroom door at three o'clock in the afternoon – a time when he was likely to be in the middle of his nap.

'Lai Hin, don't disturb your grandfather,' I whispered. From inside the bedroom came a surprising admonishment. Father's voice, though muffled, was audible. 'Let the girl come in, Daughter. I am already awake.'

Thereafter, Lai Hin took to spending an hour or two each afternoon with her grandfather, as she had with her grandmother before her death. I could hear them chatting through the closed bedroom door, Father's low rumble interspersed with childish giggling as Lai Hin laughed at something he had said. When I asked her what she talked about with her grandfather, she became coy, saying only that he told her stories. I was amazed by this. Father had been stern when we were children; he had fed us facts, not stories, and here he was having apparently stored a lifetime's worth of tales for my daughter.

Father never spoke of what happened at the Padang. My husband was equally vague and would reveal no details. I could only surmise that the Japs had beaten Father because he fell from time to time, perhaps also because he spoke mainly Chinese and only a little English. Later in the war, we learned that we in Green Town were fortunate. The neighbourhood was not considered a hotbed of Communism, and we were treated relatively well. No *sook chings* – purification parades – were ever carried out in Green Town. Others were not so lucky.

10

Before we even had time to recover from the men's unexpected visit to the Padang, four shadowy figures stormed down our driveway. One had the unmistakable bearing and colours of an officer – the tan uniform, smartly ironed and festooned with badges, and on his head a proper canvas cap with a hard lining, not the flattened cloth version seen on the ordinary soldier. The sweat cloth was also absent from the back of this man's head: here was someone who obviously did not need to endure the Malayan sun.

Something in the rhythm of the rapping must have intimidated me, for I opened the front door without delay, to be confronted by a soldier with hollow eyes. I made the customary bow to this soulless-looking representative of the Japanese emperor. While my back was prostrate, the officer figure stepped forward. I was beset by an uncanny feeling that I had seen the man, or rather his gait, somewhere before, though I could not think where. I straightened and noted that his posture was rigid, and his full lips pressed into a pout, but his narrow eyes skimmed the premises as if he were busy committing to memory every inch of our house and garden.

'Wong-san.'

I was startled that the man knew my name. His greeting, emerging more as a growl, had not been friendly, but there was no doubt that both my name and title had been used. Bowing again, I noticed the officer's black ankle boots for the first time and waited.

'You don't recognise me?'

'I – no, I don't recall, sir.' I performed a third obeisance, a deep bow which served as an apology. Though bowing was not our custom, we in Malaya observed early on that the Japs bowed a lot. We must have made a subconscious decision collectively to lower our backs because bowing became a craze during the Nippon period. We even learnt their different forms: the *rei* (ordinary bow), the *saikeirei* (deep bow) and the *kokumin girei* (bow by an entire assembly).

'I am Hashimoto-san. I came to take photographs at your mother-in-law's birthday dinner last year.'

Fear crimped my bent neck, and something close to disgust crawled over my skin. I was aware of prickles forming on my flesh, as if a swill of cold air from the limestone hills had just blown in, or as if I had been bitten by a colony of ants. I remained in the posture of the *saikeirei* with my head down and back straight. After several minutes had elapsed, when I judged it safe to raise my head, I was finally able to place the face before me with a time and a place.

Only twelve months had passed, but it felt more like twelve years. In between meal preparations and the laying of the table, I had paid little attention to the photographer who arrived. He had taken the only image ever captured of Mother-in-Law, a black-and-white still that now hung above the doorway of our outer hall. Like most photographers in Ipoh before the war, the invited professional had been Japanese, a fact which no one questioned. There were many races in Malaya in those days: Bugis, Siamese, Armenian, Eurasian, Indonesian in addition to Malay, Chinese, and Indian, so it seemed natural that there should also be Japanese.

I stared at the man before me. His face was thinner than I remembered. In truth, I had a clearer image of the paraphernalia he'd brought with him – the sleek silver camera he'd placed on a tripod, his myriad sets of photographic lights, even the fans of paulownia wood to keep us ladies cool – than of the man himself. Something about him seemed different. It took a while for me to work out that the black moustache which had hugged the rim of the photographer's top lip was now missing. Gone also was the mop of tousled hair, which had looked so different from the average man's slicked-back head. The shock of hair that had given the artist a bohemian charm was no longer present, or was perhaps hidden beneath his hard cap. Without these accoutrements, and in his uniform, Hashimoto had taken on the waxen appearance of his compatriots.

'I am sorry to learn that your mother-in-law passed away,' he said, in the tone of a family friend who had dropped in on a social visit. He gave a little bow.

I bowed in response, though what I really wanted to do was to spit on Hashimoto's leather boots. 'Very kind of you to say so, sir.' I managed to sound reasonably calm, but the words nearly stuck in my throat. I wondered how he knew about my mother-in-law's demise and how much longer this incongruous attempt at small talk would continue.

A figure stepped out of the shadows. He had remained concealed behind one of the other Japanese soldiers, but I recognised him at once, despite his attempt at an exaggerated swagger. It was none other than our policeman neighbour, Ja'afar Abu, giving me an oily grin. He greeted me with '*Selamat pagi*, Wong-san' and cast his eyes around the house as if he had never been a guest. 'Your husband here?'

'No, he is at work in his office.'

'Where is his car?' This question came from Hashimoto. 'I remember he has car, yes?'

I swallowed, nodding. With our neighbour inches from me, I could hardly lie.

'Where is his car?'

On this, I permitted myself a trickle of ignorance. Ja'afar could not possibly have known where we had hidden the family jewel. 'Petrol is expensive, and my husband shares the car with a friend. The friend has it today. I don't know where it is.'

That much was true; I was ignorant about the Austin 8's exact whereabouts. I had begged my husband not to tell me, realising early on that for as long as the Japanese ruled Malaya, the less I knew about certain things, the better off I would be. It was a strategy I also adopted with my sister-in-law Dora. I did not wish to know how she was using the secret chamber inside Dorcourt; so long as I did not ask, I would not know. Whenever I happened to see a stranger on the driveway next door, I turned away from our windows. It was better that way.

Of course there were times when I burned with questions, as happened at that precise moment. There I was, before a former photographer now bedecked in the uniform of the Nippon Imperial Army, and our Malay neighbour was standing side by side as his comrade. I was so tempted to ask what was happening that indiscretions nearly slipped off my tongue.

Hashimoto unbuttoned one of the breast pockets of his uniform, removed what looked like a small notepad from it, and tore off a sheet of paper. He then flipped out a pen and scrawled on his sheet, using the back of the notepad as support. He handed me the paper. There was an address, a date, and a time.

'Tell your husband to come. With car.'

I nodded and bowed a final time. I watched the men leave, going so far as to stroll down our driveway so that I could stare at their receding backs and know for certain that they had gone.

Afterwards, I turned over the piece of paper Hashimoto had given me. It was a page taken from the receipt book of one of the old Japanese stores in Ipoh. Weng Yu's appointment was for the next day at St Michael's Institution at 10 a.m., Nippon time.

Like the kongsi house in which we had sheltered in the jungle, Ja'afar's house was built in the traditional Malay style, with its living quarters set on stilts above the ground for added ventilation. It was made of wood, as our Green House was, but Ja'afar's house had steps leading up to the open verandah where my mother-in-law had sometimes sat with Husna, Ja'afar's wife. It was Husna who opened the door, as I expected she would. I watched her face carefully for any hint of displeasure and saw none. Husna beamed in her usual way.

'Mei Foong! Please come in!' she said effusively.

'Are you sure this is a good time, Husna?'

'Yes, yes!' She gave me a wide smile, full of brilliant teeth, and led me by my hand into the cool of her house. Their youngest child, a girl called Aminah who sometimes played with Lai Hin, was standing at the side of the living room with her arms stretched out above her head. Then, unsure where to put her arms, she let them drop to her sides while giving me a shy smile which showed a missing front tooth.

I waited on one of the rattan chairs in the living room while Husna disappeared into the kitchen. She returned holding a glass of water in one hand and a plate of colourful *kueh* in the other: round green balls dotted with white flakes of desiccated coconut. The cakes had been part of Mother-in-Law's repertoire, one of the many delicacies her expert hands had made and with which she had tempted the people of Ipoh. I was struck by a wave of nostalgia and sadness; I had to force a sigh to shake it off.

'So sorry I haven't had time to visit you until now, Husna. We came back . . . oh, I can't even keep track of time any more. It has been very hard.'

Husna reached out to touch my arm. 'I know,' she said, blinking softly at me, eyes full of compassion. 'I was here when . . . the day they came for the men.'

After a pause, she whispered, 'Is your father all right now?'

'His back is sore and he can't sleep. I want to make him chicken with ginger – that will give him some strength back – but with so little income coming in, how will we ever afford a whole chicken?'

When Husna touched my arm for a second time, her eyes were moist. 'I am so sorry, Mei Foong, it is horrible, horrible. Why did they do that to an old man? These people are not human.'

Aminah remained at the edge of the room, her big eyes full of curiosity.

'And you, Husna?' I asked, changing the subject. 'How are you and Enche Ja'afar?'

The glance Husna gave me was fleeting and, I thought, slightly embarrassed. She moved her head before saying hurriedly, 'We are okay-lah, Mei Foong, can't complain. But it . . . I . . . ,'

Husna broke off her sentence abruptly; she seemed deep in thought. 'What can I say? We live in a different world now.' She gave an agitated sigh. 'The children have gone back to school. And Husband . . . at least he has work, keeps him busy.'

'What sort of work does Enche Ja'afar do now, Husna?' I asked, rather pointedly, but I knew Husna well enough to be direct. 'Is he still a policeman like before?'

'Yes,' Husna replied. I waited for her to elaborate, but when she said nothing more, I considered mentioning his visit to our house that morning.

'Husna,' I said, this time reaching across to touch her arm. 'We have known each other a few years now, and I feel we can talk openly. Something seems to be troubling you. Am I right?'

Husna looked to be on the verge of tears. 'I . . . I don't know what has got into my husband. Some people have given him funny ideas, Mei Foong.'

'What funny ideas, Husna?'

'Before the surrender, he went off to fight. But he was not fighting the Japanese, he was helping them.'

'What? Your husband was helping the Japs conquer Malaya?'

'Oh, Mei Foong,' Husna said in anguish, 'he doesn't see it like that, he thinks he was fighting to free Malaya from the *orang puteh*. The Japanese promised to give Malaya independence.'

'And Enche Ja'afar believed them?'

'Yes, I know, I know it was silly of him. Praise be to Allah, there were not many of these crazy men. Hamid was furious. My husband could have killed his own brother! I said to him, "If you see your brother and the Malay Regiment in front of you, what will you do then?" Husband could not answer. But he still went. I could not stop him. And, Mei Foong, I . . . Look, no one knows about this . . .'

'Of course, Husna, you have my word. Enche Ja'afar came to our house this morning with a Japanese officer.'

'Oh, you mean the photographer from the Mikasa Photo Shop on Belfield Street? Mr Hashimoto?'

'Yes, do you know him?'

'He's my husband's boss. Husband reports to him when there are special assignments. Mr Hashimoto is not the only one in uniform now. All the Japanese in Ipoh were spies.'

On seeing my mouth drop, Husna nodded while adding gravely, 'Yes, every one of them – the photographers, the shop owners – they were all working for the Japanese government the whole time. They're back today as army officers. That Japanese sundry shop, I always wondered how it survived. Now I know. Husband tells me the owner is some high-up official in Kuala Lumpur.'

Husna pushed the plate of green cakes she had carried in from the kitchen towards me. 'Here, have a piece of *ondeh-ondeh*. I made them just this morning.'

◆　◆　◆

When I told my husband about Hashimoto's visit, Weng Yu's face turned the colour of chalk. He could not eat his dinner. Like his mother, Weng Yu had adopted the Malay custom of eating with his hands, but he spent the evening pushing balls of crushed tapioca around the bowl with his fingers.

Afterwards, he went out into the garden. I thought my husband was heading across to Dorcourt via the secret gate, but he remained firmly within our boundaries, his back rigid, circling the perimeter.

Father and I looked at each other. 'I'd better see how Husband is,' I mumbled.

Father rose at the same time. 'Wait, Mei Foong, I'll come too.'

We walked slowly, Father weighed down by age and his still-recent injuries, me by the baby inside. Dusk was falling, the sky turning a lovely crimson. It was a time of year when the trees were bursting with flowers and the whole garden smelt of sweetness. I sat beneath our flame-of-the-forest, admiring its scarlet crown, while Father and Weng Yu embarked on circuits. Both men remained deeply pensive. I felt sorry for my husband, who was so unsuited to war and brutality. Some men are cut out for heroism, but Weng Yu, with his gentle temperament and sensitive soul, had passions of the artistic variety. The Japanese occupation was already proving to be a torture. I was sure he would spend the night agonising over his summons by Hashimoto.

Our children, meanwhile, were enjoying games on the grass. The eldest, Wai Sung, kept to himself as usual, kicking a football in front of him. From time to time he would attempt a fancy trick, dribbling the ball or manoeuvring it up his body and over his head. His younger sister and brother were as content to be free of his company as he was of theirs. Lai Hin and Wai Kit had claimed spots in a patch of sand near the secret gate, where they were pitting marbles. All three were given repeated warnings not to approach any soldier and certainly not to speak to one, but I wondered whether the children really understood the danger we were in. What if they unwittingly repeated some of what they heard, what if Lai Hin suddenly called out, 'Bloody Japs' to a patrolling troop? Although our adult conversations seemed to splash off their backs like rain off roofs, I was sure that some of the words they heard would have permeated. I looked up at the bloom on our flame-of-the-forest tree and marvelled at the beauty of its flowers, which were orange-red with hints of yellow fanning out across the top. In the face of such majesty, I allowed myself a few minutes of happiness. Sitting on that bench listening to my children's shrieks, it could even have been an ordinary evening.

My husband was the last person to retire for the night. When he had taken his bath, he changed into his pyjamas and climbed into bed. He did not sleep, but lay quietly on his back, staring straight up at the ceiling. I could hear him sucking air in nervously through his nose.

I turned on to my side and placed an arm on his shoulder. 'Husband, they probably just want the car. Please try to get some sleep.'

'You never know what these Japs might want. They beat your father the other day, didn't they, and what for? They've gone mad, I tell you!'

Weng Yu sat up suddenly, propping himself up on his elbows. 'Imagine, betraying us like that. We would never have invited *him* to this house if we'd known he was an enemy spy.'

My husband spat out the word 'him' as if Hashimoto's name would choke him. I felt the same; I could not bear to think of the hospitality we had inadvertently extended to a Japanese spy.

'It's too late to change that now,' I said quietly. 'There's no point regretting the past. We have to think about the children. If he wants the car, you have to give it to him. If you can get anything from this Hashimoto at all – it doesn't matter what, anything we can sell for cash – take it. We need the money. Make sure he knows that Wai Sung is learning Japanese.'

Weng Yu gave me a sardonic glance, raising one eyebrow and at the same time releasing a huff.

'Do you think I like it, Husband? But the Japs are here and the white skins aren't. They ran off and left us with the enemy, remember? Anyway, what's so terrible about learning Japanese? We're speaking English, aren't we?'

Weng Yu did not reply. From his demeanour I could tell that he had no riposte. I would gladly have gone to see Hashimoto in his place, but we both knew there was no question of his missing the appointment. We sought comfort in each other's arms, for the first time in many weeks.

◆ ◆ ◆

Weng Yu's meeting with Hashimoto was to take place at St Michael's Institution, a once august school run by Catholic priests. St Michael's, as the school was affectionately known, was housed in sprawling colonial buildings opposite the Padang where my husband and the Chinese men of Ipoh had been made to stand under the full blast of the Malayan sun.

Weng Yu drove off in the family Austin shortly after breakfast. Since we had been forced to change our clocks to Tokio time, ten o'clock in the morning was actually eight o'clock by natural light. On the morning of his appointment, the change conferred an advantage: it meant that my husband would be home before the Malayan sun became too fierce. He came back on foot as expected, sweat dripping from under his *topee* but with a surprising grin on his face.

When he told me that the Japs had given him a job, I almost dropped the bowl I was carrying.

'But that is excellent news, Husband!'

I thought at once of a steady income coming in, but I was also pleased by my husband's obvious delight. Every part of his face beamed, even his neck and ears glowed, and the smile he gave me was almost tender. It hit me then that I had only seen Weng Yu so enthused when listening to music or whenever we watched plays together. The thought came like a thunderbolt. There was a peculiar sensation in my tummy, a premonition of what I was up against. Instead of anger, I felt pity, imagining a younger Weng Yu, cheeky but possibly happy too, on that fateful day when he had learnt about his father's death. The event had taken place years ago, but the man-boy before me still seemed trapped in old wounds. And yet, he had been successful, becoming one of Ipoh's few British-trained engineers. Within the folds of my compassion, a strange pride bubbled.

'Tell me, Husband! I want to know everything!' I cried out. 'What happened?'

'I went to St Michael's as instructed. The Japs are using the school as offices. At least, that's all I saw there. The signboard outside the place reads "Perak Shu Seicho" or something like that.'

'Okay, so you get there, then what?'

'I see Hashimoto-lah. He offers me a job.'

'What, you get there and straightaway you see Hashimoto?'

'Not exactly-lah. I have to pass the sentries first. At the gate, there are two of them. Ai-yahh, why do you want to know such details?'

'I'm interested! Why can't you tell me? Not hard, is it?'

'Typical woman! Wants to know all the useless details! Okay, so I show Hashimoto's paper to one of sentries, and he tells me to drive in. "Park inside," he says. I park under a rain tree in the compound and walk to the main entrance. The buildings all look the same, but there is a hole in part of the roof, on one side. The place doesn't look too bad, though. The classrooms on the ground floor are fine, and they're all occupied.'

'What, every single one is now an office?'

'I think so. There are men inside each room, and desks as well, not school desks – large office desks, like the one in my office. The Japs have obviously gone round collecting office furniture. Looks like they're doing a lot of work – their desks are piled with paper and typewriters, some men are on the telephone, there are files everywhere. Funny thing is, our Malay policeman neighbour was inside one of the offices, in his uniform, talking to one of the Japs.'

'Oh,' I said, feigning ignorance. I had kept my word to Husna and had not mentioned Ja'afar's presence in our house. 'Did he see you?'

'No, he and the man were engrossed in something, they didn't notice me pass. Then I see Hashimoto, and he asks for my office furniture.'

'He asks? Is that all he wanted? What about the car?'

'I'll come to that in a minute. First, he offers me a job. He says that he knows I am a British-trained engineer. They need good engineers in Ipoh, he tells me, as if I didn't already know. He asks, "Will you come and work for us?"'

'It's like the office furniture – what can I say? I say yes, of course. Hashimoto smiles, points upwards, and tells me that I am now in charge of all repairs in Old Town, beginning with the roof of St Michael's. And he says sorry, but my car is needed for other work and I am to hand him my keys. So I take the keys out of my pocket and give them to him-lah. Hashimoto smiles and tells me to report for work tomorrow morning at nine o'clock. Then I walk home.'

I sighed. 'And what about money? How much will they pay you?'

'Hashimoto says they are still trying to work out how much they can pay us, but that I am not to worry. "It's better to work for us than not to work for us." Those were his very words.'

The reply did not please me; I continued to worry about how we would be able to feed us all. However, Weng Yu did become a big fish – Senior Engineer – in the revamped Public Works Department. Ironically, it was the Japanese who gave my British-trained husband the role he had craved and which had been denied him by our colonial rulers. At long last, Weng Yu was able to apply the skills he had been taught in Britain to his hometown.

11

Shortly after commencing his new job, my husband initiated a singing group. Neighbours would descend on our house every Thursday evening for what we called a 'sing-song' around the gramophone. The choice of name demonstrated Weng Yu's sense of humour, for in those days the phrase carried different connotations. Cabaret girls were known as sing-song girls, even though some of them would surely have died if their lives had depended on turning out a tune. My husband's sing-song group, on the other hand, had exacting standards.

Weng Yu chose the members himself. He would first ascertain their musical tastes and whether they could play an instrument, before finding out which instrument they played and exploring any previous singing experience. On the few occasions when these initial conversations proved satisfactory, my husband would issue cautious invitations to come along on a Thursday evening.

The idea for the group had arisen from the dreaded Radio Taiso drills which Weng Yu was forced to endure from the day he commenced working for the Japs. Radio Taiso began at eight sharp. Because of the imposition of Tokio time in Malaya, eight in the morning actually meant six o'clock natural time. The skies would still be dark when Weng Yu set off on his bicycle, guided by its bright headlamp. On the first morning, my husband, who had not been warned that he would have to exercise before being allowed to sit at his desk, ended up a little sweaty, and thereafter took to carrying a change of clothing in a satchel draped over the handlebar of his bicycle. On arrival at the school he would park his bike in the compound before walking across to the Padang. There, he and Ipoh's other civil servants were expected to stand in readiness. It was obligatory for anyone working in the nearby government offices to attend, be they engineers, teachers, or policemen. From time to time, Weng Yu found himself standing beside our policeman neighbour, which was how we learnt that Ja'afar Abu had been promoted from lowly Corporal to the position of Deputy Inspector.

A few minutes before eight, one of the Japanese soldiers would walk to the front of the field. This was the signal for someone to begin blaring music. Loudspeakers had been affixed to the poles that were hastily erected around the edges of the Padang. The music, Japanese of course, was inevitably accompanied by mutterings, also in Japanese. At the beginning of the war, those who did not understand the language were excused, but it did not take long for the more perspicacious among our fellow Malayans to learn what was required.

With Radio Taiso, there was a leader whose example you followed. When he lifted his arm above his head, you had to do likewise; when he swung his arms about, you did the same. Other drills included standing on tiptoe, arching your body to touch your toes while keeping your legs straight, and all manner of the stretching and contortions, which our new rulers thought would keep us fit. Radio Taiso was an example of the sort of unquestioning discipline the Japs wanted to instil. If told to bend, you bent; if ordered to scald your toes, you scalded your toes. Nothing was impossible; it was just a matter of *seishin*, or spirit, which to the Japs meant blind obedience to the emperor. My husband, much as he loved music, hated sport. He was happy to watch football, but playing it was another matter. As for waving his arms in the air or hopping on his toes while sweeping both legs in and out like a pair of scissors, such actions he deemed completely beyond the pale. Even the accompanying music failed to endear Radio Taiso to him. But the tunes gave him an idea.

'Wife, what do you think about having a singing evening in our house?' he asked.

I peered at Weng Yu. Was it my opinion he wanted, or my permission he sought? Either instance was rare – he did as he wished in our house, a precedent set while his mother was alive, and so ossified by the time I came along that change was a lost cause. On the day Weng Yu asked about the singing group, there was a gleam in his dark eyes. He gave me a half smile, the sort of smile in which lips curve mischievously, but then straighten at once as if uncertain whether or not to smile. Before I knew what was happening, Weng Yu began humming a familiar tune, one that turned my mind back to the days of our courtship.

On my then suitor's second visit to my parental house, Father had tried to impress the young man by taking an American record out of its sleeve and placing it on the gramophone's turntable. The record he had chosen was the operetta *Rose-Marie*, which had as its signature tune the famous 'Indian Love Call'. As soon as the song came on, Weng Yu rose unannounced. I could see him clearly under the electric lights Father had had installed, which showed off in fine detail the contours of Weng Yu's angular chin and the dimpled clefts which appeared on both cheeks when he smiled. How handsome my future husband had looked, with his hair neatly combed, greased back, but not with the absurd amounts of brilliantine plaguing men of the era. Every now and again his luminous eyes would glance at the ceiling and then at us. The slight hump of his Adam's apple twitched in anticipation.

'When I'm calling you-oo-oo-oo . . .'

As soon as he opened his mouth, Weng Yu became a different person. His eyes stopped flicking nervously, which was his habit when speaking; instead, they stayed resting on me. His whole body visibly relaxed, even the tension in his broad shoulders dissipated. No longer did he sit stiffly in his armchair, but transformed into a performer who held his audience in thrall with the notes that emerged effortlessly out of improbably elastic lips. His voice was low, much lower than when he spoke, but also unexpectedly melodious. Goose pimples rose on my naked arms. Every glass vessel in the room seemed to shake. Weng Yu continued to sing, attaining depths I had not thought possible and doing so with an ease and a confidence he did not have when he spoke. He was at once engrossed and engrossing, aware of his power to arouse not only our spirits, but even inanimate matter. I knew then that if he ever asked, I would marry him.

'Indian Love Call' remained in our record collection, as did the other British and American songs we had once enjoyed. We realised that such music was now frowned upon; indeed, anything Western was frowned upon, though we later discovered that Japanese officers gorged on Western cuisine whenever they could. Western music and movies, on the other hand, were replaced by Japanese songs and films. Later on, the Japs would arrange weekly culture evenings at which other Asian music – Malay, Chinese, Filipino, Indonesian, Siamese, and Indian – was allowed. At the outset, however, the emphasis was very much on turning us Japanese. Free lessons in Japanese were offered everywhere. Newspapers took up the challenge, devoting a page or two to the teaching of the language. I never took formal lessons, but my husband and eldest son, Wai Sung, both learnt Japanese, the latter with greater enthusiasm than his father. After just two months of instruction, Wai Sung was able to decipher many of the new signboards that had sprung up in front of Ipoh's restaurants and cinemas and public buildings. These were obligatory and written in the elementary Japanese or Katakana script.

The thin air of occupation suffocated me. Flags of the Rising Sun were everywhere, or so it seemed. With each breath we took, we felt the pressure to conform, to love the emperor or 'Tenno Heika', to demonstrate how 'Nipponised' we were. Strangely enough, the Japs did not like being known as Japanese; they wanted instead to be called

Nipponese. In their terminology, Japan was Dai Nippon, Japanese men Nippon-zin, the women Nippon-huzin, and the language Nippon-go.

Those were heady days, the atmosphere fetid. I could not wait for the nightmare to end. Without having realised it, I had been content under the British, yet even I could see that, given the manner of their departure, nothing would ever be the same in Malaya. It was our treacherous neighbour, Ja'afar Abu, who had first uttered those words; months later, I finally agreed with him.

Little wonder then that my husband was pulled by nostalgia and a yearning to create a piece of the past, no matter how small. I, for my part, was keen to encourage the confidence Weng Yu had gained since his new employment.

'Good idea, Husband,' I said. 'Only, I worry that your singing will attract attention. Better to sing Japanese songs. Do you know any?'

'I don't want to sing Japanese songs!'

I frowned. 'You'll have to sing at least one or two. You can't just sing Western songs! The Japs don't only play martial music, you know, some of the Japanese songs are quite good.'

It was true that there was variety to Japanese music; even I liked some of their numbers. My husband, when scoffing, was probably thinking only of their marching tunes, and unfortunately there were rather a lot of these: abhorrent, terrifying music in which no amount of sweet trumpet-blowing could disguise the underlying beat of war. I could not understand why they were so popular in Ipoh. At the time, it was difficult to step out of the house without hearing someone whistle or even sing the dreadful 'Aikoku Koshinkyoku', the patriotic march, with its rousing insistent tune.

But there was another genre altogether – songs of an ethereal quality, many with foxtrot and rumba rhythms, which could have been Western were it not for their incomprehensible lyrics. I had no idea who the singers were or how to go about getting their words, but I had a good idea whom to ask. I had spotted her at one of the concerts organised by the Nippon Army I'd attended with Father. We had gone purely as a show of patriotism, but had ended up enjoying ourselves more than we could have anticipated.

It was the ever-garrulous Mrs Lim who had first mentioned the woman. According to Mrs Lim, one of her neighbours, a certain Mrs Chan who lived on the same road, was taking Japanese lessons avidly. 'The silly woman really adores Nippon culture!'

When I saw Mrs Chan at the concert, I remembered Mrs Lim's words. I knew also that this Mrs Chan had belonged to the Elim Gospel Hall choir before the war. Whether the woman had continued her activities in the musical domain, I had no idea, but her background made her a suitable candidate for Weng Yu's sing-song group.

When my husband invited Mrs Chan to come one Thursday evening, I could tell that she was flattered, not least by the attentions of a still-handsome man. Mrs Chan was a striking woman herself, though of uncertain age. She looked rather well-preserved, with hair that fell to her shoulders and a fringe sweeping off an as yet unmarked forehead. No one knew her real age, but she had taught History for so long at the Anglo-Chinese Girls' School that she could not have been less than forty. Mrs Chan did not walk so much as waddle. The reasons for her bizarre gait were unclear: she was not fat, and both her legs appeared to be in proportion to the rest of her body. Mrs Chan's other notable attribute – a large mouth – was perfect for delivering agreeable tones, and an equally good conduit for stinging rebukes.

The very first time Mrs Chan appeared at our house, she walked in with Samad, who had ventured the five minutes on foot to fetch her. In those days, none of us women felt safe on our own, even if the journey took no more than minutes. There were too many soldiers around, and all that was required was for one unfortunate encounter to destroy your life. The Japanese soldiers who did not assault your bodies made sure they attacked your minds because many had taken to the revolting habit of urinating openly on the streets. Only the bravest or the most brazen of females went out without a chaperone: the former in semi-disguise, wearing their hair cropped and with oversized men's shirts to conceal their curves, the latter in whatever dress they chose, having already consorted with a Japanese official and therefore being under the protection of the secret police.

Greeting Mrs Chan at the door, I admired her slick cheongsam and remembered how cultured she had been when I was still at school. I could imagine her nurturing a genuine passion for Nippon language and culture. Within minutes, our house livened up. She and Weng Yu stood near the gramophone, which fortunately sat in the inner hall where the singing was less conspicuous, while I placed myself in an armchair. My husband wound the gramophone and lowered the needle on to the record. When the sound came on, he bit his lips nervously; the record was already scratchy even though it was quite new. He looked at Mrs Chan, who in return gave him an encouraging smile. The pair proceeded with a duet of 'Silent Night' that had been made popular a few years previously by the American singer Bing Crosby. Their voices didn't quite blend. Mrs Chan's was lower than I'd imagined, with a glamorous quality to it, rather like Judy Garland's, I thought, though her vocals were of course not as smooth. They followed that with a rendition of 'God Bless America', a choice which made me squirm. I knew that Deputy Inspector Ja'afar was at home because I had seen him walking in next door and I worried that he might report us to his bosses. Every squeak on our driveway made me look up in expectation of a pounding on our front door.

As soon as they finished their second choice, I asked, 'Mrs Chan, do you know any Japanese songs? There's one I particularly like, the one that was played at the end of the concert last week. Remember?'

'Oh, you mean "Minami Kara"? "To the South"?'

'I'm ashamed I don't know what it's called. Hum it and I'll tell you.'

Mrs Chan began to sing the melody, a lilting tune which worked so beautifully in her sultry voice that she hardly needed wind instruments in the background. The following week Mrs Chan brought the record with her and wrote down its lyrics in Romanised script for Weng Yu. You would never have guessed that the song was a fascists' call to arms. We did not divine it either; brother-in-law Weng Yoon was horrified when he found out. 'Minami Kara' served a very useful purpose however; it, and songs of a similar ilk, stopped the Japanese soldiers from unduly harassing our house.

With Weng Yu and Mrs Chan meeting regularly, the sing-song group began to garner a reputation in the neighbourhood. The next person to join was Dr Pillay, also known as 'Big Ears', who worked at the District Hospital and had treated my mother-in-law during her final years. After Dr Pillay became a member, two others joined at the same time: a Miss Lee who, even before the war, preferred dressing in male attire, and her companion Miss Mak, who in contrast was one of the most feminine women you would ever meet. Miss Lee, of course, sang contralto while Miss Mak was a soprano. The two ladies had begun sharing a house in 1940, causing tongues in Ipoh to work overtime, and not always kindly.

This motley crew of five became regular crooners in our house on Thursday evenings. Weng Yu would play a selection of tunes, always in English first, before putting on to the gramophone any Japanese records which the other members had brought with them. The entire group would break into song, regardless of which tune came up. Most of the time, they sang as a group, but there were occasions when they performed duets and even solos.

On what must have been the fourth or fifth sing-song meeting, I noticed a furtive shadow in the vestibule outside the door. It was our second son, Wai Kit, performing little hops in the style of a Radio Taiso exercise in which he pulled his arms up towards his chest and then quickly released them again, and doing so to a rhythm only he could discern. Seconds later, the boy's head popped out from behind the doorpost. As soon as our eyes met, Wai Kit slunk back into his hiding place quicker than I could have blinked. He knew that his father's singing sessions were off-limits; he was meant to be inside the bedroom he shared with his eldest brother.

When it came to children, Weng Yu put into practice the severe discipline he had been taught by his mother. This included, among other things, the imposition of graveyard silence during meals. In England, my husband once told me, children were seen but not heard; during his sing-song sessions, they should not be seen at all. The only child to whom my husband granted the occasional leeway – and this only when he was in a good mood – was our eldest boy, Wai Sung, but even he was not allowed out at sing-song time.

It would have been impossible to ignore the merriment in our house on Thursday evenings. Even the servants, who of their own accord listened only to Chinese or Malay songs, kept their bedroom doors ajar. Among our children, I was surprised to see Wai Kit prowling around. I had never heard him sing or even hum and wondered where this sudden interest in music came from. I recalled only that he sashayed when he walked, almost like a dancer.

When I saw his surreptitious little dance beyond the doorpost, I put an index finger to my lips, to indicate that we would keep this little secret together. After a brief retreat, Wai Kit revealed his long and narrow face once again, and there was the tiniest of smiles on his pencil lips. The following day, when his father was not in the house, I heard Wai Kit's high-pitched voice offering a rendition of 'Somewhere over the Rainbow'. It was my turn to smile. We were nurturing yet another singer in the family.

Sing-song evenings in the Green House made the war tolerable. Come rain or shine, the intrepid crooners would turn up, and during the hour they spent in our inner hall they transported us all to a better place.

12

After breakfast one morning, Father appeared in the dining room bearing in one hand a shallow box made of sandalwood and, in the other, sheets of rice paper. The reddish-brown box, heavy but devoid of carvings, was familiar from my childhood.

Father set it down on the table alongside the rice paper and threw me an enquiring look.

'Shall we, Mei Foong?'

'Father, I haven't picked up my brushes for years. I won't be any good.'

'It doesn't matter, Daughter. When there is ugliness all around, we must remind ourselves that beauty exists in this world.'

Father looked hard at me from behind his round lenses. He seemed strangely happy, his normally stern features soft in the Malayan sunlight. 'Remember your first lesson?' he asked.

I nodded uncomfortably, throwing him a self-conscious half-smile. My wariness amused the old man; his eyes lit up and he proceeded to ignore me.

Opening the box, he removed first an ink stone and then a fine set of brushes. The ink stone, made of black slate, glowed with the same minimalist beauty which had struck me the very first time I saw it, just after my seventh birthday, when Father had invited me into his study.

I remember being surprised that Father had come searching for me. His hours in the study were his own; he asked no one in, and none of us dared disturb him. It was late afternoon, a time when the sun was still strong. After ushering me in, Father had to walk outside to let down the bamboo blinds that hung at the edges of the verandah. He left the door open, and a mild breeze blew in. I could hear the intermittent squawking and chirping of the yellow-faced mynah birds, which hopped about on our lawn when they thought no one was watching.

When Father came back inside, he indicated that I should sit at one of the two places that had been laid at a large table. In front of me was a square sheet of bamboo paper printed with grids. Next to it, a number of calligraphy brushes were lined up neatly, one alongside another, beside an ink stone – which I assumed to be mine – and an ink stick. Father had given me my own ink stone! It took a while for this radical idea to sink in. Everything looked exquisite; even the ink stick had a golden dragon carved down one of its sides. The same instruments lay in front of Father's seat, but his paper was proper calligraphy writing paper, a type favoured by experts. Made of rice and known as Shuan paper, it came without grids.

Father shook his head gravely when I picked up a brush. 'Not so fast, Mei Foong. First, you must prepare your mind. When your mind is not ready, your hands will be stilted. They will not move freely.'

Father lifted a spoon which lay inside a porcelain bowl. The bowl itself was filled with a clear liquid. 'You must use only clean water,' Father said, emptying spoonfuls of water on to the top of his ink stone. 'First, we will grind our ink.'

Father was a serious man who had a sombre air at the best of times; in front of his brushes and ink, even his thin moustache seemed straighter, as if it had to focus on the task at hand. With brow furrowed and eyes narrowed, Father looked truly frightening, and more than a little mad. He began to move his ink stick on the small pool of water he had created, making circles repeatedly across the stone. The scratchy noise, like sand being ground on a hard surface, was oddly soothing.

I copied Father's actions, but after only a minute became bored. My scratchy noise stopped.

'What are you doing, Mei Foong?'

'I'm tired, Father.'

Father resumed his continuous swirling movements. 'You will never be a calligraphy artist if you can't even make ink. Rest for a minute, take your ink stick out; don't leave it in the water.'

Father did not reprimand me, yet I somehow felt his disappointment. The ink thickened on his black slate. After another minute he dipped a brush into the ink well and then moved the pointed tip of the brush's hairs effortlessly across the piece of test paper he had set aside. The horizontal line he wrote blurred at its edges, for the ink was not yet ready. Father continued rotating his ink stick with vigorous circular strokes. As I watched, I felt ashamed. Father had never taken my elder sister into his study for a calligraphy lesson. He had chosen me instead, and I had failed him. I could not even grind ink.

Eventually Father's ink thickened to a consistency that pleased him. Glimpses of white shone through on Father's black ink stone. Still not saying a word, he tested his ink once more. This time the line which he drew across the page remained firm on the paper, with a clear head and tail. Father was ready to write.

I wondered whether Father would ask me to start grinding ink again, but he was already elsewhere, fully absorbed. He dipped his brush into the ink and then frowned as if every cell in his body was concentrating on the task at hand. With eyebrows still knitted, Father wrote out the Chinese characters for my name, Mei Foong, which means 'Beautiful Wind'. I watched Father's brush gliding across the paper like a song in the air, his hands moving with mesmerising ease. He wrote without pause, channelling all of his energy on to the sheet of Shuan paper in front of him. Every stroke was perfect, at least it seemed that way to me. When, after a few days, I was allowed to hold a brush, I appreciated Father's expertise even more, because I then understood how precisely the tip of his brush had had to be placed, with just the right amount of force and lightness. I knew then that I was observing a true master, a man for whom the brush served as an extension of his fingers.

I wanted to write calligraphy the way Father did. I knew it would take time, but I never imagined the effort it would cost, the futile years I would spend trying to force the brush, before realising that what came out had to arise from within. Father had told me this repeatedly, but I had listened with one ear closed. Though my technique improved with practice, I never became the master Father was. I could not lose myself enough, could not let every nerve relax or allow my breathing to become sufficiently rhythmic to be able to pour my soul out on to the paper. The brushes were kind to me only in sparing moments, when they would sing and dance with the sort of liberating fluidity I so longed for.

After my marriage to Weng Yu, I stopped writing calligraphy altogether, fearing that my husband would look askance at this wholly Chinese activity. The calligraphy set Father had given me lay locked in the right-hand drawer of the dressing table, alongside Mother's antique fan. I was not sure if I was ready to retrieve the box.

Father gave me a quizzical look. While waiting for my answer, he managed to wordlessly convey the idea that if my husband could have his singing, I should also enjoy something beautiful.

◆ ◆ ◆

'What is that?' Weng Yu asked. We were inside our bedroom, my husband behind me at the dressing table. His voice was unusually thick, his words a mumbled pastiche while he stood looking over my shoulder at the rice-paper scroll I was smoothing out with both my hands.

'It's an idiom; can you recognise the characters?'

My husband, I knew, had attended the Yuk Choy School in his first two years, where he would certainly have been taught to write Chinese. The ideograms I had written may have been too advanced, however. Weng Yu narrowed his eyes and screwed up his magnificent nose.

'This is what it says, Husband: "Practice makes perfect". What do you think?'

Weng Yu curved his mouth disdainfully. 'Well, it's not what one would call art.'

'But why not? If it had been done by a Chinese master, I'm sure you would think it beautiful. Of course, I cannot be a master without practice!'

To this my husband did not respond; he glanced away from my writing towards the quiet street outside. As Weng Yu continued staring out of the window, I had an urge to pummel him. I was tired of being ignored like a piece of furniture. I felt provocative, determined to elicit a reaction that was more than physical excitement.

'You know, Husband, I used to write every night with Father in our study at home. I had forgotten how . . .' – I groped for the word – 'relaxing I found it. I've seen what happens to you when you sing. The same thing happens to me when I write.'

Weng Yu arched an eyebrow, a tiny flick full of surprise and scepticism. His aquiline nose flared out at the same time, with just the hint of a sneer. Calligraphy, his nostrils suggested, was not art; it wasn't even painting or sketching; it could not possibly be compared to singing – an exalted form. He seemed insulted. 'You have too much time on your hands, Wife.'

Weng Yu cast his nose into the air, and I could see the insides of his nostrils, circular and deep, in which tiny hairs nestled. He looked decidedly less handsome from that angle. A cold sliver ran through his voice. When my husband noticed the dismay he had caused, he tried to make amends in his usual fashion.

'Well, calligraphy is beautiful in its own sort of way, I suppose. But why don't you learn to paint? Proper painting, Western painting. Mrs Chan is keen on art; you could ask her.'

I carried on smoothing out my large sheet of rice paper as if nothing had happened. I was proud of what Father and I had written; I had no intention of taking lessons in Western art, from Mrs Chan or anyone else. I had been taught art at school, but they could never have taught me Chinese calligraphy. This I'd forced myself to learn from Father over many painstaking years.

Afterwards, when Weng Yu had left me alone, I wondered where his contempt for things Chinese had come from. It could not have been from missionary school. I too had attended an English-speaking school in Ipoh, but it had not purged me of appreciation for my culture. The sound of his feet next door in the inner hall annoyed me. I was fractious even when music poured out of the gramophone, an English song of course. I remained in front of the large vertical mirror of my Italian-made dressing table thinking about what my husband had said.

When I leaned towards the glass, I saw a darkening patch on my forehead. My baby was not quite due, but I had already endured more spots and itchy skin than in my previous four pregnancies put together. I was quite sure that the baby I was carrying was a boy, and he was beginning to tire me. I resented the constant feeling of exhaustion, the little rashes that broke out, and now the changes to my colouring. There was even a glow on both cheeks, which left oily stains on the tips of my fingers when I touched them.

I sat back irritably. Next door, Fred Astaire's smooth voice came on as he began to sing 'Cheek to Cheek'. The actor had entranced us in the movie *Top Hat* in those happy early days of our marriage, before war and suffering engulfed us all. My husband was less intolerable then, or perhaps I had been blind. It was quite possible that he had always insulted everyone in the same way, with a special pique reserved for the women in his life. Weng Yu had certainly treated his mother abominably, and as I thought about it, I realised there had been someone else, a young Chinese man who was a visitor to the family house. He had been there when we went to see Fred Astaire and Ginger Rogers sing and dance.

His name was Wen Yin, and he was the son of Weng Yu's late father's second brother who lived in China; in other words, a Chinese cousin.

Wen Yin lived in my father-in-law's ancestral village and, coming from China, spoke no English. When the young man first visited Malaya, it had perhaps been a novelty for the Wong boys, but by the time *Top Hat* was released, the Malayan cousins were no longer so solicitous. They largely ignored Wen Yin, leaving him in my care. I was taken aback, yet at the same time felt pity for the young man. There was no reason why the Wong boys could not at least have paid attention to Wen Yin for a few days, despite his deadpan voice and his recitation of facts, and those bright eyes which flitted nervously from side to side. From the state of his Chinese tunics and trousers, it was clear that he was poor; from his manner it was equally obvious that he felt socially awkward and did not understand small talk. Only two subjects were of interest to him: the city of Soochow, which he had visited, and canals, which he adored, and he combined the two in conversation, Soochow being a city of canals. Wen Yin, who knew every inch of every canal in Soochow, did not tire of telling anyone who would listen which canals he had walked beside.

As we went into the dining room one night, my husband whispered into my ear, 'So, what new canal have you heard about?' with a smirk on his thick lips. The family resemblance could not be doubted: Weng Yu's own eyes flitted from side to side even as he sneered. I had felt nothing at the time other than a niggling unpleasantness, but years later in front of my dressing-table mirror, rage welled up in my chest. I thought of the way my husband preened himself in front of our bathroom mirror, how he combed his hair incessantly and inspected his chiselled cheekbones, and all I wanted to do was to run into our kitchen, grab a plate, and smash him over the head. I would have given anything at that moment to wipe the smugness off his smile.

Of course, I did not do anything of the kind. I let the moment come and go, the same way all the moments in my life have come and gone – with utter indifference, each oblivious to the fact of its passing. The young cousin never again returned to Malaya.

13

The Japanese were adept at exploiting Weng Yu's skills. Although they paid him a pittance, they gave him the grand title of Senior Engineer. They also allowed him to lead a team of workers, which would have been unimaginable under the British. Weng Yu's team went about repairing war-damaged infrastructure: the Hugh Low Bridge, which was the largest and best-known in town; rows upon rows of Chinese shop-houses with their five-foot ways; and the roofs of the numerous buildings that had been shelled. Hashimoto even hinted to my husband that if he worked diligently enough, he could be made Chief Engineer one day, unlikely though this seemed.

We spent weeks accumulating the goodwill of our new Japanese masters. We were thus surprised to hear loud rapping one night on the kitchen door. The rhythm was wild and frenetic. Though lacking the menace favoured by Japanese soldiers, it was also not the casual tap-a-tap Rokiah used whenever she came in search of salt and cooking oil. Yet the visitor must have come from Dorcourt, since no one else entered at the back.

As we sat up, my back stiffened. My nerves were already frayed, the baby I was expecting being due, and the unwelcome knocking disquieted me even more. Could an intruder have learnt about our secret gate? The thumping continued. Father, Weng Yu, and I looked at one another in alarm. We stopped eating; I remember putting down my bowl and chopsticks. The children, meanwhile, watched us like rabbits. After a few seconds Father said, 'Better open the door.' I could not understand how he managed to remain so calm when my own heart was racing.

At that moment Samad poked his head in. There was no need for him to say anything; he asked the question with his large eyes. My husband gulped, before giving a slight nod and standing up. Father rose too, and all three men went into the kitchen. I could not decide what to do. Feeling a deep dread, I joined my husband and father, knowing I would have to face whoever it was sooner or later.

As soon as Weng Yu opened the back door, I caught a glimpse of two figures outside. I could not see them well; darkness was already falling, and the electric lights in the kitchen made the outside seem blacker than it actually was. My husband's tall body also cast a shadow which obscured the visitors. However, I was quite sure that one of the grainy shapes belonged to my brother-in-law – it had his robust waistline. The next minute I heard his voice. Weng Yoon first said something mundane like, 'Sorry to disturb your dinner,' and then, without pausing, added, 'but we must come in. Something terrible has happened.' His voice was more thread-like than usual and had a definite tremor.

Weng Yoon did not even wait to be invited; he brushed past my husband and entered. His driver, Ali, came in immediately afterwards, his face grey with anxiety. My brother-in-law, impatient as ever, was unable to contain himself. Before Ali had even reached the cover of our air well, Weng Yoon blurted out, 'Bad news from Seremban. Second Brother and his children, they . . . they . . .'

He then stopped and scanned the kitchen with the inexpressive eyes of a fish. Dissolving into tears, Weng Yoon turned away to sniffle in semi-privacy. 'Sorry,' he said, muttering into the air.

'For God's sake, what is it, Weng Yoon?' my husband shouted. I was glad for his intervention: the suspense was unbearable. Even Father became impatient. 'Yes, just tell, please,' he said, with what I thought was a touch of irritation.

Weng Yoon continued standing miserably in the middle of the air well, wiping away tears and shielding his eyes. He finally turned to his Malay driver. 'Ali, you tell them,' my brother-in-law whispered, before adding even more softly, 'tell them what you've heard.'

All eyes then trained on Ali, whose shoulders were hunched and whose bowed head hung uncomfortably between them. Clearing his throat, Ali began in Cantonese: 'Uncles, Aunty, bad news, very bad . . . from Sungei Lui.'

There were murmurs all around, and the name Sungei Lui was repeated. Some of us had heard of the place, others had not; in any case no one knew where it was. My husband asked, 'Where is Sungei Lui?'

Weng Yoon replied glumly, 'Negeri Sembilan. It's a village northeast of Seremban.'

'A village, you say?' I asked. 'But what does that have to do with Weng Koon? He lives in Seremban.'

'His wife's family . . . ,' Weng Yoon began and just as quickly stopped, as if he could not move his jaw.

The words churned up a mix of fear and dread in my stomach. I knew that Weng Koon's late wife had been Chinese educated. Under the Japanese, this meant trouble: when they first arrived, anyone who had been Chinese educated was a possible target.

'Her family . . . ,' Weng Yoon resumed at a glacial pace, 'came from . . . from Sungei Lui.'

I felt sick; I asked Chang Ying for a chair so that I could sit down. My brother-in-law, meanwhile, took a deep breath of resolve. As if he had made up his mind to get the telling over with, he spoke with the speed of a swollen river.

'Second Brother's in-laws have been living with him in Seremban since his wife passed away. Someone had to be in the house with the children while he was at work. But the in-laws must have been homesick. He took them back to the village for a visit. They all went, the children too. I don't know how long they stayed, just a few days probably.

You know that Sungei Lui is mixed, right? It's not just Chinese living there, there are Malays too. Ali's cousin, for example.' At this, Weng Yoon turned once more to Ali and said, 'Please, tell them, Ali.'

The driver's head was still bowed. 'My cousin,' Ali resumed in stuttering Cantonese, 'in Sungei Lui is distant cousin. From Indonesia. He is farmer.

'It happened five days ago . . .'

Ali paused, gave a slight sigh, and then said, 'Japanese soldiers come to village, tell everyone to line up outside house. Chinese men and children one side, Chinese women another side, Malays other side, separate from Chinese.'

A collective gasp passed around the room. Ali raised his head, but instead of looking at us, he stared up at the kitchen wall, a firmament that had originally been cream but was now blackened by years of flames from the wok fires which the servants fanned high into the air. His voice turned into a squeak.

'They take Chinese men and children into jungle behind village, Chinese women into one house. Everyone hear gunshots and sound like *parang* from jungle, like someone chopping *lalang* . . .'

My hands rose inadvertently to cover my mouth, but no noise came out. Not a sound could be heard. In the kitchen no one stirred; we were too riveted to even wheeze.

'A lot of noise, children scream, men scream. My cousin, other Malay villagers, no can do anything. They know Chinese men and children die, but people no can do anything. Many soldiers there. They come, four trucks, all got guns and bayonets. My cousin no want to watch, no want to hear, but must watch, cannot cover ears, cannot go back inside house. Japanese soldier poke him with bayonet. "You also want *kepala potong*-kah?" he say. "You move, your head next." Malay men and women and children stand outside in sun many hours. No water, no food, but cannot go home. Listen to scream, listen to cry, hear gunshots, hear men dig with *changkol*, chopping noise, more scream, children cry, "No! No kill me!"

'Then, late afternoon that time, jungle very quiet, no sound except soldiers. Soldiers come back from jungle, their uniforms all got blood. Blood everywhere: on shirts, trousers, bayonets, guns. Red water in rice fields, all red. Commander give order, and other soldiers go into house with women, there also, many gunshots and screams.

'And then . . . and then . . .' Ali's eyes became moist, his voice ever more distant. 'Soldiers, they . . .'

Next he was crying openly and could no longer speak. He sniffed back tears, swallowing many times. When he tried to speak, the words stuck on his tongue, and when he finally managed to heave them out he sounded like a braying donkey. It took a long time for us to understand that the soldiers had thrown oil around the house into which they had herded the Chinese women and girls.

Ali would not look at us. He continued staring directly ahead, haunted by the flames and the terror.

'Big fire . . . ,' he whispered, 'women scream, horrible noise. Big fire, burn many days . . .'

As Ali stood sobbing, an almighty commotion broke out. There were murmurs and cries; everyone shouted and spoke at the same time. 'It can't be true!' I blurted out, my voice hoarse from shock. Our old servant Ah Hong, who had known Weng Koon since birth, buried her head in her hands and burst into tears, she and Li-Fei both. Chang Ying joined in sympathy. The men gulped and blabbered. Father asked a question. Weng Yu also spoke, though so incoherently that no one had any idea what he was trying to say.

The mayhem died down after several minutes. Then, as if in a dream, we heard Ali's hushed voice. 'Only Malays now in Sungei Lui. All Chinese die that day.'

This valedictory statement shook us out of a collective trance. When we finally spoke after a good minute's silence, our voices were disbelieving.

'How do you know that Weng Koon and his family were there?' Father asked with uncharacteristic brusqueness. 'Did your cousin see them? Does he know the family?'

Ali looked up for the first time. His eyes, which had been red and mournful in the telling of his story, grew weary at our unspoken accusations.

'My cousin know family,' he answered, with an indignation that had not been there before. 'Of course he know family! They come for visit. He see them early in morning arrive. Uncle Weng Koon, he tell Japanese commander, "We no live here," but commander no care, everyone to the jungle!'

Ali stood stroking the moustache that he had been nurturing for some weeks, a broad tuft hanging over his fat lips. He stroked it ferociously, challenging us with his eyes as if to say, 'Don't blame me, I'm only the messenger; it's the Japanese you should be angry at.'

At the time I was not angry with Ali, at least, not that I was aware of. However, the many years during which the Japanese targeted our Chinese men must have sown seeds which became an undergrowth of resentment. This perfidious web ensnared our innermost feelings, until we could not separate what Malaya had been before the war from what Malaya became during it, so that we ended up behaving as if things had always been the way they were, when the reality was quite different.

We passed a bleak evening during which my husband veered between disbelief and guilt. Weng Yu wondered whether his sing-song group could have somehow been a reason why the Japanese commander had not spared Weng Koon. He considered stopping the Thursday meetings altogether.

'But, Husband, according to Ali, the Japs didn't go after Weng Koon, they went after the Chinese in his in-laws' village. This cannot have anything to do with you. Anyway, you have access to a phone at work. Why don't you use it to call Weng Koon's school tomorrow?'

The suggestion flustered Weng Yu, who was touchingly honest about certain matters. 'I can't just call! I need a work reason!'

'Listen, go to Hashimoto and make up some excuse for why you have to call your brother's school.'

'What kind of excuse?'

'I don't know!'

We both turned to Father, who merely shrugged. 'Let's sleep on it, my children. We'll think of something by tomorrow.'

My husband lay on his back that night, unable to sleep, full of remorse for having lost contact with Weng Koon. Weng Koon's argument had not been with his eldest brother but with Mother-in-Law. It would have been easy enough for my husband to contact his second brother, but Weng Yu had never bothered. 'I've been a bloody fool,' he said, staring at the ceiling. 'I should have done it.' His voice broke. 'Why the hell didn't I just write to him? I'm such a fool . . .'

Weng Yu sobbed the way a gentleman would, with tears gushing up from a profound place yet so quietly that no one outside our bedroom would have known he was crying. A lump came into my throat for this man who was somehow an island, separate from others, even his own family. My anger did not vanish, but it thawed a little, like an iceberg whose core remains intact while small floes break away.

I remembered the conversation I'd had with my brother-in-law Liew Chin Tong in the jungles of Lahat, when he had reminded me of Mother-in-Law's sixty-third birthday party the previous year, the event to which Hashimoto had been invited as photographer. Weng Koon had come once again with his son and two daughters. It was the last time I had seen them. And now, according to Ali's cousin, all four were dead – shot and buried in the jungle somewhere. Perhaps they were not even buried; perhaps their corpses had simply been left to rot in the sun, to be overrun by flies and maggots.

We in Ipoh had seen for ourselves the spiked heads which the Japs left to hang at the gates of the Central Market. There were other warnings, insidious rumours I preferred to ignore. Mrs Lim and the members of the sing-song group often talked about the individuals we should be wary of, people like Deputy Inspector Ja'afar, who carried out their duties more fervently than was warranted.

There were also stories about the Japanese secret police, the Kempeitai, and their unspeakable deeds. I had no desire to hear these, but Mrs Lim persisted. 'How else, Mei Foong,' she would ask rhetorically, 'do you explain the screams that are heard at all hours of day and night from that building on Chung Thye Phin Road?' 'I don't know,' I would reply.

In truth, I did not wish to know. I reasoned that if we went out as little as possible and kept our ears and eyes closed when we did, we would avoid trouble. My husband could carry on as Senior Engineer in the reconstructed Public Works Department, and our eldest son would attend Nippon-go school. We would demonstrate our cooperation. The Japs never needed to know how we really felt about them. We simply had to keep our heads low until this nightmare came to an end. I had no idea when this would happen, but for as long as my husband kept his job and our eldest son attended Nippon-go, we would receive the rations of rice and sugar we so badly needed.

If anyone had called me a collaborator to my face, I would have recoiled. As far as I was concerned, we were only giving the Japs our unwilling cooperation. The story of Sungei Lui came as a warning that my survival strategy was not without risk. It seemed imperative that we learn the truth about what had happened to Weng Koon.

The next morning, we decided to come clean with Hashimoto, who had, after all, met Weng Koon at Mother-in-Law's birthday. 'We have to trust that he still has a humane side,' I said.

The day felt interminably long. When Weng Yu returned, all he could say was that Hashimoto had agreed to patch a telephone call through to the missionary school where Weng Koon taught Geography. The school confirmed Weng Koon's absence. Where he was, nobody knew, certainly not Hashimoto, who refused to divulge anything else.

We never found out what really happened to Wong Weng Koon or his children. They, like many others, simply went missing. There were no bodies, no last rites, proper burials, or cremations, let alone apologies.

14

In the course of Japanese Imperial year 2602, or 1942 in western parlance, the *Perak Shimbun* newspaper announced that we could exchange our used Malayan currency for fresh Japanese notes. The *Perak Shimbun* was a one-page sheet of unalloyed propaganda; to call it a newspaper was generous, but we were nonetheless grateful to have it. The *Shimbun* allowed us to assess how our new rulers were faring in the wider world once we no longer possessed our cherished Philco: after returning to Ipoh, we were obliged to hand over all wireless sets to the Nippon Army. This left us with no idea as to how the war was progressing. Of course, the news blackout was a Japanese tactic to keep us in the dark. Fortunately, we'd had plenty of practice decrypting British war propaganda, and we were equally adept at reading between the Nippon lines.

The *Shimbun* announcement about currency exchange came with fanfare. The exchange was to take place on a one-to-one ratio: one Japanese dollar for every Malayan dollar brought in. We could not have guessed how useless those Japanese dollars would soon be, how their value would erode from week to week (and, eventually, from day to day). If I'd had even a little foresight, I would have retained some of our Malayan dollars under lock and key in Mother-in-Law's fireproof safe. The warning signs were all there – galloping prices, the establishment of a black market, the rise of bandits and thugs to positions of power – but I was too obtuse to extrapolate the consequences. In the few months after our return from the jungle, rice quadrupled from six cents to twenty-four cents per catty, pork doubled in price, and the bar of soap which previously cost twelve cents cost thirty cents. Electrical and engineering goods suffered even more. I could not understand how the price of a simple piece of wire could have increased ten times in a few short weeks. How was a household of thirteen people, with another infant on the way, meant to survive on Weng Yu's modest salary?

Seeing the runaway rise in prices, I headed out to Old Town as soon as I could, even though my baby was overdue. The *Shimbun* had warned us that after a certain date, only Japanese dollars would be valid. Thus, on a morning when I felt reasonably well, it seemed sensible to venture into town. I did not relish the outing, but it was imperative that we procured the new notes before the banks ran out.

Samad walked out to Abdul Jalil Road, where he found a rickshaw puller, a Chinese man with a sturdy physique. Our gardener escorted the puller to our house. When the sly puller saw how heavily pregnant I was, he raised his fare by another twenty cents. What he did would have been unthinkable before the war, but in the new Dai Toa Co-Prosperity Sphere, our old norms of behaviour had been destroyed within a few short months. I shrugged in response to Samad's questioning glance. What choice did we have?

The gardener helped me into the rickshaw and then climbed in himself. The puller threw a buttery grin which made me dislike him even more. Hoisting his beam, he ran the first few paces to gain the requisite momentum, in the process kicking up puffs of dust from the laterite road. My memories are of his back, leathered and sinewy, the skin exceedingly chocolate, with large bones protruding and muscles rippling in gentle waves: in short, the back of an ox. After a few steps, the puller began to walk, and we ambled along at a steady pace.

At the corner of Abdul Jalil Road, just minutes from our house, the Main Convent missionary school had been turned into a

Japanese-language teachers' training college. The Hinomaru, the by-then ubiquitous white flag with the red sun, hung at full mast inside its grounds. Without even the hint of a breeze, the flag dropped limply in folds. It promised to be a scorching day, hot already at eleven o'clock, though of course this was really nine o'clock in our customary time. As we set off I could feel the rays of the sun sharply on my black head. I hoped we could return without undue delay. If it was this hot at nine, it would be unbearable in the middle of the day.

'Where will you go for what we need?' I asked Samad, who had been tasked with finding a replacement for the front tyre of my husband's bicycle. With daily use the treads on both tyres had become worn, but we could only afford to replace one of them. We decided to change the front tyre, given that it was the more damaged. Samad was also to search for a bolt for the bicycle pump. This small part, which in previous times had been found in abundance in Ipoh's hardware stores, was increasingly hard to come by. Nuts and bolts and all manner of hardware items were devoured by members of the Japanese military, who were willing to pay outrageous prices. In less than five months, the supply of nuts and bolts had more or less disappeared while their prices quintupled.

'I know a man, Aunty,' Samad confided in a surreptitious whisper.

I half-turned in my seat to look at him. In the bright sunlight, Samad gave me a crooked smile which displayed his dazzling teeth. This Samad, the one sitting beside me then with his curly hair combed neatly from the roots, was the loyal man I had known for years. Sungei Lui flashed through my mind, but at that moment I found I could not be angry. I trusted him instinctively. I smiled in response, warmth suffusing my heart.

'I'm glad, Samad. But do you know him well? These days . . .'

I left my sentence unfinished while Samad continued smiling. 'I have a plan, Aunty. But may take longer time. You wait for me at bank, Aunty? Okay-moh?'

We were within earshot of the rickshaw puller, and both Samad and I spoke softly and in code. We had not agreed to do this beforehand; we simply sensed that it was the best course of action. This was what the new country, called Malai but pronounced 'Ma-ra-ee' because the Japanese were unable to pronounce the *l* properly, was like. With Japan's footprints everywhere, we could trust no one, not even a rickshaw puller who happened to pass our house by chance.

We trotted at a steady pace into Old Town, heading for what had once been the Hong Kong and Shanghai Bank at the corner of Belfield Street and Hale Street. It was the tallest building in the whole of Ipoh and easily the most beautiful, with its tower, columns and colonnades, its square arches, bays, and elegant panel windows. The building remained upright and as grand as before, but the bank inside had been renamed the Yokohama Specie Bank.

Stopping next to the building, the rickshaw puller made a great show of puffing and panting in the hope of extracting a few more cents out of us. He shot me a dirty look when I gave him his fare with no extra.

'You no understand, Aunty,' he said gruffly.

'We have to live too,' I replied, but the man had already turned and was making his way down the road at an easy pace.

Samad helped me climb the steps leading up to the five-foot way. We entered a hall the size of a football pitch, with high ceilings from which enormous fans were spinning. There was an ocean of people, so dense that at first we did not see that the crowd was simply the tail end of queues which ended at six counters.

Queuing was the one habit introduced by the Japs of which my husband wholly approved. He had grown accustomed to waiting in line during his six years in London. On returning to Malaya, it surprised him that our British rulers had chosen not to enforce strict queuing here. He would grumble about the jostling he had to endure just to watch a movie. At the most popular films, it was more than jostling: there were stampedes when the box offices opened.

Such demeaning scenes were a thing of the past under the Nippon government. Queuing became the norm, and with it came pitfalls for the unwary. At the Yokohama Specie Bank I had not expected so many people at that early hour. I had no idea how long my transaction would take.

'You want me wait, Aunty?' Samad asked.

I shook my head; far better for him to run the important errands with which we had entrusted him.

'I fast as can, come back, Aunty.'

With that, Samad dashed off and I found myself at the back, huddled in the midst of a crowd that didn't so much snake as ripple occasionally, like a simmering cauldron. Somehow space would be found to accommodate a newcomer like me. I entered at some ill-defined point, a sort of bubble that was absorbed by the pot before it fanned out into distinct lines.

As I stood I felt a kick in my belly. I was still in the amorphous nether region of the crowd, unable to move forward, equally unable to leave without an escort. I stroked my belly with both arms, in the hope that a light massage would bring some relief. On finding that the pressure of my fingers helped, I searched my handbag for Tiger Balm ointment, that miracle cure for aches, pains, itchiness, and everything in between. The ointment would have alleviated my discomfort, but alas there was no Tiger Balm to be found.

Finally, I joined one of the queues and we began to move. When we were a third of the way into the hall, the woman in front of me started grumbling rather loudly. She spoke into the air, to no one in particular, in a shrill voice which drew as much attention as her immaculate cheongsam.

'So long to wait! Much better when the *ang moh* were here. At least they got things moving.'

Her mutterings, in rather coarse Hokkien, were distracting. She had the narrow, cunning eyes of a fox and a bewitching smile that seemed to invite me to criticise our new masters. I let the moment pass, smiling in return but keeping my tongue welded to the floor of my mouth, all the time thinking of our four young children and the child yet unborn. I even screwed up my lips to make sure that nothing would come out.

When the woman saw that I would not be baited, she scoured the queue for another victim. Someone to the right of us struck up a conversation with the fox. For the next twenty minutes, their gossip washed over me, before another kick in my belly made me catch my breath.

My baby, being already fully grown, was exceedingly heavy; often the child did no more than stretch out an arm or a leg, but sometimes it seemed to rock inside my liquid cocoon. It had been especially active while I was standing in the queue, irritated perhaps by the lack of air and my own discomfort. By the time I neared the counter, I was ready to faint. The ceiling fans swirled eddies around the room, but there were too many bodies, too much heat. I needed to sit down. The vast hall was not equipped with pregnant women in mind; there was nowhere, nothing – no chair or bench, not even a stool.

The earth began to spin. My legs buckled. As I fell, the words 'I cannot believe this is happening' crossed my mind. The thought came to me, but not the physical will; I was unable to bring my legs under control.

In the melee, the crowd somehow knew to make way. A wave spread out from me. Everything turned foggy: the faces, people's clothing, the grey concrete floor beneath, and above, the white ceilings hung with fans whose blades were a whizzing blur. A man jostled his way through the crowd. I could not see him, but I could feel the wave around me spreading and contracting, spreading and contracting. The man was allowed to pass; as he approached, I was sure I had seen those arms before. Even from my vantage point on the floor with my body sprawled out, my whale of a belly staring up at the world, I knew.

I opened my eyes to find Chew Hock San bending close to my face, peppering me with cigarette breath. The blood had begun flowing back into my brain, and I squirmed under his intense scrutiny. I had assumed we would never meet again. He had told me about his intention to move to another town; what was he doing in Ipoh?

'Mei Foong,' he said quietly, 'are you all right?'

Until that moment he had never called me by my name. It rolled off his tongue with ease, as if he had been practising, and with a tenderness which made me blush. Though still groggy, I remember being thrilled by the sound of my name.

I had never been in such physical proximity with another man apart from my husband and father. The blood coursed through my head. Hock San remained in that crouched position, tantalisingly close, but without touching me, so that I was awake yet at the same time felt as if I were in a dream. He seemed desperate to cradle my head, but did not dare. I thought of my husband, and even more that I had to get away.

'I'm okay,' I said, though not with any conviction. After blinking once, I pressed both hands against the floor and tried to sit up. My husband would have been proud of such an effort; he himself was not able to be stoical, but it was a British quality he much admired.

'Slowly . . .'

Being lightheaded still, I was clumsy; I brushed close to Hock San and felt the heat of his skin.

'You don't need to get up immediately, you know.'

I had forgotten what his voice was like – low, but a pitch higher than my husband's.

'Can I help you . . . when you get up?' he asked, his face red.

'I can get up myself,' I replied, more roughly than I'd intended, overcome by a rush of irritation. How I was going to manage to raise my body, I had no idea. I sat still for a minute.

'If you could give me your hand,' I finally mumbled, looking not at him but at his stubby fingers. His nails were not trimmed and rounded like my husband's, but long and unkempt. Beneath the white sliver on his third finger was a crust of dirt.

Hock San offered me his right hand while using his left to support my back. His large hands felt strong; even then, despite his bearing much of my weight, sweat leaked out of the pores on my face. It was plain to us both that I would not last much longer in that queue.

As soon as we were upright, Hock San yelled loudly, 'People! This woman can't stand any more.' He waved his arm about. 'Please, have heart, let her go first! She is carrying a child.'

Everyone stared; at the same time the crowd began to open up, miraculously, like the Red Sea in one of the missionary stories we had heard at school. Chew Hock San, with his left arm still supporting the crook of my back, led me forward. Weng Yu, I knew, would never have shouted in such a brash fashion. My husband was unlikely to have pushed me forward in the crowd; he would have waited his turn in the queue. Chew Hock San's large hand remained on the arch of my back, and I made no protest. I could think only of getting to the front, exchanging the currency I had brought with me and then going home. I was aware of being dizzy and my own loud panting.

When we reached the front of the queue, Hock San finally removed his left hand. He continued to stand close by, and though our bodies did not touch he was so close that his skin seared mine. I could hear his breathing. Every nerve in me tingled.

Behind the counter sat a male teller who had served me for years. The clerk gave me the merest wisp of a smile, so fleeting that I was not even sure whether it had been a smile. When he asked me what I needed, I handed over my wads of Malayan notes.

'Six hundred dollars,' I said. Five hundred of those dollars had been my mother-in-law's savings; even as I think about it today, I feel pained.

Mother-in-Law would have been so upset had she seen what crumbs her hard-earned cash eventually bought us.

From a drawer on his desk, the clerk brought out wads of notes, hot off the press and garish purple. The ink had barely dried on those hurriedly printed notes. Many were adorned with touching scenes of Malayan life: a Malay kampong surrounded by coconut palms, a couple of water buffalo and their keeper, and plenty of floral motifs, such as banana leaves. 'We adore your country' was the purported message from our Japanese masters. Bank notes with banana leaves were especially ubiquitous, which is why the useless pieces of Nippon currency came to be called 'banana notes'.

There were, however, no banana coins: for every Malayan five-cent coin, I was given the equivalent five-cent note in a disconcerting purple. When I left the bank, my Italian leather handbag, purchased at a time when such goods were available and reasonably priced, was much lighter than when I arrived.

Hock San accompanied me out and continued walking beside me, his big hands hanging stiffly by his sides.

'Samad asked me to wait for him here, but I should go home,' I said. 'I need to lie down.'

'Where is Samad?'

'Getting a tyre for our bicycle and a bolt for the pump.'

Hock San's eyes widened. 'Where is he going to get those without paying an arm and a leg?'

'I don't know; he said he had a plan.'

'And you believed him?'

'I've known Samad for ten years. He's family – of course I believed him.'

Hock San turned away with a look of sheepishness before asking, 'How is Weng Yu?'

'He's well, thank you. You know he has a job, don't you? Senior Engineer in the Public Works Department. We can't complain. And you – how are you all, and your wife and children?'

'Fine.' Hock San gulped uncomfortably, and his eyes moved away.

There was a pause before I asked, 'I thought you were going to move to Telok Anson, what happened?'

'They changed their minds. We're staying here for the foreseeable future.' To prevent a silence he mumbled, 'Children grow up so quickly! My girl, she's already telling me what to do. Imagine!'

He chuckled with pride at this image of his daughter and then continued chattering, though I have no idea what about. I remember only my beating heart while the rest of me felt like lead, especially my tongue. The tension made our journey home awkward, but neither he nor I knew what to do with it. Sitting in a rickshaw he had hailed, serenaded by the sound of padded feet falling on hard ground, I was acutely conscious that the man beside me would thereafter be living in the same town.

15

Ah Hong was sweeping the floor in our bedroom when we heard the clacking of boots. A thud followed, which told me that our servant had dropped the fat shaft of her palm broom. As I walked along the vestibule, I could hear the padding of Ah Hong's feet on parquet. From beside the louvre windows, she turned to me with startled eyes. Before she could say a word, the banging began: a ferocious, inhuman sound made not by knuckles or fists, but by a pole struck so hard against our front door that I feared my overdue baby would somersault inside his liquid cocoon.

My husband was at home that day. It must therefore have been a public holiday, though I cannot recall which one. There were many unfamiliar holidays in that period: Empire Day, Army Day, Navy Day, the Emperor's Birthday, not to mention the numerous Japanese festivals, all treated as occasions for educating us about Japan's greatness.

What I know is that it was a holiday, my baby was very late, and the Japs were knocking.

Father and I stood near the entrance and Samad a little behind as my husband opened the front door. We proceeded with our customary *rei* and did not see Hashimoto, Weng Yu's boss, outside until we had raised our heads. Once my husband realised that his boss was outside, he swallowed hurriedly and the lump at the front of his throat wobbled.

Another officer stood beside Hashimoto, a man with a white band around his left arm. My heart seized up at the sight of the armband: I had heard about these men. I blinked once to make sure I was not seeing things. When I opened my eyes again, the armband was still there, so innocuous looking, but there was no mistaking the ideograms emblazoned in bloody red.

The man pushed his way past, brushing against my extended belly without so much as a 'please' or an 'excuse me'. My head remained slightly bent, as it was meant to be. Under the colonials we had been unquestioningly subservient; under the Japs we only pretended, but our pretence was an important means of self-preservation. As the officer marched past, I stole another glance and saw that he stood no more than five feet five inches tall. From the side he appeared well-fed, not fat, but clearly not bothered by shortages either. He wore a neat khaki uniform with a black collar and a belt around the waist. As he swung his body around, he showed off the military cap on his head, replete with its black visor, its bright red band and the golden five-pointed star in the middle. There could no longer be any doubt that our visitor came from the dreaded Kempeitai, or secret police.

'Where he gone?' the Kempeitai man bellowed in that guttural manner in which they spoke. His demeanour was that of an enraged bull: face swollen, expression thunderous, as if about to charge. No one replied – we had no idea whom he meant. Our bewilderment only increased the man's fury. He started pounding the planks of our parquet floor with the bayonet in his right hand, shouting, 'Where he go? You say where, now!'

By then we had learnt that Japanese officers were best placated with low bows, especially when we had no answer. My husband thus performed the *saikeirei* more or less as a reflex, prostrating himself with the words: 'I'm very sorry, sir, I don't know who you are referring to.'

'Brother-in-law!'

Weng Yu and I were both so stunned that we looked up without thinking, at the same time surreptitiously casting each other a sideway glance.

'But, he is next door, sir!'

'Not brother, brother-in-law!' the Kempeitai man huffed. 'Brother-in-law, Liew Chin Tong!'

My poor husband's mouth remained open. 'Liew Chin Tong? But we haven't seen him, sir! He lives on the other—'

'We know where he live. He not there! Gone where?'

With another deep bow, my husband replied, 'I'm sorry, sir, we haven't seen much of Liew Chin Tong since his wife, my second sister, passed away.' Weng Yu followed this apology with a third ultra-deep bow.

My husband's obeisance did little to calm the Kempeitai man. The officer gave us a look of such contempt that I thought he was going to spit. Instead, Mr Kempeitai unleashed a stream of what sounded like invective at the four soldiers who had entered our house and were standing inside, stern and unsmiling, in their dirty shoes. The soldiers strode off, one towards our marital bedroom, the others down the vestibule off which the children's bedrooms were located.

At that point, Hashimoto, who had watched the proceedings in silence, said something to the Kempeitai man which made him glare. The soldiers stopped in their tracks and looked keenly at the Kempeitai man until, in another instant, the latter issued a bark, this one less harsh than the first, at which point the soldiers continued with their search.

The next minute, drawers were flung open. There followed the sound of rattling, which I assumed was my jewellery being dumped on to our bed, and the loud animal frustration of someone who had not found what he was looking for. Papers rustled, and then a door, belonging probably to Weng Yu's Italian almerah, creaked. When we heard hangers being shunted about and fabric ripped apart, I felt ill. We could not afford new clothes; as it was, we could barely afford the thread and raw cloth with which I now patched our old garments. The baby in my belly responded to my nerves by kicking against my abdomen, until the same faintness that had overcome me at the Yokohama Specie Bank began to take hold. My temples roared. The pain spread. There was an overwhelming noise, though whether the noise came from inside my head or from somewhere else altogether, I could not have said.

A soldier ran in, muttering under his breath. Hashimoto nodded. When he turned to us, he must have seen how my eyes were rolling. Metal clanged against a wall. I did not imagine this: someone was hitting a wall at the back of our house hard, with what sounded like a metal bat. I remember thinking that if I had a weapon, I would have knocked my own head too, to relieve the pain. I began swaying from side to side. I placed both hands on top of my head and began massaging my crown. I had the feeling that I would not be able to stand for much longer.

Hashimoto looked at me with concern and said, 'Are you all right?'

'No, sir,' I replied in a very weak voice. 'I must lie down.'

Hashimoto and the Kempeitai man exchanged staccato-like sentences.

'But you have safe?' Hashimoto finally asked, turning to my husband.

'It belonged to my mother,' Weng Yu replied, quickly adding 'sir' with a bow. 'Only my wife knows the code.'

'Follow her and open safe,' Hashimoto said drily. 'After, she can lie down.'

My whole body felt like lead; I could not imagine getting as far as what had once been my mother-in-law's bedroom, which was located all the way down the vestibule, past our bedroom, past the inner hall, the children's bedrooms, and the bathroom, and beyond the air well.

Yet, when the Kempeitai man gave a vociferous cry of 'Hurry up!' my legs were powered by adrenaline. Out of naked fear, they shuffled of their own accord. The walk seemed endless, though it was no more than seven yards. After just a few paces, I began gasping and thrashing like a fish out of water. Somehow, with Weng Yu holding on to my left arm and Samad my right, we reached the rear bedroom. As soon as we were inside, I collapsed on to the single bed.

The young soldier glared at me. 'Open, open!' he cried, wagging an index finger at the metal safe in the furthest corner.

I gestured wearily at the safe and then at the side of the bed, to indicate that someone would have to lift up the metal box. The soldier turned and issued a flurry of commands. While I was still staring at his rigid back, a cramp reeled me sideways. The pain dug down into my bones, and I felt as if I had been stabbed. A whooping scream leapt out of my mouth. Before I knew what was happening, liquid began trickling down my leg and then the first contraction came, a wave of pain which passed from the top of my abdomen, all around my belly and through to my lower back. The pain was excruciating even though I was lying down. In no time at all my dress was drenched, and the waters no longer a trickle but a gushing spring.

At first there was much shouting in that tiny room; the soldiers seemed to have no idea what to do. Eventually an awed silence descended. The men dropped the metal safe and simply looked at me in wonder, until Hashimoto entered and ordered everyone out. I heard my husband begging Hashimoto to help transport me to the District Hospital. He refused, but shortly afterwards the Japs left us alone. Samad cycled to the District Hospital to summon an ambulance, which arrived with two men and a midwife. In this way my mother-in-law's fireproof safe was protected and our most precious jewellery shielded from the prying eyes of the Japanese.

◆ ◆ ◆

Our fourth son, James, to whom we also gave the Chinese name Wai Foh, slipped into this world several weeks late under the watchful eyes of two women, one of whom was our neighbour Lim Choy Yoke. So preoccupied was I with the gasping and the pushing and the feverish work which only a woman can do that I scarcely registered the presence of the hospital matron, a plump Chinese lady with many years' experience delivering babies all over Perak state. I knew she was there, but I paid her little attention until James was already born and Matron stood smiling while she snipped the umbilical cord. She had a wide face, a complexion that never saw the sun, and a hefty, reassuring presence. 'You did very well,' she said as she put my afterbirth, still a fresh red, on to a white tray, from where its deep-magenta clots of blood assaulted my senses. Later, after Matron had wiped James down and handed him to me, I remembered how the previous matron had been a white lady, also the matron before that, indeed, until the arrival of the Japanese, an Asian woman had never been appointed Matron at Ipoh's District Hospital.

Weng Yu, of course, had not been present at the birth – it was unheard of in those days for men to attend such intimate events unless their medical expertise was required. In any case, Weng Yu, who fainted at the sight of his own blood, would never have survived the ordeal.

When my husband eventually entered the hospital ward, he came towards my bed. He did not touch me but searched my face while mumbling, 'Hello.' Satisfied that I was well, he smiled, went to the crib at the bottom of my bed where James was lying, and picked up our son. My husband held the newborn near his chest, but away from his face, with the same detachment he had shown towards all our children. In a few minutes the Chinese matron came to take James away, and my husband was able to return to his own undisturbed life.

By then I had reconciled myself to mine. I had chosen Wong Weng Yu; I was a wife and a mother. I had to live with the inescapable fact that five children needed me. It was my duty to learn to be, if not happy, then at least content. Perhaps our Japanese tormentors had a point; perhaps life was just a matter of *seishin*, or spirit. I hoped that if my husband and I had enough music and plays and movies in our life, we might rekindle the joy we had once known. Artistic pursuit could be the spark, our children the cement. I prayed that James, along with the four other children we already had and any we might have in the future, would bind us further.

At the time, we had other worries too. We could not help but be concerned for our brother-in-law, Liew Chin Tong, and also for his sister, Miss Liew, both of whom had not been seen for a week. We could not think where they would have gone, but the fact that the Kempeitai were searching for them gave us a clue.

Every few months, the *Perak Shimbun* would announce a great victory against guerrillas somewhere in Perak's jungles. This gloating was inevitably followed, only days later, by reports of a setback, of members of the special or military police being killed outside Malim Nawar village, or a high-ranking official being shot dead in Kuala Lumpur – events which served as timely reminders that the Communists whom they so feared had not been eliminated. The Japanese were truly terrified of the Communists; throughout their occupation, they expended inordinate resources on hunting down and killing so-called Communist elements.

I was not a fan of Communist ideology, yet I cheered every time the *Shimbun* reported an act of reprisal against the Japs. We loathed our new rulers so much that we supported anyone who dared to fight them, even Communists.

Until the Liews' disappearance, I had paid little attention to the *Shimbun*'s victory pronouncements. Afterwards, however, I sifted the news carefully, studying every nuance, checking each name, wondering all the while where my brother-in-law and his sister were and whether they had really joined the Communists.

We knew little about these hill people, though there were plenty of rumours. According to our neighbour Mrs Lim, they numbered thousands and had even been bolstered by British and Australian troops.

From the singer Mrs Chan, we learnt that the Communists had built a first-class system of intelligence, which gave them up-to-date information about the movements of Nippon officials. My friend Yik Wei, who came to congratulate me on James's birth, said that the guerrillas were experts in the art of sudden attack and quick withdrawal, which was why they were able to lure the Japs deep into the jungle and then punish them in Malaya's towns with impunity.

On the face of it, Liew Chin Tong and his sister seemed unlikely resistance fighters. They were both English educated, whereas most of the Communists had attended Chinese vernacular schools. Before the Japanese invasion, the Liews had led comfortable lives working for the British establishment. Neither of their occupations – court interpreter or English teacher – made them suited to Malaya's forsaken jungle, with its infestations of leeches and mosquitoes and where the sun barely penetrated. But if we really had Communists in our family, there was no doubt that our lives would be more perilous.

Days after the visit from the Kempeitai, my brother-in-law Weng Yoon obtained a chit from the personal assistant to the governor of Perak. This was a piece of paper with a message in Katakana declaring that Dorcourt was not to be disturbed by anyone, not even by Japanese soldiers. The paper, which Rokiah stuck on to one of Dorcourt's massive windows, must have cost Weng Yoon dearly. He was too embarrassed to tell us about the chit himself; we learnt of its existence while I was perambulating our gardens in an effort to regain my strength after giving birth. 'Big Sister,' Weng Yoon said, avoiding my eyes, 'I could not afford more than one chit, I'm sorry.'

Weng Yoon turned and backed away before I had the chance to reassure him. A chit would have been useful, but we had more pressing concerns. To conserve our banana currency, dinner that night comprised a soup of chilli leaves, picked from a garden bush, and a curry of papaya and rambutan fruits, plucked also from the garden.

I thought of Mother-in-Law as I ate our meagre fare. I was thankful she had been spared this suffering, but at the same time, I missed her, especially then. In the Dai Toa Co-Prosperity Sphere, there was a shortage of everything, even rice. To counter what was obvious to us all – that the country was in rapid decline – the Japs exhorted us to become farmers. With so many mouths to feed, I was forced to take their suggestion seriously. I wondered what my entrepreneurial mother-in-law would have done.

I looked up at her as I passed the outer hall with Samad. She lurked above our doorway, smiling grimly in the only photograph ever taken of her on her own – a black-and-white picture in which her fierce cheeks seemed to admonish anyone who dared peer too closely. The photographer, of course, had been Hashimoto, a fact which struck me as a sour joke. I tried to dismiss the bitterness from my mind; the old lady herself had remained staunchly optimistic, and it seemed fitting that I should follow her example.

As Samad and I toured the garden, I tried to survey it through my mother-in-law's eyes. I imagined her walking beside me, inspecting the fruit trees and rose bushes she had asked for. The roses had been planted not for pleasure, but for sale, at a time when bouquets were all the rage in Ipoh. With people now hungry, demand had dried up. I ordered Samad to pull them up and hoped Mother-in-Law would not mind.

Together with Samad, I measured the garden perimeter and examined the soil. Mother-in-Law, I was sure, would have been meticulous in estimating how much we could grow in our garden. She would not have wasted an inch of space, nor would she have wasted anything her garden produced. Even when she could afford fertiliser she refused to buy it, preferring instead to be hoisted on to her sedan chair so that she could follow the Sikh men as they drove their bullock carts around town. While the bullocks dumped their brown gold, Mother-in-Law would point, and Li-Fei, who accompanied the troupe with spade and pail in hand, would stoop to haul the treasure off Ipoh's streets. The servant would not have put up with the putrid odours for anyone other than Mother-in-Law. The old lady herself was oblivious to smells and the looks of amazement on the faces of passers-by. 'Always have way to stretch the family wallet, Mei Foong,' she once told me, 'but must be patient.'

In place of the fruit trees, Samad and I planned beds of vegetables: yams, sweet potatoes, carrots, cucumbers. There were also onions, garlic, ginger, and chillies, of course. A patch on the side of the garden, near the secret gate to Dorcourt, we dedicated to herbs – the curry leaves and lemongrass, mint and coriander which made bland food palatable.

Realising that Samad and I could not succeed on our own, I enlisted the active cooperation of all our servants. Together we learnt about farming. We soon became experts on planting seasons; we knew how much manure to put on which plant, which vegetables needed more water than others, and which leaves had to be pruned early. Remembering Mother-in-Law's example with the cow-dung, I made sure that nothing went to waste – not a drop of urine, not even a lump of night soil. Every stem, every leaf, and every root from the garden was eaten, dried for storage, or replanted. We embraced recycling long before it became fashionable.

For meat and eggs, we eventually reared chickens. At night we were forced to lock the birds inside a coop that Samad built, lest they be eaten by stray cats or stolen by thieves. In this way we were able to supplement our staple diet of boiled yam with a few eggs each week and with chicken meat from time to time. The one thing we could not grow, however, and which we all missed terribly, was white rice.

In the weeks leading up to the Chinese New Year of 1943, the prices of many foodstuffs doubled. We had survived reasonably well until then, but I could not see how we would celebrate the New Year unless I sold one of Mother-in-Law's bracelets. When I opened her safe in search of an item to pawn, I could feel my heart pumping. The very act seemed a sacrilege. She had worked so hard . . . I kept harkening back to the many conversations we'd had, to all that she had taught me. I could see her in the house, arranging the copper and silver coins and the precious notes she had earned during her life into stacks and counting them. I locked her safe again that night; I could not fritter away what she had toiled for, not when my husband was employed, when we were not destitute and no one was ill.

As the prices of goods continued their inexorable rise, I sifted through the old lady's jewellery once again, finally accepting that I had no choice. If I did not sell something, the children would eat boiled sweet potato and a ginger omelette on New Year's Eve. I eventually chose a bracelet made of gold, the cheapest piece I thought I could pawn. The bracelet itself would not fetch much, but the value of gold had increased many times. Removing the bracelet, I locked the safe again and stood before our altar table, asking Mother-in-Law's forgiveness.

I then went to our bedroom where I sat in front of my dressing table. The large louvred windows let in cylinders of light, which highlighted the grey hairs on my head. The metallic slivers had appeared only since the Japs arrived. I removed the offending strands at night, under the arc of the electric lights, when I could not help but also notice how my face, which had a naturally thin shape, looked even more flute-like. I'd had vigorous arms as a girl, but you could now see the bones sticking out from under my sleeveless pyjama top. My appearance, I knew, was increasingly skeletal. This was hardly surprising: we never had quite enough food, and the children and Weng Yu had to take precedence.

From a locked drawer in the dressing table, I retrieved the personal notebook I had been keeping since the birth of our eldest son, Wai Sung. This book, a small, old-fashioned Chinese exercise book equipped with large blue squares, was exactly like the one I had used to practise Chinese writing in my childhood. Using a black pencil, I would repeat ideograms over and over in my brown exercise book until

I had perfected the strokes and their order, so that each ideogram fitted within a blue square.

When Wai Sung was born, the idea came to me of recording his personal details. My maid, Chang Ying, had brought me a new Chinese ledger, and I began writing out Wai Sung's name in Chinese. I then paused to think about what else I wanted to say. I could recall every contraction, every push which had brought him into this world, but I decided that my notebook should be dedicated to my children. It would not be for me to record what I felt; the book was to be about them. I proceeded therefore with the date, hour, and place of my firstborn's birth, also his length and weight.

No one knew that I was recording such details. My husband, I suspected, would have laughed if I'd told him. Father too might have thought me sentimental. There were moments when I considered revealing the existence of this notebook, but I was afraid of being mocked.

When Lai Hin and Wai Kit were born, I wrote about them in my notebook. The records of our eldest three children were solely in Chinese, but when Robert came along, my husband and I succumbed to the latest craze and gave the boy a Western name alongside a Chinese name, at which point I began writing Latin letters in my notebook for the first time.

James's details followed in similar fashion. I wrote out his Chinese name first, Wai Foh, and then his Western name, and then the year, month, and day of his birth, and finally the hour. James's emergence was as cauterised into my nerves as the births of all my other children; I could have described each minute with engineering precision, but I contented myself with writing down his length (twenty inches) and weight (six and a half pounds).

Opening a window, I surveyed the stars. We had been taught at school that the sky was eternal and unchanging, but I was beginning to wonder whether anything, even the sky, could be truly unchanging. I thought back to the year which had passed; already, it seemed that the town in which I had grown up had changed beyond all recognition. In place of solitude and sleepiness had come a sordid bustle generated by the type of commerce which, in any other era, would have shamed its residents. Without innocence, there can be no shame, and without shame, redemption is impossible. I searched for the constellation which our Malay neighbours called the Bintang Pari, the Ray Star, known also as the Southern Cross. Its axes were missing that night, perhaps shaded by invisible cloud. I stepped away from the window, knowing I would have to wait for the clouds to pass.

PART IV

16

'Are you all right, Husband? What happened?'

Weng Yu's face bore the greenish tinge of garden grass as he stumbled through our front door in the arms of his fourth brother, Weng Yoon. I ran forward, fearing that my husband would faint. Father followed with wide eyes full of bewilderment.

The solid beat of footsteps on the driveway told me that the rest of Weng Yu's neighbourhood watch group, known as the Jikeidan, had accompanied him home. They trooped in one by one: first Misters Lim and Chan, who lived on the next road; then the good Dr Pillay himself; and finally the gardeners, Ali and Samad. Without exception, the Jikeidan boys looked tense and more than a little shaken. Samad, who was carrying the *changkol* handles he and Weng Yu had used on patrol, refused to look at me. He hurried into the kitchen.

There was a loud thud as my husband's knees crumpled. Weng Yu fell to the floor, his face no longer green but a limestone white. When I touched his skin, it felt clammy and cold.

'Please, someone, what happened?' Father asked in a clear, firm voice.

Weng Yoon's eyes flitted between my father and me, unable to decide on whom to focus. Finally, he chose me. 'There was a fight, outside the Odeon Cinema. Horrible, blood everywhere. I know we can expect such things, but it was still a shock. A group of *samsengs*, thugs, you know the type . . .'

Father released a languorous sigh. 'What is this country coming to?'

I looked at my husband, who by then lay on the *barlay*'s parquet flooring with both eyes closed. Poor Weng Yu would have been terrified: an altercation was what he had most dreaded when he had been drafted into one of Green Town's Jikeidan groups. But he'd had no choice. Being a man between eighteen and forty-five, in good health and displaying 'suitable thinking', he had been fished out and dumped into a neighbourhood watch group.

'You should have seen it, Big Sister, we turned up just in time,' my brother-in-law continued, this time with a frisson in his voice. 'The *samsengs* had thrashed a young man with batons and sticks. He was lying on the ground. There was a gash on his head, his spectacles were broken, ground to pieces, and one of the scoundrels had his hand inside the young man's trousers. Big Brother rushed at the group with his *changkol* handle. One moment later and they would already have grabbed the man's wallet. But it was crazy, man!'

Weng Yoon paused for a second, staring at the prostrate man on the parquet floor. He nudged my husband on the rib. 'This guy didn't even wait to see whether we were following him.'

It was a description of my husband which I did not recognise. A lump came into my throat; I had an urge to stroke Weng Yu's ruffled hair as he continued lying on the floor with his eyes closed and his pallor wan.

'I tell you, Big Sister, it was amazing. He and I were walking slightly ahead of everyone else, so we were first to reach the Odeon. Big Brother just charged. Of course, you know me' – at this, Weng Yoon gestured towards his still-large belly with both thumbs – 'I can't run as fast. They would have known we were Jikeidan. But they could have beaten Big Brother up before any of us got there.'

My brother-in-law looked down at the still figure with what I thought was grudging admiration. A low murmur echoed around the outer hall. The other members in my husband's neighbourhood patrol group nodded vigorously. For a fleeting moment I saw a different future. I wanted to grab hold of it with both my hands.

'What happened after that?' I asked loudly. 'Did you arrest the ruffians, Husband?'

Weng Yu did not move, did not even open his eyes; he was breathing heavily.

'No, we gave chase, but they ran off, Big Sister,' my brother-in-law said, his voice shaky.

'We chase, Aunty, no catch men.' It was Ali who had spoken. Next to him, our gardener Samad, having returned from the kitchen, mumbled, 'They run too fast, impossible. Even running champion cannot catch.'

'This is going to be a problem for me. You know that we are supposed to arrest thieves and robbers, right?' Weng Yoon said, looking at both Father and me. 'I will have to explain to the Japs how we let these ruffians get away.' He emitted a hoarse laugh. 'Let's just hope I haven't lost my powers of persuasion.'

Though Weng Yoon tried to make light of the matter, there was an uncharacteristic furrow lining his forehead. He looked paler than usual; evidently, the chit he had purchased would not save him from the 'crime' of failing to apprehend a robber.

As with so many things initiated by the Japanese, the Jikeidan had a pompous ring. The neighbourhood watch system was known as the Voluntary Vigilance Corp for Self-Preservation and Self-Protection. It did not live up to its promise. The Jikeidan was instituted in Green Town in the course of 1943 (or 2603 under the occupiers' calendar), ostensibly to increase our good neighbourliness, though no one could tell us exactly how Jikeidan would achieve this. Indeed, at the start, we weren't given even the most rudimentary details, such as who, what, when, and where.

And then, after months of hearsay and gossip, the groups were commenced in a sudden rush, with more fanfare than organisation. Tools were not issued: each member was expected to bring his own. To Weng Yu's great surprise he found himself among friends, and good friends at that. He was even given a good shift night – a Monday evening – when most revellers stayed at home to recover from their hectic weekends. Alas, their watch area was rather large, going as far as Ashby Road to the north and Anderson Road to the west, which meant that they had to patrol not only our leafy neighbourhood, but also past two cinemas (the Odeon and Ruby), a hotel (the Mayfair), and the school (the Convent of the Holy Infant Jesus) that had been turned into a Japanese language institute.

'You can't have everything, Husband,' I told him when he grumbled. 'At least you're with a nice group of people.'

My husband, being an ordinary Jikeidan member, was required only to show up and walk, whereas my brother-in-law had other responsibilities. As a Jikeidan leader, Weng Yoon was given access to Green Town's family register, so that he would know the names of everyone living in the neighbourhood. Therefore, in addition to catching robbers and thieves, he was expected to flush out anyone who should not have been there, anyone who 'looked' undesirable, and Communists of course.

At the outset, when I heard that Wong Weng Yoon had been designated a Jikeidan leader, I was astonished. Weng Yoon was even more British-loving than my husband and determined to be a thorn in the sides of the Nippon regime, though the strange goings-on next door could have been more at Dora's instigation. There were always myriad visitors with darkened faces walking down Dorcourt's driveway – people who could only get about if their true identities were concealed; in short, the very 'undesirables' Weng Yoon's Jikeidan group was meant to be arresting! His Jikeidan stewardship thus tickled me; now though, I could see that holding an exalted position under the Nippon administration was no laughing matter.

I smiled in an attempt to put my brother-in-law's mind at rest. 'At least you don't have a Communist problem. I'm sure you'll be able to talk your way out of this one.'

The lawyer frowned.

'Yes, Weng Yoon, I'm sure the other members of the group can go with you, to tell them what happened,' Father said.

To this, Dr Pillay nodded vigorously. 'We'll be happy to come with you, Weng Yoon. I'll bet Hashimoto wouldn't have been able to catch those boys.'

Weng Yu, who had remained quiet through this conversation, was lying still on the floor. When I caressed his shoulders, I found them as hard as cement.

'Are you all right, Husband?'

He opened his eyes. 'They didn't hurt you, did they?' I asked, stroking his left cheek.

'No,' he said gruffly. He seemed suddenly embarrassed and tried to stand. I held one of his arms while Dr Pillay took the other, cautioning, 'Slowly, Weng Yu, you might be drowsy.'

'I'm okay,' my husband insisted, shrugging away my hand even though his normally rich voice was thread-like. 'Just a bit tired. Too much happened tonight.'

'But, Husband, you were very brave! It's wonderful that you stopped a man from being robbed. Not many men would have been so fearless. I'm proud of you!'

Weng Yu threw me a condescending look as if I were a stupid child. 'Silly woman,' he hissed, 'you just don't understand!'

There was stunned silence in the room. Something like remorse immediately came into Weng Yu's eyes, but he bit his lower lip and held his tongue. Though Father's moustache twitched and his jaw tightened, he did not look at me; none of them did, nor I at them. We stood staring at the parquet floor while my husband hobbled towards our bedroom.

◆ ◆ ◆

With the establishment of the Jikeidan, neighbours were soon spying on each other twenty-four hours a day. It became second nature to watch what everyone else did and to denounce so-called 'traitors'. In such a cesspool, it was best to keep one's innermost thoughts to oneself.

We were surprised to see Mrs Chan of the sing-song group waddling down our driveway one Saturday evening after dinner. She was not really a family friend and therefore came only on Thursdays, and never on her own under a darkening sky.

Old Ah Hong, who had shown Mrs Chan to a chair in the inner hall, was asking the lady whether she wanted a drink when my husband and I wandered in. Without warning Mrs Chan burst into tears.

I rushed to our neighbour's side, not quite knowing what to do. Touching her shoulder struck me as overly familiar, yet to not comfort her at all seemed unkind. In the end I knelt in front of Mrs Chan's chair. When she was able to look up, I touched her gently on her right arm and was relieved that the old teacher did not shrink away.

'Has something happened, Mrs Chan?' I asked, in as easy a tone as I could manage.

She nodded. 'Yes,' she said, in a voice hoarse from crying. 'My husband, he's been . . . arrested.'

'Arrested?' Weng Yu's baritone boomed from behind me. 'What on earth for?'

'Oh, it's so silly!' With those words, Mrs Chan lost control once more and began snivelling like a child. In between gulps, she continued to blubber, her shoulders heaving.

Ah Hong had the good sense to bring in a glass of water for our visitor. The tall vessel with colourful stripes down its sides calmed Mrs Chan, and she made a concerted effort to speak. She began haltingly, but once she had regained her poise, she proceeded at a breakneck pace.

'We went to the Odeon to watch that new movie about Admiral Yamamoto – you know, the one that has Pearl Harbour and Malaya in it. The place was packed. We bumped into friends there. I don't know whether you know the Chins. He's an accountant. Anyway, my husband was chatting with Mr Chin during the interval in the foyer, and my silly hubby complained about the high cost of living. I know he shouldn't have. It was very careless, but you know how it is, you chat and you forget yourself and well, things are very expensive. Can you blame him? I mean, I had to pay twelve dollars the other day for a light bulb!'

Mrs Chan nodded gravely when gasps went around the room. 'Yes, twelve whole dollars!' she repeated. 'Before the Nippon-zin came, a light bulb was forty cents. I'm not complaining – there's much to admire in Japanese culture, but things have become crazy. Naturally, my husband said so. Anyway, when we came out after the show ended, six policemen from the local station were waiting for us; as if they needed six people to arrest one man! They said he had been overheard complaining about the high cost of living and that complaining about the cost of living was a crime.'

'A crime? What nonsense will the shorties come up with next?' my husband said, in a voice full of disdain. His indiscretion horrified me. I watched Mrs Chan carefully. Her taut face seemed to relax. For the first time that night she even smiled, and eventually broke out into a guffaw. 'Shorties,' she mumbled. 'Yes, that's very good!'

Suddenly becoming serious, she turned to me. 'Mrs Wong, I need your help.'

'Of course,' I said, 'whatever I can do. What do you need?'

'Your neighbour is a deputy inspector in the police force, and I know you're friends of his.'

'Well, it was my mother-in-law who was really their friend,' I said, hoping to conceal my reluctance. 'I know his wife Husna much better than Enche Ja'afar. As for Weng Yu, well, he only sees Enche Ja'afar from time to time.'

'That's more than I can say. Please, please.' Mrs Chan's voice dropped to a sibilant whisper. 'Intercede on my behalf. Please, Mrs Wong. Ask your deputy inspector to help my husband. He's locked up in the Central Police Station.'

The teacher leaned forward and held both my hands. Her appeal was so earnest that I could not possibly have refused. My husband cast me a stony glance, which I ignored.

'Mrs Chan, I will try, but I can't give you any guarantees, okay? I don't know how Enche Ja'afar will react. He hasn't been very friendly since the start of the war.' I attempted a smile, even though the thought of asking Enche Ja'afar for a favour made my stomach churn.

We walked out along our driveway and on to Ja'afar's. It was very dark; in the Nippon era, a disconcerting gloom settled over Green Town after nightfall, since no household wished to attract undue attention. The car which the policeman had procured at the start of the war, narrow, with a long bonnet and an ugly posterior, was parked along his driveway. The vehicle cast a sinister shadow, which for some reason reminded me of an animal about to pounce. Shaking the idea off, another bizarre image took its place – that of a person hiding behind the car and suddenly leaping up. My heartbeat quickened as we passed the beast.

I was still holding my breath as we climbed the steps on to Enche Ja'afar's verandah. When I knocked, the deputy inspector himself opened his front door. He seemed more than a little surprised to see us. There was no smile on his face; only when he realised that his wife Husna was standing behind him did he force himself to relax. Her visceral pleasure permeated the five feet of space between us as she shouted, 'Mei Foong! Mr Wong! How nice to see you! Please, come in!'

'Good evening, Husna, Enche Ja'afar. I hope we're not calling on you too late.'

'No, not at all,' the policeman and his wife replied at the same time, after which Husna repeated, in a voice full of affection, 'Please, please, come in!' The warmth of her welcome affected us all, and even Enche Ja'afar felt obliged to bestow a smile, albeit of the cursory variety deployed by Ipoh's hawkers.

Removing our shoes, I entered first. My husband and Mrs Chan followed. Ja'afar's family and the Chans knew each other by sight, which made a long introduction unnecessary. A pause ensued when Husna insisted on leaving us to prepare refreshments. I can't remember what small talk we filled those minutes with. Mrs Chan must have invented a topic, as I recall no heavy silences.

Husna soon returned with an enormous tray on which sat a teapot, cups, saucers, and a plate of two-tiered *kueh*. I let slip then that Mrs Chan was a fan of Japanese culture. Enche Ja'afar looked at her with approval.

'Go on, Mrs Chan,' I said. 'Tell Deputy Inspector Ja'afar what happened to you this afternoon.'

I watched the policeman's demeanour carefully. He nodded when he heard that the couple had gone to watch *Hawai Mare oki kaisen* (The War at Sea from Hawaii to Malaya), tut-tutted at Mr Chan's complaint, and then, on learning of the latter's arrest, remained utterly impassive. Something he did, some small movement of the shoulder or perhaps the jawbone, gave me the distinct impression that he was accustomed to being told stories like Mrs Chan's. When she hesitated, he threw her a sly smile.

After she finished her story, Enche Ja'afar nodded. His black moustache was quivering when he said, 'One bottle of Hennessy and a brand-new Sheaffer pen.'

The words had emerged so softly that I barely heard them. I looked again at Enche Ja'afar. He seemed quite collected. There was nothing at all to discern in his face. Husna, on the other hand, was flushing furiously and clasping and unclasping both hands while avoiding my eyes. I knew then that what I thought I'd heard was indeed what Enche Ja'afar had said.

Mrs Chan had evidently been prepared, for within seconds she replied, '*Terima kaseh*, Enche Ja'afar. I will bring you these gifts. Please give me time.'

I looked at Mrs Chan in wonder. Until that moment I had regarded her as an unworldly teacher who kept her head in lofty dimensions. Yet there she was, agreeing to blunt terms to secure her husband's release from a police cell.

Afterwards, when we had escorted Mrs Chan home, she invited us into her house and said, with genuine feeling in her mellow voice, 'Thank you so much, Mrs Wong. Thank you, Mr Wong.'

'Don't be silly, Mrs Chan, no need to thank us. I'm glad that Enche Ja'afar is willing . . . ,' I said, and then stopped, wondering how best to phrase my delicate question. 'Mrs Chan, do you need help . . . you know? Look, I've heard that you have many private students, probably more than you need, but still, things are so expensive these days.'

A light flickered in Mrs Chan's eyes, gratitude perhaps at my concern, though she did not look at me. 'I'll be okay, just have to find more students.'

'Is it Japanese History you now teach, Mrs Chan?'

'I errh . . . yes,' the lady replied, rather cautiously.

We looked at one another, each sensing that there was more to come. Mrs Chan then said, 'I teach Japanese History generally. But if you were, you know, to ask me, well then . . . It could be done differently.'

Mrs Chan fixed her gaze on me. My eyes were held bound. Gulping a mouthful of saliva, I said, 'Well, as it happens, I am thinking about our daughter, Lai Hin.'

I hesitated, hashing and rehashing the sentences inside my own head. I was relieved when Mrs Chan beamed. 'Oh yes, I remember Lai Hin. She's a spirited girl, isn't she?'

She then leaned forward in her chair, so that her lips were only inches from my left ear. Despite this proximity, she lowered her voice to a whisper. 'I've kept copies of our old primary school textbooks. I can use those if you like.'

My mouth opened wide. Mrs Chan was turning out to be full of surprises. Raising an index finger to her lips, she shook her head from side to side, to remind me that under the Japs, even brick walls had ears.

'How much per lesson, Mrs Chan?' I had already begun doing sums in my head, a necessity in those days of zooming inflation.

'Don't worry about the first month.' When Mrs Chan saw that I was about to argue, she stretched out a palm to silence me. 'We will discuss price after the first month – that's my condition.'

'Thank you, thank you, Mrs Chan!' I blurted out, in between the tears I found myself swallowing. 'I don't know what to say.'

'We will start the week after next,' the teacher replied imperiously. 'I will make preparations next week.'

I spent the next several days wondering what sort of preparations a teacher as experienced as Mrs Chan would need to make for a Primary One student. When she arrived at the sing-song group, I was surprised to see the enormous circular cake tin she carried in.

'Be careful when you cut it, especially the bottom edge.' That was all that she said, and off she went into the inner hall to sing.

While they had their sing-song, I cut the cake. It was a plain cake, very tall, rectangular in shape, with no icing anywhere, sugar being so dear in those days. Indeed I have no idea how Mrs Chan could have found the ingredients for her concoction; I assumed that she had managed without butter. There seemed to be a layer in the middle of her grand design through which our bread knife would not pass. I cut the parts I was able to, into slices, and then wrenched off the top. There in the bottom half of the cake sat a textbook which I recognised at once.

This textbook, along with other history textbooks, had been banned by the Japs. If we were found out, we could all have been arrested. I removed the book from the tin, brushed away a few crumbs, and wiped its hard maroon binding with a piece of wet cloth. I then locked the book inside my mother-in-law's fireproof safe. There would have to be absolute secrecy, and the children would need to understand what this meant.

The sing-song session finished around nine o'clock. When our visitors had departed, my husband went back into the dining room to roll his customary late-night cigarette. Without thinking, I took a sheet of the square white papers he had cut and began creasing it.

'What're you doing, Wife?'

'What does it look like?'

'But you don't smoke.'

I sighed. 'You're right, I don't, or maybe didn't,' I said, crumbling brown flakes of local tobacco on to the sheet of white paper. I had watched my husband and father many times, but had never attempted to roll a cigarette myself. To this day I do not know what possessed me. My fingers acted with frenetic compulsion, not stopping even for a second. I ignored my husband altogether until the cylinder was closed, tight and properly filled. When the tube of brown leaves was ready, I struck a match and lit up.

17

I had expected the first puff to be deeply satisfying. It looked so easy and elegant when Weng Yu and Father held the white sticks in between their index and third fingers and drew in breath. I imagined I would inhale and simply swirl the smoke at the back of my throat as they did. I thought pleasure would seep effortlessly into my larynx. Instead I coughed and spluttered like a bronchial patient. On my first attempt, I could not understand why anyone would want to smoke. If my mother-in-law were still alive, she would have fixed a glare on me. She'd had no vices, apart from a sweet tooth; she certainly did not approve of women smoking. I could already hear the clacking of her tongue. When I imagined her shaking her head, I could not suppress a smile.

Once a cigarette has been rolled, there is nothing to do but smoke it. I thus put my mind to learning how to hold the acrid smoke inside my mouth. I reasoned that if I began by first blowing the smoke out, it would be easier to bear. After a week I was able to tolerate the sensation of heat in my mouth. Soon, drawing the cloudy ringlets into my lungs felt perfectly natural and eventually it became even pleasurable.

My husband was surprisingly intolerant of this new habit. He stared whenever I lit up. After I released a puff, he would wave away the smoke with one hand as if it were choking him. I ignored this deliberate petulance. If he was allowed a dozen cigarettes a day, why could I not have a few? Weng Yu would rise from his chair in a huff, to escape to his world of music. He had smoked Capstan Navy Cuts before the arrival of the Japs; with the onset of shortages, he was reduced to rolling his own cigarettes, which he did with ill humour and an air of resignation.

For me, smoking brought unexpected benefits. The action of rolling and holding a thin stick gave my hands something to do, and with something to do, I felt somehow more glamorous, like the Hollywood stars we had watched in the cinemas before the Japs came. With exhilaration came confidence, alongside a stark fact: smoking salved my hunger pangs.

By then, it had been a year and a half since we had last seen a bowl of white rice. Images of food often assaulted my mind, not the meat or fancy dishes, but the fluffy steaming grains of white rice we used to enjoy. I would have given anything for a bowl of rice. The very thought made me salivate.

Before I took up smoking I had to force myself to think of something else. Or someone else, people like Liew Chin Tong and his sister. Unfortunately, whoever or whatever I thought about always brought me back to food. Memories of Liew Chin Tong made me recall the fish which Samad had caught in the pond near the tin mine, creatures with bulging eyes and fat juicy flesh. Fish, in turn, reminded me of wonderful smells – the ginger and rice wine with which the fish was steamed or the bubbling crispiness of fried fat. I would get so hungry that I thought my taste-buds would explode.

By the time I discovered that I was pregnant again – a fact confirmed by Dr Pillay – I was rolling six cigarettes a day and thinking not of Liew Chin Tong or his sister, but of sour pickles. This was curious, for I had not been afflicted by food cravings in the course of previous pregnancies. I made Ah Hong pluck the papayas and mangoes off the trees still standing in our garden and pickle them in accordance with Mother-in-Law's recipes. Ah Hong had to use a fraction of the recommended sugar and salt because the prices of these had reached extortionate levels. How she managed to replicate the desired astringency, I shall never know.

With the help of things sour, the child which was to be my sixth grew. I felt a special affinity for this baby. I was convinced she was a girl and I would call her Cecilia. When I was certain that she was real, I walked into the inner hall one night, holding my tummy in both hands. Puccini's *Madame Butterfly* was playing on the gramophone. My husband was sitting completely still in his armchair with his head laid back and legs stretched out. His eyes were closed. There was an angelic expression on his face, and his breathing was even. I wished he could be so relaxed all of the time.

'We're going to have another child, Husband,' I whispered, not daring to touch his arm.

Weng Yu opened his eyes. For a minute he seemed not to know where he was, but then he smiled as he put a finger to his lips. 'That's wonderful, Wife,' he said, almost tenderly. Our eyes locked like magnets. I felt love and happiness at that instant; I knew I was desired. I could not bear for the moment to slip away.

Weng Yu was the first to lower his eyes. 'This is my favourite aria. Doesn't she have a beautiful voice?' he asked, pointing to the record sleeve. There was a photograph of the soprano Margaret Burke Sheridan. When the final orchestral notes of 'Un Bel di Vedremo' faded into the air, my husband lifted the needle. A hard silence descended on the room, and I was overcome by disappointment, the same feeling I had whenever I left a cinema, knowing that the magical world to which I had been transported was about to evaporate. I did not want to return to my real life, the only life I had, in which nothing had really changed.

There were smiles and laughter around the dinner table when I announced the news of my pregnancy. Father congratulated us and invited me on a stroll around the garden. He could only hobble by then, but nonetheless he insisted on his nightly intake of fresh air. We set off, with Father's gnarled hands clutching the dragon's head on his wooden stick and a grimace on his face.

After nearly two years of Nippon occupation, what surrounded our house resembled more a cemetery than a garden. In place of a lawn were rows of raised beds. Instead of rose bushes and hibiscus, we had vegetables. Some of the fruit trees – the papaya, mango, and banana Mother-in-Law had so loved – had been transplanted to the garden's edge. But it was the raised beds which abounded, and Father and I were able to walk only along the narrow paths running in between them.

The old man was exceptionally quiet that night. Time and again I glanced at his stooped but stubborn shoulders, waiting for him to share what was on his mind. Father would pause, look as if he were about to speak, but then continue on his way, one resolute step at a time. Near a plot on the side of the garden bordering Dorcourt, he stopped yet again. As he stood still, an evening breeze fanned the white strands on his head. It pained me to see his back so curved that he no longer had to bend to touch the emerald leaves of a brinjal tree. I longed to be close to Father the way I had been as a girl, and was on the verge of reaching for his arm when he at last spoke.

'These are rather dry, Mei Foong. You must tell Samad to water them.'

Father looked at me, eyes brimming with sadness. I thought he was going to cry, but he swallowed quickly and resumed hobbling.

When we were about to complete our circuit, he turned to me. 'This war, Daughter . . .' His mouth was twisted into a bitter curve which shocked me – I had never known bitterness in my father. I clung to his arm as we walked down our driveway to the front door. I could feel the frailty of the bones that had once held me. I went inside, numb from unshed tears, full of fear for our future.

The gambling dens re-opened throughout Malai in November 1943. Everyone was exhorted to play. We were told there was too much money floating around; if we used our scrip inside the new halls of entertainment there would be fewer notes left in the system. This, in turn, would help reduce the prices of goods.

When it came to speculation, my husband hardly needed encouragement. He became an early patron of one of Ipoh's gambling halls. At first Weng Yu would play mah-jong only on Saturday afternoons after work, but it was not long before this newly resumed activity spilled over into Sundays as well.

Remembering the mountain of debt from which Weng Yu's mother had saved him, I became increasingly uneasy. Father knew the whole story and was fully cognisant of the large amounts Weng Yu had lost, yet he never expressed any opinion, and did nothing other than to give my husband a wistful look whenever the latter went off gambling. Father himself was no gambler: he had seen too many lives ruined to approve of mah-jong, poker, fan-tan, *chap ji-ki*, or any of the myriad games of chance and riddle in which Ipoh became engrossed.

One Sunday morning, after my husband rose from the dining table and was heading to the latrine in preparation for his usual departure, I announced my intention of following him to the gambling hall. Father looked away. Then, almost at once while stroking his cotton-wool moustache, he said, 'Mei Foong, you know that you will almost certainly lose, don't you?'

The comment provoked me. Why did Father not admonish my husband? When I glimpsed the anguish in the old man's eyes, I replied in a quiet voice, 'Father, don't worry. I don't even know how to play mah-jong! I'm going just to keep an eye on Weng Yu.'

'You will be very tempted, Daughter, trust me. I have seen this time and again. People get drawn in, and then they become addicted.'

As Father shuffled out of the dining room, I was overwhelmed by how much each of his steps cost him. He had good days and bad days, and that morning happened to be a bad day; even with Muthusamy standing at his side to prop up an arm, the old man's forehead was creased in pain. On his mouth was frozen the curve of bitterness I had seen previously. Father wound his way down the vestibule, murmuring, almost to himself. 'Just know that you can never win.'

The gambling den which my husband frequented was on the top floor of the Foong Seong building, a grand villa on Laxamana Road about twenty minutes' walk from our house. The building boasted a line of traditional windows with wooden shutters along its facade. All of the windows were open, and we could hear the din from the street. The higher up we climbed, the more noisy it became. When we reached the second floor, the noise was compounded by smoke. On entering the room itself, a haze stung my eyes. My breath caught. Even the blades of the ceiling fans were unable to cope, churning air to little effect. Everywhere, bodies generated heat and sweat which mixed with the potent fumes of elation and despair.

When my eyes and lungs settled, I saw that the room was packed with stalls offering every conceivable game of chance. There were tables catering to mah-jong players, but also tables for cards and dominoes. Lining the sides of the hall were stalls hawking riddles and stalls selling just numbers. Men and women, whether immersed in play or awaiting their turn, were utterly absorbed. Some laughed manically, others shrieked that the spirits had misled them, still others that they had come so close, if only one die had rolled a three instead of two. Colourful expletives reached my ears that I had only ever heard from Ipoh's rickshaw pullers.

After a few minutes I realised that there was a mix of languages. In the British era, Malaya's gambling halls were open only to the Chinese, but the Japs allowed everyone in. The more the merrier, since all communities had a role in combating inflation. In the sea of Chinese punters was thus a scattering of Malays, Indians, and Eurasians taking chances with their banana notes. These were no novices standing around wondering what to do, but experts who knew how to play and who shouted loudly at each other.

There were, of course, more men than women. I did not take any notice of the men at first, but after I left my husband at a mah-jong table,

I could feel their eyes flickering over my figure. This was to be expected since my pregnancy was already evident, and I hardly looked like any of the other ladies out for the day. Moreover, it was the first time in two and a half years that I was walking without a male chaperone. I stiffened as I always did in the face of male admiration, so that my back was straighter and my head higher than I normally held it. I was glad that I had powdered my face and applied a touch of lipstick before leaving the house. My make-up seemed to please the men, as did the colourful, flowing skirt I was wearing which I had matched with a plain Chinese tunic. They eyed my slender form and rounded belly, a few smiled, one even contorted his lips into a whistle as I passed the Chee Fah, or Double Tote, stall. There was a time when I would have glared or flushed with embarrassment or even become confused, but now I found that I enjoyed the attention. I felt especially proud that I could garner a whistle despite having borne five children, with another obviously on the way.

I spotted Teoh Wai Fong seated at one of the tables. We had not seen each other since our return from the jungle, but I noticed at once how remarkably bouffant she had kept her perm. Over her forehead there was even a strategically placed cowlick. From the misty distance it was obvious that the red on her lips could only have come from a foreign lipstick.

Her voice was as loud as I remembered. 'Mei Foong! How nice to see you!'

Wai Fong turned to a tall woman ensconced in the chair next to hers. 'Miss Goh, this is my good friend Mei Foong. Could you please do me a favour by giving her your seat?'

The tall woman, who suffered from bad acne, gave me a look of displeasure. I felt my face burn. 'No, no, Wai Fong, I didn't mean to disturb you.'

'You're not disturbing me at all. I want to hear all about how you and Mr Wong are. You must be well, since it looks like I should congratulate you!'

Wai Fong accompanied her final sentence with a short, shrill laugh which drew murmurs and mischievous nods. I had no choice but to take the seat vacated by the tall Miss Goh. Wai Fong must have known that it would be too raucous for conversation, but she insisted nonetheless that I sit down. When it became clear that I did not know how to play mah-jong, she emitted a disapproving noise. 'Ai-yahh, Mrs Wong, I must teach you!'

It is hard, having now played mah-jong for thirty years, to recall how nervous I was. My beginner's anxiety only added to the excitement and thrill. Mah-jong is a game of strategy and tactics, much like gin rummy, and with my head for numbers, I learnt the basics within days. In mah-jong, my skill at quiet observation was put to good use. I was aided also by an excellent memory, which allowed me to hold in my mind's eye the pattern of tiles each of my opponents had recently thrown while I continued building upon my own positions. Thus it sometimes felt to my opponents as if I had a sixth sense for which tiles to discard and which ones to retain.

From the very first, my objective was not to lose too much. Such caution, of course, determined that I would also never win outsized amounts, but in this I was content. Mah-jong was simply a way for me to pass the time while keeping an eye on my husband, who after a few months could not be dragged away from the tables on weekends.

It was a stifling afternoon when I saw Chew Hock San again. I was pregnant with Cecilia, and the tiles had not been kind. Every gambler will recognise the overwhelming despondency that prevails when the cards or the tiles or even the dice conspire against you. On the day in question my downfall was swift, and the winds ranged against me very ill indeed. I tried to renew my luck by changing seats with Wai Fong. When this brought no success, I went off to wash my hands. Such ruses often worked, but on that particular afternoon, nothing I did had the slightest effect. The tiles refused to cooperate. I could form neither sets nor sequences, and was unable to profit from even the most beautiful of starting arrangements. Fed up with losing, I rose from the table and was in the midst of giving my place to a waiting player when a man with a heavily pomaded head three tables away smiled at me.

Chew Hock San must only have just arrived – otherwise I would have seen him – but he rose when I did and started walking towards our table. With a single glance he took in my protruding belly while I had a momentary lapse, wondering what he was doing there. White noise filled my head; my limbs turned into slate; a chill flowed through my bones; and all the while he was drawing closer. There I stood, exposed in my sleeveless Chinese tunic, with nowhere to hide.

We said hello stiffly. Teoh Wai Fong had no such compunction; she yelled out her greeting with gusto and surveyed the pair of us with undisguised curiosity. There was an awkward silence until, for no reason at all, I thought of Liew Chin Tong and how he and Chew Hock San had whispered to one another in the confines of the jungle. Here was a man who might know where my brother-in-law had gone. But I could hardly have asked him with so many present.

The first thing that came into my head to say was, 'I have to go home now, the children are waiting.' This was true, though not what I had wanted to say; having come out with it, however, I was obliged to give the whole table a curt smile and to begin walking to my husband's table. I could feel eyes on me: Chew Hock San's certainly, but Teoh Wai Fong's sly glance was also on my back.

At the next table my husband sat wholly absorbed. From the large pile of chips before him, he had evidently been winning. It would have been a good time to depart, except that Weng Yu never left while on a winning streak. He was one of those able to retreat only after being thoroughly beaten, when there was nothing more to lose. As we approached, his elongated mouth shouted out, 'Pong!' He looked up at the slight ruffle in the crowd, registered our presence, and straight away glanced down again. He then picked up the tile he had sought and continued to play without saying anything. His handsome cheekbones were as taut as stretched tarpaulin.

'Husband, you remember Mr Chew, don't you? We were in Lahat together.'

Hock San stood grinning beside me. Weng Yu glanced at him as he would have glanced at a fly on the wall before mumbling a formal hello and nodding his head once. When it became clear that my husband was not about to stand up or to shake the clerk's hand, Hock San interjected, 'Mr Wong, I don't want to disturb your game. I can see you've reached an exciting point.'

A smile formed on Weng Yu's malleable lips. 'Yes, lady luck is with me today.'

'In that case, Husband, are you nearly ready to go home?' I said, taking in the beautiful curve of my husband's lips and holding my breath.

'No-lah, we only just started this round.'

I breathed out bitterly, pointing to the clock on a wall. 'Why don't you get someone else to take your place? We've been here many hours.'

My husband seemed not to hear me. He sat frowning in concentration with grooves lining his forehead. Then, half-opening his finely contoured mouth, he muttered, 'Wife, why don't you go home first?'

The words stung, no matter how many times I had heard them. I was afraid, of course, as most women were then, of walking around unaccompanied, but I did not want to create a fuss. I had not been brought up to make demands.

'Mrs Wong, I would be happy to take you home,' Hock San said quietly.

'Good idea!' Weng Yu cried out. 'Let Mr Chew keep you company!'

From behind, a familiar voice called out, 'I'll come too, if you don't mind. I've had enough for the day.'

I turned to see Teoh Wai Fong standing before us, her Western dress smoothed down, cowlick in perfect position. She had already gathered her winnings into the handbag she had taken to carrying – a creamy number made of leather, with a hard gold frame enclosing it like the crust on sliced bread.

'There! You have plenty of company, Wife. Nothing to worry about. I will see you at home.' With a broad smile, Weng Yu returned to his game.

◆ ◆ ◆

With only one bicycle between the three of us, we ended up walking. Hock San stayed in the middle, wheeling his vehicle alongside us two women. We were an improbable group: the Teoh family lived in the opposite direction to Green Town, but Wai Fong would not hear of being taken home first.

As we walked I considered whether there was a way of mentioning Liew Chin Tong casually. Each time I resolved to drop a hint, Wai Fong would turn towards me and I would think better of it. I could not help staring at the neatness of her cowlick and the foreignness of her lipstick – both items which Miss Mak, a member of my husband's singing group, had warned me about.

'That mah-jong companion of yours is knee-deep up to no-good. You know-moh, her husband is one of Ipoh's armchair brokers-ah?'

'What is an armchair broker?' I had asked, never having heard the term.

'It means he wines and dines the Japanese military. I think he specialises in electrical goods. Because of his wife, he also deals in textiles and fabrics.'

'Well,' I'd retorted, 'I know Mr Teoh has one of those textile goods distribution cards. So what? Someone must have them.'

Miss Mak saw that I did not understand how the black market worked. She threw her curled head back and gave a throaty laugh. 'Ai-yahh, you are so innocent, my dear!'

Touching my arm, she went into a lengthy explanation. 'Mr Teoh's official job is to enforce textile rationing, yes, to make sure that we in

Perak only get our one yard of cloth each per year. But you think there is rationing for the Japs-ah? Of course not!

'Do you see the higher-ups short of clothes? You think they can't get batteries or tyres? No! Hah, and why do you think? Because when Mr Teoh's military friends need textiles or electrical goods, they go to him. He scoots off to find whatever they need. He knows they will pay through their noses. Nothing is too expensive for the bloody emperor! Of course, Mr Teoh cannot work on his own: he needs middlemen. The shorties are fickle, you see; their demands make no sense. I know because that wife of his comes into our shop, poking her nose into everything. One week she's interested in electrodes, next time it's solder-ing sets. She acts as his lieutenant, but she doesn't work alone; she has an army snooping around in coffee shops, hawker stalls, hotels, listening. That's what her field brokers do – they eavesdrop, hoping to pick up a careless snippet which will lead to their next find.'

From Miss Mak's vantage point inside the Radio & General Shop, Ipoh was full of spies, brokers, and informers. There were apparently many who did the Japs' bidding and profited from trade in all manner of smuggled goods. 'You should not trust anyone, Mrs Wong. Especially not at the Foong Seong Villa. I tell you, that place is full of the worst snakes. Look carefully next time you see Mrs Teoh. Are her clothes old? Is she wearing local make-up? What kind of handbag does she have?'

The handbag in question was dangling off Wai Fong's shoulder. When my arm brushed against the satchel by chance, its leather felt soft; no one who was not close to the Japs could possibly have afforded it. Miss Mak was right: I couldn't trust any woman who carried such a new, beautifully made bag.

I had to wait another fortnight before Chew Hock San escorted me home again. This time, we were alone. I felt his slanted eyes on me, with their hint of mockery, but there was something else too, a softness that made walking side by side embarrassingly intimate. I was aware of his shoulders, his muscled arms, and also of how heavily he trudged along. The man may have lifted me into a pit, but he would not be able to waltz. When he invited me on to the back of his bicycle, I blushed. Riding pillion was not something I would even have considered doing before the war. Although it became fashionable during the Nippon era, I myself had never ridden pillion. I worried about falling off and looking like a fool, but at the same time did not wish to offend Hock San.

He sensed my hesitation, however, and surprised me by saying, 'It's okay, Mrs Wong, we can walk if you prefer.' I nodded gratefully and we carried on at the same easy pace.

I wondered when I should raise the subject. It seemed dangerous while we were still in town; there were too many people about. Passers-by milled the streets; vagrants slept rough on five-foot ways; for a short while we could not even hear ourselves as a Tokio bus rumbled down Brewster Road on its outstation run to Taiping, packed with far more passengers than the British would ever have allowed. Not only were men and women standing inside, there were even men strapped on to its roof and another two hanging on the side steps, clinging for dear life on to the metal rail edging the bus roof.

The crowd thinned as we approached Poh Gardens Lane, but I continued to hold my tongue, wary of the Japanese sentries who had now been posted at a kiosk near the Odeon Cinema. When we reached the safety of Green Town's rubber smallholdings, we slowed down. I was already feeling Cecilia's weight. With the neighbourhood's laterite roads so pot-holed from use, I had to watch where I put my feet. Whenever I glanced down at the road, I noticed Hock San's hands, large and burly, pushing the handlebars. Their thick fingers seemed knobbly for a man so young. His fingernails were still dirty, though no dirtier than before.

Just after we passed the Main Convent I asked, in a quiet but firm voice, 'Mr Chew, do you know where my brother-in-law and his sister are?'

Hock San threw me a sideways glance of surprise. He thought carefully before replying, as if each word had to be weighed. 'What makes you think that I would know, Mrs Wong?'

195

'You used to talk to each other, I remember. At Grand-Uncle's mine.'

He nodded without looking up. 'Yes.'

'It would really help if you can tell us anything – anything at all . . .'

Hock San continued walking. Then, with no warning his words came out in a rush. 'I spoke to them before they left. I helped him make contact with a friend in Papan. A close friend, someone I went to school with. I know that the necessary arrangements were made. Mrs Wong, do you understand?'

I nodded cautiously. 'I think so, Mr Chew.'

'I don't know how they got to Papan, with so many roadblocks, but they left one night. They reached safety, that much I can say.'

'Mr Chew, have you heard from them since?'

'No, but they must be okay-lah, otherwise we would know.'

We had reached my house by then. Hock San ground to a halt, made a clumsy turn, and, with his prominent jaw thrust forward, whispered, 'If I weren't married, I would have gone, too.'

I shot him a curious look. 'Why?'

He seemed agitated by the question; perhaps he had expected me to understand. Barely moving his lips, he said, with a slight huff, 'We must fight them.' A pause followed during which his square chin was defiant. 'We should all be doing something, especially me, as a man, to protect us, my family, everyone here . . .'

He stopped abruptly and looked at me with an indefinable expression. The sympathy in his eyes turned inexplicably harsh, as if he had said too much and was suddenly ashamed of his vulnerability.

In the following days, something in his face haunted me. I had a lingering yearning for better times, for softness and beauty instead of the relentless hardness of constant war. I longed for waking moments that did not merge with nightmares, light that did not dissolve into shadow. Under the Japanese there was little sense of night and day, of right or wrong; no sooner did dawn break than dusk settled. Time marched forward as it always had, but we were numb to its passing.

18

It began with a cough. My husband's morning wash, a mini concerto of harrumphing noises ever since I had known him, worsened one day early in 1944. Apart from that touch of catarrh, Weng Yu was otherwise well, his appetites healthy. He went to work as usual on Samad's bicycle.

By Thursday, we had to call off the week's singing session. Samad was despatched to the other singers' houses to apprise them of Weng Yu's malaise. They were told that there was nothing to worry about; Mr Wong had a minor cough, and it was only out of an abundance of caution that the merrymaking was being postponed.

Late on Saturday evening, I was awakened by panting in the vestibule. The space beside me in the bed was empty, which meant that the heavy tread on our wooden floor had to be my husband returning from his exploits at the Foong Seong Villa. Weng Yu was walking so unevenly that I wondered if he had consumed whisky at the gambling hall.

As soon as our bedroom door opened, he started to wheeze. I sat up in bed; in eleven years of marriage I had not heard such a noise. His back was turned to me when I asked, 'Husband, are you all right?'

Weng Yu, who was seized by a sudden a fit of retching, did not answer. I rose, flicked on the electric switch, and saw how pale my husband was. I held his arm as he staggered the few feet to our bed. He slumped down with a hand across his forehead.

'Do you have a headache, Husband?'

Again he did not reply. His eyes were closed, his breathing heavy. On reaching for Weng Yu's hand, I became aware that he was so depleted of energy that his arm would have fallen on to the mattress if I had not held it. His forehead was not especially hot, though I would need a thermometer to be sure. I went to the dining room, to the corner side cupboard in which we stored an assortment of items. I was quite sure that Chang Ying had put our rudimentary medical chest inside.

When I returned, Weng Yu's eyes were open, but they looked watery and bloated. 'I'm very tired,' he said in a weak voice.

'Of course you're tired, Husband. It's past midnight.'

'No, I . . . I have trouble breathing.'

'Why didn't you come home earlier?'

'I thought it was just the cigarette smoke. You know what it's like in there.'

I shook the thermometer and slipped it under my husband's tongue. His eyes were closed again, as if he could not keep them open. The thermometer reading was normal.

'Do you want a hot drink? We don't have Milo, but I can make a cup of tea. Or just hot water. What do you want?'

Opening his eyes for an instant, Weng Yu mumbled, 'Nothing, Wife. Just help me into bed.'

I unbuttoned his shirt and untied the belt on his trousers. The trousers were surprisingly loose – my husband had clearly lost weight. His ribs were visible; when he coughed, the exposed bones quivered. Weng Yu lay on the bed, spent, with his eyes closed but mouth ajar. He began breathing through his mouth, inhaling loudly and exhaling with the shrillness of a kettle. Within minutes his breathing had established the rhythm that kept me awake the whole night.

Every now and again I turned to touch his forehead. Though my husband groaned, he did not wake and did not open his eyes until the shadowy dawn light flooded in. I was already up and dressed. I watched Weng Yu roll over. His eyelids, still heavy, kept shutting awkwardly, but his voice had regained its normal timbre.

'Why didn't you wake me, Wife? I will be late for Radio Taiso.'

'You are in no shape for exercise, Husband.'

'I have to go to work; otherwise I won't be paid.'

'Well, I'm n—'

'Hashimoto will say it's all a matter of *seishin*. I must get up.' Weng Yu hauled himself up from beneath the blanket.

'Don't you think you should see Big Ears, Husband?'

'I'm sure it's nothing, Wife, just a bit too much smoke. Anyway, I'm already late! I have no time-lah.'

For the next few days my husband came home panting like one of Green Town's stray dogs. This was despite his not riding Samad's bicycle. It was our gardener who transported him to St Michael's in the morning and fetched him in the evening. Merely riding pillion made Weng Yu complain of fatigue. When I begged him to see Dr Pillay, he accused me of nagging. Of course, he also carried on smoking – we didn't think about our lungs in those days.

On the night before the sing-song group was due to meet, I felt a trembling in our bed. I reached for my husband's hand and found it not only hot but also covered in perspiration. At the same time his teeth were chattering. When I checked his temperature, I found it had risen past 100. I got up, changed into fresh clothes, and went to wake Samad. Enough was enough; this time, I was not going to let my husband stop me. Had Weng Yu been less languid, he would no doubt have protested; as it was, he lay silently with eyes shut and not even the wherewithal to ask where I was going in the middle of the night. Every few minutes his body was convulsed by shivers.

I arrived at the medical quarters a few streets away and rapped on the main door until the lights came on. For once, I threw good manners out of the window and did not care that I had awakened everyone. Dr Pillay eventually emerged from his room, yawning. When he saw me, he narrowed the eyes he had just been rubbing. Later, in front of the dressing mirror, I realised how unnerving I looked; my face, devoid of any make-up whatsoever, was sallow from worry, and the strands of hair strewn over my forehead gave me the appearance of the wildness I'd had on the day the bombs first fell. When I described Weng Yu's symptoms, a cloud passed through Dr Pillay's eyes. 'Give me a minute, Mrs Wong,' he said in a voice still hoarse from sleep. A few minutes later when he returned, he was dressed in his day clothes and carrying a black medical bag in his right hand. I was glad I had found the doctor. Weng Yu and I both trusted him, even though he had trained only in India. I asked what my husband's ailment could be.

'Mrs Wong, let me see the patient first. There's no point speculating.'

'But you think it could be serious, don't you?'

Dr Pillay pulled his thin lips into a smile. 'Let's just go, shall we?'

The electric lights were on in the inner hall when Dr Pillay, Samad and I arrived home. The remaining adults in the Wong household were all awake. Father and the servants, who had decided to keep vigil, welcomed us with cups of hot tea.

I tiptoed into the bedroom with Dr Pillay. My husband looked even more dazed than before. Half-opening one eye, he just as quickly closed it again. Dr Pillay placed his black medical bag on the floor. He then sat beside Weng Yu and observed his patient for a good minute, presumably taking in the eyes which refused to stay open, the beads of perspiration and the heaving on every breath.

When the doctor was satisfied, he pulled down the blanket while pulling up Weng Yu's pyjama top. From out of his medical bag came a thermometer and a folded stethoscope; the former he slipped under Weng Yu's arm-pit, the latter he straightened out and held against my husband's chest. Dr Pillay's eyes opened wide at the sounds that the ribbed ear-tips of his stethoscope delivered. As his eyes dilated, he asked Weng Yu to take deep breaths and to hold them. Finally, refolding the stethoscope and putting it in his lap, Dr Pillay said, 'There's a lot of mucus in your lungs. Have you been coughing it up?'

Weng Yu nodded.

'But my husband has always had terrible catarrh, Doctor,' I said. Weng Yu, instead of objecting to what I'd said, as he might have in ordinary times, simply lay pale and miserable.

Dr Pillay took out a small torchlight from his bag and proceeded to examine the patient's throat, ears, and eyes. Grunting softly, he tapped my husband's back with a medical hammer. Next, he asked a series of questions, which Weng Yu answered rather self-consciously. My husband reddened when he admitted to having had chest pains for a week.

'Can you describe the pain?'

'Well . . .'

'Is it a sharp pain or is it dull?'

'Sharp,' my husband said, breathing rapidly, 'Like now.' Closing his eyes, Weng Yu gasped while clasping both hands to his chest as if he had just been stabbed.

'Why didn't you come to see me?' Dr Pillay demanded, his dark cheeks deepening in colour. He looked frustrated and aggrieved, rather like a headmaster admonishing his favourite schoolboy. I felt sorry for my husband, who seemed in great pain and could only mumble, 'I – I didn't think there was anything serious . . .'

'Hmm . . .'

Dr Pillay emitted another grunt, this one loud, before turning to face me. His large ears twitched when he said, 'Mrs Wong, I'm sorry to give you the bad news, but Weng Yu probably has pneumonia. This is very serious indeed.'

◆　◆　◆

X-ray photographs taken at the District Hospital the following morning confirmed Dr Pillay's diagnosis. Malaya had become a cauldron of diseases by then. Malaria, tuberculosis, and beri-beri abounded. It was unsurprising that someone with a weak chest like Weng Yu would succumb to bacterial pneumonia.

My husband was to be sent to a hospital in the town of Batu Gajah, fifteen miles south of Ipoh. I was unhappy at how far he would be, but Dr Pillay insisted that we had no other option.

'Your husband needs a drug known as M&B 693. I know they have it in Batu Gajah – the MO, medical officer, is a friend and I've checked with him. But there's not much of this medication around, Mrs Wong. It's British-made. We certainly can't afford it in Ipoh.'

When Dr Pillay disclosed what we would need to pay to make my husband well, the earth spun under my feet. I lost track of time, until the good doctor snapped his third finger and waved his hand in front of me. 'Mrs Wong?'

M&B 693, which before the Japanese arrived had cost only eight cents per pill, would now cost twenty-five dollars to purchase – for each pill. Weng Yu was going to need at least ten days' supply, possibly more. Thoughts came to me in a tidal rush. How would we be able to afford such an expensive drug? Yet there was no question of not getting it for my husband. But how was I meant to keep the family alive when there were so many of us and there I was pregnant again and . . .

It had taken no more than a handful of words to make life feel impossible. My head pounded, I had trouble breathing. If I had been alone, I would surely have burst into tears, but there was Dr Pillay sitting across the desk.

'Mrs Wong, does any one of your children have their father's symptoms? A cough maybe? Anyone complaining of being tired?'

I looked blankly at Dr Pillay. As I sat on the stool in his office caressing my protruding belly, Cecilia made her presence felt. I was shaking inside, but I pulled up both my shoulders and resolved to be strong. For Cecilia's sake and that of my children. I know now that I was simply pretending. I pretended to be strong and, in the act of pretending, discovered a reservoir of strength I never realised I had. At the time, though, I was so scared that all I wanted to do was vomit.

19

Hashimoto screwed up his flat nose in a sympathetic manner. He seemed proud of being a dogsbody for the emperor, and wore his officer's cap even inside the office where the air was cooled by a ceiling fan with a lengthy rod and giant blades that whirred noisily.

Clearing my throat, I said, 'Sir, Wong-san is the sole bread-winner in our family. I beg you, it is now mid-March, please pay him for a month's work. He will make it up when he is well. We have a lot of medical expenses.'

Pleading was not one of my strengths. It was hard to tell whether Hashimoto thought my tone overly obsequious or not supplicatory enough. He stared when I raised my voice to compete with the ceiling fan's rotor. The dark skin on his face turned ashen. His expression was inscrutable save for the eyes, which widened before narrowing as he replied, 'Wong-san, work not yet done, but you want Nippon government . . . pay your husband?'

This last sentence was pronounced with a lilt of disbelief, quite uncharacteristic of the throaty way in which the Japs normally spoke.

'Hashimoto-san, I am not suggesting charity. My husband will make up the hours when he is better. Please,' I said, suddenly feeling parched in my throat, 'we need the money.'

Hashimoto waved a dismissive hand. He did not even bother giving me a second glance. Had I been able to call up tears at the drop of a hat, it might have helped my cause, but I have never been a woman to cry easily. I vowed not to forget that moment.

Years later, after Japan had already been rebuilt and had begun sending their wretched cars and electrical goods to our country, I took care never to give them my business. Life would have been easier if I'd bought one of their damned television sets or even their fridges, but I always thought of Hashimoto. I remembered my humiliation and refused to yield. I have never knowingly bought a Japanese product. Not one.

◆ ◆ ◆

Samad did not whistle while we cycled home. I rode pillion on the back, doing furious calculations in my head. For as long as Weng Yu was unable to work, we would lose his salary as well as the allowances the Japs had brought in by then: the cost-of-living allowance and the family allowance. Though neither amounted to much, every cent counted.

Thanks to our precarious situation, I was more aware of the vagrants who seemed to be everywhere, sleeping in the open along every inch of Ipoh's five-foot ways. There had also been beggars under British rule, but their numbers exploded in two years of Japanese occupation. There were the old and infirm, and also children whose parents had taken to the streets. As we rode on, shirtless boys ran up, sticking out emaciated arms in the hope of a banana note. I looked at their stalk-like bodies and bloated bellies and vowed that, no matter what happened to my husband, I would never allow my children to end up on the passageways outside Ipoh's shop-houses.

After Samad deposited me on our driveway, he threw me a contemplative look. I was wondering what he was thinking when I bumped into Father in the vestibule, hunched over his walking stick. The old man's eyes flashed when I recounted Hashimoto's cold reception. I told Father that I would have to enter his room. The old man gave a resigned nod, pressed his steely lips together, and twisted them into that crescent of bitterness I had previously seen.

I dragged myself into the bedroom, which had once been Mother-in-Law's. I took no pleasure in what I had to do. I sat on her bed and wanted to cry. I had never felt so lonely; I only wished the old lady were alive then. I gave thanks for my bedrock of a Father, who would know which shop I should go to.

Taking a deep breath, I opened the safe we had protected from the Japs. It stood in a far corner of the bedroom just beneath the window. From the bottom shelf I removed the remaining pieces of jewellery which Mother-in-Law had once worn and caressed them with my fingers: the silver belts, gold brooches, and elaborate hairpins favoured by the Nyonyas as well as dangly earrings of uncertain provenance. I placed the pieces meticulously on the bed. Surely these would fetch enough; surely I would not have to dig into Mother's heirlooms on the top shelf. I folded the belts, separated the brooches from the hairpins, and put the earrings to one side. With Chang Ying's help, I found a wooden box into which we were able to fit the various pieces.

As I headed to the outer hall where Father usually rested in the afternoon, footsteps could be heard along our driveway. I opened the front door to see my brother-in-law Weng Yoon walking up. A fearful noise was coming from the other side of the road.

'Hello, Weng Yoon,' I said. 'Do you know what that noise is?'

'Yes, it's your gardener-lah, felling a rubber tree.'

'What, our Samad?'

I stood on tiptoe, trying to get a better view of the figure across the road. My brother-in-law, although thinner than he had been at the start of the war, still had a wide girth, and I could only see Samad when Weng Yoon turned his head. The gardener paid us no attention. He was holding a saw in both his hands and was busy forcing its teeth into the bark of a rubber tree.

Weng Yoon, meanwhile, pressed a red envelope into my hands with an uncertain smile. 'So sorry to hear the news, Big Sister. This is to help with . . . your expenses.'

For a minute I could not speak; I did not know what to say; everything that came into my head sounded banal and trite, especially the thank you I mumbled. Weng Yoon and I looked directly at one another for longer than normal. There was empathy in his clear brown eyes and, I hoped, gratitude in mine. He took leave with a nod of his head. When I went into our marital bedroom to open the envelope in privacy, I could not have anticipated the thousand dollars I found inside. I burst into tears.

Samad rode with me in the rickshaw to Patrick Street in Old Town where Mrs Ong Heng Lai, a modern lady of Nyonya descent who had been Mother-in-Law's business rival, lived. Mrs Ong no longer made a living out of selling the *kueh* or cakes for which the Nyonya community was famed, but she had become the mistress of a senior Japanese military officer. That, at least, was what was whispered.

'Ah, Mrs Wong, what a pleasure to see you!' she crowed, as if we were old friends. In truth, we had never spoken until then. Of course we knew of one another by reputation, such was Ipoh in those days. As soon as Mrs Ong opened her mouth, her high-pitched staccato began to grate on my nerves and her superficial manner made me wary. I remembered the words Mother-in-Law had whispered – 'I tell you, that one is a survivor' – in a voice of grudging respect. This was a compliment, coming as it did from a woman feared by the entire town. Once I was inside Mrs Ong's living room, I cursed myself for not having gone to a regular pawnbroker. By then retreat was too late. Besides, I needed the cash, and both Father and my friend Yik Wei had judged Mrs Ong to be the best person for the transaction I sought.

For the first fifteen minutes I endured the chatter and *kueh* which the Nyonya insisted on doling out. In between empty phrases, I stared at the sheer voile material of Mrs Ong's body-hugging kebaya blouse. Her cakes were sweet and rich, bursting with the sugar and eggs and coconut, which those of us who were less cunning could not have afforded.

Eventually Mrs Ong asked, 'So tell me, Mrs Wong, how I can help you-ah?'

I threw a plea in the direction of her sculpted eyebrows and heavily powdered cheeks and said, 'My husband is very ill, Mrs Ong, he has pneumonia. Maybe you know he is the Senior Engineer in the PWD, but he can't work anymore. And I – I need money to buy the drugs for him.'

Mrs Ong compressed her already narrow eyes further, unleashing webs of spidery wrinkles, like rays from the sun. There was a moment of silence during which the Nyonya studied me, as if I were an animal specimen and she a veterinarian about to dissect me in the laboratory.

'Have you brought security?' she finally asked, in a tone so frosty that I began to wonder if I had imagined her previous friendliness. I retrieved the wooden jewellery box from my handbag and placed it on the large coffee table. Opening the box in such a way that its top obscured the contents from Mrs Ong's direct gaze, I took out the delicate pieces one by one, starting with the golden hairpins.

'Wahh, what beautiful pieces! They belonged to your late mother-in-law, didn't they?'

I smiled. 'How much will you give me for them?'

'Let me see what else you have, Mrs Wong, and if I like the rest too, I can give you a price for them all. How about that?'

We exchanged an uncomfortable glance. In Mrs Ong's eyes I saw desire; in mine I hoped there was hard-headedness. She did not need to be generous; if she chose to play tough, what could I do? We both knew that only the desperate pawned their belongings. I took out the gold brooches first.

The encouraging noises which Mrs Ong made as each piece appeared became more circumspect. The change was highly unsubtle. Her lack of pretence niggled at me as I sat in her living room. Humiliation dried my throat so that I could barely speak. Every word became an effort. I kept telling myself to focus, that I could not afford to get angry. At one point, while caressing a brooch with a gemstone in the middle, Mrs Ong declared, 'Well, you know, Mrs Wong, there aren't many buyers of these luxuries now. Most people don't like the Nyonya look any more.'

'I know, Mrs Ong,' I replied, giving her a pleasant smile, 'but if there is someone in Ipoh who can appreciate jewellery as lovely as these pieces, it is you. Everyone says that you are the expert.'

The remark pleased Mrs Ong, whose tiny mouth curved into a smile exposing front teeth so white they could only have been new dentures.

She frowned, though, when I brought out the silver belts. 'I'm afraid, Mrs Wong, these belts are not really to my taste.'

I shot her a stony look. 'Very well,' I said, folding the belts and putting them back into my box. Mrs Ong made a hollow noise which sounded like a laugh, the sort that is afraid of showing itself; it ebbed as soon as it had begun, as if she had just swallowed her laughter whole.

'Mrs Wong, there is no need to put your belts back. I would be happy to relieve you of all your pieces. I'll give you four hundred for the lot.'

'Four hundred. Only four hundred?'

'Hah!' The woman emitted a snort. '*Only*, you say? Well, if you think someone else can give you a better price . . .'

By then it was already two o'clock. I did not have much time. I gave the woman my most ingratiating smile and said, 'Mrs Ong, you know I would prefer to sell these pieces to you, a Nyonya, rather than to one of those Chinamen pawnbrokers on Leech Street. Five hundred, and it's all yours.'

'Five hundred? Mrs Wong, you will do me out of a living! Really.' But I could tell that her resistance was half-hearted. I wished I had asked for more; what Mrs Ong paid me would barely have bought twenty of the M&B 693 pills for my husband.

As I handed Mother-in-Law's jewels over in exchange for a few miserable banana notes, I had a premonition that I would have to sell more jewellery in the future. I felt truly sullied, as though I had betrayed Mother-in-Law and was already selling my children short.

◆　◆　◆

By the time I returned to the District Hospital, Weng Yu's bed was empty. I found a nurse who told me that he had already been transferred to Batu Gajah. I was gripped by fear, not knowing when I would see my husband next or even whether I would see him again.

I was preoccupied by thoughts of how I could visit Batu Gajah when someone called out: 'Aunty, are you all right?'

I turned to find the nurse Lim Choy Yoke coming towards me along the long corridor. 'You look very pale,' the young woman said, peering at me with concern.

I had not seen the girl for many weeks. She was a qualified practitioner by then who left home each morning at an ungodly hour. Her mother, the voluble Mrs Lim, often complained about her daughter's dedication. For all her mother's grumblings, Choy Yoke seemed none the worse off; her figure remained fulsome and her cheeks bulged with pink flesh. As I looked at her, I realised that I had not eaten all day.

'I'm very hungry, Choy Yoke, and a bit tired,' I replied, suddenly overcome and unsteady on my feet. I yearned to lie down, but we had to get home first. Choy Yoke guided me by the arm to the main entrance of the hospital where Samad stood waiting under a rain tree. I was starting to get dizzy and did not take in the instructions that the nurse shouted out to our gardener before she patted my hard, rounded belly and sent us off.

The journey to our house only involved going down a few streets, but it felt as far as Singapore. Samad had to hold on to my arm while he dragged his bicycle along the tarmac. As we approached Abdul Jalil Road, a tug came from somewhere deep in my belly. I shrieked at the strange sensation, which felt as though roots had taken hold inside my body and become twisted. Yet it was not pain I felt but a pulling. The tug vanished after I put both my arms over the rounded crest of my belly and inhaled. Once the wrenching had passed, I wondered if I had imagined it.

By the time I finished eating the boiled sweet potato and stir-fried long beans that the servants set down before me, I had forgotten about the sensation. I lit a post-prandial cigarette and gave myself over to the buzz in my head. I thought about tuition fees and the money we would need for meals. I ruminated on medication, hospital bills, and the number of trips I could make to Batu Gajah. My head began to ache. In the back of my mind was the possibility that Weng Yu might not live, a thought which nearly choked me.

I went across the road to the patch Samad had cleared. The land did not belong to us. We were trespassing, but I was confident that if the owner showed up, we would be able to come to a reasonable agreement. I discussed with Samad how we should use this second plot. Our gardener wanted to grow sweet potato and yam, our staple foods, but I was full of worry for the imminent future when Weng Yu was away and we would have no money coming in. I argued in favour of fast-growing plants – the radishes, lettuces, green onions, and baby carrots I thought we could eat within days. Alas, I was to learn that farming rewards the patient: nature takes her time. I had to adjust my expectations, because even fast-growing plants took a month to harvest.

After Samad and I reached a compromise, I continued circling the garden. I knew that staring at ladies' fingers and turnips did not enhance their growth, but counting our harvest made me feel better. I became obsessed with manure, monitoring how much we produced and used. Each morning and evening saw me supervising the collection and distribution of our night soil, with strict reminders to the children to urinate at home if possible.

In the days after Weng Yu left for Batu Gajah, I could not concentrate on calligraphy. The brush felt like a dead weight in my hand, and the ink coagulated on my paper like putty. There was no fluidity in my composition. The daubs I made were unworthy of being called art, their heads too big, their corners rushed, and their tails blotchy. Even my straight lines were crooked or smudged. Father glanced at my rice paper without a word. When, after a fortnight, my calligraphy had not improved, he reminded me of the first writing lesson we'd ever had together. In a voice which brought tears to my eyes, Father said, 'Remember, Mei Foong, it's all in our minds. Free your mind, the rest will follow.'

20

BATU GAJAH HOSPITAL

2 April 1944

Dear Wife,
I am sorry I did not have the chance to say goodbye. What were you doing that afternoon that you came back so late?

It is miserable here. I have my own room, but there is a lot of noise during the day, with trolleys being wheeled and nurses coming and going. You would expect a hospital to be quiet at night, but it isn't. The nurses are forever taking my temperature or just poking their heads in — to make sure I'm alive, I suppose. The trouble is that as soon as the door creaks, I wake up. And then I can't sleep again.

The doctor, a Dr Foo, is worried about my appetite. I told him I would eat more if I were forced to drink less. Actually, I'm secretly glad I have to drink a lot of water. The food here is terrible, as bland as the food I had in London at the YMCA where I stayed before moving into lodgings. Chillies would solve the problem. But I'm not allowed too many chillies in the regime Dr Foo has put me on.

I take the M&B 693 four times a day and drink gallons of water. There is a large jug, which is refilled as soon as it's empty. I'm in pain from having to drink so much. Just when my stomach is most bloated, the nurses come in and order me out into the grounds. They tell me I need fresh air. I walk a little bit and then sit on a bench, listening to the birds. I wish I had music. I miss my arias and the sing-song group. If only Ipoh were not so far away.

There is something I want to tell you about. I have too much time on my hands. I find myself thinking about things I don't normally think about. There was a woman when I was in London. Her name was Helen. She was my age, the daughter of my landlord. She loved music, like me. She wore the same perfume you used to like, the one which smells of roses. I wanted to marry Helen, but Mama objected. I was very hurt by what happened, but all of that is in the past now. I only feel I should have told you before. If I get out of here, I will try to be a better husband. Forgive me.

With love,

Weng Yu

My hands shook as I read my husband's letter. I could not decide what he was trying to tell me. That he had loved another woman? Perhaps he had only ever loved her. I lit a cigarette and then another. In the days to follow I smoked incessantly. I took to walking around the garden and somehow always ended up at the hospital in search of Dr Pillay. On the third such visit, he said to me, 'Mrs Wong, it will take a while for the drug to work. How about this? I promise that I will come and see you as soon as I have news about your husband's health, okay? So, if you don't hear from me, it means I have no news.'

It was early afternoon when Dr Pillay sent me away from the hospital, one of those hot, steamy days when vapour rose off Green Town's tarmac roads. I had just passed the Women's and Girls' Home when I felt a tug in my belly. The pulling was harder than I had ever felt it, as violent as the stomach cramps I used to have before menstruation, when I was prostrate with pain. After a few minutes the spasm ceased, but it resumed minutes later with increased vigour. This time I also had an urge to pass water.

As soon as I reached our house I went to the latrine at the rear. Our latrine was a hole set on top of three cemented steps, beneath which sat an enormous bucket visible only from the outside. I tried to ignore the pain as I climbed up to the gods. I hoped my discomfort would be transient.

When I saw the blood spurting out, I screamed. My first thought was of fertiliser and whether Samad would be able to use our rich effluence if I dropped blood on to it. When the bleeding did not stop, I realised what was happening. My lips began to move in a slow yawning motion, opening and closing without a sound, until a chilling howl rose from my gut. It came without warning, this eerie noise I had never before in my life made. There was banging on the door, and Chang Ying's voice shouting, 'Ah Soh! Ah Soh!'

I managed to stand. I dug my fingernails into the walls and staggered down the steps. At the bottom I gasped and, with a pull, undid the metal clasp which kept the door locked. There was a large audience outside: Father, one or two of the servants, and my daughter, Lai Hin, all staring with panicked eyes. I became conscious of my sarong not yet pulled up, of the paleness of my legs held wide apart, and of the deep redness of the clots continuing to leak in viscous strings on to the grey kitchen floor.

The contractions began as I stood there. I doubled over and cried out while cradling the hardness of my belly with both hands. I could feel her heartbeat weakening; I knew she was dying. When the pulse of her movement stopped completely, I began to wail. She had shared my body for nearly twenty-eight weeks; I had to see her. I lay on the kitchen floor and refused to move. I was still in that position, whimpering, coughing, crying, and at the same time choking from the kitchen smells when Lim Choy Yoke and Matron arrived. They stood over me as Cecilia finally emerged, a tiny being smeared in a nest of bloody entrails. There was a great emptiness in me when I looked at her; I did not know how I could continue living. I caressed the little nose that was already formed and wept.

◆ ◆ ◆

The moon. The stars. The night sky. In the months to follow my thoughts comprised such shards, with no beginning and no end.

The disjointed ramblings came as I recorded the details of Cecilia's death, which in some way also marked her life, inside the exercise book with the big blue squares and the thin brown cover. Images of the girl I had held before she was placed into a casket assaulted my mind. Our daughter Cecilia, long and thin – thin of nose, long of face, a face like mine but with hair her very own, wisps the texture of angora, and on both hands the most diminutive of fingers.

After I lost her, I was aware that I had clung to her as though she were a beacon who would be special in some way, a child through whom my marriage to Weng Yu could be saved. After she died I felt stupid and helpless, and also guilty. Somehow, I must have done something that had killed her.

I did not know how to tell my husband. I would begin by writing, *Dear Husband*, but I could not continue; the words would not come. Or rather, I could never find the right words. It seemed easier to tell him about our new vegetable patch or what the children were being taught, anything except what was really weighing on me. I could not go to Batu Gajah; I did not have the strength. I made excuses to Weng Yu which sounded hollow even to me.

Not a single day passed when Cecilia was not on my mind. Even this morning, thirty-one years later, I woke up imagining what she might be doing if she were alive. She would be a young woman by now, perhaps married with her own children. I wonder whether she would have been fiery, like her sister Lai Hin, or calmer, like me.

When Hock San came to visit, I was still in distress. I had just returned from the hospital where I had to be admitted to have my womb scraped clean of every trace of Cecilia. I was resting in my bedroom when our servant Li-Fei put her head around the door and announced the arrival of Mr Chew. On her tongue his name sounded like an accusation.

'Mr Chew Hock San?' I said in surprise.

'Yes,' the servant replied, scowling. Disapproval darkened her face.

I went into the outer hall, where I found Hock San standing by the window. He had his back to me and was looking out at our flame-of-the-forest tree which happened to be in bloom. He turned when he heard me enter. There was no mockery in his slanted eyes; instead they were filled with concern. His demeanour was serious and could even have been called grave. He did not smile until I smiled at him. In his large hands he carried a book with a dark-green cover.

'Mr Chew, long time no see.'

'How are you, Mrs Wong? Sorry to hear about your husband-lah. And you . . . I hear that you also not been well, true-ah?'

I looked carefully at Hock San. When I saw that his sympathy was genuine, I sighed and said, 'Yes Mr Chew, I – ah, the baby I was carrying, she passed away.' My mind drifted as I said this, back to those endless minutes on the kitchen floor when I had felt life draining out of me.

There was silence. Hock San seemed taken aback by my directness. Eventually he mumbled, 'I'm sorry, Mrs Wong, really, I – ah . . .'

We stood awkwardly, both of us colouring, not knowing where to look or put our hands. It was not a subject a woman would have discussed with someone she did not know well, and a man at that.

I found my tongue when I realised that our guest had been offered no refreshment. 'Please, come through into the inner hall,' I said, gesturing to a room on the other side of the vestibule. 'What would you like to drink? Tea, or maybe water? It's hot today, isn't it?'

'No need for a drink, thanks. I came to see how you were, Mrs Wong. And here, I brought you a small gift.' He held up the hardback book so that the golden peacock and the title on its cover were visible.

'*Pride and Prejudice!*'

Hock San reddened as if embarrassed. 'I thought, well, that it would give you something to do, you know, as you aren't well enough to go out. Your brother-in-law Liew Chin Tong, said you enjoyed reading. I hope you like it.'

'Yes, yes,' I said, rather loudly, excited by the gift. Father was the only person who had ever given me a book, and I felt extraordinarily grateful. 'Second Brother-in-Law was right; I do like reading. I've been going through the literary classics recently. I go next door to Dorcourt, you know. I . . .'

I stopped to smile, hoping to convey my pleasure. I was not going to tell Hock San that Jane Austen was the classical author I liked least. Nothing seemed to happen in her books; characters merely moved from one drawing room to the next, or possibly into a parlour or a ballroom. With their large noses and fair skin, the obtuse hints in which they spoke were interspersed by the author's caustic narrative. 'It's called irony, Grandma,' one of my grand-daughters would one day say, 'and Jane Austen is a genius at it.' Austen was clearly too clever for me.

Looking at Chew Hock San, who stood grinning, I could not imagine him opening a book by Jane Austen. 'Do you enjoy reading, Mr Chew?'

'Oh no, I never read,' he replied, and when I asked, rather sharply, 'Never?' he took on an injured air. He caressed the stray hairs on his chin which had been missed by the razor blade and mumbled, 'I don't have the time, Mrs Wong.'

I knew that Chew Hock San did not sing or play music, and was therefore surprised to hear that he also did not read. I could not imagine such a life.

'What do you enjoy, Mr Wong?'

Hock San cast his eyes on the floor. 'Well, I play badminton.'

Something about the way in which he said this made me think that he had dreamt up his answer in the preceding seconds. It seemed best to stop probing. Hock San was equally keen to talk about other things. Lifting his eyes from the parquet floor he had begun to say, 'About your brother-in-law,' when Father hobbled in.

Hock San and I exchanged helpless glances which Father may have caught, though he merely acknowledged Hock San's greetings with a wide, toothless smile. As soon as the latter had left our house, however, Father looked at me with questioning eyes. I waited for Father to ask what must have been on the tip of his tongue, but he remained immobile in his usual chair, stroking the two-inch goatee which fell below his chin.

Chew Hock San turned up again within days. Under his arm he was holding yet another book, this one a thick tome with Chinese writing on its cloth cover. I had anticipated this visit and had already determined what we would do. As soon as he arrived I said, 'Mr Chew, good afternoon, you were asking about fast-growing vegetables. Come! Let me show you what Samad has done.'

I whisked him to the other side of the road. When we were out of earshot I whispered, 'What were you going to tell me the other day?'

219

Hock San knelt to touch one of our lettuces. 'I got news from a . . . let's just say he's a friend. Chin Tong and Miss Liew are safe. They're now part of a unit based here in Perak.'

'What, they're here? In this state?'

Hock San looked up. 'Yes,' he said quietly. And then, more stoutly, 'Your lettuces are big and fat. What does Samad feed them with?'

I smiled. 'If I told you, I'd be giving away a secret.'

We moved to the next raised bed where our gardener had planted green onions whose shoots stuck out of the ground in neat rows. Hock San bent down again; when he spoke, his voice was barely audible. 'My friend tells me the tide has turned, the Japs are losing the war. They've lost in India.'

I went down on my haunches so that my face was at the same height as Hock San's. 'How does your friend know?' I asked, breathing heavily in the heat. I was so close to him that I could smell his sweat as we both squatted, partially shielded from view by green onion shoots, his right knee almost touching mine.

Without flinching, he said, 'I can't tell you that. I'm sorry.' When he placed his right hand on my left knee, I jerked from the spark which flew between us. Hock San did not remove his hand but kept it where it was. Continuing to look straight into my eyes, he began caressing my kneecap. Desire ripped through me, and I nearly fell over. I had not known how violent passion could be. I remember Hock San saying my name, maybe even more than once.

◆ ◆ ◆

Afterwards, a spell was broken. As we crossed the road, Hock San trailed behind me and I sensed prying eyes. I could not see anyone at Dorcourt's windows nor behind the louvred windows of our outer hall, but they must have been there, watching. Husna next door was the only person who declared her interest: she swept down her driveway in a long tunic and skirt, throwing me a quizzical look.

I waved. 'Is something the matter, Husna?'

'No, no, Puan Wong, not at all, sorry, I thought Mr Wong had come home . . .'

'Unfortunately, Weng Yu is not back yet. This is Mr Chew, a family friend. I was just showing him our garden opposite.'

I smiled as the two shook hands. Husna seemed uncomfortable at being introduced to a man who was not my husband, but whether the embarrassment was for herself or for me, I could not tell. She asked how Weng Yu was. I assured her that he was better, although progress had been slow. He would be home any day now.

◆ ◆ ◆

The book Hock San had brought was a Chinese classic – *Dream of the Red Chamber*. My father, who owned a copy, had been the first to pique my curiosity with it. At the precocious age of thirteen, I had removed the book without permission from the shelves of our home library, determined to work my way through its one hundred and twenty chapters as a sort of literary challenge. If I'm honest, I was far too young to appreciate the novel's subtleties, but nothing was going to stop me. When I put the book down after a year, its cast of characters – so numerous as to be uncountable – immediately became a blur.

Hock San's gift was second hand, its pages yellowed, some even torn, and many with scribbles on their margins. When I started reading the novel, however, I realised how much more I appreciated it as an adult. I was transported to a different realm, a land peopled by magical stones and complex women who mirrored some I knew in real life. I had forgotten the book's richness: the many myths I had heard as a child, the tenets of Buddhist-Taoism that Mother had instilled, the filial piety I grew up with and which was my duty, and even the shrill operatic music which made pinpricks crawl on my skin – all of this I found between the book's pages. When I realised that the central story involved a love triangle between a man and two women, I wondered whether Chew Hock San was trying to convey a hidden message.

On his next visit he stood rather stiffly outside our front door, his large hands clasped together.

'Good morning, Mrs Wong. I know you're busy, I won't stay long. I just want to say, if you like to play mah-jong sometimes and you need someone to go with you . . .'

Hock San stopped speaking. He looked at me directly, without reticence, burrowing into the depths of my eyes. I remembered the heat of his hand on my knee and coloured.

'I – ah – good . . .'

'How about this Sunday? You want to go then?'

I was startled by Hock San's decisiveness and agreed perhaps too readily. I had not visited the Foong Seong since my husband had been sent to the hospital in Batu Gajah. Indeed I had not gone on an outing that was not also an errand. The prospect of a few hours of pleasure was enticing. Father, who stood eavesdropping in the outer hall, frowned; he did not reprimand me, but I knew he was not pleased.

Chew Hock San became a familiar sight on our street on Sundays. We would head to the Foong Seong Villa on Laxamana Road at ten in the morning and return by six. Although we were fodder for whispers, I could not stay in Green Town writing calligraphy and perusing Dorcourt's library every single day. Mah-jong was a perfect foil to help me take my mind off Cecilia and my husband's illness and what our lives had become.

I thought the gossip would cease once it became clear that my rides with Hock San were quite proper. He would cycle while I rode pillion, and we chatted as we meandered through Ipoh's increasingly potholed roads. He told me stories about his childhood in a village near Taiping in northern Perak, funny stories which made me laugh. When he spoke about his family, on the other hand, I wanted to cry: they had been so poor that his mother would squeeze droplets of water out of the vegetables she bought in the market, to make them weigh less so she could save half a cent. This,

222

apparently, made a difference to their next meal. In such circumstances, having electric light was out of the question: like many others at the time, Hock San struggled with his homework in front of a kerosene lamp. There were celebrations when he gained a secondary school certificate, and from an English-speaking school no less – a fact he revealed with undisguised pride, as if to let me to know that, in his own way, he had achieved no less than my husband. We reverted eventually to walking beside one another – it made conversation easier. I learnt that he did actually play badminton and even teamed up occasionally with Miss Lee, the woman in my husband's sing-song group who preferred male attire to frocks and who was Miss Mak's companion. Miss Lee, who had been a badminton champion before the Japs arrived, could still humble most players in the state.

On our third walk I began to confide in Hock San. The words rushed out like air from a ruptured balloon. I told him how distraught I had been at losing Cecilia, at a time when my husband was not even present. Hock San listened attentively, not once interrupting me or grimacing at details or evincing judgment at the folly of not telling my husband. When Hock San put his hand on mine, the gesture seemed natural and full of warmth, and once again I felt the heat of his large hand. I liked his broad shoulders too; when I stood next to him I realised that he was less stocky than he appeared, it was simply his physicality which filled the space. He eventually dropped his enormous hands back to his sides, and we continued walking in companionable silence. The man's irrepressible joviality soon returned, however, and that walk, like all our other walks, ended on a high note.

A few days later, Father asked me to show him around our garden. He wished, he said, to inspect the new vegetables Samad had planted. Despite Father's legs having become noticeably weaker, he had retained his stubborn spirit and insisted on struggling by himself to the other side of our road. When we reached the additional rows of raised beds, Father nodded in satisfaction. 'Nice fat radishes,' he murmured. His voice, though not as powerful as it had once been, remained perfectly audible; when he turned to announce that he should perhaps have spoken to me before, I was worried that he could be heard in both Dorcourt and Ja'afar's house.

'Daughter, people will talk.' After a second's pause he added, 'It was one thing accompanying you home when your husband was here. But now, with Weng Yu in hospital, how can you go off gambling in the arms of another man?'

'Father!'

'Well, Daughter, I've seen you. You look forward to his visits. That's true, isn't it?'

I looked at Father's cotton-wool hair and balding crown and the back that now hunched over a well-loved walking stick. I wondered why he had not taken me aside before.

'Father, please do not worry. I go with him because I wouldn't get the chance to go out otherwise.'

'I hope that is all there is to it, Mei Foong, I really do.'

The look which Father cast in my direction, so full of remorse, made me feel truly sorry. I vowed to be more cautious from then on.

A few weeks afterwards, Dr Pillay came to tell us that Weng Yu had recovered enough to be released from hospital. My husband would not be allowed to work for another month, but he could continue his recuperation at home.

I promised the good doctor that when this nightmare of an occupation was over and life had returned to normal, he would have to come to our house for a proper meal, one which included chicken and fish and white rice. Had it not been for Dr Pillay, we might never have secured the precious antibiotics which saved my husband's life. The doctor was turning to depart when a question popped out of my mouth.

'Dr Pillay, what do you think about this business of Indian independence?'

Through March, April, and May of 1944, Malai's newspapers had been abuzz with the Japanese invasion of India. The object was apparently to rid India of the British so that, with Japanese support, Indians could govern their own country. Malaya's Indians were in ecstasy. I had seen Dr Pillay many times while the events were unfolding, but had never asked his opinion.

Dr Pillay stopped smiling and became rather guarded.

'Dr Pillay, I hope you don't mind my asking. We've known each other a long time.'

He sighed. 'It's all right, Mrs Wong. I was in favour at one point, now I'm less sure.'

He smiled once more, his large ears twitching.

'And why have you changed your mind?'

There was no one else in the room, Father being in the middle of his afternoon nap, but Dr Pillay nonetheless felt compelled to lower his voice. 'We have to get independence by ourselves, Mrs Wong, not with the shorties. They're losing in India. It's over for them.'

Dr Pillay was echoing what Hock San had told me, and yet, just the previous day, the *Shimbun* headlines had read, 'Our Forces Ready for Big Offensive Against Imphal', as if the Japs were about to gain this city in north-eastern India.

'I tell you, Mrs Wong,' Dr Pillay continued, 'it's over for them. They've lost in India. Personally, I think the tide may have turned. I think the British will soon be back.'

'The British? Really? You think so?'

At the thought of British rulers reigning once more in Ipoh town, I was filled with a relief I never imagined possible. Dr Pillay and I stood peering out of the louvred windows in the outer hall, trying to catch a glimpse of the skies beyond the flame-of-the-forest. We smiled at one another, each looking forward to the day when Allied planes would be heard in the great expanse overhead.

PART V

21

On the morning Weng Yu was to be released from hospital, I rose with the first crow of our cockerels. I had not been able to sleep. I was unsettled by the prospect of seeing my husband, at once thrilled by the promise in his letter, but conscious also of Cecilia. I had not managed to tell him about her passing away.

My hand trembled as I held the handle of my coffee cup. I lit a cigarette and smoked it while taking small sips of the dark, aromatic liquid. Li-Fei sized me up with her shrewd eyes. I turned away to shield my dread from her.

With my mind elsewhere, time flew by. Samad and I took twice as long to gather the vegetables, even though I already knew what we would pluck – stringy long beans, the juiciest of our brinjals, leafy Chinese broccoli, and plenty of ginger, onions, garlic, chillies and lemongrass with which to flavour the dishes we would prepare. The table would be full of my husband's favourite food. This was a homecoming meal I wanted him to remember.

We arrived late at Ipoh's Central Market. In hindsight, we should have gone to the grocery store first. But my maid, Chang Ying, had persuaded me to finish the morning in Belfield Street at the grocery shop, where I had reserved two tins of butter and a tin of jam. This last would just be a quick stop to allow me to pick up the goods, and then it was a straightforward jaunt home.

I was excited about the butter and jam I had ordered. We'd hardly had butter or jam since the Japs arrived. I knew how much my husband adored his Western breakfast, his fried eggs and pork sausages and the toast, which he ate with butter and jam. Western sausages were impossible to come by, but I could at least procure the butter and jam, though the condiments would cost us dearly. When I'd visited Mr Chee, the grocer, the previous week, his manner was mild until I began bargaining, at which point the wily man had turned into an unmoveable buffalo. Lacking Mother-in-Law's hard-headedness, I ended up pawning more jewellery.

That was when the reality of our lives sank in. I was conscious that Mother-in-Law's safe was almost depleted. There were only two gold bracelets left, lying forlornly on the bottom shelf, and on the top was a gift I really did not wish to part with, a delicate necklace Mother had given me, made of eighteen-carat gold with a sumptuous jade stone at its heart. It had been Mother's farewell present, picked out when she was already ill and knew that she would not live. I had nothing left from her except for my wooden fan. Whenever I held Mother's necklace in my hand, which I did from time to time, I would think of how, despite her sternness and her pencil-thin lips that were always pursed shut, she had loved me.

I could not stop thinking about her as I followed Chang Ying around the market. Part of me took in the crowd, wondering where these people – and there were many of them that morning at the market – found the money to buy as much as they did. My mind, though it flitted, remained mostly on Mother and her necklace. For the first time, I appreciated the care with which she had chosen the jade on the necklace. The stone was almost perfect in its texture and colour, an ethereal green devoid of white veins, a gem forged by the heat of the Earth over millions of years.

I trudged behind my maid, feeling both an outsider and a novice. I was jostled on all sides as we continued along the dark, grimy corridors. I swore to myself that I would part with Mother's necklace only if we were starving and I had nothing else to sell. I wanted to be able to give the piece to Lai Hin when she came of age.

We eventually reached the fish section, where the smell seeped into my nostrils and I could no longer daydream. The place had not changed: there was still that hard grey floor, slippery from blocks of melting ice, and a pungency which lodged itself in my consciousness, so that long after Chang Ying had put the black pomfrets into her basket and we had left the fish section, there remained the metallic taste of scales on my tongue. I could not wait to rinse my mouth.

Next, we waited at the pork seller's stall. It amazed me how long everything took, that buying two pomfrets and half a catty of pork could consume so much time. I knew then that we would be late at the grocery store, but it seemed best not to hurry the scrawny Cantonese pork seller as he wielded his huge cleaver. I watched him slice pieces of belly from part of the carcass lying on his stall table. My husband would have fainted at the sight of the man's sharp knives; even I feared for the butcher's fingers, the way he sawed and snipped with such gusto.

We walked into the grocer's shop two hours later than I had said we would. Mr Chee shot me a wistful look from behind the counter. There was someone else in the shop – a woman, hovering near some shelves on one side. I did not notice her at first among the mountain of tins, tubes, and cartons stacked from floor to ceiling, which was the way with Malayan grocery stores then or even today, now that I come to think of it. Despite suffering from desperate shortages in those days, Mr Chee's shop managed to maintain its trademark dishevelled look.

'I've come for the butter and jam I reserved last week, Mr Chee,' I said, smiling. The grocer looked uncharacteristically gloomy.

'Mrs Wong, I'm sorry but I – er, I thought you weren't coming.'

From the shelves near the right-hand side of the store came a slight cough and the shuffling of feet. I recalled this only later; at that moment it was the grocer who claimed my full attention.

'What do you mean, Mr Chee?'

He cleared his throat. 'Umm, well, I had expected you here at nine o'clock, you see. And so, when you had not showed up by ten forty-five, I was no longer sure you wanted the goods. And there was someone else asking for butter and jam. I – look, maybe you women can work it out between you. Mrs Chew is still here.'

She emerged like a phoenix from among the boxes of red candles, joss-sticks, silver paper, and underworld money near which she had been standing. I had not seen Chew Hock San's wife since our sojourn into the jungles of Lahat, but she looked almost exactly as I remembered her, slightly older of course, and thinner. In fact Kit Mei was almost gaunt, but with her dark glowing skin and pale lips she had retained a certain rustic beauty. The years had given her both grace and a degree of bitterness. She kept her pale lips twisted resolutely downwards and at the same time held her head higher and her neck straighter. She did not move; it was clear I would have to go to her.

'Kit Mei,' I said in Cantonese, thrusting out my hand. 'How nice to see you! How are you?'

She emitted a raucous laugh. 'What a question! Tell me, Mrs Wong, how do you think I would be, ah?'

She looked at me coldly, eyes blazing, black mole thrust forward.

I was taken aback by her shrillness. From behind the counter, Mr Chee stared in stupefaction and with unbridled curiosity. I coloured, unable to think what to say. And then I remembered the tins of butter and jam.

'Mrs Chew, my husband has been very sick. With pneumonia. He is coming back today from Batu Gajah Hospital. The butter and jam you have taken is meant for him-lah. I reserved them last week with Mr Chee. Please, can I have at least one tin of butter? Mr Chee can get more for you in a few days.'

'Mr Chee can get more for me-ah? Is that right?'

'Mrs Chew, think of it like this: if I had not reserved them with Mr Chee, he would not have had butter and jam today, ready for you to buy.'

'What? You think just because you reserve means they are yours, ah? Hah? Like that-ah?' Kit Mei's cheeks were puffed up and her eyes watery. Her speaking voice, normally subdued, had become strident.

'Mrs Chew, please,' I said, in the pleading tone I only used with the Japs. 'I need the butter. And the jam too. But they are not for myself, I need them for my sick husband.'

Kit Mei hissed, 'And I need my husband, Mrs Wong. Have you ever thought about that? Stinking cunt!'

Without warning, she lunged. I screamed until her hands found my neck, at which point they squeezed hard and I could no longer breathe, could not even croak. I began gasping and coughing. My arms flailed as I spluttered. Out of the corners of my eyes, I caught sight of Samad and Chang Ying standing nearby, wide-eyed, and wondered why they were not moving to help me. The woman had gone mad. Could they not see that? Kit Mei released my neck but then dug her nails into my bare arms. Her nails were short but sharp, like a lioness's claws; I felt the pain moments later, when round droplets oozed out and began to flow, streaking my arm in trails of red.

At last the others acted to pull Kit Mei away. Somehow, between Mr Chee and Samad on one side and Chang Ying on the other, the crazed woman was separated from me. I could no longer think about butter or jam. I wanted most of all to get home.

◆ ◆ ◆

As I washed the blood off my arm, I imagined the grocer telling his wife and children about what had taken place in his shop that day. 'Guess what,' he would begin, with a glazed look in his eyes, 'there was a fight between two women. Yes, two women! One is the wife of that British-trained architect, the other the wife of some clerk in the civil service. The fight was about him, the clerk. Can you imagine? The women really went for each other. I had to mop blood off the floor.'

I shivered inside our marital bedroom, cold and miserable. While I undressed and put on fresh clothing, I could hear Mr Chee's deep voice droning on, adding embellishments here and there as people tend to do. Gossip was what Ipoh thrived on; the scene in the store would be my undoing. I did not want to think how the tale would spread.

I headed to the kitchen. Sprawled out on the large table under the air well was the feast I had planned for Weng Yu. There were vegetables fresh from our garden lined up on the preparation table, with their roots and clumps of soil removed, and on an enamel plate lay one of our fattest chickens, its feathers already plucked and its stretchy white skin exposed, ready for chopping up. While surveying all of this, I realised I could not stay inside the house; I was simply too nervous, given to pacing up and down, my fingers fidgety. Chang Ying glanced furtively at me. I was glad it had been she who had accompanied us to the grocery store, not Li-Fei. Chang Ying would keep the incident to herself.

I went into the garden, to look at our onions and garlic and glorious greens. I began to count, estimating how long the supplies would last. When I worked out the answer, I felt a surge of pride: not only were we feeding ourselves well, but we were close to being self-sufficient. Almost everything on our table had been produced with our own sweat and ingenuity, which seemed to me a considerable achievement. Until the Japs arrived, we had been town dwellers who never imagined we would have to till the soil, yet there we were, managing a small farm, which even included chickens. If I'd had my way, we would have added goats and pigs too, but Samad told me that we had no room.

At the sound of a motor engine, my heart jolted. It was a sound I had expected for many hours, but when I finally heard it, I had trouble breathing. The moment had come; I could no longer hide behind the spinach and the brinjals. A dilapidated black Ford pulled on to the driveway. When I saw my husband in the front passenger seat, I rushed across the road, screaming with such excitement that Dora, Rokiah, and Ali came scrambling over from Dorcourt.

The driver who had brought my husband was a curly haired Indian man who looked positively fat beside my husband. I exchanged a horrified glance with Dora, scarcely believing how much weight Weng Yu had lost and how he grimaced even while pulling himself out of the car. No one knew what to say.

'Master, you so thin! We must fatten you up!'

It was Li-Fei who had shouted, the same old Li-Fei who claimed to be blind. As far as I could tell, she pretended not to see the things she preferred not to see; on anything of interest, her vision remained as sharp as an eagle's. A biting remark came into my mind, but I knew that if I let it loose, I would only sour the atmosphere without achieving anything. Li-Fei had been in the Wong household for much longer than I had, a fact she liked to remind me of through petty glances and enduring silences. She let me know that she had seen my husband grow up and would always look out for his interests.

Weng Yu beamed at his servant's little joke. The illness had brought a new haggardness to his face: creases radiated out of the corners of both eyes, and his pallor was an unhealthy grey, the colour of ash and cinders. Where his cheeks had once been, there were now hollows. The clarity with which I saw all of this when I went to him, to take his hands in mine, brought tears into my eyes. Swallowing, I said, 'Husband, you must make sure you eat properly.' I was even afraid to hold his wrists, which had become delicate and bird-like.

My husband smiled. He seemed moved by the moment, and by my concern. Tenderness suffused his face, especially when he smiled, as if being alone and near death in Batu Gajah had made him realise what was dear to him. When he squeezed my hand, a shock ran through his meagre body. His eyes at once darted about, in a thorough movement like the vigorous sweep of a steam iron which took my body in greedily.

With that single glance Weng Yu's face changed; a scowl came over it and his lips straightened. He searched my eyes for an instant before his flitted away to the distance, where they settled on the burgeoning farm I had created. There was surprise on his face, but also displeasure and his eyes turned steely. I could feel him retreating away from me into some unknowable distance a galaxy away, a place I knew I could never reach. I begged him not to go, with my eyes I pleaded and also with my soul, but it was too late.

The next moment Weng Yu's habitual look had returned, the one in which he blamed me for something. He adopted his customary posture, with his head tilted up so that he looked down on us. A fine hair inside his left nostril was visible.

'Why aren't the children at school? Is Mrs Chan still tutoring them?'

The questions, which were unexpected, sounded like barks, sullen and resentful. I could see that Dora, who stood behind my husband, was startled by their peremptory nature.

'Husband, you know that Mrs Chan has been teaching Wai Sung and Lai Hin. It's going very well – but please, let's talk about that later. First, you must come inside.'

When Dora heard the way I placated Weng Yu, as I would have a petulant child, her eyes flashed disapproval. She managed her own husband differently, but Dora's stout Protestant manner would never have suited me.

Weng Yu, for his part, feigned dull indifference. Perhaps he really did not care. It was not usual for him to ask after the children, whom he regarded as my domain, but now he called out to our eldest son, Wai Sung, who stood grinning in his Japanese army cap. When the boy went up to his father, Weng Yu stroked his head.

'Wong Wai Sung, my eldest son. You will be the head of this family after me. You will continue the family name.'

My husband's lips contorted into a satisfied curl as he spoke. He released a sigh and began walking towards the front door. He was forced to take baby steps, despite two men supporting his arms, Samad on one side and the Indian driver on the other. I followed closely behind, stunned by the little speech my husband had given. Weng Yu had never articulated traditional Chinese ideas, at least not to me. The smell of the hospital, with its disinfectants and its medicines and its bitterness, clung to his clothes. The vapour would trail him for weeks.

'Would you like something to eat, Husband?'

'No.' The reply was swift and gruff.

'Do you want to listen to music?'

He did not answer, though he followed me into the inner hall. I asked Ah Hong to bring a glass of water and also a glass of lime juice into which she was to stir two teaspoons of sugar. I would explain to my husband how precious sugar had become. I would tell him about our new garden plot, how we saved the manure and had trained ourselves to waste nothing. I would remind him that our children learned from old British textbooks; he would be so proud. There was also Cecilia to speak about. For that we would need time. And music.

I helped Weng Yu into his favourite armchair. 'Close your eyes and relax. I will put on the records for you,' I said softly. He looked up at me, eyes brimming with gratitude, and nodded.

I went to the record cabinet to retrieve Mozart's *Le Nozze di Figaro*, a special recording my husband had procured for which he had paid a handsome sum. I chose an aria we both liked and had often listened to, an easy, lilting tune, which I thought would lift his spirits and free my tongue. When 'Voi Che Sapete' came on, my husband began to hum, moving his head in time with the tune. An expression of tranquillity came over his face; his jaw and cheeks relaxed. I had planned to mention Cecilia once the aria had faded, but by then my husband's eyes were closed and it seemed easier to let him rest. Another aria came on, then another; by the time Weng Yu fell asleep, I had not said any of the things I had been storing for weeks. The afternoon passed in the same way the rest of my life seemed to be passing, running away in a direction I had never intended.

◆ ◆ ◆

Later on, the rains came. The drops pelted down hard and fast, making a terrific noise against the corrugated roof of our air well. The children sat cowed; they understood without having to be told that the old rule of not speaking at meals would be reinstated. Conversation during our celebratory dinner was stilted. Even after the thunder and lightning had subsided, no one wanted to speak.

From across the dining table, Father watched us anxiously. Now and again the old man frowned. Finally, he said, 'Son, were there many people at the hospital? Did you make friends?'

Weng Yu stopped rolling his sweet potato.

'You know that Batu Gajah Hospital was a European hospital before the war, don't you, Father? I had my own room.'

I cringed at Weng Yu's sarcasm. Father, on the other hand, sat with Zen-like equanimity, without any outward sign of being riled, but at the same time not taking his eyes off my husband even for a second.

'Hmm, yes, indeed yes,' Father replied, nodding slowly. 'And of course Mei Foong told me what you wrote to her. But you never mentioned friends. I thought perhaps you might have met someone else, another patient, for example?'

The pause which followed lasted so long that I thought Weng Yu was not going to reply. That would have been too great an affront, and even my husband did not dare.

Eventually, he said, clearly with great reluctance, 'There was a Chinese man. I used to see him in the garden sometimes when I went for walks. We would both sit on the benches and stare at the trees.'

'And what about your—'

'Father, I'm very sorry . . .'

My husband's voice trailed in the air; he seemed truly agitated, on the verge of breaking down. There was a mortifying silence around the table. The electric lights accentuated Weng Yu's gauntness and made him somehow diminished. I understood then that the agony, the sheer misery that was etched into his face, went beyond illness. The weeks I had spent in distress over Cecilia now seemed self-indulgent. I was full of guilt and remorse.

'I really don't want to talk about the hospital. I'm home now,' Weng Yu added in a whisper. 'That's what's important.'

I could have hugged my husband at that moment. I began telling him about the land opposite our house. 'We now grow most of what we eat. What do you think of that?'

Weng Yu half-smiled, half-grunted as he helped himself to a spoonful of minced pork steamed in beaten egg.

'We should take a walk after dinner. I can show you what we've done. The neighbours come and look at Samad's vegetable beds – they want to learn our secrets. You must see our chickens too, so happy and fat.'

Weng Yu chewed contentedly on the drumstick I had saved him. His appetite was hearty for a man so skinny. When he finished the chicken leg, he used his fingers to fashion yet another piece of sweet potato into a ball. I realised how much I had missed watching his sculpted fingers work: he was the only one in our house who had adopted the Malay tradition of eating with his hands. As long as he enjoyed the food we prepared, it mattered less to me that he and I did not speak. He bit into the crunchy pak choi before turning to the eggs, which our most prolific hen, Flora, had laid. By the end of the meal, Weng Yu's plate was swept clean.

Afterwards he agreed to tour the garden with me. I was delighted, but also afraid. The rain had brought renewed vigour to our plants, giving each leaf an emerald glow. The air smelled of cleansed earth.

As I held my husband's forearm, his bones dug into my skin. He was not emaciated, but he was feeble and extraordinarily fragile next to me. Despite this, he clearly resented having to hold my arm, as if being supported by his wife was a sign of weakness. Beside a bed of marrows, Weng Yu nearly fell. He tried to shake off my arm; when he realised that he could not, his face turned black. He grabbed my baggy Chinese trousers, at the same time gnashing his teeth and emitting choice Hakka words.

We did not speak until we reached the chicken coop. Weng Yu had calmed down by then. He said nothing about our vegetables, but laughed when I told him that we had given our prized hen a name – Flora. Flora had beautiful feathers in different shades of brown. She seemed to know her name and would run forward when called. She would sit while the children stroked her, like a treasured pet.

Weng Yu smiled indulgently at this story. The next minute his face turned red, and he asked, in a bristling tone, 'Wife, why didn't you tell me?'

'Husband, I . . .'

I felt suddenly stupid. As soon as I thought of Cecilia, I found I could not speak. But then I looked at my husband, who stood before me just skin and bone, and I was moved by pity.

'I told you about Helen,' he blurted out, his voice caustic. 'But you . . .' – at this point he shook a forefinger at me – 'how dare you keep something like that from me. This was my child.' The smirk on Weng Yu's face concealed a simmering violence. I could feel its volcanic force and feared he would erupt unless I took great care.

'Forgive me, Husband,' I said, deciding to tell him everything. I would continue even if he became angry, no matter how pathetic I sounded. 'I wrote it down many, many times, but the words all seemed . . . useless. I couldn't send the letters.'

In an imploring tone I recounted how I'd told the servants to burn the missives in the wood fire in the kitchen.

Weng Yu stared at me with disdain. 'You had no right not to tell me. You are my wife. You have no right to keep secrets from me.'

I looked him in the eye to make sure I had not made a mistake. His irises were brown and clear, the whites surrounding them full of implacable hardness and righteous anger. It dawned on me, with something akin to an earthquake, that the man to whom I had been married for eleven years was more traditional than I'd ever imagined.

'Husband,' I said haltingly, 'since when have you kept such old-fashioned ideas?'

Weng Yu's laugh was filled with scorn. 'No husband wants to be a laughing stock. Even an Englishman would object. It's a universal idea.'

'Husband, I should have told you sooner. Forgive me. But as for secrets, you know, it's not always easy to tell everything at once.'

'Why? Are you keeping something else from me?' he asked, rather sharply.

'No, of course not.'

He seemed satisfied by my response, which had come quite naturally and without guile. When my husband took my arm, a faint smile graced his dimpled cheeks. He had said his piece; we could now go inside.

When I helped him undress, I finally saw the toll his illness had taken. Weng Yu, though a slim man, had never had bones sticking out at his front and sides. Running a finger along a rib, I said, 'Husband, we really must feed you.'

I was close to weeping. After my husband fell asleep, I continued to lie awake, besieged by a feeling that I did not really know the man I had married. The good-looking British-trained architect who appeared at our house had seemed westernised, and yet the more I thought about it, the more I realised that Weng Yu's British ideas were limited to superficial things, such as the clothes he wore and the breakfasts he ate. Of course, he read English books and listened to Western music, but the values he held dear were not that different from my own Confucian ones. As the eldest son, my husband was deemed head of the entire Wong family; as the man in our house, he was naturally the head of ours, a position that had never been up for discussion. Weng Yu regarded all of this as quite fitting. I myself was not sure where I stood on the thorny issue of equality between men and women, though I knew I did not like the way my husband condescended to us. It wasn't that he did not like women; on the contrary, Weng Yu was fond of female company, and even fonder of feminine beauty, so long as the sources of such pleasure did not challenge him.

When his mother had tried, soon after his return from London, to question his business ideas, Weng Yu sulked for weeks – she had told me this herself. Mother-in-Law had managed a thriving business selling Nyonya *kueh* for nearly forty years, yet Weng Yu never once sought her advice, deferring instead to other men. Perhaps my husband had felt threatened. His own mother was a force larger than life, her words more piquant than the most fiery of chillies. She had been the head of Weng Yu's family even when her husband was alive, a fact she relayed to me one memorable afternoon when I went to seek her help with my husband's gambling debts. While outlining a course of action, she recounted her own marriage. I listened in stupefaction, unable to imagine Weng Yu ever handing me his income month after month.

My husband, I realised with a touch of horror, was actually quite old-fashioned. We even addressed one another in the traditional Chinese fashion, instead of calling each other by name, as Weng Yoon and Dora did next door. Watching the rise and fall of Weng Yu's chest, I was astounded I had not noticed before. How blind I had been during our courtship, and so naive! I thought back to those halcyon days and to our wedding – a wondrous celebration that had been the talk of Ipoh town. Father had footed the bill for the festivities, of course, in the same way that he had paid to install us in a rented house. Though Father never breathed a word, I knew that he gave plenty of work to Weng Yu over the years to ensure that we were well-provided for. Another radical thought struck me then, so forcefully that I felt as if my spine had been spliced. Goose pimples erupted all over my skin. I had always thought that I'd made a good match with my marriage, which was certainly what everyone else also supposed, but Wong Weng Yu had made an even better one. With Father as his backer, my husband was like a fly landing on butter. What an excellent catch I'd been, and I hadn't even realised it.

I turned to the skinny man by my side. I wondered whether he had really chosen me for my supposed beauty and refined manners, and the elegance with which I carried myself. We were both acutely aware of status, proud to be seen with one another, in many ways the ideal match. Few women in town were able to appreciate Weng Yu's singing the way I did; I adored his voice, and he loved my adoration. All of this I knew to be true, but perhaps Father's deep wallet had also been an attraction. Sourness invaded my throat. What would happen now, now that Father was made poor by the war?

I held back the tears which came. Beside me my husband continued to sleep quite soundly. At some point he turned on to his side and started to snore.

22

In the course of 1944 rumours about Japan's war losses spread like forest fires. Weng Yu's sing-song group, which had resumed as soon as my husband returned from Batu Gajah, became a repository of titbits. There was as much chattering in our house on Thursday evenings as there was singing. Though I had never been keen on war talk, I was so impatient for the curtain to fall on the Nippon era that I took an unseemly interest in the campaigns being fought.

From Dr Pillay, I heard about Japan's abysmal failure in India. According to him, the Japs were also in trouble in Burma, though you would never have known this from the local papers. In July, it became clear that the island of Saipan had fallen into American hands. We learnt this from an unexpected source: the Japanophile teacher Mrs Chan.

She waddled into our dining room one morning in a state of great excitement. Clapping and waving both hands she cried, 'Good news!'

'Has something happened, Mrs Chan?' I asked cautiously, putting down the calligraphy brush I had just picked up. Father, who was seated beside me, put his brush down, too. He eyed Mrs Chan, whom he had never fully trusted. My daughter, Lai Hin, sat up like a startled cat in the chair opposite.

'Yes! The Americans have taken Saipan. Isn't that wonderful? The shorties are being pummelled.'

Father spoke English well enough to understand what Mrs Chan had said. He grunted with pleasure, his cotton-white moustache dancing across lips that were stretched into a wide smile. 'Daughter, let's not start writing yet. Let's wait till the children begin their lesson,' he said, 'so that I can first have a cigarette to celebrate.'

'Of course, Father.' I returned his smile, equally delighted that the tide had turned. The Japs were losing; it would now only be a matter of time. Their failure in Saipan was excellent news. But we still had the children to consider. My daughter was only eight and full of curiosity about the world. She sat watching us, taking in every word, too young to grasp the hazards we faced, yet old enough to be dangerous.

'Lai Hin,' I said as casually as I could, 'you are never to call any Japanese person you meet a "shorty", do you understand?'

Mrs Chan let out an overly hearty laugh, as if newly aware of what she had done and suddenly embarrassed. 'Yes, Lai Hin, you must never repeat what we grown-ups say. You will remember, won't you?'

'Of course I will remember, Mrs Chan,' my daughter retorted, knitting her eyebrows together. 'I'm now already eight years old. I would not call the Japs shorties anyway. It's rude! You should not be rude!'

'Very good, Lai Hin,' Mrs Chan said, patting my daughter on the head. The teacher and I exchanged looks of amusement. 'Now I have an idea. Why don't you go and get your brother? The two of you can get your books ready in the outer hall and turn to the next History chapter.'

'But I want to watch Ma and Maternal Grandpa paint calligraphy.'

'Well, Lai Hin, we won't be starting until your lesson begins,' I told her. 'Go and get ready.'

The girl's face fell, conveying unfettered disappointment in the way only an eight-year-old can. The blow would be forgotten within minutes, when the next interesting thing came along. Mrs Chan liked teaching our two, especially Lai Hin; that, at least, was what I thought, for the teacher had recently talked me into adding art lessons. My daughter had long been doodling everywhere: on sand, on paper, on the palms of her hands, and very occasionally, when the urge to disobey overtook her, on the walls of our house. From an early age she had sketched people and trees and strange animals, which were figments of her wild imagination. Some were grotesque, others fantastic, yet others quite real, such as her cartoon image of the mongrel that had bitten her third brother's hand when he had teased it. I was grateful to Mrs Chan for nurturing Lai Hin's talent.

She now bundled the girl off to the door and checked that it was properly closed before taking my arm and whispering, 'I thought I should tell you, the gossip has spread. I know about your fight in the grocery store.'

Next door in the inner hall, I could hear a piano concerto being played on our gramophone. At that moment I wanted to be somewhere else, in another world, another life, anywhere but where I was. Of course, it made sense that the scene in Mr Chee's shop would be passed on and dissected and commented on. I had somehow hoped for another ending, as if each event in my life could splinter into different trajectories and I could choose the outcome I preferred. I knew deep down that this could never happen, that I would be the object of malicious tongues and curious stares; real life rarely evolved kindly. Yet, when my fears were confirmed, there was a moment when time stood still. I imagined my husband, who had not yet returned to work, resting in the armchair with his head laid back, eyes closed.

'Well?' Mrs Chan prodded. 'Is it true?'

'She came at me, Mrs Chan,' I said softly. 'What could I do?'

For a minute the teacher was pensive. 'Hmm . . .' Then, putting her mouth close to my ear she said in a low voice, 'You must tell him to stop visiting here. And don't come home alone with him from mah-jong.'

'Mrs Chan, I tell you, coming home with him was never my idea. But I need to get home, there are the children, and my husband won't stop playing until very late. What am I supposed to do?'

Mrs Chan had just opened her mouth to say something when the door opened and my husband shuffled in. The teacher was not remotely flustered; she moved away from me and exclaimed with tremendous gusto, 'Mr Wong, how are you today? You're still not putting on enough weight. The heavier you are, the more powerfully you sing, you know!'

Weng Yu threw her a distant smile and me a sour look. 'Tell my wife that. She doesn't look after me enough, just sits around all day doing nothing.'

The teacher rolled her eyes. My husband would not have seen it though – she had her back to him. 'Mr Wong, how can you say that? Mrs Wong was managing the house the whole time when you were sick. It's not easy these days, you know, with five children. You men just don't appreciate what we women do for you! They don't appreciate us, do they, Mrs Wong? Now, I must see what the children are up to.'

With a wave of her hand, Mrs Chan left the room. My husband, I could tell, was itching for a fight; his face was black and he held his body rigidly. Merely seeing his wretched face drained me. I did not have the energy for a confrontation. I followed Mrs Chan out to where the children were waiting.

◆ ◆ ◆

The more heavily the Japs lost, the worse their behaviour became. Any sense of proportion they previously had evaporated into thin air. The Kempeitai, led in our town by a certain Sergeant Yoshimura, was particularly active. I had never seen this Yoshimura because the secret police kept a low profile, but he was reputed to be sadistic. Ipoh was awash with rumours. There were more arrests than before, and blood-curdling howls could be heard with increasing frequency from a hospital on Chung Thye Phin Road, which had been requisitioned early on.

Even the sentries at the kiosk into Green Town, who had treated us with benign indifference for two years, became suddenly hostile. The change happened overnight. It struck us that a new decree must have been issued in which the guards had been told that *seishin* now required overt demonstrations of aggression.

Every other Saturday afternoon in those days, our eldest son, Wai Sung, played football with boys from the neighbourhood. The boy had been playing since our sojourn into the jungle and at some point during the previous year, had begun participating in neighbourhood matches. He was first given a stint in defence followed by one in attack, after which Wai Sung settled into his preferred role of goalkeeper. He would stand at one end of the field, ready to throw himself at the oncoming ball or to butt heads with another player to deflect the missile. The football pitch, a field really, was not far away, but since the boy was still only ten, Samad accompanied him. The games were events which our son looked forward to and never missed, and I was surprised by the long face he pulled on returning one day.

'What happened, did you lose?'

'No, Ma, the guard slapped me.'

Wai Sung turned an inflamed left cheek towards me. There were fresh finger marks on his skin; his ear, bright red, stared indignantly up.

'What did you do?'

'I didn't do anything, Ma.'

'Then why did he hit you?'

'He said I didn't bow low enough, but I bowed the same way I always do.'

I looked at Samad, who stood helplessly folding and unfolding both hands in front of him. 'Same bow, Aunty. Wai Sung make same bow.'

'Which guard was it?'

'The new one, Aunty. You see him last week. Fierce, no smile.'

I remembered the guard very well, or rather, the shape of his lips, which seemed to me malignant from the moment I set eyes on him. There was something about his posture, how he stood like a pillar in front of his pathetic little kiosk, which conveyed much about his attitude. While massaging the soft flesh on Wai Sung's cheek, I thought about the Kempeitai. For reasons we did not understand, they had never returned to our house, but with a brother-in-law known to have joined the Communists, we had to keep vigilant.

'Wai Sung, my boy, listen to me. The Japs are losing the war. They will leave Malaya one day. But until then, we must be very careful. We must not make them angry. Do you understand?'

My son responded with an unhappy nod. I stroked his hair, thick straight strands, the texture of which brought pleasure to my fingers. I remembered his birth and my relief when the white matron, Mrs McDonald, at the District Hospital in Green Town, told me I had borne a boy. I had felt a surge of triumph, knowing that a son was what Weng Yu wanted. Since my husband's return from Batu Gajah, he had not ceased repeating the mantra that Wai Sung was destined to continue the Wong lineage. His father's attention was going to our son's head: the previously obedient boy was now cocky and surly when not given his way. If truth be told, I was secretly pleased by this incident with the Japanese sentry. I hoped it would put an end to Wai Sung's strutting about, arms swinging, in imitation of the soldiers outside.

My relations with his father had not improved. Weng Yu had plenty of visitors – colleagues from the Public Works Department, members of both his singing and Jikeidan groups – to keep him company. With them he laughed and joked; with me he was sullen. I could do nothing right: the coffee I offered was too thin, the tea not sweet enough, I woke him when I got out of bed in the mornings.

In those days I held my head high and did not know how to make myself scarce. Instead, I went to great lengths to secure what I could, so that the servants were able to prepare my husband's favourite dishes. My only reward was that the more weight Weng Yu put on, the more irritable he became. Three weeks after returning from hospital his face had regained much of its flesh and colour, and he was well enough to go on walks around Green Town. But he remained morose, oblivious to how the air which he dragged around him drained the life out of us all.

Late one morning I went into the inner hall where Weng Yu sat listening to music. I looked in on my husband whenever Father and I took short breaks from our calligraphy, in case I could fetch an item or be useful in some way. Of course, I wanted Weng Yu to notice me, but at the back of my mind were calculations too: the sooner my husband was well, the sooner he could work again. Paganini's 'Caprice no. 24' was playing on the gramophone when I entered. It was my husband's favourite piece at the time, and he kept replaying the record. I found him sunk in his armchair, like a snail which had retreated into its shell, with his eyes closed. His face, however, looked peaceful.

I cleared my throat before touching him gently on the shoulder. 'Would you like a cup of coffee, Husband, or maybe a glass of water?'

The eyes which opened glowered at me. 'The trouble with you, Wife,' Weng Yu hissed between gritted teeth, 'is that you know nothing about music. If you did, you would not be disturbing me in moments like these.'

The force of his bitterness rooted me to the floor. For a minute, I was unable to think or even feel.

'Husband, I . . . It's true I don't play an instrument, but I enjoy listening to music. I've always—'

'Don't argue with me, woman!' he shouted. 'I could have had a different life! Now it's too damned late.'

I stood rooted to the spot as I absorbed my husband's wave of rage and unfettered resentment. Then, in a moment I shall never understand, I fled. I was stung, certain that the whole house would have heard his outburst. We had a visitor that day, Mrs Chan, who was then in the middle of her lesson with Wai Sung and Lai Hin. I did not like an outsider hearing our marital quarrels.

There was no sanctuary anywhere in the house except in front of the dressing table in our marital bedroom. I sat before the mirror for a few minutes, trying to gather my thoughts. The glass told me that I still looked young, which I suppose was a relief. My fine features were intact, if a little the worse for wear, the shiny hair on my head largely black, my narrow eyes on the whole unlined and my figure that of a slim, unmarried woman. What, however, was the point of looking pretty if your husband paid no attention?

When I eventually went back into the dining room, Father was waiting. 'Give him time, Daughter,' he said very quietly. 'Weng Yu was an angry young man when I first met him. His anger will subside, as it did before. Be patient.'

Father himself did not sound convinced. Without replying I began grinding more ink. I had little choice. When had I ever truly had a choice? The future had knocked at an unexpected moment, when I was only seventeen. It had called with options which at the time seemed grand: Wong Weng Yu, or one of the other young men who were interested in my hand. I had chosen the handsome civil engineer with the British diploma, the one who wooed me with flowers and song and whom I thought would one day rebuild our entire town. I did not realise the enormity of what I was doing, that I was choosing my future, and by choosing it, I would exclude other possibilities. I could not have foreseen that one day I would sit before a mirror wondering if I had not made a grave mistake.

◆ ◆ ◆

Light was streaming in through the air well where I found Father sprawled out with his head down, a tangle of arms and legs. His fall had been preceded by a reverberating thud and a volley of screams and shouts. In the clear light Father's blazing indigo jacket stood out against the grey cement floor.

Thankfully, the old man's head was not bleeding, though his face was pale. Fearing he might have trouble breathing, I pleaded with the servants to stand away. Weng Yu, who had by then returned to work, was not there, but the children were nearby, gawping with their eyes wide. When Lai Hin began to cry, I motioned to old Ah Hong to take the girl into her room.

Father, meanwhile, moved his eyelids from time to time, so that I knew he was awake. His forehead was cool when I stroked it. I asked one of the servants to fetch a glass of water before sending Mutu, Father's driver, to the hospital for an ambulance. The old man would normally have protested – he hated fuss – but on that day he did not lift his head.

At the hospital, Dr Pillay was satisfied that Father had not suffered a concussion. Nonetheless, when the doctor began to ask a series of questions, Father admitted to suffering from stiffness in his joints. It had been many months, he mumbled, strenuously avoiding my eyes. I could not believe my ears. Father began staring out of the hospital's folding doors which also served as a large window. By the time Dr Pillay's interrogation was over, he had drawn out confessions which amazed me, such as that the stiffness had begun first in the old man's elbows before moving to his knees. The pain had worsened progressively over the months until, in the last week, Father was even feeling it in his bones.

'Is the pain worse in the morning, Mr Kwok?'

Father nodded, still avoiding my eyes. 'Yes, it's so bad that I have to lie in bed until the sun is shining and the air warm. Then I get up.'

'Why didn't you tell me, Father?' I asked in exasperation.

'Exactly for this reason, Mei Foong,' Father replied calmly. 'You would have worried. Daughter, I'm an old man now. Of course I will have aches and pains.' He said this with a hoarse laugh.

Dr Pillay snorted. 'Well, I can give you aspirin to help with the pain, Mr Kwok. That's what I'm here for!' Twitching his oversized ears, he added, 'The pills won't make you younger, but your pain will definitely get better-lah!'

The good doctor turned to tell me that each tablet cost a dollar and fifty cents, but he assured me they would ease Father's morning pains considerably. This was an expense I had not counted on; it meant I would almost certainly have to sell the last of Mother's jewellery. Outside, the leaves of the rain trees rustled in the breeze.

On our short journey home, the world looked cruelly perfect, the sunshine somehow brighter and Green Town's trees more vivid. Even our lettuces seemed juicier than before. Nippon occupation, I realised, would soon end; if only Father could hold on for a little while longer, he would live to see the day. I looked at his hands, so hard and knobbly that they now resembled a chicken's claws. When I recalled how those same hands, then unlined, had lifted me up and placed me on his lap, I had to swallow a tear. How quickly the years had passed. It seemed only yesterday that Mother had left us.

In the days immediately after her demise, Father had been less distant. He had sensed my desperation, how much I needed to keep him close and never lose sight of him. He was patient, letting me watch his morning tai-chi exercises in a garden wet with dew and afterwards entering the study with me for calligraphy practice. I looked again at those stiff, wrinkled hands and realised how much they had taught me. The thought that I would never see them again one day brought on a feeling of utter desolation.

But I did not cry. Nor did I hold Father's hands in mine. I could not bear to let him see my sadness.

23

The day after Father's collapse, Chew Hock San came to visit. I had thought about him many times since the fight with his wife, but seeing his stocky body in the flesh, installed on a chair inside our house, was a shock. He sat with Father and then asked if I would show him our vegetable beds. His wife, he said, was about to have another child and he would need to expand his home farm. He had attempted many of our fast-growing plants, but somehow, they did not flourish the way ours did. He wanted another tour, so that he could ascertain for himself what we did differently.

My pulse quickened as we walked out of the house. Li-Fei's silver head, with its distinctive bun, peeped out from around the corner. I could feel her eyes, their animosity undiminished, following us all the way across the road. Hock San gave no hint of concern. I wondered if he had heard about his wife's fight with me. He waited until we were among the raised beds before speaking.

'Mrs Wong, so sorry that I haven't come for a few weeks. Are you well?'

'Mr Chew, I don't think you should come here any more, not to see me anyway. Your wife tried to strangle me in Mr Chee's shop.'

Hock San looked as if he had seen a ghost.

'What?'

'I met her in Mr Chee's grocery store. We had a fight. Or rather, she had a fight. She flew at me and put her hands around my neck. And then she scratched me.'

'What the hell did she think she was doing?'

'Mr Chew, you need to tell her the truth.'

'The truth? The truth?' he shouted the words out with a caustic laugh. 'Do you want to know the truth? I'll tell you the truth!' Suddenly aware of a possible audience in the houses opposite, he lowered his voice. 'Have you read the book?'

'Mr Chew,' I replied, as calmly as I could, 'it is a rather thick book! With so many characters, I got a bit lost. But yes, I read it.'

He brightened when he heard this. And then, with his eyes boring into me, he nodded and at the same time pronounced gravely, 'I'm glad.'

There was a flutter at a nearby bush. A monitor lizard peeked out, its head raised, claws spread out, ready to scurry away. I turned my back and carried on walking so that I would not have to face him. But Chew Hock San did not follow. After a few paces, I realised that he was exactly where I had left him – beside the scallion shoots where I had seen the reptile. I slowed down, praying that Hock San would catch up. We had reached the bed of lettuces when he declared, 'Sometimes I feel like Chia Pao-Yu.'

He was referring to the hero in *Dream of a Red Chamber*, the second novel he had given me. Hock San lowered his voice in synchronicity with mine. We found ourselves squatting down beside the lettuces as if we had planned it. As soon as we were partially hidden by the brinjal trees further ahead, he grabbed my arm. 'Mei Foong, I need to tell you . . .' His voice was husky, his eyes resting on a distant shoot.

'My marriage to Kit Mei was arranged. We accept one another, obviously, but . . .' He gulped as if in pain. 'When I'm next to you, I'm in another life. I never give books. But you, you make me think of new things.'

Hock San was on his haunches, scrutinising me, leaving me shorn and vulnerable yet also eminently jubilant. No one had ever said the same things to me. I remember shivering.

'I feel like Chia Pao-Yu,' he repeated, still holding on to my arm. When he looked away, something like sadness flitted between those slanted eyelids. His voice turned into a gravelly whisper. 'But I'm trapped, caught, I have nowhere to go. I wanted you to know that, Kwok Mei Foong.' Chew Hock San rolled my name out slowly as if it were a delicacy on his tongue.

◆　◆　◆

The swelling in Father's joints worsened. His bedroom, which had been my mother-in-law's, was situated at the rear of the house where it enjoyed the best of Ipoh's breezes. He took increasingly long to leave his room in the mornings, despite Dr Pillay's heavy prescription of aspirin.

One sweltering morning when there was still no sign of Father at noon, I tapped on the bedroom door. He was lying on his back, asleep. His hands were folded together and resting gently on his chest, on top of the thick blanket keeping his body warm. From beneath the blanket, a skinny calf stuck out, which throbbed with greenish veins.

I pulled up a chair. The large window was open, and a refreshing breeze blew in from the limestone hills. Father's head lay propped up on two pillows. His face was pale, his cheeks taut; from time to time he ground his teeth and groaned. I watched his wavering chest, how he coughed every few minutes. After a severe bout of retching, the crinkly eyelids lifted and I saw the semblance of a smile.

'Is that you, Daughter?' he asked in a frail voice.

'Yes, it's me. How are you, Father?'

'I'm as . . . as well as can be, Daughter.' He coughed softly, stirring the phlegm in his throat. 'But it feels like the time has come for me to go.'

'*Chay*, Father! Don't say things like that!'

My hands reached out to caress a gnarled knuckle. I felt the hard, scaly lump and the stiff bone beneath, digits which not long ago were writing unaided and painting with horsehair brushes.

Father gave another cough. 'Everyone has to go sometime.'

As I continued moving my fingers across the unyielding landscape of Father's hands, I said, 'The Japs will be gone soon.'

Though the old man lay still, I was certain he had heard me. After a few minutes he opened his eyes.

'Mei Foong, there are a few things I need to say.'

His voice was croaky. I poured water from the pitcher beside his bed into a glass. With some urgency, he said, 'I have not much time left, Daughter. I want to say I'm sorry, so sorry, about you and Weng Yu.'

My trembling hand spilled water on to the side table. 'Father please—'

'No, let me say this. Mei Foong, when I brought him home, I thought he would be the best husband for you.'

'Of course, Father. I don't blame you for anything. No one forced me.'

'He is not the man I thought he was.'

When I heard the melancholy and disappointment in Father's voice, I knew that his heart was breaking, as mine was. My head emptied of all thought. I saw before me only air and static. I held the glass to his lips, noting the bulge and contraction of his throat. I wanted to cry.

'About you and Chew Hock San . . . I know you've told me that there's nothing between you—'

'It's the truth, Father.'

'I believe you, Daughter.'

Father closed his eyes and paused to catch his breath, exhausted from so much talking. When he opened his eyes once more, he said, 'Not everyone will believe. I know what this town is like.'

Another few seconds passed. 'Remember what I've said, Mei Foong.'

There was a peaceful expression on his face when I left him. I went to Ah Hong, to ask that she give him a glass of tea with plenty of sugar. I then headed to the vegetable garden for my customary tour with Samad.

We finished around noon. When Samad and I returned, we found a commotion in the house. Everyone, even the children, had gathered around Father's bed. The old man, it seemed, was having trouble breathing.

Horrified by the number of people standing around, I chased them all away. My daughter, Lai Hin, clung to my knees and had to be dragged, screaming, by Ah Hong into her bedroom. Placing myself on the chair next to Father's bed, I held his hand. His chest was no longer rising and falling evenly; in between coughs and gasps, it shuddered. When the fits of trembling passed, he would gulp for air. Every time his breathing settled, I placed a finger beneath his nostrils, fearing the worst.

Father died with his eyes open. He gave me no warning, no jerk or grimace, not even a cough. There was such a tranquil expression on his face that I had no idea his heart had stopped. One minute there had been a pulse, weak but present, the next it had gone, and the breath of life no longer warmed my finger. I gave a cry.

I closed Father's eyelids, first the left and then the right. As I rested my lips on his forehead, I thought how fragile life was, how Father had been with us just a minute before and now he was somewhere else. Though his body remained, something vital, a palpable presence, had left us.

From that moment on, the colours around me seemed to fade. Everything was dull and bland, and I was gnawed by an emptiness I could not shake off. My husband sensed this and was gentle with me. For a few days, united in sorrow, we were able to regain a degree of intimacy. Weng Yu himself was much affected by Father's passing away.

He had looked up to the old man, had relied on his advice; he confessed to being sorry for having taken Father for granted. Weng Yu wept, as did our children, especially Lai Hin, who had loved her grandfather. I, meanwhile, could shed no tears. I was devoid of regret and of feelings of any sort. My heart felt cold and my brain numb. I could not answer any of the questions posed by the monks who miraculously arrived despite not having been summoned by me.

Somehow, we muddled through the funeral arrangements. There was a wake presided over by drumming monks, followed by a procession to the Sam Poh Temple in Ipoh's caves where my mother-in-law had also been cremated. I have no idea what I said to our guests, or they to me. I remember our neighbour Husna sitting beside me on one night of the wake. She joined our cortege, staying close to our children during the walk to the crematorium. My husband held my hand, to make sure I did not stumble and fall. Chew Hock San and his family were there, too. When I nodded at them in greeting, his wife responded with an icy smile.

The immediate aftermath of Father's cremation is a muted blur. I was sunk in a maze of muffled whispers, without any idea whether the whispers were real or if I had imagined them. Food lost its taste, and time became a nebulous concept in which the seconds, the hours, and the days flowed one into the next while I wandered down alleys leading nowhere.

One day, strange new aircraft were heard over Ipoh. The roar of their engines jolted me out of my trance. My heart beat fast as I ran outside, knowing that I was taking a risk, but I had to look. There was a squadron in the air, too many planes to count. These were large machines – much wider than the Japanese planes we had seen – and they made a deep, gut-wrenching noise.

Days later we learnt that the planes were B-29 bombers, which America had developed. Fifty-three B-29s had been deployed in Singapore and had put a dock out of action. If Allied aircraft could fly so brazenly over Malaya in broad daylight, Japan was definitely losing the war.

I thought at once of Father lying on his bed, how his eyes had suddenly opened as we were washing him. I'd had to close them again before combing his mop of hair, which was soft like angora. If only Father had been able to hold on for another week. At that moment it hit me that I would never see him again. The tears gushed out, rivulets at once salty and bitter, which flowed furiously down both my cheeks.

◆ ◆ ◆

It was inevitable that Weng Yu and I would seek solace at the Foong Seong Villa. It was equally inevitable that there would come an evening when he would wish to play for longer and I would need to be accompanied home. And who other than Chew Hock San should jump at the chance of chaperoning me? A frisson passed between the other gamblers at my husband's table when they heard who would be taking me home. The looks of recognition were subtle: a blink here, an aversion of the eyes there, a tightening of the cheekbones. I was convinced that they had all heard about my fight with Hock San's wife.

'What a good idea, Wife! Let Mr Chew take you home,' my husband said, without once taking his eyes off the tiles in front of him. I touched Weng Yu on the shoulder, praying that he would glance up so that he could see how troubled I was.

'Husband, Mr Chew has walked me home many times. I don't think we should trouble him again.'

'No trouble at all, Mrs Wong, really,' Hock San said softly.

'There, you see! Mr Chew doesn't mind! Do you, Hock San?'

'Not at all, Mr Wong, I have to go in that direction anyway.'

'But, Husband,' I pleaded, 'why don't you come home now? It's almost dinnertime and Wai Sung had a big football game today. He would be so excited to see you.'

'No, no, no, Wife! Pong!'

With that simple bellow, Weng Yu picked a tile off the table and was fully immersed. I could not see how I would drag him away. Once again, I was left to walk home alone with Chew Hock San.

Fortunately, it was early in the evening, and there were too many people on the streets for us to talk about anything consequential. However, I knew it would be quiet once we reached Green Town. I dreaded what Hock San would say. Father's warning was fresh in my mind, and I feared for myself and my reputation, and even more that my resistance could crumble under another onslaught.

It was with relief that I spotted Dr Pillay just after we had entered Poh Gardens Lane. Big Ears seemed in a good mood; he could not stop grinning. He turned around to walk part of the way with us. Once we were well beyond the Japanese sentries he said, 'Have you heard the news, Mrs Wong?'

'No, Dr Pillay, what news?'

'They're losing Iwo Jima!'

'Really?' I cried, 'Are you sure?'

Until a few weeks earlier, in February of 1945, none of us had heard of this fantastical place. Brother-in-law Weng Yoon, being a keen studier of maps, explained that Iwo Jima was an island, an insignificant dot south of Japan and north-east of the Philippines. In short, a Crusoe-like place in the middle of nowhere, bleak and wind-swept, but ideal for landing planes and stationing troops.

With Iwo Jima having been invaded by US Marines, Japan was going to lose a strategic asset. I jumped for joy. It had taken the Americans long enough, a battle lasting over a month, even though the island was supposedly much smaller than Singapore.

Dr Pillay raised his eyebrows when he saw the little jig I broke into. 'Why, Mrs Wong,' he exclaimed with a wide smile, 'I see you're quite a dancer! And you look very fetching in that dress. You should wear dresses more often.'

Japan's losses were piling up, and our nightmare was finally coming to an end. For the first time in three years, there really seemed to be light. I felt ecstatic; I would have happily fallen into Dr Pillay's arms if he were a twirling man. I had never thought him handsome, but he looked marvellous that evening, freshly bathed and shaved, his whole face radiant. I suppose I must have looked striking too, in the orange-red Western dress I had put on, with its golden flowers. I did not usually wear dresses, but the Chinese blouses and trousers I had for going out in all needed darning, and I had not had time to mend them.

'Dr Pillay, you don't know how happy you've made me!' I said, giving the doctor an involuntary hug. I remember surprising myself; the only man I had ever hugged was my husband. I had not even hugged Father and have no idea why I felt compelled to hug Dr Pillay, except that it felt like the right thing to do.

Hock San stopped abruptly. Standing with his legs a little apart, he stared at the doctor and me. His nostrils flared like a bull's. When Dr Pillay said something like – 'Isn't she something, Mr Chew?' – Hock San looked as if he would charge at the doctor and butt him. He pretended to smile, but those slanted eyes could not conceal a simmering hostility.

Eventually, Dr Pillay went on his way. As his figure disappeared down the road, Chew Hock San whispered furiously, 'How could you!'

'How could I what? Why did you have to be so rude? Dr Pillay has been very good to us. He helped get Weng Yu a place in Batu Gajah.'

'So you have to flirt with him, ah?'

I studied Hock San carefully. I resented the insinuation and the attitude, as if I should somehow have to account to *him* for my actions. My indignation boiled over into rage, and I found myself yelling.

'If I may say so, it is none of your business! How dare you!'

My voice was quivering; I was so angry. If we had not been outside in full view of the street, I would have flown at him, pummelled his breast or at the very least scratched his arms. I had the urge to gouge his eyes out and damage him in some way. All of the resentment I had ever felt, a mountain of bitterness and outrage, came gurgling out of my chest.

'Don't be so bloody ridiculous! You are not my husband!' I screamed in English, not caring whether the entire street heard me.

Li-Fei opened the front door. She stood at the threshold, watching us with a mixture of suspicion and displeasure. She was still there when Hock San walked away, his face crestfallen.

While Iwo Jima was being fought over, our daughter Lai Hin learned to paint with a brush. Naturally, when Ipoh's Propaganda Department decided to host an art competition for children under the age of ten, Mrs Chan hovered in our house to persuade me that Lai Hin should enter it. Incredibly, the topic of the competition was 'Asia, Arise'! The competition must have been conceived to impress upon us the idea that Japan's *seishin* would prove ultimately invincible. Politics, however, were far from Mrs Chan's mind.

'Your daughter is really quite good,' she told me in a serious voice. Then, with a wink and a nudge, added, 'Wouldn't it be great if she won? Imagine!'

I searched Mrs Chan's youthful face and did not know what to say. I felt uneasy about participating in such a farce. There was also the question of cost: the tubes of paints to purchase, the paper and the brushes. A bar of local soap cost ten dollars by then, while charcoal could only be bought for two hundred dollars a picul. Every time I thought prices could rise no higher, they confounded me by going farther up. If essentials were at such lofty levels, how were we to afford paintbrushes and paint?

As if reading my mind, Mrs Chan added promptly, 'I can give Lai Hin what she needs. I have brushes she can borrow and paints she can use. And I can spare a few sheets of paper. I know how dear those are.'

The teacher stood in our house with her hands at her sides. Her eyes did not let mine go. 'Well?'

Thus the matter was settled. Under Mrs Chan's guidance, my daughter put brush to paper and created pieces which student and teacher inspected closely while making indecipherable noises. What Lai Hin finally showed me was a canvas of bleeding lines and dark dots, intersected by polygons and circles whose outlines were so fine, they looked as if they had been scraped out by a knife. Perhaps a knife had been used. This was so-called 'modern art'. Many of the circles were painted a rather realistic shade of blood red, which would have made my husband faint.

Both Lai Hin and Mrs Chan waited expectantly for my verdict. 'Hmm . . . yes, it's very colourful, my girl. But, what do these lines and dots actually mean?'

The nine-year-old's rose-bud mouth exploded at my ignorance. 'It's quite simple, Ma. These dots are us Asians, the circles are our countries, the polygons are the Europeans who came. And now, with the help of Japan' – at this, the girl pointed towards a red sun – 'and its soldiers here' – she put a finger on an ochre line that shimmered down from the centre of the page – 'we will kick them out.'

I exchanged a puzzled glance with Mrs Chan. I did not understand modern art. It seemed best to say nothing, especially since I did not think such a painting would win.

The Japanese must have developed a penchant for the avant-garde. Instead of the rice planters in revolution, which they would normally have favoured, they chose Lai Hin's painting as one of three runners-up and awarded my daughter a cash prize of fifty dollars. I sighed at the thought of so much money and watched enviously as my daughter slipped the banana notes into her piggy bank, a piece carved out of dark wood with a palm leaf painted on its curved back.

While staring at the vessel, I remembered that it housed a considerable amount. Lai Hin was a keen saver who hoarded all of the *ang pows* – the red packets she received each Chinese New Year – inside her palm-leaf piggy bank. When I had lifted the children's piggy banks surreptitiously one night, I had been amazed to find Lai Hin's receptacle twice as heavy as Wai Sung's. I recalled then the store of British coins our daughter had dropped into the pig's slot and regretted not being able to use the money for household expenses.

A fortnight after the art competition, there was tight rapping on our kitchen door. It came at an early hour, when it was still dark outside and my husband had not yet departed for work. In the murky dawn light we saw Weng Yoon's robust figure and, beside him, a rather flustered Dora.

My sister-in-law rushed in to hug me. 'Good new! It's official, Big Sister: Germany has surrendered!'

'Are you sure?' I asked, frozen in shock.

I had waited so long to hear those words that I could not quite believe them. A German defeat had seemed inevitable and yet fantastic at the same time, like a horrible dream from which you knew you would one day wake. In the same dream, another part of you remained bewildered, unwilling to truly believe it could happen, in case it never did.

Weng Yoon clapped my husband on the back.

'What do you think, Big Brother? Isn't it wonderful? We should get a bottle of Hennessy and celebrate with the Jikeidan boys.'

My husband frowned. 'Too early to celebrate, I think. The Japs aren't going to give up that easily.'

'Oh, come on! You can't be serious, Big Brother! Are you telling me you don't think the war is as good as lost for Japan?'

'I think Japan will lose, of course I do. I hope so anyway. But it's not clear when. She hasn't lost yet, you know. She's still fighting.'

What Weng Yu said was quite true: the Germans might have surrendered, but the Japanese were continuing to fight. Despite losing Iwo Jima, Weng Yu's boss, Hashimoto, insisted that Japanese troops were valiantly defending the motherland. They weren't cowards like the Germans; the world would see what Japanese *seishin* was made of.

In the face of Weng Yu's caution, my exhilaration deflated like a punctured tyre. We had seen for ourselves how cruel the Japs were in victory; there was no telling what they would be like in defeat. If anything, worse could yet be in store. I was so engulfed in pessimism that it did not occur to me to wonder how Weng Yoon and Dora had heard the news so quickly. Eventually, I concluded that they must have kept a wireless set. This was, of course, illegal; we were meant to have handed our wireless sets over to the Nippon authorities. However, I was quite sure that there was still one inside Dorcourt and that it would have been Dora's idea. For the first time I felt grudging admiration for my sister-in-law. I was ashamed I had not resisted more.

As I looked into the mirror that night, I put my shame away, in the same place where I kept all unwanted emotion. If I had confronted the loneliness I really felt, I would have turned mad with rage, a rage so terrifying that I would have broken every single plate in the Green House. I could not let self-pity take hold; otherwise I would have risked being consigned to the mental asylum in Tanjong Rambutan. What would have become of my children then? There was always someone else to think of, if not the children, then the servants, for whom I felt a keen sense of responsibility. There was no place for anger in my life and no one to console me. I buried the turmoil somewhere deep, unaware that it gnawed away at me in the dark.

24

One by one they fell, like tiles in a game of dominoes. After Okinawa and Burma came the Philippines and Borneo. Everywhere, the Japs bore a heavy toll. On mainland Japan itself, major cities were bombed daily by the B-29 planes we had seen.

All of this I learned from visits to Dorcourt. Either Dora or I would scramble through the secret gate to exchange the latest gossip, so desperate were we for news. At the same time, we were uncertain what to believe and whom to turn to. We would dissect what the *Perak Shimbun* deigned to tell us, lay bare what our husbands had heard in town, and share the snippets passing through Green Town's houses. I felt like a biologist gathering specimens for laboratory examination. Dora and I would sit down in Dorcourt's dining area and pore over the disparate pieces minutely. These sessions brought us closer. I became fond of Dora, and it is probably no exaggeration to say that she grew to like me too. We would sit at the pine dining table her husband had had imported, two young women prematurely aged by war, our heads streaked with silver and with miniature crow's feet fanning out from the edges of our eyes. Dora, however, had succeeded in retaining her elegance: though her kebaya blouses and sarongs were shabbier, she had lost neither her poise nor her fair skin. I, alas, looked every inch the poor farmer beside her, with my own face sun-scorched from so much walking outdoors. Dora, whose crescent-shaped eyes had regained their sparkle, reminded me of the young woman I'd once been, the one who had led a protected life in my parental home on the Gopeng Road, surrounded by servants and beautiful objects. I yearned to hold an antique vase once again in my hands. More than that, I longed to be able to walk down a street without fear, to know that my place in this world was safe. Suddenly, I wondered where my life had gone.

Dora eventually trusted me enough to show me her wireless set. Without a word, she tuned into the static-infused British news programme that was being broadcast across the seas from Colombo, but even Dora with her Anglophile nature did not fully believe what the British were telling us. I didn't either, not after what had transpired at the start of the war, when our erstwhile rulers had so shamelessly trumpeted their 'defence' of Malaya.

The trouble was that we were even more sceptical of the Japanese. We knew that the *Perak Shimbun* would contradict everything we heard elsewhere, but its full-throated denials took our breath away.

'We will fight until victory!' screamed the *Shimbun* headlines. The analysis, such as there was, explained that Japan would prevail, because one hundred million people moulded out of *seishin* could never be beaten. Their defiance made me think that Japan's fall could take years, not the months everyone was claiming. For once, my husband agreed with me.

It was a dizzying time. Rumour had it that Mountbatten would soon reclaim Malaya and Singapore, though no one had any idea what 'soon' meant. Weng Yu came home one day with news that a convoy of Nippon military trucks had been seen heading down Brewster Road. We wondered where they could be going and rushed next door to Dorcourt, where we sat around the dining table with Weng Yoon and Dora, a map spread out between us.

'The trucks were covered up with tarpaulin,' my husband said. 'They must have been carrying equipment, not soldiers.'

Weng Yu added that the convoy had been travelling south towards Gopeng Road. But since the Gopeng Road led on to Kuala Lumpur and thence to Singapore, the fact that the Japs had taken the Gopeng Road could mean any number of things. To confuse everyone, another convoy was seen several hours later going in the opposite direction: north along the Brewster Road.

Similar processions appeared the next day and the day following that. This flexing of military muscle was accompanied by ominous new headlines assuring us that the Imperial Nippon Army would defend Malai to the last man.

Before the convoys stopped, we beheld another strange sight: a trail of Buddhist monks and nuns dragging their heels into town from the Gopeng Road itself. At first this devout procession was small, but after a day more monks and nuns followed. Some headed down Hugh Low Street; those who turned right on to Brewster Road walked past the entrance into Green Town. We heard about them from Samad, who spotted a group of stragglers at the corner of Poh Gardens Lane. He reported that each person was carrying either a suitcase or a cloth sack, as if they had a destination in mind. Samad, always a quiet man, had been too shy to ask where they were going.

I sat pondering the news with Dora. In between sips of tea, we surmised that the monks and nuns must have come from the cavernous temples built into Ipoh's limestone hills. The Sam Poh Temple, where Father's body had been cremated, was one of the temples situated on the outskirts of town – a good four miles away. I wondered whether the monks who had presided over Father's funeral were among the refugees now fleeing.

Late one morning, Dora and I walked with Ali and Samad to the corner of Poh Gardens Lane. A dusty, bedraggled, yellow-robed troupe was filing in. They looked a sorry sight, their faces dazed, shaved heads leaking with sweat, robes blackened by grime. There seemed to be no one senior to speak to; the leader of the group must have been a long way off. Dora, who'd had the foresight to bring a canteen of water with her, ran alongside one of the younger women to offer a drink, which the novice took gratefully. While the woman was gulping water down Dora asked, 'Miss! Where are you going?'

In between mouthfuls, the nun told us that the Nippon military had arrived and had dumped weapons inside the caves. One did not have to know about war, she continued, to realise that the cache was menacing; there were clearly guns amongst them, and cigar-shaped tubes which must be bullets, and probably bombs too, though she could not be sure. When the Nippon Army first arrived, the monks and nuns had been at a loss as to what to do. The munitions were in the caves and their own temples were set slightly apart; nonetheless, with bombs and rifles and bullets and eventually even cannons so close by, their community had taken a collective decision to evacuate. Other cave temple communities had also chosen to leave. As I listened, I remembered what the *Shimbun* article had said, and realised that the Japs were serious about defending Malaya to the last man. Despite my bitterness, I was impressed, because their determination stood in stark contrast to the British retreat we had seen with our own eyes. We would simply have to hope for the best.

July came and went. There was another conference, another set of pompous words in what was called the Potsdam Declaration, issued with a warning that if Japan did not surrender, it would face consequences. Throughout the verbal barrage, Japan remained standing. The *Perak Shimbun* even scoffed at the possibility of an unconditional Japanese surrender. 'We will fight on until the final victory!'

On 6 August 1945, Dora and I heard via the British news broadcast that the world's first atomic bomb had been dropped on the city of Hiroshima. Quickly taking out a map, we saw that Hiroshima was a port town on the western part of Japan's main island. In those days none of the photographs of the horrific injuries which the victims would have suffered had yet been disseminated, but I had learnt enough science to realise that the bomb would have released an unimaginable amount of energy. The devastation must have been great. The announcer mentioned 'a huge cloud of impenetrable dust and intense fires springing up'. Surely Japan would capitulate within hours.

Together with Weng Yoon and Dora, my husband and I sat up in Dorcourt that night. We kept vigil for the next two consecutive nights, expecting to hear that the Japs had surrendered. Weng Yoon even set aside a bottle of champagne. Instead, on the morning of 9 August, Dora and I learnt that a second atomic bomb had been dropped by another American B-29 plane, this time on a port city called Nagasaki.

Even then, Japan did not issue a surrender decree. 'They are mad!' my sister-in-law cried, jumping up from her chair. Her nervous energy filled the air as she paced the living room, wringing both her hands.

Japan's procrastination was unfathomable. I sat immobile, feeling Dorcourt's hard dining-room chairs bite into my buttocks, unable to say a word. I could only stare at Dorcourt's cathedral-like windows while I counted the motes of dust which danced in a wedge of light. When the servant Rokiah appeared with Ali, thinking that the war had ended, we had to explain that another very large bomb had been dropped on Japan. I remember passing through the secret gate, mired in the knowledge that our nightmare had not ended.

Nonetheless, after Nagasaki, a change descended over Ipoh. The town seemed somehow quieter, more sombre, as if part of the bomb's toxic cloud had drifted across the South China Sea into Malai. Weng Yu came home saying that his boss, Hashimoto, who previously had been overflowing with confidence, had turned gloomy. The damage in Japan was very bad indeed, so great that the top brass had called a halt to fighting. There would soon be a cabinet meeting. Hashimoto had apparently put his head into his hands and wept.

'What did you do, Husband?'

'What could I do? I went to my desk and did what I've been doing for the last two years – I pretended to work.'

The rumours resumed. This time, there was no stopping the tide. The boldness of Ipoh's inhabitants returned. Those who had been afraid to venture out at night began taking evening strolls. Neighbours dropped in to gossip, among them the teacher, Mrs Chan, and the nurse's mother, Mrs Lim, both of whom claimed that Japan had already surrendered. Dora and I knew better; the radio service we listened to had said nothing, and we were sure that the British would have announced an event as momentous as that.

In the middle of this chatter Chew Hock San appeared, waving his arms frantically. He had obviously been running and needed a few moments to catch his breath.

'I have news!' he said, while gulping in air. 'About Liew Chin Tong and Miss Liew. They are well. They're coming down from the hills and will soon be here in Ipoh!'

'Really?' I shrieked, almost grabbing Hock San's shirt collar in excitement. 'Are you sure, Mr Chew?'

'Yes, yes, a school friend is in touch with them.' There was a furtive look in Hock San's slanted eyes, and he changed the subject abruptly. 'And Japan,' he announced, 'has surrendered!'

I smiled, asking mildly, 'What makes you say that?'

'My school friend told me! He says that the villagers are already slaughtering chickens. They are celebrating; the hill people who have come down told them. These hill people have secret informants from Britain, you know.'

Hock San opened his mouth wide and curved his lips. He appeared to have forgotten about Dr Pillay. Despite myself I smiled back, caught in an upsurge of profound happiness. I had a sudden desire for Hock San's small, fully stretched mouth. We stood grinning like idiots on the driveway. Though I knew that Japan had not surrendered, I hoped peace could finally be around the corner.

◆ ◆ ◆

Within days, the Ipoh gambling farm, the Foong Seong Villa, and other centres of 'entertainment' closed their doors. The closures appeared to confirm the general rumours that were circulating, but until I heard the facts relayed by an official channel, I could not allow my emotion free rein.

On the morning of 16 August 1945, our British news programme at last announced that Japan had surrendered the previous day. Dora and I flew off our chairs, delirious with joy. We hugged one another, jumping up and down and stamping our feet like children. In her excitement Dora ripped the brown and green sarong she was wearing and my eyes misted up, but neither of us cared. I was relieved, and so happy, but at the same time part of me could not believe that it had finally happened, that the Japs were no longer our masters. I continued to weep as I went home via the secret gate.

Outside, everything looked the same. The security kiosk remained at the corner of Poh Gardens Lane and Brewster Road, and it was still manned by swaggering sentries. Our friends dropped in: Mrs Chan, Mrs Lim, Miss Lee together with her companion Miss Mak, and Dr Pillay of course, who invited us to a private celebration. In the midst of this were the Japs, impervious as ever, not for a minute looking like a defeated nation. In the Public Works Department, Hashimoto continued to be Weng Yu's boss and gave no indication that change was imminent. The Japs were outwardly so calm that I began to fret. Could it be that separate arrangements had been made for each of Japan's conquered countries and that the surrender did not apply to Malai?

And yet, there were signs. Another fleet of B-29 planes flew overhead, and this time they dropped leaflets. The white paper which my husband brought home read: 'The Japanese capitulated on the 15th of August, 1945. Until the arrival of the British military authorities, the Malayan Peoples' Anti-Japanese Army will take charge.'

'But that's what Mr Chew said!'

My husband scowled.

'You remember, Husband, when he came to tell me about Liew Chin Tong and Miss Liew? Mr Chew mentioned that they were coming down from the hills.'

Weng Yu's face turned black with annoyance, so I said no more.

Shortly thereafter, the rush began. Provisions shops throughout Ipoh flung their doors open. The large shop on Belfield Street was one of the busiest. Known simply as the Ipoh Provision Shop, it was among the oldest in Ipoh, and it seemed that the entire town passed through its doors on the week of 13 August. Prices rose by the hour. When I heard from the servants what the merchants were demanding for basic foodstuffs, I ventured out myself. By the time I reached the Ipoh Provision Shop, local rice was going for seventy-two dollars a catty, each egg cost twenty-eight dollars, and even small bottles of coconut oil were being sold for sixty-five dollars. No matter how high the price, there was a taker; someone would open up her purse, and as soon as she did, another followed. The frenzy was the worst I had ever seen, worse than the most awful of Chinese New Year seasons, nothing short of panic. And then I realised the reason: everyone wanted to deplete their banana notes before the British returned. I too opened up my purse, waving my banana notes at the shopkeeper's daughter.

That night, when the children were asleep, I sent Chang Ying and Li-Fei into the children's bedrooms with instructions to bring all the little piggy banks into the outer hall. We would have to split the pigs open; it was the only way we could get our hands on the notes I knew the children had kept.

Old Ah Hong was the first to object. 'But mistress, Lai Hin upset. She save hard. She work. Also win competition.'

I looked at the servant's wrinkled face and the eyes squinting accusation.

'Ah Hong, we must use up these notes – they will have no value when the Japs have gone.'

Ah Hong stared in incomprehension. 'No value-ah? Money, how can have no value?'

'Ah Hong,' said Chang Ying, 'like when Japan people come-lah! You remember, English money then no value, remember?'

'Oh, yes. But Lai Hin save so hard . . .'

I turned away from Ah Hong towards Chang Ying, who was holding a Chinese cleaver in her hand. Ignoring the sliver of guilt that crept in, I said, in a rougher tone than I'd intended, 'Open the first one.'

There was an almighty crash when the metal of the cleaver collided with the thick wood out of which Wai Sung's piggy bank was made. The pig's rounded back was sturdy, and Chang Ying needed two blows to split it open. As she moved to the next piggy, Li-Fei counted out the money that had already been released. The pigs fell like Japan's dominions: first Wai Sung's paddy farmer, next Lai Hin's palm leaf, then Wai Kit's fisherman, and finally Robert's coconut tree. After half an hour the bundle of notes in my hand had grown thick and the servants retired to bed.

As I turned to switch off the electric light, I spotted a figure peeping out from behind the door of Lai Hin's bedroom. I blinked; when I opened my eyes, I saw that the door to her bedroom was closed. Perhaps I had imagined it. I tiptoed over, to find that the door to Lai Hin's room was in fact closed. It was dark inside; the girl seemed fast asleep. I approached the lime-green bed in which my daughter slept and stroked her head. She was tucked in under her checked blanket and dead to the world. My guilty conscience must have been playing tricks. I continued stroking my daughter's hair, listening to her breathing. But when I eventually crept out, I was unable to shake off a niggling feeling that my daughter had witnessed our dark act in the middle of the night and that she would hold it against me.

25

The Japs dug their heels in, determined to show that they were still our bosses and therefore superior. Hashimoto said nothing to my husband about leaving. As for the sentries at the kiosk into Green Town, they were as well-entrenched as on the day they first appeared, the only difference being that we no longer had to kiss their feet. As for the British, there was no news of when they might return.

Finally, on 21 August, Japan's official surrender was published by the *Perak Shimbun*. It began:

> *To our good and loyal subjects,*
> *After pondering deeply the general trends of the world and the actual conditions obtaining in Our Empire today, We have decided to effect a settlement of the present situation by resorting to an extraordinary measure. We have ordered Our Government to communicate to the governments of the United States, Great Britain, China and the Soviet Union that our Empire accepts the provisions of their joint declaration.*

I burst out laughing. The official statement was such a literary gem that I took it at once to Dorcourt, where Dora and I spent hours poring over its many pages. We perused the document more than once to make sure that our eyes were not playing tricks. Neither of us could see the word 'surrender', no matter how many times we read through the pronouncement. Surrender was obviously too humiliating a word for the Japs. In the years to come, Japanese semantics would be taken to new heights. In their own history books, Japan's barefaced cruelties would be diminished, occasionally even wiped away. Official ways would be found to pretend that Japan had fought for a just cause; indeed, to claim that she herself had been a victim.

Several cups of tea and many cakes later, I decided to return home, not via the secret gate, but by walking openly down our driveway. We had avoided this simple act for three and a half years, preferring not to be seen. As I walked on the street towards our driveway, I saw none other than our policeman neighbour Ja'afar Abu returning home. He was on foot, his car having mysteriously disappeared. The deputy inspector had also lost his swagger. He looked confused, out of sorts, like a rich man who suddenly finds himself homeless.

'How are you, Enche Ja'afar?' I asked.

The policeman gave me a look of anguish, and his answer, when it came, was a rhetorical statement. 'I suppose you must be happy, Puan Wong.'

'And you're not happy-ah, Enche Ja'afar?' I said with a weary smile. 'I know they treated you better, but they were cruel to us Chinese.'

The policeman gazed at me derisively with his clear brown eyes. I had, I suppose, assumed that once the Japs left, the policeman would metamorphose back into the good neighbour he had been before. As we stood on the street that day, the street on which we had both lived for many years, it hit me that I might be mistaken. A seething silence followed in which I felt acutely that my race had become unwelcome to Ja'afar Abu.

To soften the febrile atmosphere, I mumbled the first thing which came into my head. 'Well, things may be um, ah, less expensive from now on, Enche Ja'afar. Maybe we won't be short of everything. I mean, a shortage of coconut oil even, how can that be? We have so many coconut trees here, cannot be right-lah!'

The policeman grunted. 'Puan Wong, you may have won for now. But our day will come.'

With those words, our neighbour performed the Japanese bow and turned to walk to his front door. I wondered what his wife, Husna, would say. I made a mental note to call on her the next day while the policeman was at work.

Husna's delight at seeing me could not have been faked; she radiated warmth and pleasure as she greeted me on the verandah of their home. A smile stretched across every part of her face, even along the creases lining her skin. She grabbed both my hands in hers and pulled me towards her. There was a smell of lemongrass on her baju panjang, the long-sleeved tunic she favoured. Before I could greet her, Husna blurted out, 'So good-lah, Mei Foong, at last the Japanese are going!'

'I'm glad you say that, Husna, because I saw your husband yesterday. He does not seem so happy.'

Husna stopped smiling. 'Would you like something to drink? I cannot offer food, but maybe tea or water?'

She looked uneasy. Though I declined the drink, she was not to be put off. Husna went straight to her kitchen. While she was there, I inspected their living room. Numerous artefacts had been added since my last visit, which had been some two years before with Mrs Chan. On one wall a copper-tooled painting hung, a piece with the image of a Malay farmer tilling the land, set against the timeless backdrop of paddy fields and palm trees. On the circular coffee table was a silver betel box with intricate floral motifs carved around its top and sides. My mother-in-law had kept a betel box too. I wondered where it had gone. I was going through the list of places in which I could have stored it when Husna returned with a glass of water.

'I didn't know you chewed betel nuts, Husna.'

She laughed. 'Only sometimes-lah, Mei Foong. I used to chew with your mother-in-law. But I think we enjoyed the gossip more than the chewing.'

I sipped my water. For the next few minutes we talked about Mother-in-Law, how much we missed her still.

'I'm glad she did not have to face these last few years. It would have broken her heart, Husna, to see what has become of our country.'

Husna's face took on a sudden serious expression. 'Mei Foong, my husband, how to say, he is a good man, a good husband and father. I don't agree with all of his ideas. I am glad that the Japanese will go.'

Outside, the most obstreperous among our cockerels, the one with the least sense of time, began to crow; it must therefore have been noon, or two o'clock Tokio time. Husna whispered her next words. 'I remember your last visit to our house, Mei Foong. I felt so ashamed. That will now end, and I'm glad.'

I leaned forward to touch Husna's arm. We sat for a while, content to enjoy the peace which we hoped would return to Green Town.

When we heard that British marines had landed in Penang on 3 September, Weng Yoon finally opened the bottle of champagne he had been saving. I asked Samad to slaughter two of our chickens and to gather the ripe vegetables from our garden. Foodstuffs we had not seen for many years magically found their way back into the shops and at reasonable prices too, and we were able to feast on grains of fluffy white rice. We celebrated late into the night, eating as if we would never eat again, our thirst slaked by water, tea, the bottle of Hennessy that Weng Yu's sing-song group shared, and Weng Yoon's champagne. Even I partook, not because I liked the taste of alcohol, but because it felt right to be drunk.

No one wanted to go to bed. Late in the evening, my husband wound Strauss's *Blue Danube* on the gramophone. Weng Yu led me to the *barlay* in the outer hall, where he took me into his arms and whirled me around to the sounds which shivered through the horn. It was the first time we had danced together. I had no idea how graceful a dancer he was, so light on his feet, able to steer me effortlessly as the pace quickened. I wondered whether he had danced with the Englishwoman, if it was her from whom he had learnt his steps. In those moments as he held me close, our past travails – the war, his illness, the child we had lost, Father's passing on into the next world – seemed far behind.

There was a moment when Chew Hock San came into mind. I had no reason to reproach myself; he would never have fitted in the company we kept that night. Weng Yu swung me around until I was dizzy. I begged him to stop and we laughed manically, still not believing that the British were back, for they had not yet appeared in Ipoh. I looked at my husband, a man with greying temples and a proud nose who was a product of Great Britain. He could have lived in London, but instead he had come home to please his mother.

Weng Yu lit a 555 cigarette and handed it to me, the woman he had chosen as his wife. I was proud of this fact, prouder still to be his wife, this man who was admired for the way in which he danced. In turn, I had given myself to him. By then I had sold everything I ever owned: every piece of silver, an inheritance which at one point had seemed too bountiful for me to ever fully spend. It pained me that Weng Yu seemed not to have noticed. Though I had no material possessions left, I was glad I'd had the means to see us through those years of darkness. I wondered then whether my husband appreciated what I'd done, and whether it would ever be enough.

◆ ◆ ◆

On the day of the parade, we saw them. I was shocked by the colour of Liew Chin Tong's face. His complexion, which had previously been a deep tan, now had the greenish tinge of the jungle. I thought at first that he must be ill, until I spotted his sister among the women behind, sporting the same sickly hue. When my eyes ranged further around I noticed that all the guerrillas had muted complexions, a shade somewhere between jungle green and khaki brown, matching the uniforms they were wearing.

There was something else that struck me. Although there were men and women, and older as well as younger members in the group marching, they all bore an uncanny resemblance to one another. The Communists were mainly of Chinese extraction, of course: we had already heard through word of mouth that most came from Chinese vernacular schools. But as I watched them step forward, obviously happy, safe in the knowledge that they had served their country heroically, they seemed to share a peculiar sameness, a fervour in the way they swung their arms and marched, almost as if the war was not yet finished.

When I waved to Liew Chin Tong, he did not smile back. He was smiling, but not at me. Perhaps he had not seen us. But he made no effort at acknowledgement even when I stepped out from behind the crowd. Gone was the man who had once told stories and made jokes; in its place stood a creature with a stern chin. His jawbone was set, like the marble which limestone and clay become. The things Chin Tong had seen showed in his harrowed eyes, which were full of pain as he walked past without so much as a nod.

'I never liked him. I don't know what Second Sister saw in him,' my husband remarked drily.

I looked up in astonishment. 'Well, that's the first time you've said so, Husband! Anyway, Second Brother didn't use to be like this. We talked a lot at Grand-Uncle's tin mine. I wonder if he's avoiding his old friends too.'

'Obviously not. Look!'

I turned to where my husband was pointing, further ahead in the crowd. A short, stout man with glistening hair was being embraced by Liew Chin Tong. I recognised Chew Hock San at once and also his wife, Kit Mei, beside him, welcoming home a senior officer of the Malayan Peoples' Anti-Japanese Army, a hero of the Nippon era.

The minutes thereafter had a surreal quality. I was awake, able to see all that was happening and upset by Liew Chin Tong's snub; the shapes and outlines are clear, yet no matter how many times I go over those minutes, they continue to be veiled in a strange, dusky light. I remember Liew Chin Tong passing, then Hock San raising his hand to wave. Hock San was yards away, and there were countless bodies between us, but when he smiled I had to turn away. There was something in his gaze I could not bear, a feeling that he could discern every tremor going through me. My husband, who saw this, sulked all the way home.

◆ ◆ ◆

When Weng Yu confronted me, he was standing near the dressing table in our bedroom. In one hand he brandished the Chinese novel which had been Hock San's gift.

'When did he give you this?'

My husband shook the book so hard that for a minute I thought it would fly out of his hand. His lips were quivering, and he could barely get his words out. It took a few seconds before I realised what must have happened.

'Who gave you permission to go through my personal drawer? How dare you!'

'Is this what you do while your husband is dying in hospital? Gallivant around town with another man?'

'And is this what a husband does: rummage through his wife's dressing table, searching through her things?'

'It's what a husband does if his wife has been unfaithful.'

'Husband, I have not been unfaithful. And I did not "gallivant around town", as you put it.'

'No? That's not what I've heard. Everyone has been telling me how friendly you are with Chew Hock San. Silly me, I defended you. And now I find this!'

'Husband, calm down,' I pleaded, looking at his crimson face. 'You are making a mountain out of a molehill, as the British would say. I couldn't go anywhere after I lost Cecilia, you know that. Mr Chew was kind enough to bring me books to read.'

Weng Yu narrowed his eyes. 'Don't call him Mr Chew him in front of me. It says here, "To Mei Foong, With my love, Hock San". Now, I'd call that intimate, wouldn't you?'

I could have kicked myself for not tearing out the page with Hock San's handwriting. I had known there was a risk, but I thought it small, not having foreseen any reason why my husband would find the book. I kept it locked inside the top right-hand drawer of my dressing table. As for its key, I placed this inside an envelope in the left-hand drawer, hidden between other items: other keys, old purses, and cheap earrings in boxes. Weng Yu must have spent time rifling through my belongings. Unless, of course, one of the servants had told him where to look; they cleaned my dressing table and would have known where I kept my keys.

'Li-Fei warned me. As soon as I returned from Batu Gajah, she told me what you'd been up to.'

My husband's voice turned steely. 'And in case you think I don't know what this novel is about, let me remind you that my father was a Chinese classical scholar. He told me about *Dream of a Red Chamber* when I was still a boy. So don't think you can fool me!'

Weng Yu was gradually raising his voice again. I could tell, from his sullen face, that he would work himself into a frenzy.

'If you really haven't been unfaithful, tell me why his wife would have charged at you in a grocery shop? Why would she do that, ah?'

I stood in the mute and frozen posture of one who was guilty. For a minute my body did not belong to me; when I tried to speak, nothing came out. Everything seemed far off, most of all that fateful day in Mr Chee's store.

'And to think I could have died!'

The idea of this infuriated Weng Yu. He began striding forward as if he were going to hit me. His face shone with resentment, and I could see, in those deep-set eyes, the glint of malevolence. For the first time in our marriage, I felt afraid. Though not an athlete, Weng Yu was lithe and stronger than I ever could be. I had no defence other than to rely on his continuing goodwill, his ability to exercise self-control.

'You are to leave this house. You are not to sleep here tonight.'

Weng Yu did not yell out these last words; he said them slowly with cold, quiet precision. The command was no less incisive for having been made without fuss; rather, his calm delivery enhanced its sting. I had nowhere to go and he knew it.

'Please, Husband, give me another chance,' I said, overcome by sudden shame at the adultery I had committed in my heart and also in my dreams. I desperately wanted to make up with my husband. But I regretted the words as soon as I said them. They left a bitter taste, even though at that moment what I felt most were agitation and confusion. It was only later that I became cognisant of how I must have sounded, as if I had caused my husband terrible injury, when I had done no greater wrong than every married man in town would have been guilty of.

'You are to leave,' Weng Yu repeated, even more imperiously than before.

He then turned his back and headed for the door. When I thought that the entire street would have heard our argument, if not the exact words then certainly the gist, tears rose up. In all of my life no one had ever dismissed me, not even the teachers at school. I could not bear to ask my husband again for another chance; my pride would not allow it.

I wiped my eyes with a handkerchief. Weng Yu, who had by then reached the door, was in the midst of walking out. I was not going to let him have the last word.

'Know this, Husband.' Weng Yu swivelled around, surprised no doubt by the seething whisper which emanated from my throat. I hardened my voice further. 'If I leave now, I will never return. Do you hear me? Never.'

26

I spent the night in Dorcourt. Dora's manner with me was brusque. Remembering how keenly she had dissected events just before Japan's surrender, I expected to have to parry questions, but my sister-in-law was surprisingly uncurious. When I started to say, 'It's not what you think,' she put a hand out. 'That is not my concern. I don't need to know.'

The statement sounded neutral except that Dora's studied avoidance of my eyes told me she had already reached her own conclusions. Christian compassion obliged her to offer me the guestroom, though she made clear that I was to stay for no more than one night. As soon as was decently polite she left me alone with my brother-in-law in the large living room, where yellow light from the gas lamp on the street was pouring in through Dorcourt's cathedral-like windows.

Weng Yoon seemed equally embarrassed, whether by what had happened or by the mere fact of my presence, I could not tell. For once he was at a loss for words. He walked about the room shaking his head. From time to time he would look at me and ask, 'Are you sure you don't want me to talk to Big Brother? Everyone says silly things in the heat of the moment.'

I thought back to the scene in our marital bedroom and shook my head. My husband had been in control of himself; he had known what he was doing. The humiliation which washed over me had a tingling sensation on my skin, like a layer of fine dust.

Needless to say, I did not sleep. The guestroom in Dorcourt was next to the library downstairs where my brother-in-law locked himself up that night. I doubt if he was working, but he was restless. I heard him pacing the heavy parquet floor while I lay awake thinking about the children. As I stared at the fragment of yellow light which slipped in through the tiny gap beneath the door, I finally realised what my husband's game was. He intended to punish me. He would deprive me of the children. Our children, my children.

When this thought dawned, I became indignant. I was their mother; how dare he do that to our little ones. What would become of them? I thought about each one of them in turn and wept as I had not wept in years. They were still so young. The eldest, Wai Sung, was only eleven, the youngest, James, barely three. Three years old! I had vague memories of being three. It was an age when time had meant nothing, when one day slipped into the next and anything that was not before me was immediately forgotten. James would forget me. I could not even be certain that the older ones would remember.

And how would they manage? I was sure that Wai Sung, a solitary creature, could survive, but what about the others? What about Lai Hin, the only girl among them; she would surely need her mother. Did my husband not consider that? Or her brother Wai Kit, a boy who loved singing and dancing and sewing and who was different from other boys. Did my husband not realise how much Wai Kit would need me? Then there was cheeky Robert, already nearly five. Without my guiding hand, I was sure he would grow up to be just like his father. I could not leave them, I simply could not.

And yet to stay was impossible. I had already asked my husband for a second chance. I knew now that he would not change his mind; even if I were to crawl on my knees, he would not relent. This was the man who had refused to speak in Chinese after returning from London. He had known very well that his mother could speak no English; if he could have punished his mother so, he would surely punish his wife more. I had seen the grim determination on his handsome face, the arrogant raising of both his nose and his chin. The more I recalled those minutes, the more incensed I became. How dare he behave so self-righteously, he who had not given a moment's practical thought to feeding our family during the war.

My sobbing was broken only by the gurgle of pipes inside Dorcourt, which came to life whenever someone flushed the English toilet Weng Yoon had had installed. There would first be a rumble as the chain was pulled, and then a sloshing of water. In the still of the night, the bab-bling noises had a salutary effect: I stopped crying and began counting the drips in the bathroom. I wondered what I would do. I thought about all the relatives we had. I wished my uncle who lived on Belfield Street had returned to Ipoh, but he was still with cousins in Pusing, a one-street town I did not relish travelling to. I would have to go some-where else for a few days, maybe even a few weeks. Thereafter, though, I needed to earn a living.

The thought terrified me. How I wished then that I had fought harder with Mother to go to teacher training college after I left school, or on to something else, anything that would have provided me with a qualification. I had a good brain, I knew that, and I'd spent years at school, yet I had nothing to show by way of achievement other than a school leaving certificate, a thin piece of paper which so many others also carried. When I considered what else I could produce to show for my life, I realised there was nothing, nothing except five healthy children and the antique fan Mother had given me. It was too late for regrets; I had chosen this easier life, the one I led with Weng Yu, and now I would have to find a job. I resolved to take any opportunity that came my way, no matter how menial. I wondered what this might be. I knew how to cook and clean, of course, and cleaners and washerwomen were always in demand. I could be a secretary if I knew shorthand and typing, except that I didn't; I would have to take a course. And even if I were able to type and take dictation, what business would employ a thirty-year-old woman who had never worked in her life? Who in Ipoh would give me a job? I could not imagine; I foresaw only the whispers and gossip and pity that would be heaped on me. The thought made me cringe.

But if I were to leave town, there were the children . . . As soon as they came to mind, I started crying again. I dug my face into the pillow so that no one would hear me. I knew I was already the talk of the street; there was no need to add to general conjecture. By the time I turned my head towards the air to breathe, a dreary light was already creeping into the gap under the guestroom door. One of our cockerels next door began to crow. Soon I would have to face the children.

They were certain to ask what had happened. I could not think what I would say.

◆ ◆ ◆

There was an expectant hush when I entered the Green House. The children were nowhere to be seen. I could hear neither the patter of feet nor the clanging of pots nor even the squeak of a door, though I knew that everyone was there, waiting.

It did not take long for me to pack. I removed my Chinese tunics and trousers and Western dresses from the hangers in the almerah and folded them. I swept up the only jewellery I had left, the earrings and bracelets of fake pearls, which I placed into a second suitcase alongside little notes I had written. At the very bottom of that suitcase I packed the novels Hock San had given me and, on top, Mother's fan and the brown exercise book in which my children's details were recorded. Even if I could not be with them on their birthdays, I would think about them; he could not deny me that.

I knew, without having to be told, that personal effects were all I was allowed; family photographs would be out of bounds. I went into the inner hall where we entertained our guests, so that I could have a final glimpse of the framed images of our wedding day. These had been taken in black and white and hung on a wall. They showed a jubilant man and woman holding a knife to the bottom tier of an enormous three-tiered wedding cake. Next to it was an electrifying image captured by a local journalist, in which the shock on my face was evident, as a pair of pigeons clambered out of the cake and flew into the air. The photograph had been taken when one of the pigeons was flapping its wings, and my mouth had curved into an *O*. I looked astonished but elated. I'd had no inkling there would be live birds. I loved the novelty and the glamour.

Moving away from the wall, I went to the side table where a large family photograph sat. This had been taken more recently, in the months before the war when my mother-in-law was celebrating her sixty-third birthday. It was Hashimoto's photograph; the bottom right of the paper bore his name. Some of the people in the photograph – my husband's second brother Weng Koon and his children – were now dead, and those of us who had survived looked more haggard than we had four years previously. Among our children, only the eldest three peered at me from the yellowing paper.

A whimper in the room reminded me of why I was there and that I could not stay long. I turned to find my daughter, Lai Hin, her eyes red from crying.

'Where were you last night, Ma?' she asked in a strained voice.

'Next door, at your fourth paternal uncle's house.'

'How come you have bags, Ma?' Lai Hin pointed to the packed suitcases on the vestibule floor. Her voice was just a squeak.

'Your Ma has to go away.'

The nine-year-old seemed to understand what this meant. She ran to me, throwing herself against my knees and wailing in earnest. A lump came into my throat.

At last, everyone emerged from their hiding places. They entered the inner hall all at once and with great commotion: old Ah Hong, my maid, Chang Ying, and the gardener, Samad, none of whom had a dry eye between them; then the boys Wai Kit, Robert, and James, whose footsteps resounded on the parquet floor. Once the boys trooped in, they stood open-mouthed with their arms by their sides, as if they knew that something momentous was happening, which called for stillness and silence.

Only Li-Fei stood apart, surveying me with a detached air. When our eyes met, hers had an insolent light which seemed to issue a challenge, to see whether I would dare ask what she had told my husband. I ignored her; I had no energy left for a fight.

Just as I was wondering where our eldest son, Wai Sung, was, he appeared, wearing a neatly ironed white shirt and a pair of dark-blue, mid-length trousers. The trousers came down to his knees and were held up at the waist by a thin belt of black leather. I had chosen the belt myself for the boy's tenth birthday. It had been purchased with my husband's income, of course, but it was I who had arranged the purchase, just as I had arranged all of our children's presents.

With this belt around his waist, Wai Sung came directly to me. It was clear that he had not slept and had been crying. In a rasping voice he said, 'Please, Ma' – and at this he broke down – 'please don't go.'

For as long as I live, I shall never forget the next moment, when my son began to bend his legs until he was kneeling on the wooden floor. The top of his head came just below my waist. When he looked up, tears were streaming down his face. 'Please, Ma, I'm begging you.'

I covered my mouth with both my hands and closed my eyes. The air felt thin, I could neither breathe nor speak. I swallowed once, and then, after opening my mouth to take a gulp of oxygen, I removed the folded tissue I had tucked into the fold of my collar and wiped my eyes. I have an abiding memory of waves crashing against a shore, rendering me mute. My son was only eleven; how could I have explained? Was there anything I could have told him, and what purpose would this have served? My throat tasted of salt. Opening my eyes, I raised Wai Sung from his knees and hugged him close. The boy had a lean body; he would grow up to inherit his father's figure.

When I let him go, I patted him on the head. 'Son, your Ma cannot stay. Be a good boy. Please, don't hold this against me. Try not to forget me.'

Wai Sung gave me a look filled with disappointment and reproach. I had hurt him, of course I had, but there was little else I could do.

I began the long walk out. Chang Ying and Samad insisted on helping with my bags. I knew I could not look back. When I heard Wai Sung and Lai Hin sobbing, I yearned to stay another minute, to tell Lai Hin that she should continue her drawing and her painting, but I could not. I knew that if I stopped, if I looked back for even a second, I would crumple and sink to the floor and become the madwoman I did not wish my children to see.

As I approached the front door for the last time, I felt a sudden need to hold our youngest child. I took James from Chang Ying and carried him all the way to the end of our driveway, where I knew I would have to put him down. I cradled him for many moments, unwilling for this time to end. When I kissed James on the cheek, he smiled at me happily, but then looked alarmed as I handed him back to Chang Ying. Once he was in her arms again, however, he seemed content. He stared at my suitcases, apparently aware that I did not usually go out with large bags. As I walked away, I was haunted by the dazed look on his three-year-old face. The future hit him when he had least expected it. The future had come too soon.

POST MORTEM: 3 JULY 1975

It is said that death is preceded by poignant memory.

If this is true, it may explain why Wong Weng Yu asked to see me the year he was ill. He was then at the Lady Templer Hospital in Kuala Lumpur, where our eldest son, Wai Sung, had sent him.

I was surprised by the late-night telephone call, and even more surprised to hear the anxious voice of my daughter, Lai Hin.

'Ma, please,' she implored in a high-pitched whine. 'Pa says that for three days and three nights, he saw you by his bed.'

My husband – for throughout the years Weng Yu remained my husband in name, never having bothered to file divorce papers – had been diagnosed with advanced prostate cancer. We all knew the implications.

'What does he mean he saw me by his bed?'

'He says he saw you sitting there, beside his bed, for three whole days and three nights. Pa really wants to see you.'

I realised, not without satisfaction, that Wong Weng Yu was remembering our final moments together. What did he hope to achieve by asking to see me now? Had he forgotten what I had said to him then – that if he made me leave, I would never return?

There was only one question I needed to ask.

'Is your father of sound mind, Lai Hin? Does he know what the date is and the name of Malaysia's prime minister?'

Lai Hin giggled as if I had said something funny. 'Ma, of course he is of sound mind. I wouldn't be asking you to see him otherwise. But Pa is weak. The doctors give him only months.'

Though I knew what my answer would be, I knew also that I would take my time. If the man wished to say sorry, it was too late; I had no intention of absolving him. The idea of letting Weng Yu stew for a few days, and maybe even a few weeks, brought a satisfying shiver.

'I have to think about it.'

'Of course, Ma, and you know that if Uncle Hock San were still alive, I would not have asked you, right?'

My daughter did not pronounce Hock San's name with equanimity. When I put the receiver down, my hands were trembling, the way they once had in the house I had shared with Weng Yu. Flashes of those minutes came back, when I had been humiliated and ordered to leave. If I had known then how all traces of me would be expunged from our familial house, I might have swallowed my pride and fought harder to stay, or at least fought like a tigress to see the children. Our children. For they are my children too; he had no right to stop me seeing them or to burn every photograph of me, of us together, family photographs, as if I were dead.

'Your mother is dead.'

I can imagine Weng Yu saying this to the children. Or perhaps he never mentioned me; perhaps in his mind, I was as good as dead, and it was only during his final months on this Earth that he discovered how ghosts can come back to haunt. Maybe there are gods after all.

When I left Green Town, I did not go to Chew Hock San. No one knows this; everyone believes that I ran away with him. I have no doubt that my husband fed our children the same lie. It is true that I fled Ipoh. I had to, for there wasn't a single street I could walk down where I was not an object of curiosity and contempt or worse, pity. I was the woman everyone talked about, the fallen woman whose husband had kicked her out of the house for having an affair with another man. This is what people said, though no one really knew what happened.

Despite the gossip, I would have stayed in town if I'd been able, to be near the children. But Malaya had just been at war. Everything was scarce, and what few jobs were going were certainly not going to a woman with a mere secondary school certificate whose husband did not want her.

No one knew me in Kuala Lumpur. I had an aunt and uncle who received me and gave me lodging while I searched for a job. I was washing dishes in a restaurant when Chew Hock San found me. He appeared one day, hair still pomaded, slanted eyes full of tenderness, but with a few days' growth on his chin. He looked as if he had been sleeping rough. 'Mei Foong, I've looked everywhere for you.'

With those simple words, every feeling I'd ever had for him came back, stronger than before. I threw caution to the wind. I had already lost everything; there was nothing else to fear. The people who thought that I ran off with Chew Hock San – which was pretty much everyone – could not see why I would have exchanged marriage to a suave, British-educated man for elopement with a stocky clerk who was hardly handsome.

Hock San may not have been as good-looking or as educated, but he treated me with respect. With him, I felt equal. And for a woman not used to being an equal, this counted for a lot.

Life with him was hardly a bed of roses. We were so poor at one point that we had to rear pigs. I was in charge of feeding the pigs and cleaning the sty. Despite our poverty, I was able to express the entire gamut of feelings I had, never once having to hide my fears or resentment, my anger or, for that matter, my love. I did love him, eventually. At least, I grew accustomed to him. And what is love, if not getting so used to another person's presence in your life that you depend on it, and then want it and need it?

Chew Hock San was a jealous man, as I'd already discovered. There were times when I could have killed him, and times when I very nearly did. I charged at him once holding a cleaver in one hand. This could never have happened with Weng Yu; he would not have allowed it.

Was I happy? This question I cannot answer; I can only say that I was content. We settled in Telok Anson where Hock San was finally sent by the Malayan Civil Service, and I bore another six children: four boys and two girls. Alas, two of the infants died at birth. I recorded the facts in the little brown book I had taken with me and which I open every month around the time of the birthday of one or another of my children. I know all of their birthdays by heart. I open this book and think of the child whose birthday it is. I do this especially for the children I see rarely or not at all. I pray for them, to the extent I still know how to pray, to ask that they be kept safe so that I may see them again.

Chew Kit Mei was never reconciled to my presence. A month after we arrived in Telok Anson, Hock San mooted the idea of moving his other family down too. It was, he said, the only way he would see his children easily. The flicker in his dark eyes told me how much he missed them. Nonetheless, he added that if I objected to Kit Mei's being so close, he was prepared to travel twice a month to Ipoh. How could I have said no? I did not have the heart, and Kit Mei ended up living on the other side of our small town.

Of the children I had with Weng Yu, only Lai Hin keeps steadily in touch. She visits with her children, always with lips pursed. She too thinks that I ran away with Chew Hock San and left her behind. She does not know how her father commanded me to leave, that I had no say in the matter, nor is she aware of my diary and how she is on my mind every year on 12 March, her birthday.

Among the Wong boys, our second son, Wai Kit, sees me from time to time, as does our fourth son, James, but the eldest, Wai Sung, has never forgiven me. He has told his daughters that his mother is dead. This is hard for me to hear, but it must be harder for him to say. As for our third son, Robert, I have not heard a word, even though I initiated contact a few years ago. I can only assume that he believes I abandoned him.

One of my grandchildren, a precocious ten-year-old, asked the other day whether I regretted anything in my life. I thought about this and realised that I did. The first is not fighting to see my children in Green Town. Recrimination is easy now; women had few rights then. But I know, in the softness of the nights when I dare to search my soul, that I was not as brave as I should have been. My sister-in-law Dora, had she been in my position, would have somehow clawed her way in and won.

Weng Yu did not want me near the house, and I did not fight him. I never fought him, on this or anything else. A bare three months after casting me aside, he took the nurse Lim Choy Yoke into the household as his wife. When I heard the news, I felt a stab, though I was also glad. The children needed a mother, and I had always liked Choy Yoke.

What hurts is that there are two sides to every story, and mine has never been told. Instead, every trace of me was obliterated from the Green House. The children grew up hearing only what their father told them. I was not able to protest or say otherwise.

Another woman was there, but she did not know what had happened. I do not blame Lim Choy Yoke in any way; she was not the culpable party. Choy Yoke did her best; it could not have been easy being stepmother to a whole brood. I am grateful to her for tending to my children, and even more for letting me see them behind their father's back. If it weren't for her and Chang Ying – and Ah Hong, when the latter was still alive – I would not have seen my children at all. Choy Yoke and I met one last time after she herself had left Weng Yu. She was a matron by then, her figure even more fulsome than in her youth. I was fifty but remained sylphlike, a fact that Choy Yoke commented on. She laughed, saying that Weng Yu had always had a good eye, not only for women but also for the financial resources they brought.

My other regrets? Not being able to share in my children's successes, and for that matter, not being there to share in their pain either. For this, I have only myself to blame. Also, I regret that my Wong children do not know my Chew children. The latter, of course, know about the former, but most of the siblings have never met.

The result is a gaping hole in my life, which no amount of activity or children or pretence can fill. I miss my Wong children; it's as simple as that. I did not have the chance to watch them grow up, and now that they are adults, I have lost the right to see them regularly. I have not watched any of the musical performances our second son, Wai Kit, puts on or the concerts at which our fourth son, James, sings. Lim Choy Yoke attends these as she pleases with their father while I, the boys' mother, remain banished. Like Weng Yu, James is a promising baritone, but with perhaps greater depth and flexibility; he will surely be known one day in Kuala Lumpur for his voice. Wai Sung, the son for whom I am dead, has made a name for himself as a heart surgeon; unlike his father, he has never feared blood or gore. He is a proud man by all accounts and, like his father, speaks little.

You may ask whether, if the Japanese had not occupied our country, the Wong family would be intact. Perhaps yes; indeed, I think it quite likely. Our family, like our country, would not have been wrecked. Malaysia would be a different place. I may not have been any happier with Weng Yu, but I would also not have lost my children. And for that opportunity, I would live my life a second time.

Earlier today my daughter, Lai Hin, called again, this time with sadness and accusation in her voice.

'Pa just passed away,' she said, using that tone of her father's, full of blame, as if I were somehow responsible.

I had known that this moment would come, but I had assumed it would close a chapter. I expected to feel relief at Weng Yu's death; instead, I'm full of anguish and remorse. And doubt. A million and one doubts over whether I should have gone to see him. I keep hearing his voice, that baritone which once made my skin tingle. When he asked to see me, all I had wanted was vengeance, to humiliate him the way he had once humiliated me.

I took my revenge, but even in death my husband is not letting me rest.

For with the genius of hindsight I see that a different future would have been possible. In this future, Wong Weng Yu lies on a reclining white bed. He is having trouble breathing. Our sons, willowy silhouettes with angular faces just like their father's, stand beside the bed. At its foot is Lai Hin, whose rosebud lips announce my entrance.

Weng Yu turns as I walk in. His eyes are as deep-set as I remember, his cheekbones still chiselled. He remains the handsome devil he always was, if a little crinkly at the edges. He gives me a toothless smile. He knows he has not much time.

'I am so sorry, Mei Foong, for what I did. Please forgive me.'

The voice is low and mellifluous, a voice I never thought I would hear again. But even in this other future, I do not know whether I'm ready to forgive. Absolution is not why I have come.

'Weng Yu, tell our children what happened.'

At this point, the image vanishes. Hard as I try, I cannot wind it forward, as if a mechanism in my brain has jammed and the spool is stuck. I can only hear Weng Yu's voice, now weak and trembling.

'Boys, Lai Hin, it was not your ma who wanted to leave. I made her go.'

The words ring in my ears, words I have so yearned to hear. I can no longer hold back the tears. Thirty years earlier I had not cried in front of my children; now the droplets come unbidden, gathering with force in the folds of my eyes from where they have nowhere to go but out. The tears roll relentlessly down both cheeks, rivulets of pain and relief, but also despair.

Pain because thirty years have passed, relief that my Wong children have at last heard the words. They are in the room, their presence palpable to me. I feel them in the way only a mother can, these beings who once shared my blood and the very air I breathe. In my vision the children are blurred, tenuous and phantom-like. I try to imagine Wai Sung and Robert as grown men, to catch hold of Lai Hin and Wai Kit and James, but my brain will not settle. I do not know whether my children are crying or how they feel or what they are thinking. Despair sets in. I know too well that this other future will not come to pass because when the opportunity came, I squandered it. I let the moment slip away, just as I have let so many moments in my life slip away.

'Please, give me another chance.'

My own voice is clear, if a little husky. When I said those words, I was not to know that I would be given a second chance thirty years later and that, when this moment came, I would spurn it. Despite my advanced years, I still had not learnt that the future wove itself into your life and arrived when you least expected it.

Wong Weng Yu has come and gone. His passing brought no release, only questions. Questions about what I could have done differently in my life, what I could still do differently now; whether I should have gone to see him, and because I did not, how my children will ever find out what really happened.

At some point today I thought I would go mad. I stood for hours in front of the altar table, shaking three lit joss-sticks and watching their tendrils of smoke rise to our smoke-charred ceiling. All the while I pondered the question burning in my mind: who will tell my children, now that Wong Weng Yu is dead?

Even as I asked it, I knew the answer.

I knew too that the opportunity had not yet passed; I could still reclaim my children. The moment had come.

This future is here now, and I am terrified by the vistas it brings. The fear I have is as visceral as the terror which struck me on that fateful day when eggs fell on Ipoh and the ground beneath us shook. There is a tremor in my bones. The dentures in my jaws are clattering. I'm choking, I can barely breathe. I know that I and I alone must do this; no one else can do it for me. The future is pressing. I must find the courage to reach out, to grasp the moment.

ACKNOWLEDGMENTS

This second book in the Malayan Series was completed in record time, thanks to the hospitality of my parents, Siak Choo Wah and Chin Fee Lan, who indulged my quirky hours and habits during an extended escape from the European winter. Freed from daily chores, I was able to let my imagination roam in the glorious Florida sunshine.

I am indebted to my grand-uncle, the late Chin Kee Onn, whose classic book *Malaya Upside Down* proved invaluable in delineating the realities of the Japanese Occupation. It was my late uncle and aunt, Datuk Malek Merican and Datin Chin Yew Gaik, who referred me to the History Channel documentary, *Rising Sun over Malaya*, from which I first learnt about the Sungei Lui massacre. My late uncle Tan Sri Yuen Yuet Leng also shared his memories of the Nippon era over many hours, and my greatest regret is that neither he nor Uncle Malek and Aunt Yew Gaik have lived to read this book.

As always, my British development editor, Nathalie Teitler, was on hand to provide candid and sometimes bruising criticism of my work. Some of the best ideas in this story have emerged from the flames of our discussions – testament to the importance of feedback in my writing process.

The Woman Who Breathed Two Worlds was a difficult debut novel to follow. I was therefore relieved when my agent, Thomas Colchie, and his wife, Elaine, loved this manuscript as much as they did the first, and am grateful for their continuing faith in me.

I am fortunate in having a wonderful editor at AmazonCrossing, Elizabeth DeNoma. I cannot thank her and the entire AmazonCrossing team enough for their dedication, responsiveness and supreme professionalism.

A writing life would not be possible without the steadfast love and support of my partner, Svetlana Omelchenko, who remains my biggest muse and most trusted first reader.

GLOSSARY

- Air well

  Open-air courtyard found inside many traditional shop-houses and houses

- *Alamak*

  Oh my goodness (Malay expression)

- Amah

  Servant whose primary responsibility is to look after one or more children

- *Ang moh*

  Red-haired person or Caucasian

- *Ang pow*

  Red packet (literal translation) intended as a gift and thus containing money Traditionally given to children at Chinese New Year

- *Apa khabar*

  What's the news or how are you

- ARP

  Air Raid Precautions

- Baju   Tunic or shirt; also a generic term for attire

- Baju panjang   Long tunic, usually worn with a sarong

- *Barlay*   Raised wooden platform found in houses for sitting or sleeping on

- *Belukar*   Cleared land which has reverted to jungle

- Betel nut   Seed of the areca palm which is chewed and traditionally offered to guests in the Malay tradition. Acts as a stimulant

- Brinjal   Aubergine

- British Resident   Title given to the highest-ranking British civil servant in certain Malay states, who pretended to merely 'advise' the state's ruler, the Sultan. This smokescreen was abandoned after WWII

- Catty (s), catties (p)   Traditional Chinese measure of weight, equal to 604 grams.

- *Changkol*   A hoe

- *Chap ji-ki*   A form of lottery

- *Chengai*   A tropical hardwood

- *Chin-chuoh*   Marriage in which the bridegroom moves into the bride's family

- Dai Toa   Greater Asia, as in the Dai Toa Co-Prosperity Sphere

- Enche   Mister (Malay)

- Five-foot way   Open verandah in front of shop-houses, usually five-feet wide

- *Habis*   Finished (Malay)

- Hokkien   The dialect of Chinese from the Fukien province in south China

- Kakak   Elder sister

- Kampong   Malay village

- Kebaya   Intricate top, usually of sheer material, worn by Malay women with sarong

- Kempeitai   Japanese secret police

- *Kepala*   Head (Malay)

- *Kepala potong*   To chop off your head (Malay)

- Kongsi   Benevolent organisations formed among overseas Chinese communities. The word also means a commercial company; to share or shared

- Kuan Yin   The Goddess of Mercy

- *Kueh*   Cake (Malay)

- Kwangtong   Guangdong

- *Lalang*   A type of weed

- Mah-jong   Game traditionally played by four players for money using tiles

- Main Convent   Popular name for the Convent of the Holy Infant Jesus, one of Ipoh's main missionary schools

- Makche   Aunt

- MBC   Malayan Broadcasting Corporation

- *Mesti chepat*   'We must hurry' (Malay)

- Nightsoil   Human waste.

- Nyonya   Female descendant of Chinese traders who settled in southeast Asia with local women

- *Ondeh-ondeh* Sweet cake of rice/tapioca flour, filled with palm sugar and garnished with desiccated coconut.

- Orang Asli Generic term for the indigenous aboriginal peoples of Malaysia

- *Orang puteh* White people (literal translation), meaning the colonials (Malay)

- Padang Playing field

- *Parang* Machete (Malay)

- Picul Unit of weight in southeast Asia equal to 100 catties or approximately 60 kg

- *Potong* To chop off (Malay)

- *Puan* 'Mrs' (Malay)

- Rickshaw A vehicle with a hood capable of seating two, pulled by a running coolie

- *Samseng* Ruffian or thug (Cantonese)

- Sarong Large tube of fabric worn around the waist by men and women

- *Selamat pagi* 'Good morning' (Malay)

- Soh   Cantonese or Hakka for Mrs

- Songkok   Traditional hat worn by Moslem men

- *Sook ching*   Purges carried out by the Japanese in Malaya of persons, mainly of Chinese descent, who were suspected to be hostile

- *Takut*   Afraid (Malay)

- Tapioca   Technically cassava

- *Terima kaseh*   'Thank you' (Malay)

- *Terok*   Terrible

- Tokio   Old spelling for Tokyo

- *Topee*   Hard hat

- *Tualang*   A tropical rainforest tree; scientific name *Koompassia excelsa*

- *Tuan*   'Mr' or 'Master' (Malay)

- Yam   Taro

ABOUT THE AUTHOR

Photo © 2014 AM London

Selina Siak Chin Yoke is the author of *The Woman Who Breathed Two Worlds*, her first book in the Malayan Series. Of Malaysian-Chinese heritage, she grew up listening to family stories and ancient legends, always knowing that one day she would write. After an eclectic life as a theoretical physicist, investment banker, and trader in London, the heavens intervened. In 2009, Chin Yoke was diagnosed with cancer, the second major illness she had to battle. While recovering, she decided not to delay her dream of writing any longer. She is currently working on her third book and also writes a blog about Malaysia at www.siakchinyoke.com/blog.